The Swimming Group

THE
SWIMMING
GROUP

BELLA ELLWOOD-CLAYTON

JOFFE BOOKS

Joffe Books, London
www.joffebooks.com

First published in Great Britain in 2025

Cover art by Nick Castle

ISBN: 978-1-83526-959-6

For my mom, Gwenda
My first — and favorite — storyteller

PROLOGUE

Ocracoke Island, Outer Banks, North Carolina

A perfect day for a swim. Sunbathers on the beach, families and umbrellas dotting the shoreline.

I kept an even pace despite the choppy water, my freestyle strong and easy, goggles tight around my eyes. I planned to swim past the ferry, then circle back and keep going until my legs ached, my daily ritual.

I almost collided with another swimmer, a teenage girl, blonde hair plastered to her face, one strap of her black bathing suit twisted.

"Help!" the girl screamed, eyes wild. "My mom — she's gone!"

I yanked off my goggles, treading water. "What happened?"

"She got dragged out! We were swimming, and then—" The girl pointed out past the ferry landing. The horn bellowed, its deep sound carrying across the water like a warning.

A shark could've got her mom.

I squinted, the water a sheet of white glare as the girl thrashed and waved for help. I turned toward the beach. No lifeguard in sight. The nearest people were a family making

1

sandcastles, the bearded father shaded his eyes and looked our way. Down by the pier, boys splashed around, oblivious.

"How long ago did you see her?" I asked.

"Six minutes . . . seven?"

No good. I'd watched what riptides, sharks too, could do in less than a minute.

A man swam over from the shore, breathing hard, his beard spreading like seaweed in the water. "What's wrong?"

He shouldn't have come in. If there was a shark all of us could be bait.

"My mom—" the girl choked out, eyes fixed on the horizon. "I have to find her."

"No." I blocked her. "Shore. Now." To the man: "Call the Coast Guard. Portsmouth station." He headed back, but the teenager didn't budge.

"I have to keep looking," the girl said, teeth chattering.

"Listen to me. We have to get out of the water. The Coast Guard will be here soon."

The girl sobbed, allowing herself to be guided to shore. My chest tightened as we shoved through the shallows. Seven minutes under. That wasn't a rescue. It was a fatality.

CHAPTER ONE

Provincetown, Cape Cod, Massachusetts
11 months later

Tragic Wives WhatsApp chat
8:30 p.m.

Hannah: *Who's up for a swim tomorrow morning?*

Serenity: *At art show tonight — too much champagne to swim, lol.*

Miguel: *Count me out. Toddler draaama!*

Li-Ping: *Can't, I'm training.*

Hannah: *Ok, let's leave it.*

Em: *I'll sleep in. See you all soon :)*

Guardie: *I'm away in Boston for the week. Will miss you all.*

Miguel: *Not swimming is fine by me. Another day not in the water is another day Jaws doesn't get us! [[eggplant emoji]]*

CHAPTER TWO

Harbor Beach, Cape Cod
A week later, 5:17 a.m.
Plunge count: 78

The only sounds are my breath and the lapping water. The sky is still dark, save a sliver of light on the horizon. I'm the first one here. Shivering, I shift my weight and my sandals sink into the sand. Usually, Hannah and Carol arrive first, greeting us as we gather near the beach-facing Sandbar Café, but another nightmare woke me up early and I couldn't get back to sleep. I swallow, wishing the cozy café was open right now, and I was in there sitting across from Miguel and cupping a steaming cappuccino, not outside in the cold.

It's spring in the Cape, but the weather gods don't seem to know it. These early mornings feel like the dead of winter. Then again, everything feels that way — seems like true spring will never arrive.

The beach stretches as far as I can see. To my right, MacMillian Pier stands proud, extending far into the harbor, the gateway to Provincetown. A ferry from Boston will dock here in a few hours, full of tourists even though the high

4

season is still a month away. They'll pound down the wide pier in their hunt for clam chowder and saltwater taffy.

The flat sea mirrors the moon — stark and exquisite — but the calm surface is misleading. This past year I've become an expert on cadaver recovery or the lack thereof. No matter how safe the ocean appears from land, underwater currents can move a body so far away it might never be recovered. It happens more than you think. I've googled it, memorized facts, specific cases — useless, morbid information that wouldn't even give me a leg-up at a trivia night. I hate that I know this.

I zip my puffer jacket up to my neck and check behind me. Commercial Street, the main street in Provincetown — or P-town as the locals call it — runs parallel to the beach. From here, it's all shadows, rooftops, the backs of buildings, and the Pilgrim Monument, a narrow granite tower that dominates the landscape, shooting skyward like a rocket.

It's probably smarter for me to wait on Commercial Street under the streetlights. I take a step, then stop. If my younger sister Britta were here, she'd say, "Don't be such a *mes*," which is the Swedish equivalent of a wimp, but directly translates as "titmouse, softy, namby-pamby." Even as a child, she was never afraid of the ocean, dark places, or strangers. Turns out she should have been.

I place my swimming bag onto the weathered bench and roll my shoulders, muscles tightening in anticipation of the plunge. "It's good for you," I say to myself. "Don't ruin the streak." Even though I've done this once or twice a week since I moved here from Manhattan almost a year ago — I have a count of seventy-eight plunges so far — there's always the same bracing feeling, an instinct to run back home and snuggle up in my warm bed.

Well, it's not technically *my* warm bed. I'm staying in a decadent beach house owned by my ex's family, one of their many properties that form a coastal charm bracelet from Cape Cod to Cape Hatteras. After we split up, and Britta died, I could barely function. The property was empty and on the market, so my ex said I could stay there until it sold if I made sure everything looked its best and dealt with the real estate agents — which was the least he could do after blowing up our lives in such a clichéd way.

I needed time alone. That was the original plan, anyway. The Cape seemed the perfect spot for a sea change, so I could figure out what to do next with my life.

Yawning, I twist my neck from side to side.

No point in thinking about bed. Grieving people don't sleep in or fall asleep easily. The basics are so hard. That's why I keep returning to the cold water. That shock rewires my nervous system. One day it'll work, and I'll look to the future again. At least, that's what my psychologist says.

"Em."

I glance over my shoulder. "Hey, Miguel."

"Morning, *hermosa*."

His miniature frame is swallowed by a Louis Vuitton robe and a beanie. He looks like Ricky Martin in the "Livin' La Vida Loca" video — Latino good looks and thick, swoopy hair. He could be a model if not for his height.

He hugs me, kissing my cheek, his goatee scratching my skin.

"You smell edible," I say, picking up notes of black pepper, neroli, vanilla. Miguel has an extensive collection of colognes and believes people are too focused on making a good first visual impression rather than a good olfactory impression.

"Of course I do." His phone rings in his pocket. He takes it out, glancing at the screen. "Hang on. Ronald's in London — I need to take this."

I sit on a bench and hug my knees, listening to Miguel talk. With him by my side, it doesn't feel quite so cold.

A star twinkles in the sky and small waves crash on the shore as I breathe in the salty air.

It still seems strange that I ended up here.

P-town is a coastal resort village with a year-round population of just over three thousand, and a summer population as high as sixty thousand. Vacationers love its beaches, harbor, art culture. No one loves it more than LGBTIQA+ communities. During the early evening the women have their restaurant soirées, while the boys host pool parties at lavish homes. Later a t night, groups come together in bars adorned with flags of every color.

Britta and I were raised in Boston, but in summer holidays our parents took us to the Cape, escaping the city. As we drove to the beach, we used to say, "You eat a Mashpee Sandwich in Hyannis" — those are three towns that we would drive through. We loved the long summer days, building sandcastles, eating mayonnaisy lobster rolls, fried clams, steamers. Britta and I used to spend hours searching for periwinkles and whelks in the tide pools, fighting over who got to keep the prettiest ones. I always gave in. Once Britta set her mind on something she was like a cargo ship, no steering her off course. During the evenings, we'd hang out at the hotel, breaking into our usual pairs: Mom with Britta, me with Dad, until bedtime.

Miguel takes his phone away from his ear. "Em, you're shaking. It's arctic out here." Using his free hand, he passes me two rechargeable electric hand warmers from his pockets before returning to his call.

"Thanks." I smile up at him.

A self-confessed "vanity whore," Miguel only joined our cold-water swimming group, the Tragic Wives, for the purported beauty benefits. "I follow all the different cultural beauty hacks," he'd said, "and a well-known Korean beauty trick is to soak your face in ice water. It constricts blood vessels to tighten pores and reduce redness. If it's good for the face, it's good for *all* my body parts." Although he swears his skin is more glowy from regular plunges in the Atlantic, I'm sure his twice-annual Botox regime helps, which he started at the age of twenty-one. "If you're not taking preventive measures, babe, you're not even trying."

We met six months ago looking at the same sculpture at the local Bowerstock Gallery.

"What do you think it is?" he'd asked.

"Ahh, an homage to Race Point Lighthouse?"

"A lighthouse?" He'd elbowed me with a wicked grin. "If so, it's very well-endowed. I'm Miguel, nice to meet you."

"I'm Emma — Em."

Miguel managed to tell me his life story in a few short minutes: he met his soulmate, Ronald, when he was in his late twenties, back in New York. An indie film producer, Ronald summered here in P-town. Now they're married with a three-year-old daughter they had by surrogate, and Miguel lives here full-time. Even though he has his own business, Miguel bears the brunt of the parenting while Ronald's film work keeps him away — currently London, usually New York. Luckily they can afford a manny to give him some time to himself.

"What do you do?" he asked. "Let me guess. Thirty-ish . . . comfortable in your own skin . . . tight-laced. Pharmacist? With a secret sexy side."

"*Haha*. Thanks, but no." I was turning thirty-five in a few months. "I'm a research assistant at Barnard, specializing in women's chronic illnesses."

"Fun!" He looked pitying.

"Invisible" illnesses are complex, and the women who suffer from them are often doubted. Being believed is important. How awful to have the people in your life thinking that you're deceiving them, or that you're lazy, let alone hearing the ultimate anti-female putdown, *"It's all in your head."*

As the art gallery filled, Miguel inquired about my hobbies, and I mentioned the swimming group.

"Can I join?" he asked. "I need friends here outside of toddler moms, who are the most vicious people I've ever met. Take a snack from your diaper bag that isn't organic and gluten free and watch them attack. Rottweilers."

I laughed. "You need to have a tragedy to join."

"As if anyone has a tragedy in this zip code!" he said. "Poor me, I have to spend another week in seaside heaven eating clams and swanning around in white linen . . ."

8

True. The Tragic Wives name was partly ironic.

"Being in a rainbow family in a hetero world has its struggles," he said, "but I'd rather do it here than anywhere else in the world. So, what's your sob story?"

"My boss took my research and used it as her own." If only that was the worst of it.

"She did not!"

"This shit happens in academia. Lesser-known researchers are shafted all the time." Although my PhD was on the maternal healthcare experiences of refugee populations, I'd ended up specializing in my boss's area of interest on her recommendation. I knew the work was important; still, it was her research focus, never mine.

"Scandalous. I'm sorry."

"Give me your number. I'll add you to our WhatsApp swimming chat. We meet a few mornings a week before sun-up." I put his number into my phone. "The group was named after that band — remember the Tragically Hip?"

"Erm, no? I'm a millennial. That band probably *needs a hip replacement* by now." He smirked. "And who cares about Canadian music? Let's be real."

"Bitch!"

"Always." His eyes followed a handsome man nearby, balancing a platter of champagne flutes.

The swimming group was a mix of mostly women — wives, or people married to their work. Each had ailments, physical, metaphysical. Would Miguel fit in? One thing is for sure: he'd lift everyone's spirits.

He hooked his arm through mine as though preparing to square dance. "Come on. I'm desperate for more champagne. But if the waiter seems *thirsty*, you disappear."

"Aren't you married?" I can't disguise the judgment in my voice. Cheaters deserve to have their bodies cut up and tossed into shark-infested waters.

"Yes? So? Only sensitive cis losers write monogamy into their vows. Yawn! Come on." He dragged me away from the lighthouse erection. "Bottoms up."

As I sit behind the café's sandy makeshift eating area, waiting for Miguel to finish his call, the cold works its way into my bones. I pull up the hoodie of my puffer and stare out at the inky water. The rhythmic pulse of waves hits the sand. The dark sky spreads all the way to New York City. To the home — the life — I used to have.

Miguel puts his phone away. "Sorry about that."

He always apologizes when he uses the phone — even to check the time. It's a "dumbphone" rather than a smartphone and, though it can run WhatsApp, it doesn't have email or an internet browser. Apparently, dumbphones are making a comeback, popular among those seeking a break from the intrusions of the modern world. His business, SNAIL GIRL ERA, advocates a slowed-down lifestyle prioritizing well-being versus being overworked.

I check behind me. "No one's here yet anyway."

"With the recent shark sightings, do we blame them?"

Despite it being only May and well before peak shark season, there has been an unusual amount of shark activity. The twenty-foot great whites haven't stopped us, but we agreed to swim in groups, safety in numbers. That's why our dips these last few weeks have only been chest-level, all of us dog-gy-paddling in a circle. It's a part of life in the Cape, but no one wants to be shark food.

"Maybe everyone slept in," I say.

"Brrr." Miguel grimaces and tightens his robe around him. "Don't tell me I could've snoozed for another fifteen minutes. Why do we have to meet at this barbaric hour? Sunset would be more civilized."

I rise from the bench. "It's the best way to start the day."

"No, sex followed by crispy bacon is the best way to start the day. When are you gonna get your priorities straight?" He puts his arm around me, snuggling close. "I know you want to be a born-again virgin, only eat green things that sprout, and go to bed at six p.m. and wallow, wallow, wallow, but never underestimate the power of . . ."

I hang on his words.

"A vacation fuck."

I shove him. "Could you not?" Besides, I'm not on vacation. Like it or not, this is my life now. "Oh, look" — I spot silhouettes near the Sandbar Café — "the rest of them are coming. Behave."

CHAPTER THREE

"Hi, Em. Hi, Miguel," Hannah says. "We would've got here earlier but *someone* insisted on turning all our compost heaps before we left . . ."

Beside her, Carol smiles good-naturedly. Joined at the hip, the long-time couple are the founders of Tragic Wives. In their fifties, both wear Kathmandu jackets.

Carol's known as Compost Carol around the island; even Carol occasionally refers to herself this way. She does spend a lot of time talking about her compost, why other people should compost, and if they don't, how they are personally responsible for climate change. She even tends to dress in compost colors: browns, from tan to earthy soil, spinach green, and the occasional moldy gray. The thing most people notice about her first is her hair: worm-farm silver-brown curls. She's a wonderful, larger-than-life New Englander whose ancestors came over on the *Mayflower*.

"*De nada*," Miguel says as I pass him back his hand warmers. "You two lovebirds are here now, that's all that matters."

Our group meets at 5:20 a.m. and there's a ten-minute window while we wait for everyone to show up before we plunge together.

Hannah yawns and tucks her bob behind her ear. "I stayed up last night reading a fantastic domestic noir. Had to find out who the killer was." A voracious reader, Hannah does most things full pelt. She's a senior management consultant with one of the Big Four and is our undisputed swimming group leader. Her parents were killed simultaneously in a car accident about four years ago, a side-impact collision at an intersection — that's her tragedy.

"Oh, have you started the novel I lent you?" Hannah asks me.

"Yeah, absolute page-turner." The novel is set in Belfast, and I suspect she recommended it partly because she knows I have Irish ancestry, on my father's side. "I always love your recommendations."

"And I love your 'soup bombs.' Just what the doctor ordered."

I like playing around with recipes, experimenting with different ingredients and healing foods. Hannah was sick last week so I dropped off my miso bone broth, heavy on the garlic and ginger.

Compost Carol wraps her giant scarf around her neck. "I've had late nights all week," she tells me. "Big proposal due about food scraps at restaurants." As for her tragedy, her nephew in Portland, Oregon, was a victim in a mass shooting.

"Work, work, work." Miguel groans. "Don't spend all your mojo on such ungodly pursuits."

Miguel believes we all have a certain amount of energy and if you spend too much time working, not only do you age (poorly), your creative energy is zapped from everything else, and the pleasure ratio is wrong.

Miguel, Hannah, and Compost Carol discuss shark sightings — just a week ago, a swimmer had a close encounter at MacMillian Pier. I tune them out and unzip my beach bag, shrugging my towel around me like a blanket, and think of work despite Miguel's spiel.

Since relocating here, I spend about three days a week doing casual marking for colleagues and some low-key research

13

from home. I don't miss the full-time demands of academic work, the constant pressure to maintain my research profile. I've negotiated a reduced schedule with my department, which sounds much better than admitting I'm struggling. Does anyone say "mental health break" anymore? Besides, it was more of a weepy, can't-get-out-of-bed break.

Having Natalie, Britta's teenage daughter, living with me now has forced me to pull it together. Someone's got to be the grownup.

A white-and-gray gull with an ominous hooked yellow beak approaches Miguel, leaving tracks on the sand.

Miguel kicks out at the bird. "Shoo! Parasite of the sky." He hates every sort of bird due to a traumatic incident with a chicken when he was a kid. A cock, quite fittingly.

As the gull retreats, Hannah pulls her jacket tighter and glances toward the buildings lining the shore. "Any prospective buyers for your house?"

"A couple came for a few tours and seemed keen but then ghosted the agent."

Honestly, I don't give a shit about the weirdness of temporarily living off my ex's generosity. It could be considered spousal support. Although we weren't married, we'd lived together, talked about rings, wedding venues, and at the same time he was . . . He was an asshole. Five and a half years of devotion, of supporting him while he was in med school, tiptoeing around the house while he studied, making extravagant celebratory dinners each time he passed an exam — for what?

Nearly a year ago, I came home from work early and walked into the brownstone William and I shared, admiring a fresh delivery of burgundy peonies from the local florist in a vase on the entrance table. William was thoughtful like that. Every two weeks he went to the florist and chose flowers for me. *Pink roses because of the color of your cheeks. Forget-me-nots for the blue of your eyes.* Standing there in the entrance hall, smelling those fluttery, bosom-y fresh peonies, I'd felt smug. *This is my boyfriend — a doctor — and I'll be getting flowers chosen for me bi-monthly forever.*

Bursting with gratitude, I walked into our bedroom only to find my partner on his knees devouring the "flower" of our cute young florist.

So much for "women's intuition." I'd had no clue, no forewarning whatsoever.

William said the affair was "just physical." But he didn't fight to win me back. He kept doing "just physical" things with the florist, and now they live in my former house.

At the time, I thought nothing could be worse than William's betrayal, but life laughs at you when you think like that.

We're minuscule grains of sand, unable to control anything.

As though sensing my shift in mood, Miguel comes and stands between me and Hannah. "Earth to Em." He touches my nose with his finger. "I command thee to cease thinking depress'd, morbid thoughts."

"I'm not."

"Don't try to play a playah." He pats my behind. "With a booty that plump, you have nothing to sniffle over."

"Your ass *is* exemplary." Hannah grins, her freckles on display.

"Oh, please."

"Morning!" Li-Ping, who's my age and a former Olympian skier, arrives next. Trailing behind her are two Waspy blondes who rarely show up; they're not my kind of people, too shallow and gossipy, so I usually keep a polite distance. (Their tragedies? Miguel claims it's their botched filler injections, but he was in a bad mood when he said that. They're both divorced and have kids in high school, which means they need to find work outside of the house. One of them recently said, "Ask moms what the hiring landscape is like when returning to paid work post kids — *tragic.*")

I'm a blonde too. Britta and I inherited our white-blonde tresses from our Swedish mom; Natalie has them too. I'm frequently told (mostly by nerdy boys at bookstores) that I look like Daenerys from *Game of Thrones*, minus the long hair.

I keep mine shoulder-length and am no Mother of Dragons. Mother of Nobody, more like. That was another problem with William, he kept expecting me to change my mind — as if suddenly I'd want to pop out children, even though he told me because he'd have the bigger career, I'd have to do all the childrearing, be a "single married mom." I guess we both wanted miracles, because I kept expecting him to respect me. In the end, we both ended up disappointed.

Honestly, I miss his family as much as him. His mom is a philanthropist of the arts, and an amazing conversationalist. With every boyfriend I ever had, I ended up developing a tight bond with their families; their mothers all treated me like a beloved daughter-in-law to be. Shame I can't date them.

Li-Ping wraps me in a bear hug, her ubiquitous Prada fanny pack squished against me, and I'm barely able to breathe. It feels like a superhero is squeezing the life out of me, but I appreciate the body heat.

"How's things?" I ask, disentangling myself.

"Hectic. Still unwrapping wedding presents."

As a newlywed, three things occupy Li-Ping's mind: sports, Christ, and her most amazing, do-men-like-that-even-exist new husband, Todd.

"I know you don't cook," I say, "but my present is a very special cast-iron pot that someday you'll grow to love."

She wrinkles her nose. "We'll see. Gotta warm up." Li-Ping moves off to start her stretches, leaving me to observe the others gathering in their usual clusters.

The blondes chat to Miguel about beauty products. Compost Carol strikes up a conversation with Li-Ping while she's doing her acrobatic pre-water exercise routine, and beside me, Hannah rubs her hands together, shoulders hunched up tight, and scans the beach, never abandoning her role as leader. Her gold Star of David pendant around her neck shines against her skin. She calls out to the group, "We'll wait another five minutes before going in." Little puffs of visible breath come from her mouth.

"Cold this morning," I say.

"Forty-three degrees. Not as bad as last week."

The sky's transformed. Gone is the horror movie darkness, replaced by a watercolor, dusky gray and blue, so beautiful it seems like tragedy couldn't happen here. But there is no geography for disaster: it strikes anytime, anywhere.

Even on a holiday.

When Britta called last June, we hadn't talked for months. She said she and Natalie were going to the Outer Banks for a holiday, that I should come. *"It's been too long."* It wasn't often that my sister invited me anywhere, especially since she'd relocated to yet another city — Cleveland this time — and moved in with . . . Joe or Mike . . . I can't remember, but I turned down her offer without a second thought because William had a few events on and wanted me by his side.

While I accompanied William to a charity ball, a tennis match, and a luncheon, Britta and Natalie went to the Outer Banks in North Carolina for a long weekend at a three-star hotel, visiting tourist destinations, taking long walks. On their final hot afternoon, they went to Ocracoke Island and decided over ice creams to take a dip. Locals suggested a beach near the Hatteras ferry landing.

As always, Britta swam too far out. Nothing new, she was a rule breaker and liked flirting with danger. Look at her taste in men — most of the guys she dated had a criminal record.

The water was choppy that day, but nothing unusual for experienced swimmers like Britta. Then a rip current pulled her into the deeper water. Natalie saw it happen. She called and waved for Britta to swim back, shouted for someone to help. A swimmer came to her aid, and they rushed to shore and called for emergency assistance.

By the time help arrived, it was too late. Britta's body was never found.

My chest is heavy as though I'm the one drowning. The irony is not lost on me. I've become just like the women I study. My chronic invisible illness is heartache.

17

I was the stronger swimmer.

I'll never forgive myself for not joining them on that holiday. When a family member reaches out and asks for something, the only answer should be yes.

I touch the silver bracelet on my left wrist; it's inscribed with images of Dala horses — the traditional carved wooden statues of Sweden. They represent faithfulness, wisdom, and dignity. A few Christmases ago, I gave matching bracelets to Britta and Natalie. Britta jumped up and hugged me. "We can all wear them! Never take them off!"

My gaze flits to the ocean. Soon, I'll be in the water, able to shut my eyes and float. Despite everything, it's the only way I can relax. Afterward, the endorphins will bolster me up, giving me the energy to keep going — to try to reinvent myself after losing two of the people I loved most in the world. Because as much as I hate William — god, I loved him.

"You can do better than that, Carol," Li-Ping shouts. She's filming Hannah and Compost Carol doing jumping jacks, probably for social media. "Ten left to go. Put more power into it."

"I can't!" Compost Carol uses her elbow to support her very large bosoms. No woman with D+ cups should be forced to do jumping jacks.

"You can endure all things through the power of the one who gives you strength," Li-Ping says, face red from the cold. "Amen!"

Five years ago, Li-Ping represented the US in the women's freestyle skiing at the Beijing Olympics, falling just short of a medal. Although she no longer competes after suffering from complex knee injuries — her tragedy — a combo of severe ligament tears, meniscus damage, and cartilage destruction, she has a 458k TikTok following. She joined Tragic Wives to aid post-performance recovery because cold water reduces muscle pain and soreness after training sessions. She's definitely more hardcore than the rest of us: she swims every day during the winter and stays in the water longer than anyone else. Once, when she came out of the ocean, her skin was blue.

"When are we going in?" a blonde asks Hannah.

"Soon."

We're all members of the Tragic Wives for a reason. Miguel claims he joined for the sake of beauty — the elixir of salt water to make him young and desirable — but the real reason is because he hates being alone. The waves wash away Miguel's inability to keep his own company. Hannah and Carol created the group for the community, but I think it's to keep their relationship alive, a common interest, a spark. Although Li-Ping says she comes for the exercise benefits, I suspect she longs for something to cool her ambition, her never-ending drive to outdo herself.

Why is it always easier to see what other people need? Me — I need a good night's sleep and a time machine.

Miguel elbows me. "Girl, you ready?"

"For what?" I jog on the spot to keep warm.

"Three o'clock, Magic Hands approaching."

Guardie appears in sweatpants and a long-sleeved T-shirt. Neither of those disguise his muscled body or diminish his bright brown eyes and warm smile.

Oh, damn. Why did *he* have to come this morning?

CHAPTER FOUR

Guardie, the newest member of the Tragic Wives, and certainly the hottest, only shows up sporadically. He's Canadian, in his mid-thirties, single, and has a way about him that makes women, men, and the genderqueer salivate. He was being flirty the last time I saw him, as we doggy-paddled in the ocean, teasing me about how I'd quit city life. But he's probably like that with everyone. Even if he isn't, I'm not the least bit interested. He's about as opposite to my type as you can get. Besides, romance is for the fools who believe it will last.

I didn't expect him to be here this morning. There's at least thirty of us in the group, although, most of the time, only the eight core people show up.

"Sorry, guys," Hannah says. "Rachael's texted that she's on her way. We'll just wait another few minutes."

Miguel puts a hand on his hip. "If she's always late, why do we always wait for her?"

Hannah shrugs. "Tradition."

Guardie steps close. "Hi, Em. Miguel."

Miguel and I both say hi, with me saying it half a second slower.

He wears a crystal necklace. Amethyst, on a black leather strap. His windswept hair is pulled back into a man bun.

Usually, it hangs down his neck, and once it was in a French braid.

"How'd you sleep?" he asks, like he always does.

Or not sleep is the question. It's common knowledge among our group that I have insomnia. "All right, thanks."

Miguel tsks. "If people regularly get less than six hours, their face pays — hanging eyelids, red eyes, droopy corners of the mouth."

I scowl at him and Guardie says to me, "Don't worry. Your eyes aren't red. And the corner of your mouth isn't droopy."

"Thanks. Best compliment ever."

"Oh, you want a real compliment?" he asks.

"I didn't say that."

He lifts his chin, not an ounce of reserve in his kind, open face. "Because I *think* lots of compliments about you."

I squint and share a look with Miguel. Who says stuff like that?

Guardie smiles. "But it's a little creepy to come out and say you're stunning. And intimidatingly smart. And have a very fine doggy-paddling style."

Miguel and I laugh. *Good-looking and funny.* The flirty banter warms me more than any heavy-duty puffer jacket, but I like my men older, more established, and not quite *un*attractive, but let's say I prefer cerebral over cut. My exes were all high-achieving, future-orientated men who had some repellent personality trait, like arrogance, or soapboxing, or being argumentative, that put most women off but I found strangely endearing. I was the one always trying to get them to take a break, enjoy themselves more, and not be so grumpy.

Hannah claps and steps onto a mound of sand, her al fresco podium. "Okay, everyone, we can't wait any longer. Ready to hit the water?"

"Hold your horses! I'm here!" Rachael calls out in her raspy Southern drawl as she runs down the side of the Sandbar Café, a gold-and-pink bag slung over her shoulder. "Bye-ee," she says into her (also gold-and-pink) phone. "I'll send you the article by EOD. I just have one more interview left."

Miguel side-eyes me — he's long suspected Rachael enjoys these dramatic last-minute entrances. An actress-turned-writer, Rachael pulls off the artist aesthetic well: notebook usually in hand, clothes always rumpled (designer, naturally), and smelling of incense and poetry. It's hard to tell exactly how old she is — somewhere in the thirty-five to forty-five range. She's all strawberry-blonde lioness tresses, big-boned, with curves in the right places. Her tragedy, according to her, is a history of B-grade movie roles and a graveyard of novels that haven't been published.

"Nice nails," one of the blondes says to Rachael.

"Thanks." Rachael lifts her Barbie-pink talons, filed to daggers. "Just had them done."

Rachael was the person who invited me to join the Tragic Wives in the first place. It was only a month or so after I'd moved here, and I'd lost my purse. I'd walked up and down Commercial Street, retracing my steps. When I returned to the library, I felt completely defeated.

She was smoking in front of the library entrance in a tasseled leather jacket and a jean skirt, looking like she'd wandered off a Nashville stage and gotten lost in Cape Cod."

"What's wrong?" she asked.

"I lost my purse." Embarrassingly, tears filled my eyes. "I lost everything." My sister, the man I thought I was going to marry, our house, my New York life . . . And now the thought of replacing all my ID and credit cards and getting new keys cut overwhelmed me.

"I can't help you with your purse," she said. "But I can recommend something to take that heartbroken look out of your eye. We meet at the beach, early, and swim. It's a powerful thing. You should come."

"I don't know," I said. It was a small town, and I'd rather keep to myself than be forced to interact with strangers and answer all types of questions.

She stamped out her cigarette and said, "I'll see you there tomorrow morning, just near the Sandbar Café. Don't disappoint me, babydoll."

At my next Zoom meeting with my well-respected New York psychologist (monthly sessions were part of my healing process. Why is healing invariably so *expensive*?), I discussed the idea of doing cold-water swims.

"You're living steps away from the beach," she said. "Cold-water immersion's great for your mental health. It raises your endorphins, lowers cortisol levels. It can help with insomnia. Exposure therapy is cathartic too — you may find closure."

The idea of closure felt as flimsy as a shark net.

"The ocean's the last place I want to be after what happened to Britta," I told her. It seemed macabre.

But in the Atlantic, I've found a connection with my sister. The ocean I swim in is the same ocean where Britta departed this world, albeit hundreds of miles from North Carolina. It makes me feel closer to her.

"Okay! Strip time," Hannah says.

Li-Ping belts out something about leaving your hat on while Miguel accompanies her with the bluesy musical beats.

Rachael laughs. "It's all fun and games until you actually have to get butt naked in front of a camera crew, makeup people, and the other actors . . ."

As Li-Ping and Miguel keep singing and goofing around, everybody tosses their clothes on the café chairs. Hannah and Compost Carol are in shorts and cropped sports tops — Carol wears a straw-at-the-bottom-of-the-compost color and Li-Ping flaunts racing stripes while the blondes show off in floss-up-your-butt bikinis. Guardie sports tie-dye trunks and Rachael is in a fifties-style Marilyn Monroe number that showcases her cleavage.

I slip off my jeans and catch Guardie glancing at me. Cool air bites at my skin, sending shivers down my spine. My bathing suit is a classic navy one-piece Speedo. I cover my thighs with my hand. Ever since moving to the Cape, food has been my only indulgence, and it's starting to show. No more donuts! Actually, bring on the honey-dips. A little padding's hot these days — not that I want to be hot.

Guardie's eyes flit to my butt, then away with a guilty grin.

"Come on, people!" Miguel disrobes, revealing a pair of peacock-printed Speedos. He runs toward the shoreline before whipping around and shimmying as though on a catwalk.

"Work it!" Li-Ping calls after him.

"I'm doing my best! I've only got a boyfriend dick." A boyfriend dick, he once explained, is a penis of reasonable size that one can enjoy on a daily basis — not too big, not too small — as opposed to a vacation dick which is so big it proves too uncomfortable for long-term use.

"No one go in the water yet." Hannah takes out her phone. "Let me check Sharktivity." The Atlantic White Shark Conservancy has an app to track shark sightings in real time in the waters off the Cape and surrounding islands. People can report sightings directly in the app, adding details, photos, and the precise location.

After scanning the app, Hannah nods. "All good. We're not going to die today. Let's do it."

CHAPTER FIVE

"Oooh! Colder than a reindeer's antlers," Compost Carol yells as she enters the water.

The hairs on my legs bristle as I follow behind her, each step making me clench my fists, but when we all go in together, it's not so bad. "Colder than a day-old dumpling," I call out, kicking away seaweed that's wrapped around my ankle.

"Colder than a grave-digger's shovel," Hannah says, our little game easing us into the frigid water.

The sky is lighter now, a diffused aqua. Hannah and Compost Carol huddle together for warmth and hold hands. The blondes follow. I walk with Li-Ping and, just behind us to the right — I can see them from my periphery — Rachael chats with Guardie. She sways her hips, her hand briefly touching his elbow. A pang of jealousy catches me off guard. Silly — I have no right to feel anything like that — but nonetheless the pang strikes again, making me clench my fists tighter.

Jealousy is something I've battled with my whole life. I don't crave status, beauty, or wealth, but I find myself desperate for attention — growing up in a family where affection was doled out like bargaining chips does that to you. And, yeah, that's something I discuss with my psychologist.

Cold, foamy waves assault our ankles. The water rises to our knees, hips, torsos. Goosebumps break out on my arms, all my body parts screaming, *Get out of the water!*

Rachael laughs at something Guardie says. Like Guardie, she's also very single. Twice divorced, she's told us before that she should be anointed the queen of the Tragic Wives. A professional dater, she often regales us with stories about the men she meets on various dating apps, experiences which she chronicles for magazines under her byline.

Now and then, when Miguel and I catch up over a drink we read her articles together, laughing at her clever one-liners.

Miguel runs ahead and dives in, making a huge splash, and everyone curses at him (except Li-Ping, who never curses).

Instinctively we face the sun, which is peeking over the horizon. It feels witchy, pagan; all of us in a semi-circle worshipping Mother Nature.

"Okay," Hannah says. "Starting now . . . Fifteen minutes."

We dip lower, making sure our chests are submerged. That's the key to the plunge: total body immersion. It resets the nervous system.

"Kill me now!" Miguel cries as he swims beside Guardie.

Somehow, I end up between them. Heart racing, I kick to stay afloat.

"How's work going?" Miguel asks Guardie.

"Bit slow." His bare shoulders poke out of the water like boulders. The man is *fit*. Miguel often sings the highest praise about Guardie's "perfect six-pack" — he's physically perfect everywhere, but for me, his glaring gorgeousness is a potential battleground with other women. *No, thanks.*

Guardie shrugs. "Business will pick up when the tourists get here."

Life on the island is defined by off season or in season. Off, it's a quiet, laid-back, New England-vibe town full of locals. Then bam — the warm weather hits, and it's a bustling, bicycle-riding, gender-fluid mecca.

Guardie is a masseuse at the Cape Cod Spa (hence why Miguel and I christened him Magic Hands). Truth be told, Guardie has quite a reputation as the person to go to for a good "deep tissue." He lives in a shack behind Harbor House, a sprawling mansion in the East End. The owners are in Europe, and Guardie oversees the grounds — that's what Miguel told me. Miguel makes it his business to know everyone else's business.

"If you're looking for clients," Miguel says to Guardie, "I'll let my friends know when they come up from Boston."

"I'd appreciate that. Oh, well. There's more to life than money, eh?"

"More to life than money?" Miguel gapes. "*What?*"

"Good health. Staying present. Tousling with the sea." Guardie gestures to the water.

I can't argue with that. Our healing, ritual swims.

Miguel laughs as we paddle to keep afloat. "Nothing keeps you in the present like swimming with sharks."

I'm not exactly sure what Guardie's tragedy is — something about a family estrangement — but Miguel says the tragedy is that he's poor. Whatever money Guardie makes, he often gives away, getting rid of it as quickly as he earns it.

I've always saved every penny. As a child, I had a red piggy bank decorated with hand-painted flowers, which I took enormous pleasure filling with coins — until Britta emptied it during a sick day from school and stocked up on junk food from the corner store. Mom didn't punish her or make her pay the money back. I shouldn't have been surprised — she played favorites — but from then on, I made sure to open a bank account.

"Ten minutes left." Hannah's keeping track. I bet she had a piggy bank.

The blondes swim over to Guardie and start asking him questions, so I put more power into my arms and create some distance.

After Guardie attended his first Tragic Wives swim four months ago, Miguel and I debriefed at the café. "Sooo?" he said. "What do we think?"

"I don't trust him," I replied. "A crystal necklace?"

27

"Forgive him. He's from the West Coast."

"He talks about *manifesting*." I rolled my eyes. "Do we know anything about his name?"

"We do. It's from Il Guardiano del Faro. Means 'guardian of the lighthouse'. His mom's Italian."

Wow, sexy. Instead of sharing any of my thoughts about how fascinating I found Guardie's anti-materialism, his friendliness, and his habit of going out of his way to make the people around him comfortable, I said, "He's like an ambulance chaser."

"Huh?"

"Well, not an ambulance chaser, a grief chaser — everyone knows that people who are trying to heal are ready to empty their pockets." Light therapy, EFT tapping, micro-dosing, EMDR.

"The lady protests too much," Miguel said. "It wouldn't kill you to have some fun. The chemistry between you two — combustible."

I was secretly pleased Miguel had noticed, that it wasn't something I'd misread, but lust was a laneway to lunacy; Britta had proved that over and over. "You know I'm off men for the year. I may never go back to them."

"Eight minutes," Hannah calls out, as a few seagulls squawk overhead.

Submerged in the sea, the lower half of my body has gone numb. I move my toes, attempting to sense the gritty sand. The waves sweeping across my chin make me jump even though I see them coming. I'm an ice cube bobbing in an ocean cocktail.

As I turn back, Guardie chances another appreciative glance. I've grown used to his awareness of me. A blush rises to my cheeks.

I swim back to the group, joining their conversation about the retired judge in our group who was recently catfished on Facebook.

"He was planning to propose to her too," Hannah says. "You have to be careful who you trust."

"Oh, by the way, did you try the *thing*?" one blonde asks the other, as she looks up at the sky.

"Honestly? Um, yes!" The other blonde peels into laughter. "It's just a healing thing I'm trying. I mean, I've been so sick with flu after flu, I'll try anything, and I saw them talking about it on *Real Housewives of New York City*."

"What is the *thing*?" Miguel front-crawls over.

"Seven minutes to go," Hannah informs us.

"Yoni bathing," a blonde says. "You need a window that starts at floor level. Then you stick your butt up against the window. Lift your legs onto the glass, and let the sun penetrate your vagina. Or you can do it outside."

A few of the group laugh — someone groans.

"Are you *naked*?" Miguel asks, a gleeful smile on his face. He loves anything out of the ordinary and is probably trying to figure out how to monetize it for SNAIL GIRL ERA.

"Obviously."

"I'd hate to be your neighbor!" Miguel says.

Guardie, now a few feet away from everyone, seems to be in his own world, a distant look in his eyes. Maybe he's thinking about who to give his next wad of cash to, which beauty to take out for a stroll on the beach, or his own tragedy.

As I paddle, I overhear Rachael ask Hannah, "Can I drop by tonight for a chat?" Hannah says yes and not a minute later, pink-dagger nails slicing into the water, Rachael swims to Li-Ping and asks the same question. Looks like she's doing the rounds.

Rachael has been friendlier to everyone lately. She's throwing a party at Lobster Pot next week and has invited us all.

Rumor has it Rachael is writing a book of poetry or essays or something. She's published a few op-eds in the *Huffington Post*, so who knows? Her cousin holds a prominent position at a big publisher, meaning the book could happen. She isn't just another writer waxing lyrical about a quarter-written book that will never see the light of day. That seems harsh, but there are a lot of people like that in New York and before long (unless they marry rich and suck the proverbial teat — or cock) most of them are forced to abandon their artistic dreams. I can't see Rachael doing that. She has a stubborn streak and doesn't like being told what to do. She once admitted to us that she was fired from a few films for refusing to take direction.

"Six more minutes," Hannah says.

Treading water like this, it's hard to keep my breath. But I'm not chilly anymore, thanks to the release of endorphins.

I watch Rachael, wondering what exactly she's up to with all these house visits. She came over for dinner last week with Li-Ping, and I served them and Natalie a New England "white" clam chowder — milk, butter, potatoes, pork, onion, and clams — accompanied by oyster crackers. I prefer the Manhattan style, but I didn't want to be thrown off the island for making it. We shared a six-pack of a local New England IPA. Afterward, Rachael said she needed to stay back and make a call, and I walked Li-Ping to her place, only a ten-minute stroll from William's family's beach house. I got delayed because Li-Ping's paranoid and her husband was away, so she made me check that no robbers were hiding under her bed or in the butler's pantry, or in any of the million rooms in her clifftop mansion. By the time I returned, Rachael had made her own way home.

A few members swim deeper and Hannah calls, "Not too far!"

"Unless you like living dangerously!" Miguel pipes up, breaking into the *Jaws* theme song.

"Dude, stop," Guardie says to Miguel. "We're trying to chill."

Miguel grins. "Oooh, Daddy, I like it when you're bossy."

Guardie and I laugh and our eyes find each other before I glance away.

He paddles over to me.

No, don't come over. At the same time, *Do!* Warmth spreads in my chest, an aliveness I haven't felt in ages.

"How do you put up with him?" Guardie asks me.

"It's a hard job. I want to strangle him and kiss him at the same time."

30

"Kiss him?" Guardie cocks his head.

The word kiss coming from his mouth makes me automatically stare at his lips. "In a friendly way as opposed to . . ."

"An 'I wanna rip your clothes off' way?"

A smile, more meaningful eye contact, followed by a low whistle from Miguel, whose eyes have ping-ponged back and forth between Guardie and me. Luckily, he's far enough away he can't hear us.

"So, Em . . . ?" Guardie says.

There's a question in his voice and I don't want to hear what he's about to ask me.

"Did you want to grab dinner sometime?"

"Ah, sorry, I'm . . . not really in a 'grab dinner' headspace right now." And if I ever am, I need someone predictable and comfortable — like my grumpy exes — not something knees-weak electric.

I bicycle my legs under the water, using my arms to spin away. No more flirting. The salt spray hits my face, and something about the smell and the taste brings me right back to happier days — I'm twelve again, teaching Britta how to do backward somersaults in the waves.

I keep my focus on the horizon: the line where earth meets the sky, the great divide from where few are lucky enough to return.

Britta, how could you swim out so far alone in waters known to be unsafe? Why didn't you ever learn to be careful?

I take a gulp of air and submerge, the coldness shooting straight to my head as I propel myself deeper, arms locked in a diving position, and kick lower and lower. My chest constricts, craving oxygen, but instead of rising, I loosen every muscle in my body, going completely inert. Buoyed by the saltwater, arms splayed like a starfish, I float. And there it is . . . peace: no worries, no thoughts, no pain. Each minute that passes, the relaxation deepens, a sense of losing myself into the wider expanse, dissolving into the sea.

Once I surface, Hannah says, "Time's up, if anyone wants to head back to shore."

As we stand on the sand, towel-drying, Miguel sidles up. "Coffee?"

"I have to get home. Aunty duties call." Although I'm speaking to Miguel, my gaze flits back to Guardie. Damn, he's watching me. From now on, I have to be less friendly. Less chatty. Less hot eye-contact-y. The last thing I want to do is encourage the man!

CHAPTER SIX

I step into my house and murmur "*Fan*," under my breath, a Swedish curse word useful on any occasion.

The kitchen looks like the beach after a storm — the Carrara marble counter is covered in crumbs, Natalie's rubbish discarded here and there, and a scattering of empty sour cream and onion chip packets. How can one person eat so many chips and stay so slim?

Despite the junk, William's beach house is a thing of beauty, an architectural wonder. It's ridiculous, really. Set on a cliff, it overlooks the sand dunes, a long stretch of beach, and vast ever-changing ocean. There's even a charming snow fence-lined path right down to the beach.

The best view is from the kitchen, through large, well-placed windows. The palette is coastal — white and light blues with moody gray. Cane barstools are tucked under the island counter, perfect for lazy vacation eating.

But right now, the beauty is hidden beneath the debris. It's as though I'm back in the bedroom I shared with Britta when we were kids, her stuff everywhere, piles of dirty clothes, half-finished craft projects, wet towels, homework ripped from notebooks on the floor — total disarray. She had the ability to hyper focus and come up with creative left-of-field ideas, but she was also prone to impulsivity and quickness to temper.

I'm more your plodding, try-to-keep-things-tidy person, so I scoop up some chip packets and shove them in the recycling. As for William, when we were living together, he'd have a proper fit if the condiments weren't aligned just so, labels facing out, in the fridge door. Just wait until the florist accidentally puts the soy sauce in the fridge instead of the pantry. How thin his lips will get, almost white, as he takes a breath before asking with forced pleasantness, "Next time, can you please put it in the proper place?"

Fuck you, William. Did you put your dick in the proper place?

The fact he is still with her adds insult to injury. I sometimes get hives thinking about it. William is a scion of one of the foremost families in US politics; there are a bunch of senators and governors in his wider family tree. Shame all that class didn't rub off on him. I thought he was such a good person — his work for nonprofits, how he visited his grandmother each week, preparing her dinner, and keeping her company while she watched gameshows, his vision for better health care for everyone. He was a fraud.

People who deceive the ones closest to them are the lowest of the low. Being honest may cause discomfort, but I can hold my head high.

I open the pantry door and reach for the container of gummy candy that I get shipped from Sweden, grabbing a loose handful for now and stuffing a small bag in my pocket for later. Thanks to the "candy salad" mania blowing up on TikTok, the whole world has discovered Swedish candy, which uses plant-derived colorings and real sugar instead of corn syrup, and comes in a plethora of textures, shapes, and flavors.

Chewing on a salted licorice gummy, I walk down the hall to the first of six guest rooms. For a beach shack, this is a palace.

"Natalie?" I stand at her bedroom door. I'll ask her politely to put her things away. She's grieving, robbed of her mother, and I have to be extra patient. I knock, nibbling on

34

another gummy which is so sour my lips pucker. "The morning's getting away from you."

I lean my back against the wall. This is not what I expected when I packed my belongings and relocated to the Cape. I wanted peace and solace; I didn't want to be caretaker to a distraught teen. That sounds awful, and of course, there was no question that I would look after Natalie. It's an honor to be given that role, and I take it very seriously, but it wasn't part of the plan.

After Britta died, no one was lining up to take Natalie in. Her dad was never in the picture and moved back to Sicily when she was four years old. I always wondered if he was a mafioso — his attitude, some of the things he let slip — but I tried not to pigeonhole him just because he came from Sicily. My parents in Boston are in their mid-seventies and Dad has dementia; I couldn't see them adjusting to life with a grieving teenager. Mom didn't need someone else to care for. Which left me. *Ah, Britta, you got me, didn't you? Knew I never wanted kids and gave me a last parting gift.*

I knock again and, met with silence, call, "Honey, it's nearly lunchtime. C'mon."

Groans from the other side of the wall.

Natalie is almost eighteen, nearly an adult. I want to say, *Pleeease. Get the hell up and clean up your mess,* but I pretend I'm the kind of aunt who sees every obstacle as a teaching moment. "Meet me in the kitchen in ten minutes. I'm making French toast."

Food is my love language. It doesn't involve talking.

In the kitchen, I open the windows to let in the fresh salty air.

The ocean view steals my attention. Often I spot seals bobbing their heads, and occasionally the spout from a whale's blowhole, followed by the arch of the back of the whale or its dorsal fin. I spend most of my free time on the deck, cocooned in a blanket, looking out at that sea as though it will provide answers about what happened to my sister.

35

Right now, a little girl in a red sunhat and a woman I assume is her mom are traipsing down the beach, carrying matching L.L. Bean bags. The mother's is large with pink handles and the little girl has a pint-sized version. The girl stops every so often and bends, looking for seashells.

I remember gathering treasure with Britta. Back then, I didn't know that the treasure was the time spent together, not the prize of the shell.

As I stack Natalie's dishes and set them aside — she can wash them herself later — a vision appears in the doorway, rubbing her eyes.

I take a small breath.

It's like seeing Britta, or my mirror reflection: five foot six, white-blonde hair, stocky legs. The same silver bracelet inscribed with Dala horses. But aside from the hair, Natalie inherited her father's Sicilian coloring: dark eyes, sun-kissed skin, and an undeniable allure — not an attribute you necessarily want your seventeen-year-old niece to possess.

She's wearing a black kimono which she sewed herself, numerous gold necklaces with crucifixes although she is not religious, and heavy black eyeliner smudged under her eyes.

"Sorry." Natalie slides onto a stool at the kitchen island and flicks hair out of her face. I try not to stare at her scalp where her hair is thinning in patches. "I couldn't get up."

I pour her a cup of coffee, heavy on the cream.

Her eyes flit to the dishes. "Uh, I was going to get to those."

That reminds me of Britta too. Mom never made her do the dishes. Britta just left her breakfast bowls on the table and strutted off. Mom expected me to help though, I suppose because I was more compliant. I didn't care about doing the dishes. I cared that I got treated differently. It made me want to smash something, and once when no one was home, I grabbed Britta's leftover bowl of Cheerios and hurled it against the wall. So satisfying, the *smash*, the broken pieces. Not so satisfying was realizing I'd have to clean it up, then wrapping the evidence in a newspaper and hiding it in the garbage like a psycho.

My phone rings on the marble island. When I don't answer, Miguel texts: *I have TEA. Call asap. [[Eggplant emoji]]*

Miguel often adds an eggplant emoji at the end of his texts as his signature "wink," if you will, so in this context it means nothing. The tea — gossip — he wants to spill is probably Ronald drama. Miguel and his husband often get into "apocalyptic" fights, which are worth it, Miguel says, because they're followed by "apocalyptic" makeup sex. Then again, the tea could be about Guardie . . . I'll call Miguel back after Natalie and I eat.

"Don't you have school today?" I ask Natalie.

"Yeah. I'll do it later."

The dishes or school? *Later.* Everything with her generation is later. Why can't they do things now?

"You know you need a B average. I'm happy to help and can edit any of your assignments if you like. Just say the word."

Natalie's in her last year of high school, but she's taking her remaining classes through an independent online program designed for students requiring flexible education options. A long-time dream of hers has been to study fashion design at the Fashion Institute of Technology in Manhattan, one of the top five fashion schools in the world. Even as a child, she showed artistic talent and spent more time on a sewing machine making outfits for her bunny than having playdates with her friends. Luckily, she has a killer portfolio, and won a conditional acceptance to FIT off the back of it. An up-and-coming singer/songwriter wore one of Natalie's designs on her album cover — a lime-green faux-fur playsuit — which created a lot of publicity. But she still needs to get the grades if she's going to take up her place at college — plus funds to live in New York.

FIT wouldn't have been a viable option because of how expensive it is, but when Natalie turns eighteen, she'll receive the life insurance from Britta's death — a jaw-dropping

$3 million. Until then, I'm anointed with the power of attorney.

Natalie sips her coffee and props her elbow on the kitchen island. Resting her head on her hand, she sighs and looks out at the water.

Our house is a symphony of sighing. We take turns. Throughout the ages, women's anger has often manifested this way. What does a sigh say? *Resigned.* A bitter, quiet form of anger that simmers like water in a pot.

I yawn, last night's lack of sleep catching up with me, then reach into my pocket for red jelly lips. I pop two gummies into my mouth.

"You're such an addict," Natalie says.

"I know. It's bad. Not because of calories or anything. In Sweden, you're only supposed to eat candy once a week."

"Okay, that doesn't sound like a Big Brother dictatorship or anything."

I smile. I lived in Sweden for two and a half years when I was thirteen. My *mormor* (grandmother) had breast cancer, and Mom wanted to be nearby to help out, so she took us girls to Gothenburg and enrolled us in school there despite the fact we didn't speak a word of Swedish. It didn't take long to become fluent. Nor did it take long for the cancer to take over other parts of Mormor's body, but that's another story.

"There's a Swedish custom going back to the sixties called *lördagsgodis*, meaning 'Saturday sweets,'" I explain to Natalie. "Families go to the candy store after school on Fridays and select a bag of pick-and-mix. There's gummies, chocolates, and the most delicious marshmallow–taffy hybrid. And so many shapes — discs, diamonds, skulls, buttons, and twists. You walk around town and see kids everywhere, clutching their bags of candy, but they have to wait until Saturday to eat it."

"Why?"

"A long time ago Swedish medical authorities recommended sweets as a once-a-week treat to limit tooth decay, but it became like training for kids about money management.

Delayed gratification. We'd save our allowance for the sweets. Except your mom." I laugh in an offhand way.

I have Natalie's attention now. She often says she doesn't want to talk about Britta, but her eyes take on a heated interest.

"By the time we got to the store on Fridays, Britta would've already spent her allowance on other things. I'd get a big bag of candy, and each time, Mom would cave and hand Britta money. 'It's not fair,' I would complain. And Mom would nod, and say, 'You're right. Next week, I'll make Britta miss out.' But she never did."

"That explains why Mom's so bad with money."

What I don't tell Natalie is I later found out that although candy was supposed to be a Saturday treat, Mom secretly got two other bags for Britta which she handed out to her throughout the week like dog treats. "Don't be mad," Mom told me when I found out. "You don't need motivation. You're my easy one. A dream."

Those whole two years I was in Gothenburg, I was home-sick, not for a place, but for my dad. Ever since I could remember, I was "Daddy's girl," and Britta was "Mommy's girl," and everyone was happy with that. But with Dad in Boston, all the ways Mom and Britta were closer to each other became like giant weeping sores. Mom always pulled Britta in first for a hug. Walking down the street, she'd take Britta's hand, their steps in sync, while I trailed behind. Holidays meant doing what Mom and Britta wanted — they never asked for my opinion. I'd stay home during their hikes. I had more rules, more chores. "Because you're so helpful," Mom would say, handing me another list. I hated how she was nicer to me when I was helpful, and how I craved her approval. But with no Dad, I was the *tredje hjule*, the third wheel.

Why am I thinking about any of that now? The past doesn't matter. Although, with Dad's dementia — he often slips back in time and has conversations with his mother and little brother — I'm starting to realize how his memories define so much of his life.

Natalie takes her phone out of her pocket and starts texting, angling the screen so I can't see.

"Who's that?" I tease. "A boyfriend?"

A scathing look. "Pretty old-fashioned to assume I'm just into boys."

"Right you are. My bad." I'd only known her to have boyfriends, and not many of those.

She keeps texting. "I'm meeting Kristen later." Her one and only local friend shares a love of classic cinema, and the two of them often catch movies at Waters Edge Cinema. Kristen is an extrovert who chats nonstop and wants to be a marine biologist. We've had a lot of great conversations — she's always teaching me something about the harbor ecosystem.

Reinforce positive activities, Natalie's psychiatrist advised me. *Especially those outside of the house.* "Time with friends is important."

"Says you," Natalie scoffs. "Who, like, never goes out."

"Not true." I take regular walks along the beach, have cocktails with Miguel, and occasionally friends visit from New York. But, mostly, Natalie's right: I'm house bound, grief bound. I've become a recluse.

I need to be a better role model. "I had my swim group this morning."

Natalie frowns. "Yeah, and that's not weird."

She doesn't understand my fascination with the water, my compulsion to return to it over and over again.

"It makes me feel better. But, yeah, so do carbs."

I grab stale bread from the bread box — stale is best for French toast — and cut four thick slices. It's a wonderful kitchen to cook in, with stainless-steel appliances, a professional-grade range, and a subway splashback with tiles in a herringbone pattern. Into a bowl, I break two eggs, add brown sugar, a dash of milk, cinnamon, then my secret ingredients — vanilla and rock salt — before whisking everything together. Such divine scents.

My phone vibrates with another text from Miguel: *Bitch! Mayday! Mayday. Answer me. You NEED to hear this. The tea is hot!!*

40

CHAPTER SEVEN

I'm dying to find out what Miguel knows, but Natalie is in one of her dark moods this morning, so I promise to call him in fifteen minutes. At the stove, butter sizzles on the cast-iron skillet. I glance at Natalie, who hasn't answered my last two questions, then dunk two slices of bread into the mixture and lay them onto the hot skillet. "You okay?"

She turns to me. "Huh?"

This is how she operates — normal-ish, spaced out, then sad.

"How are you feeling?"

"Fine." Her eyes glisten with tears.

"I know you're not fine. Neither am I. But one of these days, we're going to wake up and feel not quite so bad."

She mumbles something.

"Pardon?"

"Maybe I want to feel bad." She squirms uncomfortably in her seat. "Maybe it's a way to — to feel close to her."

I don't quite know what to say, so I give her a hug.

This is shit. Missing Britta is shit. Being stuck together on this island — also shit, really. My job as her guardian is to get this girl into FIT and help her set herself up in New

York. We've been reading about student housing on the FIT website. We've also had a few "discovery trips" to New York.

What will help her heal? I'm banking on time, a fresh start, and being in a program that's tailored to her, where she can shine. After that, who knows if I'll return to New York and my job at Barnard? Regardless, as soon as this house sells, I'll have to pack up and decide. The agent called earlier and told me there's another viewing tomorrow morning. Truthfully, it's tempting to leave raw fish out overnight.

Back at the stove, I flip the slices of French toast, and once both sides have browned, I slide them onto a pretty plate, add a handful of fresh raspberries, syrup, and dust everything in powdered sugar. Placing the plate before Natalie, I tell her, "Eat up."

She nods and says, "I'll try," as though I've passed her a mountain of uncooked broccoli.

Since Britta's death, I can't sleep, and Natalie can barely eat any real food. Junk food, no problem, but she has difficulty swallowing anything full of nutrients and life and love. The doctor put it down to psychological distress, which is understandable given she was in the water when Britta got taken. How traumatizing to watch your mother get swept out to sea, to be unable to save her. She must have felt so powerless.

Once Natalie and I finish eating (she gets down one of two slices, which is good progress), she starts on the dishes, and I head for the deck overlooking the ocean to return Miguel's call, so I can talk to him without Natalie overhearing.

Whoa! Despite it being spring, the wind is near gale force, so I weave around the concrete chairs that surround a concrete coffee table, and head to the corner for some protection from the weather.

"What's the tea?" I speak over the wind.

"Thanks for keeping me waiting," he snaps.

"Just tell me. I know you want to."

"I talked to Hannah. You'll never guess what Rachael's been writing . . ."

"What?"

Two birds fly into the wind, like bullets suspended against the force.

"A book about us," Miguel says. "It's called *Secrets of the Tragic Wives and Guys*. It's the salacious secrets of a group of characters who live in Martha's fucking Vineyard!"

"What?" Martha's Vineyard is only a ferry ride away. "It's a rip-off of our lives?" I touch my neck, a hot rash spreading over my décolletage. Have I said anything too personal to Rachael? I run through our interactions — swimming once or twice a week, usually followed by coffee at the Sandbar Café. Our conversations are a jumble of things. Sometimes vapid, about weather or local happenings. Sometimes intimate, sharing deep thoughts. The highs and lows. Have I ever talked to her about Britta? Rachael definitely knows my sister died, but as far as I'm aware, has no details.

"Did you tell her anything damning?" Miguel asks, clearly reveling in the drama.

I pace the deck. "She came over for dinner last week and I confided in her about William and the florist. I said I had a proper breakdown. *And* I mentioned the investigation William's under for overprescribing medication." Benzodiazepines and ketamine, specifically. Something William's utterly ashamed about. "She wouldn't write about that, would she?"

"Obviously, yes, bitch. Any scandal involving his family is PR porn."

I face-palm myself. "Rachael laughed when I told her about him eating the florist's flower, and said, 'That's a great one-liner!'"

No matter how close William's mom and I once were, if his family hears about me blabbing about the investigation, they'll kick me and my seventeen-year-old charge out of the beach house. I shouldn't have said anything. The hives on my chest are becoming raised itchy welts.

Natalie is watching me through the kitchen window. She averts her gaze.

"Anyway—"

"Are you in a wind tunnel?" Miguel says. "Or skydiving? It's fucking loud!"

"Sorry, I'll go inside."

In my room — boasting a four-poster bed dressed with crisp white linens, flanked by weathered nightstands on hardwood floors — I throw myself on the overstuffed armchair. "I can't be the only one in our group who told Rachael too much. This morning when we went swimming, Rachael was asking to meet Hannah and Li-Ping. Maybe she wanted to talk to them about the book."

"Probably!" he says.

It's only then that I notice the pure terror in his voice.

"*Mi-gue-lll,*" I draw out his name. "What does Rachael know about you?"

"Oh, gawd." He makes a mewling sound. "Never mind."

"Tell me."

"Nothing, really."

He's lying. I rise and walk to the white-painted brick fireplace, running my hand along the mantel where a carefully chosen "cabinet of curiosities" is placed: shark teeth, dried wildflowers, sea glass, and shells. Plus another half-eaten bag of candy and a candle that reads: "Smells Like a Red Sox Win! Lucky Game Day Candle," which I got for both Dad and me last Christmas. He loves baseball, Ireland, and his family, in that order. "Don't authors have to get your permission to write about you?"

"It's not a memoir, babe, it's a thinly veiled novel."

"Why not write a memoir?"

"Because everyone will *sue* her. This way she gets to share the same material but fictionalize it. I wonder if she can make me tall? Like six foot four?"

"Lots of writers don't finish their novels." I'm thinking on my feet. "They just talk about them."

"It's not a work in progress. It's done. *Terminado.* Apparently, Rachael found her missing chapter."

"What are you talking about?"

"Rachael discovered one secret so good — so twisty and unexpected — she said it'd guarantee the book would be a bestseller."

"*Whose* secret?"

Miguel is silent. When he possesses Molotov gossip, he waits until we're bar-side, sharing a cocktail before offering up the goods. That, or it's his secret — and he's stalling.

"All I know," he says, "is that Hannah told me Rachael is about to send the manuscript to a contact at a major publishing house."

"Shit! What will the rest of our group think?"

Miguel snorts. "That's obvious, *chica*. They'll want to strangle Rachael Walker with their bare hands. But they won't have a chance if I get to her first."

We say goodbye. When I open my bedroom door, Natalie is standing in the hallway, head tilted as though she's mid-thought.

"Everything okay?"

She blinks slowly. "Um . . . I finished the dishes, so . . ."

She looks like she expects a standing ovation. The slightly bitchy thought is unfair. I'm supposed to be her lighthouse in dark waters, not resentful and wishing I had no obligations. It's exhausting, that's all. How am I supposed to figure out the rest of my life when I spend so much time caretaking?

Natalie rocks a little on her feet then clutches her stomach with both hands. Her cheeks puff up.

"Oh no!" she cries. "I'm gonna—"

I race after her to the bathroom. A geyser of French toast and raspberries spews from her mouth, landing just footsteps from the toilet.

Without a second's hesitation, I cry out, "Hang on," and run to the laundry room to grab my "vomit kit" (a bucket containing paper towels, cleaning spray, and facecloths). Muscle memory by now — I've cleaned up after Natalie more times than I can count.

I sigh. Another day in paradise.

CHAPTER EIGHT

Harbor Beach, Cape Cod
Three days later, 5:18 a.m.
Plunge count: 79

Dawn is breaking and I'm the first at the beach again. Well, actually Compost Carol and Hannah were here first, but they left their swimming bag at home and biked back together to grab it.

I rub my hands to ward off the chill. It's slightly warmer out than last time. In front of me, only the tips of the white waves stand out from the darkness. Above, a sliver of a moon rests in the sky, impervious to our mortal troubles below.

I'm halfway through a yawn when Guardie approaches. We've never been alone before.

"Morning," he says, probably getting a good view of my molars. His hair is loose, falling just above his shoulders, and he's wearing a poncho and shorts, revealing muscular legs. Is he immune to the cold? He looks like he belongs in Sedona, or at some New Age surfer festival.

"Sleep okay?" he asks.

"Not great, thanks."

I'm lucky to get three solid hours. During the day, I complete basic tasks — marking for my colleagues, reviewing research papers, serving a nutritious dinner for Natalie and me, then binging on European movies in bed — but at night, between two and five, I'm victim to a whirlpool of swirling thoughts.

"You should visit our spa for a treatment. Ice bath, massage. We have awesome sleep herbs."

"Hmm, maybe." I fidget with the drawstring of my yoga pants.

His eyes linger.

Why are there always these weighty looks between us? It makes me uncomfortable (and a wee bit tingly). I'm ultra-aware of every nuance to our exchanges. Some people, regardless of compatibility, or looks, or life stages, just have good chemistry. Is that us? He said he thought I was stunning and smart . . . "So, we're the first," I say, inhaling the salty air.

We both stare pointedly at the vast ocean.

A gust of wind blows our way, and I shiver. "Did you hear about Rachael's book?"

"That's going to cause a lot of waves. Excuse the pun."

"I wonder if she'll show up this morning."

"It would take some guts, eh?"

"Everyone's probably worried her book's going to expose their secrets." I cut him a sideways glance, gauging his expression.

He nods. "I told Rachael a lot. Maybe too much."

If he likes me, why confide in Rachael? I fight off a wave of insecurity. *Urgh, stop being irrational.*

"What about? I mean, if you don't mind me asking . . ."

"My parents mostly. They're back in Vancouver. I said how disappointed they are to have a son who they can't boast about at the golf club."

"It's like that, is it?"

"Sure is. But I was born to heal. Not through conventional medicine; with these." He holds up his hands. Scratches mark his right knuckle and fingers, thin red lines standing out against his skin.

"What drew you to massage?"

"Trial and lots of error. It was the only thing that felt right. Helping people unlock energy blocks."

William has absolute disdain for alternative medicine. The man could give a TED Talk on what a crock he thinks reiki is. *Healing a person by hovering your hands over their body. Ha!* When William gets fired up about something, he list-rants. "One: Lack of scientific evidence. Two: Placebo effect. Three: Get those people on some good antidepressants. I can recommend loads of SSRIs." And prescribe he did . . . *over*prescribe, perhaps.

I don't know if Guardie offers reiki at the spa. I get the feeling his clients are there for skin-to-skin contact. Maybe I'm not the only one who feels chemistry with him.

"Hopefully your family will accept your calling." My hobby — cooking — was quickly shut down as a career option when I was younger.

"Not sure about that. I might have made a scene last Christmas." He cringes. "At the dinner table. Mom left in tears. She didn't even serve her Nanaimo bar trifle. Not my finest moment. But there you go. We haven't spoken since."

"That's tough." I'm touched he's opening up; he either trusts me or he's so in tune with his emotions he feels comfortable sharing his wounds with the world. Mine are solely reserved for the person I pay $180 an hour to talk to them about.

"What made your mom upset?"

"Let's just say they wanted me to do something I wasn't okay with. I called my parents out on our unhealthy family dynamic, especially about my brother, the 'golden boy,' which is just another term for someone who's gutless and does what their parents tell them to do."

I stiffen. "That's harsh. The 'golden child' label can be given to kids who go out of their way to help others. It's not necessarily a bad thing."

"Fair point." He looks thoughtful. "I pointed out that despite all their success, none of them seemed happy. Sometimes, I'm too honest."

48

"No such thing." In fact, there is nothing more important — and attractive — to me in a relationship than honesty. Would Guardie's secret make its way into Rachael's book? Hot Canadian healer confronts family on favoritism and superficiality? Not that riveting. Maybe he told Rachael more than he's letting on.

Guardie reaches for the pendant on his necklace, a gold crystal that shimmers in the light.

"What's with the crystals?" I ask.

"Each time I touch them, they remind me of my daily intention. A quality or virtue I'd like to cultivate."

Now I wish I hadn't mocked him behind his back about his necklaces. He reveres them like a rosary.

"Humans have always used amulets for protection, luck, or for spiritual purposes. In Ancient Egypt, Ancient Greece and Rome, Asian and African cultures. And my own."

"Which is?" I pretend I don't know Miguel told me his mom is Italian.

"My grandmother was Squamish," Guardie says, sounding proud of his Indigenous heritage. "Coast Salish. Here, check out this one." He holds the pendant away from his chest. I step forward and take it from his hand, our fingers touching.

"It's, uh, lovely."

"Tiger's eye. Supposed to mend broken relationships."

I think of William, and we share a sad smile. Maybe other people can throw themselves into new relationships, hearts smashing like ships on rocks, but not me. I don't want any involvement. That's what I tell myself, yet as Guardie draws his hand through his hair, something in me wants to skip the preliminaries and touch those dark curls. A blush burns my cheeks despite the frigid air.

"But, yeah," he says, "it's good to have a reminder like, 'Today I'm going to try to be more forgiving,' or 'Today I'm going to live in the present.'"

I'm in the present right now. And I feel kind of horny. What's happening to me?

Please tell me you sometimes eat at McDonalds and watch crap TV?"

He chuckles. "McDonalds, no. TV, yeah. I like watching arm-wrestling matches."

"*Arm-wrestling?*" I laugh. "Now you've lost me. Well, as long as you don't really believe in manifesting things, we'll be okay."

His eyebrow quirks. "Of course I believe in manifestation. Why else am I having a conversation with an intoxicating Swedish Irish American right now?"

"Ha!"

He smiles but then it drops. "I thought we were the first here but it looks like someone's started without us." He points toward a bundle of belongings I hadn't noticed on the sand, halfway between our stretch of beach and MacMillian Pier. I can't make out much more than a heap with a towel on top.

"Oh. I was sure I was alone." I search the ocean for arms slicing through the water, but there's nothing, not a ripple. "The swimmer's probably so far out we can't see them."

"Maybe," Guardie says. "The water can play tricks on us."

"You're right." I step away, Rachael's book and the fickleness of romance on my mind. People can play tricks on us too.

Which is precisely the daily reminder I need. No crystals necessary for that.

CHAPTER NINE

The others arrive in dribs and drabs.

Li-Ping sporting an Adidas sweatsuit and her fanny pack.
The lovebirds, Hannah and Compost Carol, with their shared
swimming bag (Carol carrying a basket to collect litter on
the beach after our swim; she long ago stopped asking us to
participate). The blondes. And Serenity the sculptor — a year
younger than me, tall, monosyllabic, gorgeous — whose work
was recently featured in *The New Yorker*. She hasn't attended
the last few swims.

"Serenity! Great to see you." Compost Carol gives her a
hug. "We've missed you."

Serenity tends to dress in white and wears her hair in
a topknot. Originally from Tehran (and originally named
Firuzeh), she and her family moved to London when she was
a girl, and to America when she was twenty-one, but she still
has an English accent. Her tragedy, she said, was intergener-
ational violence and trauma from living under a dictatorship.

She'd been generous with my niece Natalie from the
moment they'd met, inviting her to visit her studio and offering to introduce her to some arty New York bigwigs who were
visiting P-town.

51

I glance across the beach at the abandoned stuff down by the water then check the ocean for signs of a swimmer. Nothing.

Peggy, a middle-aged mom with a pixie cut streaked with hints of silver, is also here today. You can't miss her because she always has two accessories: wireless earbuds, ready to catch up on her favorite podcasts, and a pair of chic cat-eye glasses that add a touch of vintage charm to her appearance. She's a crime podcast aficionado who steers all conversations into "I heard a podcast about . . ." She experienced her tragedy in childhood — her best friend in middle school was poisoned by a family member, which no doubt is where her obsession with true crime stems from.

I study the ocean, looking for an arm, a head poking up . . .

Miguel shows up last, in his Louis Vuitton robe, uncharacteristically ungroomed, hair messy, bags under his eyes. "Sorry, everyone. My bubba woke up when I was leaving the house. I had to wake up the manny." Miguel and Ronald's fit friend from New York doubles as the couple's child carer.

Miguel avoids my gaze. What secret did Rachael find out about him?

I'm not the only one with Rachael on my mind. There's a buzz in the air, snatches of conversation about her book.

". . . What a bitch . . ."

". . . And I don't know why I told her anything . . . It just slipped out . . ."

". . . I thought she was just making conversation . . ."

". . . The nerve! . . ."

Hannah stands on her sand podium. "Everyone ready to swim?"

"Sure, but Guardie and I" — I feel oddly juvenile pairing our names — "just noticed a pile of someone's stuff on the beach. We weren't sure if one of the group was already out there."

"Let's check it out." Miguel's the first to answer, a bloodhound's scent for drama.

The group marches toward the pile of belongings.

A plush towel is draped on top of a bag.

"It's Rachael's!" I recognize the gold-and-pink design of the beach bag, her Havaianas, also gold — her signature color, she once told me. There's another bag too. Full of . . . I peek inside. A yellow notebook, a pack of cigarettes, and books, lots of them, hardbacks and paperbacks. Sometimes Rachael takes books to the café and, after we leave, stays on and reads.

I look back at the group, who are all watching me. "I've been waiting here at least ten minutes and haven't seen her."

"Maybe Rachael got here first and crossed paths with a creep." Peggy often injects possible near-death scenarios into our conversations. She's in the wrong profession. Instead of being a "needle nurse," saving the world one wrinkle at a time, she should be a Hollywood scriptwriter.

"Could she have swum so far out we can't see her?" Compost Carol asks — unlikely, considering Rachael was always late and there was always a fuss about her being late. Plus Rachael wouldn't have gone into the ocean alone. It was an unspoken rule among our group: Wait for a swimming buddy.

Serenity adjusts her topknot. "She's probably in the loo." It's the longest sentence I've heard from her in weeks.

"The café's closed." Hannah frowns. For some reason, everything Serenity says seems to annoy her.

"Rachael knows not to swim alone," Miguel says. "Not with Jaws out there . . ."

It's a serious concern. If Rachael went out swimming before sunrise, a shark attack is not out of the question. Sharks feed at dusk and dawn, and these waters, come May to October, are where most of the adult great whites in the world like to gather.

"It wasn't so scary to swim ten years ago," a blonde says. "Now we have to think about sharks every time we go in. Damn seals are everywhere."

"And the fishermen are furious," Peggy adds. "Listened to a podcast about it. Catches down, bait shops closing all over the Cape."

"Whatever you do, don't use the C-word," Miguel warns.

"C-word?" Serenity asks.

"*Cull*," he mouths. "Can't suggest it with the Endangered Species Act, even though the seal population's more than recovered."

"Hello?" Hannah cuts in. "We need to focus on Rachael."

Is it my imagination or does Guardie step a little closer, like he's ready to protect me if shit goes down? Or am I reading too much into things? Given he's Canadian, perhaps he's exercising his natural-born right to chivalry.

"Have you checked Sharktivity?" Li-Ping asks.

"Let's hope Mr. Spot Claw, Fruit Loops, or Big Daddy aren't around," Peggy says. Sharktivity names lots of the great whites. Besides the three just mentioned, off the top of my head, there's Luke, Squidward, Portal, Cheerio, Scarface, and Scoop, There It Is.

"Let me look." Hannah scrolls through her phone then glances anxiously at the water.

Li-Ping's eyes widen. "What is it?"

"According to Sharktivity, Big Daddy's monitoring tag pinged near the pier twenty minutes ago," Hannah says. "No visual confirmation, just the automated detection system."

Miguel presses a hand to his face. "Shit."

The mood of the group shifts — glances and raised eyebrows all around. The beach itself feels charged.

"Has anyone talked to Rachael?" Carol's voice is high-pitched. "Or checked the chat?"

"I'll look," Hannah says.

Our WhatsApp chat is pretty active; besides coordinating swim meetups, sometimes we post about the weather, share jokes or Sharktivity information.

Guardie crosses his arms, his attention on the horizon. "Look!"

I follow his gaze. Out in the water, two seals glide in and out of the waves.

"Not good," Li-Ping murmurs.

Everyone knows seals and sharks go hand in hand. Add jumping fish and circling birds, and you've got yourself a problem. I look up at the brightening sky — bird-free. Phew.

"Rachael was on the chat last night." Hannah flicks through her phone. "Guardie sent that group message — *Not sure if I'll make it in morn. Don't swim too deep* — and Rachael gave it a thumbs-up."

I'd noticed Rachael liked all of Guardie's messages, but a thumbs-up is innocuous, and none of my business, although I guess as Rachael is writing a book about our lives and seems to be currently MIA, everything she does now is our business.

Peggy turns to Guardie. "Why'd you change your mind?"

"About?"

"Coming this morning."

He shoves his hands into his pockets. "Just woke up and decided it'd be good."

"You got here first?"

"I got here first," I jump in. "No, actually, Carol and Hannah were here when I arrived and then they went back home to grab their swimming stuff."

"I'll just ring her," Hannah says, lifting her phone to her ear. She waits patiently. "Voicemail," she says.

Li-Ping reaches for Rachael's bags. "If her phone isn't here it means she's probably somewhere nearby on a call."

"Stop!" Peggy yells. "No touching."

"Why?"

Carol's face gets as serious as when she's talking about single-use plastics. "*It could be a crime scene.*"

"Let's think," Hannah says. "Why would Rachael be here early? Maybe she went for a walk and ran into someone."

"She wouldn't go too far when she knows we're all coming," Li-Ping says. "Maybe she tripped and fell."

"She might be nearby and able to hear us," Carol says. "Rachael! Rachael?"

Carol and Peggy head in different directions calling Rachael's name.

Miguel and I hurry to the shoreline, the icy water a shock to my toes.

"Unlikely to be a shark," I say quietly. There hasn't been a shark attack here since 2018.

"Rachael would have a greater chance of being hit by lightning." Miguel looks over his shoulder before whispering, "Are you thinking what I'm thinking? It's like she's disappeared."

Or someone made her disappear — our eyes meet in understanding.

Given her impending "tell-all," there's a long list of people in the Tragic Wives who'd be grateful if Rachael Walker was shut up for good.

CHAPTER TEN

Everyone gathers in a circle and speaks at the same time.

"We need to keep checking the water!" I say.

"Try her phone again!" Compost Carol orders.

Hannah dials and puts her phone on speaker. It goes straight to voicemail again: *"Hi, you've reached Rachael. Don't leave a voicemail. Email or DM. Unless it's my agent, you can do whatever you like. Bless your heart."*

"Bad sign," Peggy the podcast fanatic says. "It went to voicemail because her phone's off. If someone's got her, they'd turn off the phone first."

Carol glares at her. "Rachael could be talking to someone, like Li-Ping said. Her phone could be on 'do not disturb.' It could've died. Or she turned it off to save battery."

"Or," Peggy says, "her rapist stole it, or she was kidnapped."

Most of us give her a dirty look, and Miguel says, "Not helpful!"

Hannah glances around. "I'm calling Rachael back and leaving a message. If she turns the phone on, she'll know we're looking for her." When Hannah reaches Rachael's voicemail, she says, "Rachael, the swimming group is near the Sandbar Café with your bags. Call us back. We're worried."

My eyes are glued to the ocean. A few beachgoers are scattered across the sand, a couple speed-walk down the shoreline, and an older woman with three dogs is headed for the pier.

"We need to call search and rescue," I say, but Hannah's voice overrides me.

"Has Rachael posted anything?"

We check her social media for any recent updates — no posts since last night. Hannah leaves DMs asking her to make contact.

"Here's what we'll do." Hannah takes charge. "Split up and search the beach."

"Looking for . . . ?" Serenity asks.

"For Rachael!" Miguel snarls.

"We don't really know if there's anything to worry about yet," one of the blondes says. "There's probably a logical reason — Rachael got stuck talking to someone or forgot something and ran home to get it. Let's get coffee at the bakery that's open and see if she shows up."

Dammit. My heart pounds. We can't keep standing around talking, or DM-ing her, or, god forbid, sipping cappuccinos when Rachael could be drowning! "No!"

Everyone turns to me. Did I shout?

"Rachael could be in the ocean," I say. "We have to call search and rescue. Quick."

A ripple of tension moves through the group. Hannah nods sharply.

I take out my phone and dial 911 and they direct me to the local Coast Guard operator. In the background, I can hear one of the blondes saying that we're getting ahead of ourselves. But all the reasons a body cannot be found in water are etched into my mind.

A swimmer can get caught in a powerful rip current, which swiftly pulls them away from the shore and into deeper water, and their body is carried out to sea.

Drowning incidents in less frequented areas like this mean delayed response times, reducing the chances of recovery.

Sharks can consume a drowned person's body, leaving little or no trace.

I'm starting to feel dizzy. I look over at Miguel, but he's caught up in a conversation with Li-Ping.

Over time, a drowned person's body can decompose, disintegrate, or become unidentifiable due to water conditions and natural processes. If the weather is hot — like it was in the Outer Banks where Britta and Natalie holidayed — decomposition is even quicker.

If the incident goes unnoticed, the delay in initiating search and rescue operations can make recovery impossible.

As I end the call to the Coastguard, a hand on my elbow jolts me. "Are you okay?" Guardie asks gently. "Are they on their way?"

I nod, not trusting myself to speak without showing how upset I am.

"Have some water." He takes a rainbow water bottle out of his bag, passes it to me, and I chug it back. "What are you thinking?"

As the others talk among themselves, I struggle to get the words out. "It's just, I know the sort of things that could've happened." I breathe heavily, bringing a hand to my throat.

"Hey, it's okay." His arm comes around my shoulder, steadying me.

"My sister, she — she got swept away in the sea." The search and rescue teams did everything they could to locate her. Natalie witnessed the direction Britta was dragged in, so the teams concentrated their search in that location, using special equipment and techniques — sonar, underwater cameras, and divers.

Still, no luck. No Britta.

"I'm so sorry." Guardie's eyes mirror my pain. I'm not sure if he knows anything about it; probably someone in the swimming group gave him the run-down.

"Carol," Hannah says, "while we're waiting for the rescue team, post an update to Sharktivity, and tell them we suspect a woman went swimming thirty minutes ago and now she's nowhere to be found." Next, she divides us up and gives us tasks. We get into groups. Miguel and I will check the beach from the café to the pier. Guardie and the blondes (the women quickly volunteered when they heard Guardie was going) will search the beach in the other direction. Hannah and Carol will bike ride to Rachael's house to see if she's there. Peggy and Serenity will check the local coffee shops and parking lots.

Guardie leans close to me and whispers, "I'd rather be partnered with you."

"You can't help being so popular," I reply with a wobbly smile.

"Okay," Hannah says. "After, we'll reconvene at the Sandbar Café. Ask people if they've seen Rachael. Show them her photo — she's in that recent group photo on our chat. If you notice anyone shady, take a pic. For those on shore search, keep your eyes on the water, but don't go in. Make sure your phones are on and with you at all times."

"We should stop people from swimming," I add.

Hannah scans the shoreline. "Only a few locals are out at this hour. They'll have Sharktivity."

"Not necessarily," I say. "Some people still don't use it."

Li-Ping volunteers to stay with Rachael's things. She lowers her eyes. "Isaiah 41:13. *For I am the Lord your God who takes hold of your right hand and says to you, Do not fear; I will help you.*" It's obvious she's seconds away from tears.

"We'll find her." Guardie briefly touches Li-Ping's shoulder.

"Why are we all not saying what we're thinking?" Li-Ping asks the group, her voice breaking. "Rachael's *book*? We hear she's writing the book then she goes missing?"

"There's no time to talk about that now," Hannah says.

Peggy adjusts her cat-eyed glasses. "In the Bhagavad Gita, it says, 'Motive is the root of all actions.' I was listening to a podcast comparing scriptures and . . ."

I don't bother listening to the rest.

We're about to leave when Li-Ping asks, "What happens if we don't find anything? What happens if search and rescue don't find anything?"

"If it comes to that," Compost Carol says, "I'll call my sister."

I catch Miguel roll his eyes, and I can imagine he's thinking: *Just what we need, another crunchy hippie.*

"How can your sister help?" Li-Ping asks.

"My sister" — Carol hoists her shoulders back — "is a police officer."

CHAPTER ELEVEN

Tragic Wives WhatsApp chat
6:15 a.m.
Rachael missing: 1 hour

Hannah: *Anyone find anything? Rachael's phone is still going straight to voicemail.*

Miguel: *Nothing so far.*

Li-Ping: *The Coast Guard have sent a couple of boats. Just finished talking to one of their people. They're not picking up signs of anyone in the water, and no sharks about. Are you at Rachael's house yet?*

Hannah: *Nearly. Got waylaid asking people if they've seen Rachael.*

Li-Ping: *If you need to get into her house, there's a key under her tomato plant (sorry Rachael if you're reading). And just putting it out there . . . Are we looking for the manuscript? Did Rachael print it? Is it on her laptop? If Rachael's missing and the police get involved, we don't want a book about our secrets getting into the wrong hands.*

Hannah: *DON'T TEXT ABOUT IT. You do realize Rachael is on this chat and might be reading it . . .*

Li-Ping: *Ok. Sorry.*

Hannah: *I'm deleting this chain of msgs. From now on ONLY talk in person. I'm starting a new chat with just us.*

CHAPTER TWELVE

6:45 a.m.
Rachael missing: 1 hour, 30 minutes

"Rachael? Rachael?" I shout.

Miguel and I have searched the beach from the Sandbar Café to MacMillian Pier, but found no signs of Rachael. We've poked around the pier and shown half a dozen people her picture.

US flags line the wooden structure, flapping in the wind. The shops and businesses are all closed: the ferry terminal, the Whydah Museum, the Shark Center with its protruding Jaws head stuck above the entrance, and the kiosks that serve as offices for whale watching and fishing charters.

"Let's comb the beach again," Miguel says.

The clouds have mostly cleared, and the sun is out, the promise of blue sky, the acrid scent of brine. Seagulls cry overhead and a few morning walkers dot the shoreline. A couple of Coast Guard boats patrol back and forth across the water. I hope there's nothing out there for them to find — that Rachael would come hurrying down to the beach now to reclaim her abandoned bag. We move closer to the shrubs that run parallel to Commercial Street.

"Rachael!"

"I don't think a sea monster got Rachael," Miguel huffs, charging ahead. "More likely a Tragic Wives member dressed in sheep's clothing. Or a towel and a bathing suit."

I step over some driftwood, the sand uneven beneath my feet. "You don't really think one of us had a secret deep and dark enough to be worth stopping the book from coming out?" It's a leading question — maybe he'll spill whatever he told Rachael.

"If we were being dramatic, that would be the assumption," he says. "But Rachael will probably show up any minute, apologizing for making us worry."

As much as I want to believe him, optimism isn't my strong suit anymore. Academic ambitions once drove me — pursuing my own research instead of everyone else's, a life partner, wandering foreign markets for new spices and flavors. Now my goals are on hold, and I can barely remember what it's like to want something badly for myself.

"Rachael!" Miguel calls.

"What was with Li-Ping asking about the manuscript on our chat? Not smart to put herself out there like that."

"Rachael obviously has some dirt on her," Miguel says.

"Li-Ping's an angel." The former Olympian is a queen of self-discipline, trains daily, offers senior citizens free weekly exercise classes, and doesn't miss a Sunday at church.

"Everybody's got skeletons in the closet," Miguel says, stopping in front of some tufts of beach grass.

"In Sweden we have a similar saying: 'He doesn't have clean flour in his bag.'" I cast my eyes over the little mounds of sand, shadows and light, and scattered seashells.

"Weird. Anyway, sometimes they're not even our skeletons. They belong to the people we live with or work with. Guilt by association."

I sigh, barely listening to him.

"Guardie sure likes to help a damsel in distress," he says archly.

I'm no damsel. But distressed? Can't deny that. I use my sandal to kick through the sand, as if a clue to Rachael's whereabouts will surface.

"He likes you, Em. If you don't snap up his attention, he'll find a more willing horse to bet on. Go for it. I know you've got a slutty thoroughbred in you."

I'm about to tell Miguel to shut his trap when I spot a man by the shoreline. He's wearing a very sophisticated outfit for a morning stroll — dark jeans rolled to his calves and a pastel button-down shirt.

Miguel and I exchange a look and head to the water to cut him off.

"Hi." Miguel approaches him. "Nice day for a walk."

"*Scusi?*" The man gives him a quizzical look.

"Have you seen this woman?" Miguel shows him a photo of Rachael on his phone, her heart-shaped face framed by swathes of red hair, heavy mascara, a slight smile on her lips. Full of glorious life.

"I have seen no one," the man answers in an Italian accent.

"Are you a tourist? Local?" I ask.

He sneers and keeps walking but not before I whip out my phone and capture his profile.

"Let's keep looking," I say to Miguel, shivering despite the sun. I send Natalie a quick text asking what her plans are for the day. It's hard to motivate someone when you feel unmotivated yourself, but no matter what's going on, I need to be her cheerleader, her life coach, her private chef, whatever it takes.

Miguel scans the beach methodically.

I don't know what we're looking for exactly . . . anything out of place or clues Rachael was here. We return to the sandy shrubs closer to the street. I bend and part the shrubs in front of me, their leaves rustling in the breeze. What secret could Rachael have discovered big enough that someone might want to silence her?

I think back to the night when Rachael and Li-Ping had dinner at my house. Why had I told her so much? All the

66

tawdry details of William's betrayal. She seemed genuinely curious — empathetic, even. We bonded because she told us about this English movie producer who she dated in her twenties who cheated on her with her co-star. I don't know whether to believe it now. She was probably just trying to get material.

"Anything new on the chat?" I ask Miguel.

He checks his phone. "Nope. What about search and rescue?"

"Li-Ping said they'd call if they find anything."

A few jagged shards of glass stick up in the sand. I pick them up and place them into the pocket of my purse so no one will step on them and slice their feet.

"Aren't you a citizen of the world?" Miguel says. "Here, let me get that seaweed or whatever it is off your forehead." He leans close and flicks between my eyebrows, then gently brushes my cheek. "You know, there's things you can do about your little scar."

"It's not a big deal. Character, right?" In high school Britta had stolen a popular girl's boyfriend (something she was fond of doing), and the ex-girlfriend and her friends stalked and harassed Britta for weeks, threatening to beat her up. When they finally cornered her at the school bus stop, I was there to protect her. It turned ugly fast — hair pulling, scratching, those long, sharp nails raking across skin. I sure understood the term "cat fight" after that.

"Well, if you change your mind, LED light therapy is the bomb," Miguel says. "NASA invented it to heal astronauts' wounds. Now every bougie bitch is at home using her infrared to keep the age monsters away."

"Getting old is a privilege." I point to an area where some small boats are overturned. A privilege Britta will never have that chance. "Let's search over there."

"Rachael!" Our voices echo across the beach.

About a month after I joined the swimming group, I forgot to pack a towel. When we came out of the water, Rachael offered to share hers. It was a cold morning, and we huddled like toddlers on a bench seat at the Sandbar Café under her pink towel, wet hair in our faces. She dropped her normal brash persona and showed a soft longing, mentioning that she wanted to live by the ocean someday when she had kids, walk the beach with them, collect shells, and build sandcastles.

"I've been pregnant twice before," she said. "Bad timing; I had to make hard decisions. I thought being a mom would hurt my acting career, but, yeah, turned out that happened all on its own."

By the time we reach the halfway point between the pier and where Rachael left her bags, I'm out of breath. "I wonder which Tragic Wives member is most worried about their secret coming out?"

"Who knows? It's a guessing game." Miguel hurries ahead. Usually when something's fishy, he loves dissecting it.

"What do people keep secrets about? Money? Family issues? Career struggles? Lifestyle choices? Mental health? Definitely sex — and who with." No more beating around the bush. "What secret did you share with Rachael?"

Miguel strides ahead, calling, "Rachael?"

I race to catch up to him, sinking into the sand with each step. "Hey! Spill."

"Nooo. It's humiliating. I don't even know why I told her."

Why would Miguel confide in Rachael and not me? That envious feeling snakes into my chest, making my skin hot. I should be ashamed of myself. Jealous of a missing woman. "Tell me!"

"Serenity is the dodgiest person in our group," Miguel deflects.

"Don't be a xenophobe." I keep looking back at the waves, searching for a swimmer, eyeing the Coast Guard boats that had moved further out to sea.

"We've all heard the rumors about Serenity's 'patrons.' Believe me, that's definitely going in Rachael's book."

People certainly gossiped about Serenity's artist-patron "relations." AKA sex. It's true that Serenity has dated some wealthy people, usually around the time she needs to fund a new show. "Meh. That's old news. What did *you* tell Rachael?"

He hesitates, his expression wistful.

I reach for his hand.

"It's embarrassing." He bites his lip. "I have an . . . addiction."

Oh, Miguel. Alcohol? Cocaine? He liked dabbling in both of those, but I thought it was more of a party thing.

"Another man." Miguel screws up his face. "I'm addicted to my AI, ChatGPT. I call him Gentlemen's Personal Trainer, GPT."

I smack my head. "This is what you're worried about? Being addicted to your phone? For Christ's sake. I thought you were serious. Let's just focus on finding Rachael. That *is* serious." I forge onward.

"Em, I am totally fucking dependent. I'm such a hypocrite promoting SNAIL GIRL ERA and dumbphones when I ask GPT everything. What should I have for breakfast? What should I masturbate about? What does it mean that I masturbate about those things, and is there something wrong with me? What time should I go to sleep? What bedtime story should I read my daughter?"

"Yeah, okay, not a good look considering your brand, but still — not that serious." I pick up my pace, eyes trained on the sand.

Where the heck is Rachael?

A green vape is discarded on the sand near a bush. I nearly pick it up, but stop myself — *fingerprints* — and snap a photo instead and then keep moving.

"It all happened because Rachael mentioned she'd never used ChatGPT," Miguel prattles on. "I said, 'Confidentially, I can't live without mine.' And I explained I had two phones. Rachael said, 'Show me.' I did! And she spent five minutes scrolling and scrolling and I went to the bathroom and when

I came back she was taking pics of the chats. I didn't realize how fucking weird it was till last week when Rachael told me the main character in her book is this totally neurotic woman who is in love with her AI! Can you fucking believe it? I'll be a laughingstock."

I'm no longer listening. A pink-and-gold phone with a marble-patterned PopSocket lies in the shrubs.

"Call Carol," my voice wobbles. "Now."

"Why?" Miguel follows my gaze.

"We need the police here. Now."

CHAPTER THIRTEEN

9:15 a.m.
Rachael missing: 4 hours

The Sandbar Café is bustling with the morning crowd, oblivious to the turmoil our group is in. An airy space with high ceilings and pastel yellow walls, it's decorated with antique lobster traps, colorful wooden buoys, and carved gulls, everything positioned to celebrate the beach view. Not the kind of place you'd expect to discuss a missing friend in.

Our group is sitting at the big table near the window.

"Where're Guardie and your friend?" Miguel asks the blonde at the table.

"They stayed at the beach with Rachael's bags."

"Because I freaked out," Li-Ping admits. "Standing there all by myself, just waiting. So they took over and we" she indicates the blonde "—searched the beach together."

We return to speculating about Racheal in heated whispers, all competing for airtime, trying to get our thoughts across before Compost Carol's sister, the police officer, arrives. She was on shift nearby when Carol called — she'll be here soon.

Coffees and pastries clutter the table. How can anyone eat right now? I'm having trouble even keeping my breathing steady. I chug back my water and refill the glass again.

Ever since we got here, Miguel has been bouncing his knee, his hand darting toward his pocket before he stops himself. Damn ChatGPT. He really is addicted.

Li-Ping speaks over everyone in a whisper-shout. "All I'm saying is, I don't think it's necessary to tell people we're worried about Rachael's book. Because you know what that makes us?" She lowers her voice. "*Suspects!*"

As the word leaves Li-Ping's mouth, a woman with a hefty build enters the café. She has wild brown hair and serious eyes. She's dressed in a navy-blue uniform, gun on her belt.

"Hi, thanks for coming," Carol says to her sister before inhaling some vegan nut bar.

"Good you called." She sits at the head of the table. "I'm Officer Winn, with the Provincetown Police Department. I'm going to ask some questions, take a missing person report."

A missing person report? Already? This is getting real.

"But twenty-four hours hasn't even passed." Know-it-all Peggy shows off her crime nous. Behind her cat-eyed spectacles, her hazel eyes burn with vibrancy.

"Common misconception," Officer Winn replies. "In many jurisdictions, no specific amount of time has to pass before a missing person report is accepted." She opens her tablet. "Hey, waiter? Latte, real sweet with two sugars, thanks."

Soon afterward, the officer's drink arrives, along with Guardie and the blonde. Guardie sits by me and gives my arm a reassuring squeeze, which means, *We've got this*, or *It's going to be okay . . .* or something.

"Your names?" Officer Winn slurps her coffee. "Then tell me how you know the missing person."

After we go around in a circle, Officer Winn asks, "The missing person's full name, date of birth, and physical description?"

"Rachael Walker." Hannah instinctively takes the lead. "Rachael's somewhere in the range of thirty-five to forty-five.

She never told anyone her exact age. Red hair. Curvy. Five foot eight. She's a writer and former actress. Just small roles." She shows the officer a picture on her phone. "You can find out more on her IMDb page."

"Current address and contact information?"

"Her place is over on Conant Street, close to the beach." Hannah passes her a slip of paper. "I prepared a list with her social media and contact details."

"Known vehicles?"

Hannah gestures to the left. "Her bicycle's locked up in front of the café."

"Circumstances of her disappearance?"

Hannah tells Winn about Rachael's abandoned bags, how I found the phone in the shrubs, and that the shark, Big Daddy, was pinged this morning at the end of the pier. She says she and Carol checked Rachael's house, but the lights were off and when they knocked on her door, no one answered. I mention the Italian man on the beach and the green vape I spotted near Rachael's phone. Li-Ping says that Coast Guard are still looking, but they've stepped down the search to a single boat.

"Nobody saw her go into the water, so they'll probably call off the search this afternoon." Officer Winn takes another slurp. "So none of you saw Rachael this morning?"

"No," Hannah answers.

"Last night? Yesterday?"

Everyone shakes their head.

Beside me, Guardie shifts in his seat, his poncho brushing my arm.

"Day before?" Officer Winn asks.

"I thought I saw her go into a shop around four thirty." Two blotches of red appear on Li-Ping's cheeks. "But I can't be sure. She was by herself."

"Which shop?"

"Um . . . Toys of Eros."

Officer Winn's left eyebrow quivers.

As a proud pro-sex queer destination, Provincetown has lots of adults-only shops. Still. Imagine the headline: *RACHAEL WALKER MISSING! LAST SPOTTED: TOYS OF EROS*.

And come to think of it, it's a little strange for Li-Ping, a raging Christian, to loiter outside Toys of Eros. Maybe she was there to pick up something for herself and Todd. Newlyweds are frisky like that.

Although I brought my vibrator from New York, the whole time I've been in the Cape it has remained tucked away in my bedside table, batteries dead, just like my sex drive. Well, until Guardie came into the picture.

"Walk me through your morning swims," Officer Winn says, snapping me out of my sex thoughts. How can I be thinking about vibrators in the middle of filing a missing person report? "Who usually shows up first? How long do you swim? Do you hang out after?"

Hannah spouts off the answers.

Officer Winn turns to me. "Why were you there first this morning when usually it's Hannah or Carol?

"I, ah, had a nightmare. Couldn't get back to sleep." I explain that Carol and Hannah were there first but went home to get their bag.

"A nightmare, huh? Guilty conscience?"

That itchy, hivey feeling creeps up my neck. "No, nothing like that."

"You woke up and then?"

"I drank some water, got into my car and made my way to the Sandbar Café." Shit, is that my official alibi now?

"Did anyone see you?"

"I don't know. I think there were a couple of cars on the road?"

Miguel says he made a thermos of coffee before he drove to the beach in his Porsche.

Guardie meditated, gratitude journaled, then walked to the beach.

Gratitude journaling? Geez. His New Age stuff makes me feel old.

Serenity added a few elements to her art installation and drove to our meeting spot.

Hmm. I recall Serenity once saying she only works on her art *after* lunch, as her creative juices start flowing in the afternoon . . .

Peggy had a bowl of Cornflakes and speed-walked to the beach.

I thought she hated breakfast cereals. I swear she ranted recently about a podcast on everyday foods with low nutrient density and refined carbohydrates.

Li-Ping — she weight trained and vlogged. Would Officer Winn like to join her online community?

"Excuse me?" Serenity clears her throat.

Officer Winn swivels her head toward her. Serenity can often be so silent that you forget she's there, just like the inanimate sculptures she creates. Then she speaks, and you're like, *We have a goddess in our midst.*

"May I leave?" Serenity asks in her clipped English accent. "I have an upcoming exhibition and I'm meeting someone who has driven up from New York."

"I'd appreciate it if you wait till I finish my questions." Officer Winn asks Guardie and Miguel to repeat their alibis and double-checks a few details. Is this because men are statistically more likely to be perpetrators in missing women cases? She asks them to recount when they moved to the Cape, their involvement with Rachael, and if they've ever had any incidents with the police.

"Uh, um, I guess there's one thing." Miguel stares at the floor. "I may have received a 'drunk and disorderly' last year."

"For?"

"Property damage."

How could I not know that? He never said a word. Was that the real secret he told Rachael about? Not the lame chatbot stuff, but an anger management problem?

"Ronald — my husband — and I got into a disagreement. I'd had one too many mojitos. I overreacted."

"How so?" The officer has a hungry expression on her face.

"Might've, um, keyed his car."

"Temper, huh?"

"I'm in therapy," Miguel answers hotly.

"You'll find most of us here are in therapy," I step in, hating the officer's unsaid insinuation that Miguel is the worst person at the table because he once got into trouble with the law. In the heat of passion, people do things they regret, although I can't see Miguel keying a car. That's a whole lot of rage. I vow to be more here for him, make sure he knows he can rely on me, and he can talk about his feelings no matter how dark.

Unfortunately, my bladder might burst from all the glasses of water I've drunk. I rise. "Excuse me, I'll be back in a moment."

Guardie gives me a look as though he's checking if I'm okay. I nod at him and then weave through the café, feeling shakier with every step.

Where are you, Rachael? Has someone hurt you?

CHAPTER FOURTEEN

Officer Winn glances up from her tablet when I approach our table. The buzz of the café feels obscene now, all those cheerful voices floating around us when Rachael is missing.

I slide in beside Guardie and our thighs touch. I move away, but the warmth lingers, my body tingly from our contact.

"So," Officer Winn scans each of our faces in turn, "tell me about Rachael's dating life. Is she seeing anyone?"

"No one permanent, I think?" Hannah peers at the rest of us to check. Everyone's blank. "She writes dating columns for magazines, so she has lots of first dates. She's on all the apps."

"Maybe she had a secret rendezvous this morning," Miguel says.

Being put on the spot and forced to answer questions about Rachael, I realize there's so much we don't know about her. It's like she never showed any of us the real her. Why so secretive? Maybe she was running from something in her past.

The officer scratches her arm, watching him carefully. Is it because she's annoyed that civilians think they know it all from watching *CSI*, or is her interest piqued that someone who knew Rachael would jump to this conclusion?

"Where's her family?" Officer Winn asks.

"She was raised in Georgia," Hannah answers. "Parents live there, divorced. A younger sister and brother."

Serenity, forced to stay for the interrogation, makes a show of checking her phone. As if artists have more pressing matters than a missing person.

"Didn't she have a fight with her brother recently?" Li-Ping asks.

"That's right." Hannah brings a finger to her mouth, forehead furrowing as though she's trying to recall something. "I can't remember what it was about. Sorry."

"How do you communicate about your swimming group?"

A small pause — everyone's probably thinking about Li-Ping's damning message. Hannah told us earlier she'd erased the messages, but the police could probably recover them.

"We have a WhatsApp chat," Mr. Too-Honest-For-His-Own-Good Guardie says.

"You can read it on my phone later," Carol tells her sister.

"Since Rachael was a former actress," Office Winn says, "anyone know if she had any overzealous fans?"

A few mumbled "don't think so"s and head shakes from our group. Hannah opens her mouth like she might say more, then closes it.

"She stopped acting about ten years ago, I think," Li-Ping says.

Next come questions about Rachael's daily routines, habits, and activities.

"Rachael seemed sad lately," Serenity says.

"Sad? How so?"

"At the new exhibition at Schoolhouse Gallery, I saw her weeping in the bathroom. I guess she could've been moved by the art."

"Maybe Rachael was depressed," Peggy jumps in, "and she planted her bags and phone and ran away to start a new life."

That woman has listened to one too many podcasts.

"Another scenario," Peggy says, pushing up her cat-eyed glasses. "Rachael suicided. She wanted us to think she got taken by a shark when she actually gulped too much Nembutal from China and is now dead in some cheap motel in Boston."

The whole table stares at her. Miguel raises his palm in a "girl, no" gesture. I can't help thinking about Peggy's friend who was poisoned in high school. It's not healthy to be so obsessed with gruesome deaths.

"Leave the scenarios to me." Officer Winn frowns. "Has Rachael disappeared before?"

Everyone shakes their head.

"Any recent life events, changes, or stressors in her life?"

On the precipice of submitting her manuscript, Rachael was probably jittery with excitement.

"We don't think so," Hannah says. Why is Hannah lying? Does she have something to hide? I suppose submitting a manuscript doesn't account for a "life event." As for Miguel, I've never seen him so quiet.

"Did Rachael express any plans or intentions before her disappearance?"

To publish a "tell-all" about us. Fuck.

"She didn't say she was going anywhere." Hannah neatly dodges the question.

The officer takes a slow breath and leans back in her chair. She runs her tongue over her teeth, and I get the feeling she senses our deception, that a motive — or motives — are being withheld.

"Any places she may have gone?"

To personally deliver the manuscript to her contact at the big publishing house?

My body feels like it's going to burst with the tension.

"Rachael has some family in New York," Hannah says, "so maybe there. But that doesn't explain why her phone was in the sand."

"Did Rachael have any current conflicts or disputes with anyone? Is there a reason someone would want her out of the picture?"

This is the moment. We need to tell her.

Silence.

I scrutinize the faces around the table as the question hovers between us. I'm met with twitching eyes, suspiciously blank expressions.

Goddammit. It seems like there is a real chance a member from Tragic Wives — a person at this table — is involved.

No way. These are my friends. But some of them are more like acquaintances, aren't they? We never really know people. Not even the ones we spend so much time with.

"There's a book Rachael's writing," Guardie says. The words crackle between us all, everyone stiffening. "It's fiction, but kind of about our swimming group."

Officer Winn knocks back the last bit of coffee in her cup and makes eye contact with each of us. Although her face is deadpan, it's as though she's biting back a smile. "Any reason none of the rest of you mentioned that?"

We answer at once:

"Not that big of a deal."

"Unlikely it'll get published."

"Just forgot."

"All righty." Officer Winn rubs her hands, confidence dripping off her. "That's all I need for now." She stands and turns to me. "Ms. Brennan, you were the first person on the beach this morning."

"No, I–I was the third." Do I seem too defensive? I uncross my arms. Under the table, Guardie squeezes my knee.

"You might've been on the beach at the same time as Rachael," Officer Winn says.

Which means I could've been nearby when Rachael got grabbed, gagged or . . . No. Don't think about that.

"You're also the one who found her phone and the vape," she adds.

Am I in the middle of tragedy again? I twist my Dala horse bracelet, and everyone's eyes bore into me.

I have nothing to do with this!

"I suggest none of you leave the state." Officer Winn addresses the group, but her gaze locks on me. *I'm watching you*, it says.

Her stare scorches my face like a sunburn.

CHAPTER FIFTEEN

10:15 a.m.
Rachael missing: 5 hours

Guardie walks me to my car on Commercial Street. Usually, Miguel accompanies me, and it's tough to break loose because he always has one last witty thing to say. But as soon as Officer Winn left the café, everyone divided up with different plans. Compost Carol and Hannah were going to make missing posters and put them up around town and Li-Ping was already posting on social media to see if she could find Rachael that way. The rest of the Tragic Wives scuttled away like crabs, even Miguel, without a wave.

"It's a bit of a walk," I tell Guardie as we head up the street. I'm parked near a bookstore where I was planning to find a birthday gift for Natalie.

Guardie has never offered to walk me anywhere before, but I have a hunch he feels sorry for me.

"Officer Winn shouldn't have singled you out like that," Guardie says.

"She's just trying to do her job." I don't feel well. My shoulders are as hard as rocks. Rachael disappearing, possibly in the water, is beyond triggering.

I scan the tourists loitering on Commercial Street, wondering if they've crossed paths with her unawares, or were somehow involved in her disappearance. If she's been attacked, then anyone could be a suspect.

Even though it's May, and still the slow season, the street looks festive. Trees are bursting with fresh spring blooms. The narrow three-mile stretch is full of used bookstores, art galleries, and chichi places like the jewelry store where I bought Natalie a crucifix necklace for her collection. Above us, as far as the eye can see, bunting crisscrosses from shop to shop, an awning of US flags and Pride banners zigzagging back and forth, giving the strip a permanent holiday feel. But no amount of bunting can change the sinister mood.

"Excuse me, have you seen this woman?" I ask a young couple, holding up a picture of Rachael. They study the photo before shaking of their heads.

On the road, runners fly by in neon outfits. Guardie keeps pace beside me as I check my phone for an update on our group chat, hoping to read, "Rachael's showed up! It's all a misunderstanding!"

"Try not to worry," he says. "She's probably got talking to someone and lost track of time. We're just taking the necessary steps in case."

"In case" is the problem. *In case . . . Rachael's in danger. Or worse.*

The strap of my swimming bag digs into my shoulder. When a large group approaches wearing matching tour group shirts, I step onto the bicycle path to make room, shifting the bag to my other side.

"Watch out!" Guardie yells.

Oh shit. A man on a mountain bike, his attention on the phone in his hand, is heading straight for me.

"Em!" Guardie yells again, but I'm frozen. I always have slow reactions — but this is different — I *can't* move.

I squeeze my eyes shut at the same time as Guardie grabs me and pulls me out of the way. The bike rider crashes into Guardie, sending him to the ground. Guardie grimaces, one hand shielding his thigh, which seems to have taken most of the impact.

"Sorry, man! You all right?" The bike rider helps Guardie up.

When the man leaves, Guardie mutters, "Good thing years of snowboarding prepared me for people hurling into me from out of nowhere."

"Well, thank you. Very gallant."

"Gallant, eh?"

I give him a hug and just like that we're embracing on the middle of the sidewalk, and the smell of him, peppermint and herbs, and the delicious warmth of his body . . . why, again, am I so reticent? He's a kind, decent human, and he's the only one of us honest enough to tell the police about Rachael's manuscript. I like him, he likes me, so there's no need to be afraid.

"Um, you're still holding me," I say.

He doesn't release his grip. "You're hugging me."

I laugh, pleasure bubbling up. "You. Are. Ridiculous." I step away and we carry on walking, Guardie limping slightly.

Guardie shows Rachael's photo to the next people we come across. They haven't seen her either.

"Any updates on the chat?" I ask.

He scans his phone. "Nothing since Hannah's last message."

We pass Lobster Pot, a white building with red signage. It's a P-town dining institution, and the place Rachael had planned to throw her party. Was she going to tell us all something about the book then? To the left, there's a clear view of the pier, jutting into the Atlantic.

Dread gnaws at me. "Why would Rachael have left her bags like that? And her phone?"

"We'll get answers soon." Guardie rubs his leg where the bike hit him. "I feel like she's nearby."

"You do?" I hold my arms close to my body, wondering why Guardie would think that.

"I kinda feel drawn to the pier."

"As in . . . energetically? Are you psychic?"

He shrugs. "Just intuitive. It runs in our family. My grandmother was Coast Salish, had a sixth sense."

"Did you know her?"

"No, but the stories about her have been passed down. Most people have psychic abilities. There's so much about the human brain we don't understand."

"True. My dad has dementia. He's fading fast."

"I'm sorry." Guardie looks like he means it.

"So, you feel Rachael nearby?" My eyes are drawn back to the pier. She could have had an accident and been stranded somewhere. Or met with trouble out there. So far, the search and rescue team and Sharktivity haven't found anything — or, at least, they haven't informed us.

He nods. "All life is part of the quantum field. We're all connected, whether we recognize it or not."

Britta and I were once so close it felt like we could read each other's minds. When did we stop being so interconnected? Probably when she got pregnant at fifteen . . . It's hard to watch someone you love make so many bad decisions. Not that I regret having a niece like Natalie. But then a few years after Britta had her, Britta got into drinking and drugs, and moved away, taking her little girl with her and shacking up with different boyfriends. It was physically painful watching her life unravel.

At the next corner, an older woman is talking to two identical black poodles. "Have a drink, girls." The woman looks up. "Oh, hello there. Aren't you two a lovely couple."

We don't bother correcting her; instead, I show her Rachael's photo. She recognizes Rachael as a local actress, but hasn't seen her today.

The dogs gravitate to Guardie, circling his legs. He bends and strokes their necks and their tails wag.

Even dogs like him . . .

Not all men are like William, I tell myself. But William seemed so considerate at first, the last person anyone would ever think would cheat. Who can I trust? Even nice healer types with six-packs who wear crystals and always inquire about my well-being might be phony.

"Let's go." I check my phone — no new messages. Hard to believe so much of the day lies ahead. The weight of each passing hour presses down on me.

"You told me before your dad is a huge Red Sox fan," Guardie says. A few beach swims ago, we'd chatted about US and Canadian sports.

"Yep, Dad's the biggest fan. We had box seats as kids." He worships old-school Americana — his god: baseball. Watching the Red Sox with Dad was part of the fabric of my childhood.

"And your mom's from Sweden? You lived there for a while, right?"

"Gothenburg," I answer, pleased he's remembered our previous conversations. "It's a big city situated by the Gota alv river. Think canals and leafy boulevards. Really pretty."

"What was your highlight living there?"

"Spending time with my grandfather. He was the head chef when they had their family restaurant, Sjo och Smor. That means 'Sea and Butter.'"

"Yum," Guardie says. "Some of my favorite things." Then he asks a few questions about work, maybe to soothe me by talking about ordinary life. When I mention I'm exploring POTS, a poorly recognized autonomic nervous system disorder characterized by an excessively fast heart rate, mostly presenting in young women, he says a few of his clients at the spa have it.

A group of men in drag spill out of a bakery.

We show them Rachael's picture — no luck.

Guardie and I walk wordlessly, bodies close. "Sorry," I say when our arms knock together.

"Not a crime. You can touch me all you like."

Is he like this with everyone? It's awkward being away from the rest of the swimming group, with their banter and big personalities. And if Guardie has psychic abilities, he might know that I want him to hold me, kiss me, and make me feel good again.

If that hug on the sidewalk was an appetizer, bring on the main meal.

Whoa! Where did that thought come from? Normally, I can keep my walls up, but with today's events, raw emotions are breaking loose. The need for connection . . . for him — or *anyone* — to take away the fear.

We pass a toy store, and Guardie says, "You mentioned earlier your sister recently passed."

For some reason, it feels right to confide in him. I tell him what happened, and he listens, seeming to take in my every word, and there's no awkwardness now, only a sense of connection and support.

"So, that's why I'm looking after Natalie," I finish. "I never wanted kids and here I am. I'd give myself a C plus as a surrogate mom on a good day, C minus on a bad day."

"Awww, I bet you're great at it. You seem like the kind of person who's great at whatever you put your mind to." He continues walking briskly, his poncho swaying. "When my family pressured me to do something I didn't want to do, I bailed."

I'm about to ask what it was when he says, "What're you up to later?"

"If Rachael doesn't show up? Probably worrying. Then worrying some more. Followed by not sleeping."

"Have you had an ice bath before?"

"No. The Atlantic is cold enough for me."

"You should drop by the spa for one."

"Sure, maybe next week." I try to sound cavalier. Although part of me wants to spend more time with him, the other part would prefer to kayak to an island called Stay Home, Eat Homemade Pistachio Ice Cream, and Date No One.

"Ice baths are good for insomnia."

I manage a small smile. "It might not be the worst idea. I could see for myself what everyone raves about." Hailey Bieber,

Miguel has informed me, regularly posts her ice plunges. I can't remember the last time someone really cared how I'm doing. Do I want to be alone with Guardie after hours? From the buzzy flutters spreading through me, my body is a hard yes on that front.

As I take my car keys out of my purse, a young man of nineteen or twenty skulks by, wiry, shoulders hunched. He's wearing a blue jacket with a ferry insignia on it. He has a mustache, pimples cover his face, and he's sucking a vape. It's gray, not green like the one I found near her phone.

"Have you seen this woman?" I shove my phone toward him.

The vape drops from his hands. "Fuck." He snatches it from the sidewalk and walks the other way.

"Hold up," I call out. "You didn't say if you've seen her."

When he's gone, Guardie says. "Got him."

"What do you mean?"

"A picture of that shady vaper. I'll send it to Carol and ask her to make sure her sister sees it."

"Good plan." The bookstore comes into view, but I'll save shopping for Natalie's birthday present for another day. Before going home, I need to drop by the grocery store. "My car's just around the corner. See you around."

"I finish at four this afternoon. Just saying."

"Huh. Today. Okay. Um . . . let me think."

"The first ice bath is on me, and I can make you a wicked chai afterward."

Chai is catnip to me. "But is it the powdered kind you mix with water?"

"Who do you think I am, Starbucks, eh? Freshly brewed, traditional-style. Cardamon, star anise, cinnamon sticks."

I nudge him. "You didn't mention peppercorns or cloves."

"Yeah, yeah, those too. We buy it from a witch in Boston. She puts 'love' on the ingredients list."

"Ha! Now that I have to taste."

"Does that mean . . . ?"

"I'm coming." Did I just say that? Crap. "Um, there's my car." I hurry for my Honda, my heart racing. Have I agreed to more than chai?

"Cool. Drop by after four."

"Sure." I give a casual wave.

This can't be a date. Who would go on a date when a friend has disappeared? Receiving therapeutic services, well, that's another story.

CHAPTER SIXTEEN

When I get home from grocery shopping, I can't find Natalie. She's probably gone to town to pick something up or she's walking on the beach. She doesn't usually stay out long. We're both homebodies since losing Britta.

I set my shopping bags down and send her a text, then open the swimming chat to see if there's any news about Rachael. Nothing.

On the drive home, I spoke to Hannah and asked what I could do to help the search, but she said to stay put and she'll let me know if she hears anything. I hate feeling useless.

My eyes fall to my laptop on the counter. All those articles I should review about chronic fatigue syndrome. There's no point starting right now, with too many thoughts circulating in my brain about Rachael, and Britta . . . and Guardie.

I call Miguel — no answer — then text: *Call me. I have tea (not Rachael related).*

Now what? I yawn, only running on a few hours of sleep. I crave a nap, but that will only mess up my (nonexistent) sleep cycle. I have a few hours until I'm due to meet Guardie.

I need a hot bathing suit.

I head to the master bedroom and open my closet. There are so many drawers that I'm able to have a "tank top drawer," a "cardigan drawer," and a "pretty underwear drawer." This is why rich people are so put together. Space.

I touch the fabric of my emerald-green one-piece which covers most of my butt and still looks sexy.

Time for a shower.

The master bedroom en-suite continues the beachy palette — whites, blues, and sand. There's a custom-built vanity and, above it, an ornate mirror that reflects the New England wainscot walls. Monogrammed towels hang on heated racks and the ceramic tiles resemble pebbles.

Once the secrets in Rachael's manuscript come out, and William's family learns I've defamed their eldest son, my tentative position at Barnard will be done. It will be back to the rat race of New York, fighting for research opportunities. But maybe I shouldn't return to my old life, maybe there's a future out there that isn't yet written.

I strip, leaving my clothes in a bundle, and stand under the powerful rainhead shower.

I'll miss this.

The hot water pummels my back, easing some of the tension. I exfoliate my arms and legs with a body scrub, pumice my heels, shave my armpits, apply leave-in conditioner, and check my bikini line. It's been a long time since I prepared my body for a man.

I dry myself and throw on boyfriend jeans and a fitted white tee.

Miguel is calling. I answer.

"Officer Winn sure had a hard-on for you," he says by way of an opening. "Don't worry, I'll visit you in jail."

"More like I'll visit you. Car keyer."

"Touché." He laughs loudly, maybe to cover his embarrassment. Or because he's partly excited at the prospect of being the center of a scandal.

"Any word on Rachael?" If anyone can find something out, it's him.

"There are lots of posters up around town. Statistically, each hour we don't hear anything, it's less likely she'll be found. My Gentlemen's Personal Trainer keeps giving me horrific facts."

I bite my lip about his source of all knowledge, and walk to the fireplace in my bedroom, picking up a shark tooth from the mantel.

"My theory," Miguel says, "is that while Rachael was busy collecting our secrets, she was hiding her own."

"But what? And who knew?" I set the tooth back down.

"There must be a dodgy dude from one of her dating apps involved. Or a family member. Li-Ping said Rachael got into a fight with her brother recently. I asked around. Ex-addict, kicked out of boarding school, flies off the handle sometimes."

"The police will be onto that."

As we dissect the people in Rachael's life and their possible motives, I scoop up my dirty clothes from the corner of my bedroom and make my way to the laundry room, which is so spectacularly designed it makes you want to wash and fold.

In one corner, there's a set of white cabinets, in the other, a farmhouse-style sink. The shelves are neatly organized with wicker baskets and labeled bins for eco-friendly detergents and fabric softeners.

"I was thinking about how Rachael got my secret out of me." I open the washing machine, ready to start a load. The reek of mildew hits my face. Yuck. Natalie has left her wet laundry in the machine again. "By bonding over cheating exes. How'd she get your secret?"

"Rachael said she didn't know how to use ChatGPT, and the conversation went from there," Miguel says. "In retrospect, I was being played. She's no AI virgin."

"We can't know that." I drop my laundry in one of the wicker baskets. I'm going to have to rewash Natalie's clothes before I do mine. I pour in detergent. "Lots of writers use it and pretend they don't. Hmm, I wonder how she got the rest of the Tragic Wives' secrets."

"It's a mystery, my dear Em," Miguel says as though he's Sherlock and I'm Watson and we're in 1890s Victorian England, not current-day New England.

"Do you know any Tragic Wives' secrets?"

Miguel's silence is the only answer I need.

"You don't want my tea? Give and take."

"Bitch!"

"You'd do the same." With Miguel, everything in life is negotiation.

"Fine!" he says. "Compost Carol has a doozy."

"She has a thing for Serenity?" Everyone noticed how obsequious Carol became in the sculptor's presence — more chatty, more open.

"Pffft, *no*. Carol has a pastime she enjoys and — if her circle knew — if Hannah knew — their relationship would be done. Carol is a gun nut. She collects fucking firearms."

In this neck of the woods, that's the equivalent of collecting nuclear bombs.

"She's a great shooter," Miguel says.

Everyone in Carol's life is an advocate for gun control, no one more so than her wife. Hannah often wears a T-shirt that says, *Gun violence is the leading cause of death for children and young adults in the US*.

"I can't believe it," I say. "I've seen Hannah's posts on social media about the need for fewer guns. She goes on marches."

"I know. Girl got a lot to hide. Question is: How far would she go to keep the secret?"

"How'd you find out?"

"Well, Ronald likes guns too. We were at a gun show and saw Compost Carol of all people there. She tried to avoid me, but I was like, 'I've caught you! What are you doing here?' Turns out she sees the value of guns for self-defense, especially for women. You know her nephew was killed in a shooting a few years back. Changed her views on everything."

"So, Rachael found out about the guns and was going to put it in her book?"

"That's my guess," Miguel says.

"Where does she store her gun collection? How many does she have?"

"Not sure. But everything's going to come out."

Christ. Stress about my own secrets sideswipes me. I don't want to get kicked out of our Cape home. Natalie needs stability and I've grown attached to P-town. "There are so many things we already know about our group — the poisoned friend, the nephew in the mass shooting, the lost Olympic dreams, Serenity's shady past."

"Aren't we a wholesome lot?" Miguel says. "Don't forget Li-Ping knew where Rachael hid her house key. *Why-eee?* They're not that close."

"Interesting." I pause for dramatic effect. "And we're back to talking about *keys*."

Miguel makes a scoffing sound. "This is a mess. All the Tragic Wives are suspects. Let's meet for dinner later. I need to keep blabbering anxiously."

"I'm, um, actually visiting Guardie at his spa today. That's my tea."

"Oooo! Magic Hands! Find out what you can about his secrets. You can be a double agent."

"No, I'm going there to have an ice bath."

"Ice cubes are sexy. If you hold them in your mouth at the same time as you go down on—"

"Stop."

"But—"

"I mean it, Miguel. None of this is funny. If Rachael doesn't show up soon, I'm going to be really scared."

"That makes two of us."

When I get off the phone, Natalie is standing before me, mouth agape.

"What's wrong?" I ask. "You look like you've seen a ghost."

"Who were you talking about on the phone? Rachael? Your friend who came over for dinner last week with Li-Ping?"

"Yes."

"Is she, like, okay?"

"She's missing."

"Missing?" Natalie parrots.

"We don't know where she's gone." I see her frown and add lamely, "Maybe just for a holiday or something."

"Why did you sound worried?"

I take a breath and tell her the truth. "Rachael left her bags on the beach, and her phone, but nobody's seen her this morning. We've filed a missing person report."

The color drains from Natalie's face. She spins and runs down the hall.

I chase after her.

Flinging open the kitchen door, she storms onto the deck.

The cool beach air sends goosebumps up my arms. Of course she's upset at the unpredictability of life. A woman who sat at our dining room table just the other day, who told funny stories about taking a creative writing workshop and being asked to write from the perspective of a vegetable, has vanished.

Natalie turns to me, torment in her eyes. "I need to talk to my mom!"

I grab her. "It's okay."

"No! It's not!" Natalie tugs away. "I want to talk to my FUCKING MOM!"

"So do I! So do I . . . I miss her so much."

Then we're both crying, and I hug Natalie tight, and she hugs me back. We're clinging and weeping like drifters at sea.

"It's too cold out here." She pulls away. "I need a pill."

Natalie has had a number of panic attacks since Britta died, so William wrote me a bunch of prescriptions for Valium to give her in case of emergencies. When I can't sleep, I'm tempted to take one myself. "I'll get you one. Have you eaten?"

"Nuh." She drops her chin.

"Good thing my twenty-four-hour deli is open."

I hook my arm through hers and guide her back inside. I get her to lie on the couch, tucking a pillow under her head and putting a blanket over her. It's a red crochet blanket Mom made; in retirement, she's become a craft fiend.

"Wanna watch New York apartment reels with me?" We often do this together, analyzing square footage, unique storage hacks, and creative styles.

"Not right now."

Once Natalie's had water and a pill, I head back to the kitchen. Opening the fridge, I call, "Spinach and tomato frittata?"

"No thanks," she says from the other room.

"Bacon breakfast wrap with guacamole and a side of paprika hash browns?"

Another decline.

"You can't say no to waffles . . . ." This is met with silence, and I smile. I might not know what to say to her, I might not know how to physically comfort her, but, as I reach for the milk and butter, I have faith I can do one thing right.

CHAPTER SEVENTEEN

A girl

Newcomb Hollow Beach, Cape Cod
1:15 p.m.
Rachael missing: 8 hours

"Mr. Crab?" The girl pokes her finger in the water. "Where are you? I know you're hiding." She squats at the tide pool, her feet squishing in the wet sand. Her red sunhat slips over her eyes, and she yanks it back.

She's already found lots of pretty shells today but she needs a crab. She's been looking for ages. She's not giving up.

"Time to go!" Mom calls from the beach. She's carrying all the bags, using one hand to hold her hat so it doesn't blow off.

"Just five more minutes!" She glances back at the tide pool. Mr. Crab has to be in there somewhere. She lifts the big rock in the center of the pool, searching for tiny legs in the sand, but can't find any.

She walks to the next pool. The waves tickle her toes. A fly buzzes. Another fly darts near her ear. "Go away!"

Then she spots treasure. Under a bit of seaweed, a silver-and-blue shell shaped like an ice cream. She snatches it.

What's that in the next tide pool? Something pale, half hidden by seaweed—

A seagull swoops near the girl, opening and closing its mouth. Stupid bird. It's so loud! It'll scare the crabs.

She looks back at the tide pool . . . and screams.

It's a hand.

She wants to look away, but she can't.

Those are fingers. Barbie-pink nail polish.

"MOM!!!! There's a hand!"

CHAPTER EIGHTEEN

P-town, Cape Cod
4:15 p.m.
Rachael missing: 11 hours

What the hell am I doing here in Guardie's lair? The Cape Cod Spa, a restored two-story Cape Codder, glows with rose quartz Himalayan salt lamps and pendant lights, their woven shades resembling fishing nets.

Standing in the empty waiting room, I wonder if his "drop by after my last client" invitation might qualify as an actual date. When I'm with him, I'm awkward, undeniably, but in a strange way, less broken, someone who feels hope again. But I shouldn't read into it — he's a professional and this is just another ice bath session.

I can't decide whether to remain standing or to curl up on the couch. Where is Guardie? Massaging a Pilates babe in the dark somewhere? Or in the staff kitchen, giving himself a pep talk, nervous as I am?

The air is scented with essential oils, lavender and eucalyptus. A gentle babbling sound comes from an indoor fountain, a rock feature in a small pool. My shoulders soften as I drop onto the couch in a cozy corner dedicated to a collection of books and magazines about wellness and the local history of Cape Cod. Yawning, I rub my eyes. If I weren't so keyed up, I could nod off here.

Thoughts of Rachael trigger thoughts of Britta, and then Natalie, who's at home, rewatching old seasons of *Project Runway*. Kristen's with her, I remind myself. She's not alone.

Maybe I should call off seeing Guardie. It would be easy enough to make an excuse. "Sorry, but my sister's dead, my niece is loaded on Valium, there's a manuscript out there with my secrets, and Rachael is missing. An ice bath can't solve my problems."

I'm about to take out my phone when a girlish sigh precedes a tousle-haired beauty emerging from a suite, gushing, "Thanks, Guardie! You're the best!"

Guardie appears after her and smiles when he spots me. "Em, glad you could make it."

He's in the same shorts and tee he was in before, but this gentle light makes him look even dewier, more ethereal. He's in his element here, that's for sure — amid aromatherapy, ambient lighting, and babbling water.

"Be with you in a moment," he says to me. "I just have to tidy up. There's a room there if you want to change into your bathing suit and grab a robe and slippers."

"Watch out," the woman says when he's out of earshot. "He's addictive." Her laugh tinkles.

After I change, I find Guardie in the waiting room.

"I wasn't sure you'd show," he says.

"Neither was I. But you promised me chai."

The eye contact! *Intense.*

Flustered, I break away. "Have you heard anything more about Rachael?"

"Afraid not."

"I keep checking our group chat."

"We'll find out something any time now," he says.

That's what people expect when someone they care about goes missing — that news will follow shortly after, tidbits of information that will help them make sense of the disappearance. Those are the fortunate ones. True torture is not finding out what happened and still trying to sleep at night.

Through a door, we're transported to a Balinese-style garden: spring flowers, grasses, and sunbeds dappled by a moody, early evening light.

"We offer clients the 'fire and ice package.' Sauna" — he gestures to a wooden building — "and ice baths. Or you can just ice." Three barrels full of ice are lined up under a Japanese maple tree and a large basket of rolled towels sits nearby.

Brrr. Ice cube clusters float at the top of the barrels, the reflection of leaves shimmering on the surface.

"Just dunk in and out?" A cool gust of wind blows hair into my face. Even though the luxe garden is walled in, wind whips around the courtyard, swirling the fallen flower petals at our feet.

"Longer than a dunk. A few minutes. I'll ease you into it. The body needs time to acclimatize. You can work yourself up to stay longer."

"Got it. It's not the size of the barrel that matters," I quip, "but the duration."

He laughs, teeth white.

Miguel would be proud of me. He always tells me to loosen up, that at thirty-five, I'm too young to act so old.

"What's the difference between ocean swimming and ice baths?" Another cold gust makes me rub my arms and want to huddle next to him.

"Immediacy. Ice baths hit harder because of the controlled and colder temperature. Don't worry, you're a pro. You're used to cold water."

The romance of running barefoot into the open sea is different from squeezing into a barrel of ice. Haven't I read an article recently about a murderer storing bodies in wine barrels?

Is Rachael safe? Has she run away to start a new life? Is her body being carried out to sea, or inside the belly of a shark? Or is she being tortured by some psychopath somewhere?

"If you like, we can start with some pranayama," Guardie says. "Breathwork."

I cinch the robe tighter as I stare at the ice barrels. "Every cell in me is saying 'hell no.'"

"The monkey mind can't always be relied on. Your ego is telling you not to risk trying something unfamiliar."

"Pretty sure my ego's more foul-mouthed than that. Remind me again why this is a good idea?"

"Cold water resets your parasympathetic system."

I move toward the barrel. The ice cubes clink together, radiating a forcefield of cold. It's as inviting as spreading your legs at a gynecological appointment.

"Cold-water healing has been around for millennia," Guardie continues.

I drop my robe, dip my toe into the ice bath, and break out into more goosebumps.

"Eeee! Colder than a landlord's heart," I cry.

He smiles. "It has an antipsychotic effect, almost like electroshock therapy."

"Maybe skip the part about electroshock next time you're selling this to a client." I grip the side of the barrel and crouch into the icy water, thighs tingling. "Ugh. Colder than a hair on a polar bear's ass."

I earn another smile. "And cold-water therapy can lower your blood pressure and cholesterol levels."

"Shut up, would you? You don't have to convince me anymore!"

At the same time as he laughs, I submerge.

Ooooh! The ice is numbing — like when your hands sting from the snow — but rather than just my hands, my entire body becomes a popsicle. Vanilla with a Twist of Sex-Craved.

"I want out!"

"Keep breathing," Guardie coaches, blowing up his cheeks like a husband mimicking the Lamaze method. "You can do it. Stay in for another minute."

"I can't!" I'm freezing to death, my heart jumping errat-ically in my chest. But I do as he says, and wait until he calls me out before launching myself into the oatmeal towel in his arms.

"Thank god that's over."

"Good job," he says, proud of his student.

"Have I earned a chai?"

He clicks his tongue, looking contrite. "Funny thing — when I got here, I discovered we're out. I source the supplies, but the owner took all the chai to his other business, a hotel. I'll grab more from my witch friend in Boston soon. Sleep tea instead?"

"If it works."

"It has valerian root, passionflower, and black cohosh."

He brews the tea, and we sit and talk about where we've traveled, what our experiences were like when we first moved to the Cape, and he tells some funny stories about Canadian stereotypes. "I promise you, we're not all nice." My body is still reacting to the cold, little shivery currents rippling through my bloodstream.

We share a smile and I sip the tea, which tastes like grass mixed with mud. I catch myself yawning — certainly not out of boredom, but I'm exhausted.

All the same, it's as though there's a mini-Miguel in my head, magicking the words out before I can stop them: "It must be hard being estranged from your mom."

"I guess that's what happens when you bring up capitalism at the Christmas dinner table. My brother's a stock trader and the whole family is status obsessed." It must be hard for someone so free-spirited and unconcerned with materialistic pursuits to feel accepted in a family like his. "There's lots of money — and emotion — involved."

So, Guardie felt pressured by his family to do something he didn't want to do. His brother plays the market. I can't help thinking the two things are connected.

"Did Rachael know about the money part? For her book?" And is it true Guardie gives away his earnings? Each generous act must be a perfect "screw you" to his parents.

"Would you like some more tea?" he asks.

Noted. Topic off-limits. Not fair — I opened up about Britta and Natalie, and now he brushes me off? But then his brown eyes are back on me, his easy smile. "I want to know more about you," he says. "Were you always drawn to academia?"

"Hardly. I wanted to be a chef. Couldn't decide between pastry, fine-dining, or fusion — I loved it all."

"Still could."

"Being a student again, working kitchen jobs, those hours? Not for me. I'm happy cooking as a hobby." My university work isn't the most stable, but it pays well, I have connections, and the research matters. Besides, I've invested years in medical research. "I mean, who really loves their job?"

He just looks at me.

I laugh. "Okay, the lucky ones who've found that magic equation: work that doesn't feel like work."

"Why did you become an academic, then?"

"Long story." The memories flood back as I drain the rest of my tea.

When I was about sixteen, we had to fill out these forms for the career counselor about our interests post-high school. Mom was at home when I started filling out the form. I was sitting at the kitchen table and had written "cook" as my first choice, excited about a life where every day I got to be around food.

Mom leaned over my shoulder. "Erase that."

I angled the paper away from her. "I can't, it's pen."

She rolled her eyes, yanked open the junk drawer, and passed me Wite-Out.

Mom had been in a bad mood a lot of the time. Her work in software sales was stressful, and Britta was failing her classes and had started sneaking out of the house at night to meet older boys.

"Em, we've discussed this before. Cooking means late nights, and it's hard on the body." Mom had always resented how little time she'd got to spend with her parents when they'd owned Sjo och Smör, plus all the weekends she'd had to work (unpaid) at the restaurant.

"You're smart," she said, "and, unlike Britta, you're sensible." I flushed warm with those words, being singled out, chosen as the better one. Now that Britta was spiraling, it was like Mom could finally see me. The worse Britta got, the brighter I shone.

Mom put her hand on her hip and nodded at me. "You go to university, do your undergraduate studies, your master's. Use that sharp mind of yours. Then visit the restaurants and have people serve *you*."

I ached whiting-out "cook," but Mom's proud smile almost made up for abandoning my dream.

I set my tea on the side table, aware Guardie is studying me. "Sorry, lost my train of thought."

"C'mon, let me show you my workspace."

I follow him. I've already noticed how buff he is — that's hard to miss in our ocean swims — but his body has taken on another dimension in close confines. No wonder he has such a loyal clientele.

I blink as we enter a cave-like room, a massage bed in the middle, moss-green walls, a single lamp in the corner, ferns and greenery everywhere — a womb-like jungle. The music is tribal, rhythmic, and the drum almost sounds like a heartbeat.

"Since you're here," Guardie says, "want a massage?"

Shit, shit, shit. Shouldn't I at least experience these famous magic hands? But the intimacy will be too much. All the touching. Being so sleep-deprived, I might get carried away with pleasure . . . Am I ready for it?

"I don't always offer these for free." Guardie flexes his hands with a grin. "But, your call."

Am I mad? Who would turn this down?

Reading my mind, he hands me a towel and heads for the door. "I'll let you undress."

"Wait. I'll pay for the massage."

"No way. I'm not letting you pay."

"I'm not letting you give me an afterwork freebie. That feels . . ." *Sleazy. Porn-like.*

"We could swap services? What're you good at?" Although he asks it in a perfectly ordinary way, *SEX* screams in my head. *I'm good at sex. I want sex, with you.*

"Um, baking. What's your favorite dessert?"

"Pumpkin pie," he says. "Food is the way to my heart."

"Easy, then. I'll make you one." Did I just imply I *want* a way into his heart?

"Cool." With that he leaves me to strip off my clothes.

Fuuuuckk!

CHAPTER NINETEEN

I slip off my jeans and tee, mentally high-fiving myself for having the foresight to choose pearly-pink underwear with lace trim.

Okay, here we go. This is really happening.

I lie down, bare breasts against the massage bed, using one hand to grab the nearby blanket to cover my butt. Within minutes, Guardie's hands will be all over my body and we'll be locked in this primal place with its lush greenery and throbbing heartbeat.

Repositioning myself on the massage bed, I'm alert for Guardie's footsteps. How did I end up here, today of all days? Why's Guardie suddenly so interested in me now? Has he been interested in me this whole time?

I picture him and Rachael talking to each other a few days ago as they walked into the water, her reaching for him, her swaying hips and gale of laughter.

Guardie reenters the room. "Is the temperature okay?"

"Um, yes. I've left my phone on the chair there in case there's news about Rachael."

He nods. "My phone's been on vibrate all day."

"Rachael can't just have disappeared off the face of the earth."

"Look, I know it's hard not to think about Rachael, but let's spend this next hour helping you relax. You care for other people a lot. This is your time. Ready?"

"Yes." One word, but it feels like agreeing to more than just a massage.

He places a hand on my lower back, then another hand, strong and powerful, on my neck. He rubs warm oil over my body, scented with lavender. A jolt of electricity zigzags through me. I cringe, embarrassed by my reaction. I take a deep breath. It's natural. *Relax*.

He applies more pressure until I sigh — not one of my usual dissatisfied sighs, but full-bodied relief.

This is the right place to be. I realize I haven't felt this safe in so long.

He dedicates the next ten minutes to my back, from the bottom of my spine upwards. He's so good at this. The perfect pressure; smooth, circular strokes. His thumbs dig into my shoulders, skillfully easing out the knots.

My mind drifts to my last time with William. He took great pride in his ability to make me orgasm. It always seemed like an achievement on his part though. A+, William, your pointer finger dexterity was perfectly angled and timed, ideal flicks per seconds. He knew how to work my body, but my heart . . .

My phone buzzes.

"Do you mind passing me that?"

Just a news alert, not about Rachael. But the reminder jolts me back — her belongings in the sand, Officer Winn at the café. What is happening as I lie here? Are the police going through Rachael's phone and laptop? Have they discovered her manuscript? Have they read all the Tragic Wives' secrets?

Is Rachael *dead*?

God. No.

Guardie takes my phone back and I think about Big Daddy at the pier, how often sharks are in these waters. The idea of Rachael swimming by herself is unlikely. So where is she? I run through everything our group said when we were questioned by Officer Winn at the café, replaying the alibis.

"If only we knew Rachael's movements," I say as Guardie massages me. "Where she was yesterday and if she spent last night with anyone." Another sigh releases from me. "I feel so bad feeling so good at a time like this."

"There's nothing we can do right now about Rachael. Focus on your breath. In . . . and out . . ."

My sense of time is lost as Guardie kneads my sore muscles and limbs, applying the exact amount of force I can handle in a cycle of pain, then releasing.

Oooh . . . That sleeping tea is working its magic too.

All those women I study with their chronic illnesses, their invisible pain and the frustration from not being seen as they are by their families, lovers, and colleagues — I know what they need: a Guardie, a healer.

Even though Guardie's hands are on my back, heat builds between my legs, which is mortifying, but impossible to control. I can't believe how much I feel like sex. I haven't felt like sex since the breakup, yet something about Guardie flicks a switch. It's even weirder that I want sex now, with everything going on.

"Pressure okay?"

It would be even better if he was on top of me, naked, his hand slipping off my underwear.

Em! The man is trying to heal you, and here I am being mentally sexual assaulty. I bury my face in the pillow. If Guardie is psychic, we've got ourselves a problem.

"Turn over." Guardie lifts the blanket for privacy as I shift onto my back. When the towel settles over me again, I exhale. He traces even strokes along my collarbone. I keep my eyes shut — I can't handle eye contact with him leaning over me, his breath warming my skin.

"You have blocks around your heart center," he says. "Too much focus on the past."

Too much focus on how close Guardie's hands are to my breasts!

He works down each arm — shoulder to forearm, ending with gentle circles at each wrist.

My exhales lengthen . . .

The music changes to raindrops hitting a tin roof. At first, there are moments of silence between each drop, but then the rain falls heavier, waves of sound with no start or finish. Guardie's touch becomes softer and as he massages my arms, jaw, scalp — everything loosens. I'm not a grieving sister, a scorned girlfriend, or a runaway academic on an island . . . I'm a soul.

My eyes are so heavy . . . The blanket cozy and warm. Raindrops . . .

. . . I'm standing at the edge of the swimming pool. Daddy is urging me to jump in.

. . . I'm in the Outer Banks with Natalie and Britta. We're sitting on a blanket at the beach, licking ice cream that drips down the cones onto our fingers. We're entering the water, chatting, one sentence interwoven with another. Britta splashes me, the shock of the salt water on my face, but before I have time to splash her back, she runs in deeper.

Beside me, Natalie calls, "Mom, come back!" but Britta rarely listens to anyone. Warning her only makes her more reckless.

I kick through the waves, knees high to move faster. Ahead, Britta's arms slice through the water, her white-blonde head bobbing up and submerging. I get closer. The sky darkens. The riptide is coming.

Det är inte en undervattensström, det är Kraken. It's not a riptide, it's the Kraken. In Swedish folklore, this monstrous giant octopus drags ships under, creating whirlpools with its tentacles.

Hurry, hurry! I must save Britta.

I swim faster. I've nearly reached her.

"They found her . . . on the beach?" A man's voice cuts through my dreams. "An arm? You're certain it's hers?"

"Britta!" I sit bolt upright, shouting, "Have they found my sister?"

Guardie hovers by the bed, his expression stricken. "I'll call you back," he says into the phone. "I need to tell Em."

"Tell me what?" Crap, the blanket has fallen, my breasts exposed. I clutch the blanket back up.

"It's Rachael," Guardie says. "A body part washed up nearby on Newcomb Hollow Beach, a woman's hand. Severed by a shark, Hannah said. We can't be sure but . . . the fingers had pink nail polish. Barbie pink."

I cover my mouth. "Poor Rachael." Tears spill from my eyes. I drop my head into my bent knees and cry hard for Rachael, for Britta, for Natalie left motherless.

Guardie hugs me, his arms cocooning my ripped-open heart.

I have to face it: what happened to Rachael may have also happened to Britta. Both were swallowed by the sea.

CHAPTER TWENTY

Open seas
9:35 a.m.
Rachael missing: Over 28 hours

Officer Winn told me not to leave the state, but she didn't say anything about leaving the island.

"Yes, Dad," I say into my phone. "I'm on the ferry now. I'll be there soon." I lean on the deck railing, salty sea spray blasting my face, the crisp, briny scent of the ocean filling my lungs.

"What time exactly?" Over the last few months, Dad's dementia has worsened, and he's taken to being very specific about details. As I tell him I'll arrive just before noon I can picture him getting out his notepad and writing it down so he doesn't forget.

We've been sailing for nearly fifty minutes, which means there's another twenty minutes or so until we reach the shore. My mind is a little fuzzy because I took one of Natalie's Valiums. Word is that a little girl found a severed hand in a tide pool. Horrific. Everyone's certain it's Rachael's. The torment for Rachael's family, not knowing what she endured during the shark attack, or whether it was a shark attack.

"When you get here let's rewatch the last Red Sox game," Dad says. "Kutter Crawford, pure magic. I've been saying he's underrated for years."

Once we've said our goodbyes, I tuck my phone into the pocket of my windbreaker, give my sunglass lenses a clean with the cuff, grab my backpack, and sit back on the deck. The dampness of the air clings to my skin, refreshing and soothing all at once. It's blue in every direction — the sea, the sky — a moody palette of faded jeans and windswept gray.

Ten or so people brave the outside seating: an older couple beside me, binoculars around their necks; two teenagers huddled by the railing; a family with small kids, the children walking around with their hands in the air like tipsy scarecrows, teetering as the boat rocks back and forth.

Behind us lie the Cape's intricate bays and harbors, quaint coastal towns, lighthouses dotting the horizon. Now we're in open sea.

The last twenty-four hours replay in my head — Rachael missing, Officer Winn's questions, Guardie's massage, the news of the gruesome discovery on the beach. Then me crying, and Guardie comforting me before I rushed back home.

When I arrived for our swim yesterday morning, did I miss a clue or detail? Rachael could have been ripped apart a hundred feet from where I stood. Was there a chance Rachael survived the shark attack and got away after her hand was bitten off? Could she be out there somewhere, waiting to be found? Sharktivity hasn't recorded any signs of a shark attack. I'm still holding out hope it's someone else's hand.

If Mom hadn't called last night asking if I could come to Boston and look after Dad, I wouldn't be setting foot outside of P-town. Her friend is unwell, and Mom is staying with her overnight. Dad can be left alone, but not at mealtimes. With his dementia, he's twice put dinner on the stove and forgot about it. The last time, smoke filled the kitchen and triggered the alarm, bringing the local fire department. Although he's under direct orders to never make spaghetti bolognese again, we can't trust him. Mom even hides the tomato sauce before she pops out to the corner store.

Covering my mouth, I yawn. I got almost no sleep last night — I was too wired about Rachael, but now the Valium has curbed some of my anxiety.

I wish Natalie was coming with me to Boston, but she had schoolwork and plans with Kristen. The trip would do her so much good; feeling the cold sea spray and seeing the rest of our family. At least she'll have company, though, and won't spend another day sleeping until noon, snacking on junk food before retiring to the couch and watching hours of reality television. If only there were a "healed" button on grief. I left her a veritable health food store of nutritious homemade meals — vegetarian chili and corn chips, leek soup and crusty bread rolls, apple and cinnamon muffins — as well as a stack of fashion books from the library.

I prepared the pumpkin pie pastry for Guardie too; after all, a deal is a deal. But once I give him the pie — not a sexual metaphor — that's it, no more alone time together. I can't trust myself not to get physical with him, and although that may be what my body wants, my head is smarter.

I'm not ready for any kind of relationship, casual or otherwise. I need to focus on figuring out the next steps in my life. Am I going to return to New York? Rebuild my professional reputation?

The boat ventures farther into the Atlantic and I yawn again, shutting my eyes. The breeze kisses my face, there's the sound of waves and babble of voices . . .

I'm startled awake when a woman beside me says, "Look, Virgil."

Ahead, birds skim the water's surface. The couple have binoculars up.

"Get a picture," the man orders his wife, and at the same time my phone buzzes.

A new message on our Tragic Wives chat. Ever since what we believe was Rachael's hand was discovered on the beach, there have been a flurry of messages, condolences, and prayers. There's nothing like tragedy to bring people together.

The message is from Compost Carol. I swallow, mouth dry. I don't want to open it. If it's news about Rachael — confirming a shark attack or, god forbid, her death — I don't want to see it.

Adulting up, I tap the message.

Carol: *Good and bad news. Good: the hand discovered on the beach wasn't Rachael's. There was a boating accident & a woman's hand got severed. Bad: we still don't know where Rachael is.*

I jump off my seat, the wind whipping strands of hair into my eyes. I'm not happy about another woman's misfortune, but — THANK GOD — *Rachael could still be alive.*

Miguel's response comes a millisecond later: *You're 100% sure it wasn't Rachael's hand?*

Carol: *100%*

Peggy (the podcast fanatic) texts: *The police aren't doing enough. 630,000 people are reported missing each year. Around 90,000 are never found.*

Li-Ping: *I spent all day praying. Lord, we are asking for your divine protection and guidance. Please bring Rachael to us.*

Guardie: *I'm not in town, but if anyone needs support and wants to talk, just reach out.*

Serenity: *Who was the woman in the boating accident?*

Carol texts a link to an article:

TRAGIC BOATING COLLISION
SEVERELY INJURES WOMAN
Provincetown, Cape Cod

At 4:32 p.m. yesterday, a boating collision near Provincetown resulted in severe injuries to 58-year-old Joan Agostino. A mechanical malfunction caused two boats to collide, entangling Mrs. Agostino's hand in rapidly displaced ropes and leading to a traumatic amputation.

First responders arrived quickly and transported Mrs. Agostino to a nearby hospital. Authorities are investigating the malfunction.

For updates, follow CCN, Cape Cod News.

I push my hair out of my eyes, face tilted toward the sun. Could Rachael really be okay? There's no proof anything untoward has happened to her, besides her bags and phone on the beach. My lungs expand. I can smell the sea. The sky feels brighter, more beautiful.

As the ferry passes a cargo ship, my ringtone blares — Miguel.

He's talking so quickly I can't understand him. At first, I assume it's about the boating accident, but he keeps rambling. "It's gone!" he yells.

"What is?"

"Rachael's yellow notebook. The one that was in her bag at the beach. You saw it! The one she uses to record all the secrets! Someone stole it!"

CHAPTER TWENTY-ONE

The binocular couple seem to be eavesdropping on my conversation with Miguel, so I relocate to the deck stairwell where no one else is around.

"Backtrack, Miguel," I say, picking up from where we left off. "Start with how you know Rachael's notebook is missing." I take a handful of elderberry gummies from the bag in my pocket and nibble away.

"I relied on the font of all knowledge."

I hold back a groan. "ChatGPT?"

"He has a name! I gave Gentlemen's Personal Trainer all the info, and he advised me not to leave Carol's side. The odds were that hanging out with Officer Winn's sister would pay off. I've been at Carol's all day, helping her compost, listening to her wax lyrical about worms, mulching mediums, then forced to eat her tempeh and mung beans. But Gentlemen's Personal Trainer was right. I overheard Carol talking to her sister on the phone. Officer Winn leaked that Rachael's notebook was taken from the swimming bag before they arrived. And the notebook was where Rachael wrote all the secrets."

Missing woman, missing notebook. Not good.

"So, did the notebook disappear when — ah! *Ouch!*" A toddler with heavy boots walked right into me.

"Em? What?" Miguel gasps.

"Nothing." I wave to the parents, who are wearing matching apologetic expressions. "When did the notebook disappear?"

"It's easy to narrow down the suspects." Miguel sounds too happy for a man whose friend has been missing for over twenty-four hours. "Ask yourself . . . *who* was guarding Rachael's bags at the beach?"

During the initial search, we divided up at the beach, and later, some people volunteered to wait with the bags while the rest of us went to the Sandbar to meet the police. Li-Ping wanted to stay with the bags, but she was on the verge of a panic attack, so Guardie offered to keep her company, and one of the blondes, who's usually glued to his side, remained too.

Come to think of it, why would they need three people to stay with the bags? It would've made more sense for one to guard while the others helped search.

My stomach drops. "So, either Li-Ping, a blonde, or . . . Guardie."

"I'll happily interrogate Magic Hands."

"Attention passengers," a voice booms over the loudspeaker. "We're in luck today! We have a humpback whale sighting. If you look to starboard, you'll get a great view. Enjoy the spectacle."

The last thing I want is to be surrounded by people, so I hurry to portside, against the crush. Given binocular man was previously excited about a few ordinary birds, a humpback whale has probably given him a hard-on.

"The police should consider suspects outside the Tragic Wives," I speak quietly into the phone. "A work colleague or maybe her shady brother took the notebook to protect their secrets?"

"Em! They weren't at the beach. Her book is about us — it's called *Secrets of the Tragic Wives and Guys*. Not *The Secret Life of Office Workers*."

The Valium is killing off my brain cells. "Anyway, it's interesting Rachael added 'guys' to the title. The only guys in the group are you, Guardie, and that retired judge."

118

"Guardie's name does keep popping up, doesn't it?"

Ignoring Miguel's insinuation, I say, "Don't forget the last time Rachael was seen she was entering Toys of Eros. Could be important."

"*Allegedly* seen. Li-Ping said she saw Rachael going there, but given Li-Ping was also guarding the bags, and knew where Rachael kept her house key, she's a prime suspect. The whole Toys of Eros thing might be to throw people off."

Li-Ping is a good friend, not a murderer. It's like imagining opposites. Britta, alive. Natalie, healthy. Me, healed.

The loudspeaker switches back on, "Hope you're enjoying viewing the humpback whale. It's 'logging,' which means resting near the surface. Occasionally, humpbacks will arch their backs or raise their flukes out of the water before diving deeper. Thanks for your attention and enjoy this unforgettable experience."

"Let's review the Tragic Wives' secrets," I say.

"Okay. We've got Carol's pro-gun stance and her weekends away at gun conventions, and how it could tear apart a loving environmentalist marriage."

"Guardie's fall-out with his family," I add. "I forgot to mention that before. He told me he opened up to Rachael about the estrangement a few weeks ago."

"Why are they estranged?"

"Not entirely sure, but reading between the lines, his brother's a stock trader and the family were pressuring Guardie to do something, maybe related to stocks, and now he's not speaking to any of them." I take some gummy colas from my pocket and jam them into my mouth.

"Nah, weak motive. Gotta be more than that. Men that good-looking always have secrets. Trust me. Moving on, there's *our* secrets. My Gentlemen's Personal Trainer addiction which will obliterate my SNAIL GIRL ERA brand."

"And your 'drunk and disorderly' key art."

"Just shut your trap about that."

Perhaps Rachael has more on Miguel. Maybe he pressured her to remove some mystery secret from her book, and an innocent conversation turned deadly. I remember being surprised when Miguel told me he'd trained in taekwondo, earning whatever belt comes before black belt — it seemed unlike him, I thought he'd be too concerned about the potential of being kicked in the face. But then he explained about defending himself against homophobes and skinheads who'd attacked him in his youth.

But, no . . . Miguel hurting Rachael? That's ridiculous.

"For me, there's William's infidelity and the overprescribing investigation. It'd really hurt him and his family's reputation. And I'd get thrown out of my home."

"Meh," Miguel says as a ferry crew member in a blue jacket walks by, swinging a bucket in his hand. "You knew from the start it was temporary. Not enough to kill or steal evidence for."

"So. Everything points to the secrets from Li-Ping, Serenity, Peggy, or Hannah being juicier."

"I'm going to find out." Miguel loves nothing more than a mission. "I'm having dinner with Li-Ping tonight. I'll pry it out of her."

"Tip? Li-Ping loves after-dinner drinks. Port wine, amaro, Grand Marnier — pair it with some sweets or crackers and cheese, and after three drinks, she'll be an open book." I feel guilty sharing this, but desperate measures.

"Perfect. Once I gather all the Tragic Wives' secrets, I can figure out who has the biggest motive. But, honestly, I'm getting fatter by the hour. All this anxiety has turned me into a rabid snacker. Sit, eat, jibber-jabber, sit, eat. I need to find some Ozempic, stat, before I become a lard-ass. Ronald does not do belly rolls."

"Ronald should love you as you are." With Miguel's husband always in New York, no wonder Miguel is addicted to his chatbot. "Missing him a lot, hey?"

Miguel huffs. "Ronald knows I'm ADHD — attention desperate for hot dick."

The joke falls flat. I see through his pain and know how much he longs for quality time with his husband. "Talk to him."

"Not easy when he's never here."

A tall, white lighthouse, Boston Light, appears ahead, perched on the rocks of Little Brewster Island. Beyond it, the city's skyline comes into view — the Bunker Hill Monument, the USS Constitution, and downtown's skyscrapers: the John Hancock and Prudential buildings. The trip is coming to an end.

"What's going on with you guys?" As transparent as Miguel is about everything else, he holds the emotional status of his relationship close to his chest.

"Ever since having our bubba, I don't feel as desirable. It's not only baby-carriers who get postpartum. I feel . . . burnt out, unappreciated."

"Emotions fester if you don't express them."

"Oh, and you're so evolved, spending all your time hiding out in your ex's mansion, sitting on that stupid deck, staring at the ocean, avoiding your whole fabulous New York life. These are your prime years! The waves aren't appreciating your fine booty."

I laugh, despite the sting. "See, you don't hold back with me. Ronald won't magically make changes if he doesn't know how you're really doing."

"It's his fucking *job* to know!" On the other end of the line, Miguel clears his throat, and I can tell he's trying to collect himself. "Whatever. It's not that deep. So, here's the deal. I'll work Li-Ping. You work Guardie when you see him next. Learn more about his secret. Double-check details, look for any inconsistencies or aberrations."

"I have enough on my plate. I'm not actively sleuthing on the guy I have feelings for."

"*Feelings*, huh?" Miguel says as water taxis and fishing vessels crisscross in front of the boat. "How'd yesterday go at the spa? Did Guardie . . . Rub. You. Down?" Nose of a bloodhound, that man. All I'd told Miguel was that I was going there for an ice plunge.

Now it's my turn to clear my throat. "Turns out Guardie's a skilled masseuse." And I will *never* lie half-dressed on his massage bed again, lest I jump the poor Canadian.

"Yasss!" Miguel cheers. "There is hope for you after all. Promise me if the opportunity arises, you'll go for it. You WASP-y, vanilla, monogamy, Disney-brainwashed New Englanders wrap everything into future coupledom."

"I'm Swedish, Miguel. I do what I like. You just haven't seen me *like* anyone. The whole time you've known me I've been a hot mess about William and grieving over Britta. You're getting way ahead of yourself. All I care about right now is finding Rachael."

And that Natalie is okay.

Besides, I was only testing the waters with Guardie. I'm happy to know I'm not dead below the waist but I'm not ready to deal with my heart.

The ferry approaches Boston Harbor, showcasing the city's revolutionary history, the iconic Boston Tea Party Ships and Museum. Sailboats and yachts dot the water; the waterfront shops and restaurants on Long Wharf are already buzzing.

I say goodbye to Miguel, and walk to the edge of the balcony, taking it all in. I can't wait to see Dad.

Behind me, the light shifts; a shadow. I can feel the weight of someone staring at me. I check over my shoulder — it's the ferry worker who walked by earlier.

The young man shuffles over, eyes on the deck floor before giving me a furtive glance. "You look like Daenerys Targaryen," he says. "Or should I say Khaleesi?"

The *Games of Thrones* comparison happens quite a bit. It's the combo of my white-blonde hair, dark eyebrows, and small stature. I have no dragons at my disposal, unfortunately, no arsenal, and no magical skills beyond whipping up something good to eat at a moment's notice.

"Thanks." He seems harmless enough, probably only a few years older than Natalie, a mustache, a few pimples around his nose and mouth.

"Dead ringer," he says with a shy smile.

Wait. A strange sensation comes over me.

As he turns away, I whip out my phone and manage to capture a quick profile shot. Then I forward the image to

Guardie along with the message: *Hey. Is this the same guy we saw yesterday on Commercial Street? You took pic of him.*

As I wait to disembark — squashed among about fifty passengers — I overhear the binocular couple arguing because all the photos the wife took came out blurry.

My phone pings with Guardie's reply: *Same guy. I'll forward the picture to Carol to show her sister. Stay away from the dude, alright?*

Ok. I'm so worried about Rachael.

Guardie: *Me too.*

A minute later: *I've been meaning to ask, want to grab a bite this week?*

Bite? Bad word choice lol.

Guardie: *Oops. Let me know when you want to grab dinner. I'm out of town until Wednesday.*

I slip my phone into my pocket without replying. I'm not interested in dating potential murderers. Which describes pretty much anyone from Tragic Wives. Though maybe that's just easier to tell myself than admit what's really bothering me: he's someone I could easily catch feelings for. Hook, line, and sinker.

CHAPTER TWENTY-TWO

Dorchester, Boston
12:25 p.m.
Rachael missing: Over 31 hours

I head up the walkway to my parents' house in Dorchester, a middle-class Boston suburb with Irish roots. The neighborhood is full of elaborate Georgian, Federal, and Victorian-style buildings. Our multi-story family home is plain by comparison, with modest New England features — brick siding, pitched roofs, bay windows.

"You're a sight for sore eyes," Dad says when he opens the front door. He towers over me, face craggy, kind blue eyes under bushy eyebrows, and wraps me in a tight hug.

Thank goodness he recognizes me today.

I soften into his arms, my face pressed against his faded checked shirt, and for a few moments, my stress is completely dissipated, but then when I open my eyes and spot the framed family picture on the wall behind him, and Britta's crooked grin, all the tension returns. My sister, gone. Rachael, gone.

"Nice trip?" he asks.

"Mmm-hm, a humpback was spotted."

"The tourists must've liked that."

I follow Dad down the hall, through the living room, to the adjoining kitchen. Despite the house being super organized, it's dated; its last renovation was in the early nineties. It looks the same as usual — stark and orderly, as Mom likes it. She's an avid practitioner of *döstädning*, the Swedish art of death cleaning, where you eliminate unnecessary items from your home so loved ones won't be burdened with the task after you pass.

"Your mother's out looking after Rhoda. Pha! Don't know why she can't leave me on my own, made you travel all the way here."

"Not a problem. I get time alone with you."

Dad has always been madly in love with Mom, which is, of course, the childhood dream — happy, devoted parents. But it also meant he always chose her first: to cuddle on the couch, to cater to, to side with in arguments. Sometimes I think my sister's anger, her rebellions, could be pinpointed to being relegated in his affections. Deep down, I knew the order: I was his favorite child, we shared a similar personality. I should've felt guilty about that, I wish I had, but I clung to the security it gave me, that warm feeling in my chest. And besides, in Mom's hierarchy, my place was clear.

Dad and I stand by the kitchen counter, between us a fruit bowl full of lemons. Mom cuts one in half each morning to put in her water.

It's nice being here. All the familiar potted plants; the floral-printed curtains, dishcloths, pillows. The furniture is a mix of Scandinavian and Shaker style, effortlessly creating *mysa*, a sense of coziness and comfort.

Dad rests his hands on the counter. "Anything new?"

I don't want to worry him. "Not much."

"How's Natalie?"

"Normal teenage stuff, plus dealing with her grief." Puking up every meal. Unable to rise from her bed. Hair falling out, clumps in the shower drain.

I keep Mom abreast of Natalie's situation, that's enough.

Dad opens his mouth then shuts it. "Sometimes, I think . . . nah, shouldn't say it."

"Say what?"

He kneads his hands. "Sometimes I think you do a better job mothering Natalie than Britta ever did."

"Dad! Britta was a great mom. I mean, there were areas for improvement, but she loved Natalie more than anyone."

"You're right." His eyes get misty, and he shakes his head as if to get rid of the emotion. "Won't argue with that."

"I miss her so much."

He nods, grief etched into the creases of his face. "I miss her too." Moving slowly, he shuffles to the cupboard, takes out two glasses, and pours us some water.

The kitchen clock ticks.

"Any special men in your life?" he asks.

Guardie's text, wanting to catch up for a bite. A *date*. "I had tea with a cute boy." I laugh it off. "He's Canadian."

"That's a shame," Dad says. "Inferiority complex, those Canadians. Does he support the Canucks or the Oilers?"

"Haven't asked."

"You always forget the most important questions."

"Ha! He said he likes watching arm-wrestling matches."

"They call that a sport?" Dad frowns. "I thank my lucky stars I didn't end up with that William son-of-a-bitch as a son-in-law. As Babe Ruth said, 'Never let the fear of striking out keep you from playing the game.'"

I make an exaggerated sigh. "Please, not Babe Ruth quotes again." He doesn't return my smile.

"Something wrong, sweetheart? You look tired."

I'm drained, sleep-deprived, and the Valium is making my eyelids heavy.

"Getting much exercise?"

"Morning swims."

"Pha. For the birds." He gives a dismissive wave. He hates that I swim so often, and believes I'm tempting fate after what happened to Britta. He's given up trying to talk me out of it though.

"Winter swimmers have higher levels of a 'cold-shock' protein called RBM3," I tell him. "The same protein is found in hibernating animals. An experiment with mice found that some of them could regenerate synapses under induced hypothermia."

He furrows his heavy eyebrows. "And again in English? I've never doubted you're the smartest one in our family." I sigh again. He sometimes said that in front of Britta. He shouldn't have.

"They think cold-water swimming could help find a cure for dementia."

"Dementia? It's god's favor. Don't have to remember all the bad stuff . . . or the chores your mother nags me to do." He winks and walks to the living room. "Ready to watch the highlights?"

I smile and nod, chest tight. It's bittersweet being with him during these lucid moments, knowing they won't last.

"Let me put my stuff away and get you some food first." I turn away, feeling tears coming on. I remember Guardie's vow to honor the present moment. I should do the same: Dad's with us now. What's the point of grieving him when he's still here? But the familiar him is gone, the man we knew coming and going like the tide. It's so sad, all of us edging closer to death. I swallow hard. "Hungry?"

"No. I had a tuna sandwich already."

"But Dad" — I freeze as he reaches for the remote control and pulls the footstool to the couch — "you hate tuna." Britta was the only one in our family who liked it.

He flicks on the TV. "A nice tuna sandwich, lots of mayo, hit the spot. Come on. You gotta see Kutter Crawford's play. Mind grabbing me a Samuel Adams from the basement?"

I head downstairs to the basement, which has three rooms: a guest room, an adjoining bathroom, and a large pantry with concrete walls. Like the rest of the house, it's as though I'm in a time warp. I flick on the light. Mom's really stocked up. The shelves are lined with preserves, homemade cranberry jam — her substitute for Swedish lingonberry — peaches, and pickles. You'd be forgiven for assuming she was Amish or Mormon. I take a six-pack from the mini-fridge. Samuel Adams has been Dad's favorite brand for as long as I can remember. Bostonians take beer drinking very seriously. Beer and baseball — the city pillars.

As I shut the fridge, I notice a brand-new sink. When did my parents have that installed? I suppose if Mom's doing more preserving she needs to wash the jars here and doesn't want to trek up and down the stairs.

I head to the living room with the beer.

Dad and I watch baseball replays — he yells at the players when they do something dumb, then pats my knee when they do something spectacular. It feels like I'm a kid again and any minute, Mom and Britta will walk through the door, and Mom will roll her eyes good-naturedly and say, "You, two, off the box. You need fresh air."

I lean back on the couch and pull the quilt over my lap, lulled by nostalgia from all Mom's homey touches throughout the room. The vintage Swedish rocking chair across from me and the bright folk art on the walls. Wooden candleholders and family photographs are neatly positioned on the coffee table.

Natalie should come down here soon, maybe for her birthday. Family is important. She can't spend all her time in her room or in dark cinemas with Kristen. After her last therapy appointment, the psychiatrist told me she'd like to see Natalie once a week instead of once every two weeks.

Dad puts his arm around me. I shut my eyes, snug and safe at his side . . .

* * *

A while later, I come to. "Sorry, Dad." I think that's the third time I've dozed off today.

"You were snoring like a jackhammer."

"What? I don't snore."

"Joking."

I rise and stretch my arms. "What do you want for dinner?" It's still a few hours away, but I like to plan these things. My enjoyment in life stems from breakfast, lunch, and dinner lists; often the anticipation of the meal is as pleasurable as the food itself.

"Got some TV dinners in the freezer."

"Not on my watch." I gaze at his balding head, stooped shoulders, and aged hand cupping the beer bottle. How many dinners do we have left together? The life expectancy of someone after an Alzheimer's diagnosis is eight to ten years, and he was diagnosed four years ago. "Tonight, I'm making you any dish you want."

"You don't have to do that."

"What are you craving?"

"If I was about to get executed, my special meal request would have to be seafood linguine."

"You got it. Scallops, shrimp, garlic, parmesan. I'll head to the market now and come back and make the best pasta of your life." He'll be fine for a short while, especially if I leave him with a supply of snacks. Mom often goes out for three-hour stretches.

He nods, not looking up from the game.

Once I've grabbed my stuff and used the bathroom, I cross the living room to the front door.

"Em!" Dad beams, rising to give me a hug. "Did you just get in from the ferry? I didn't hear you knock on the door. Nice trip?"

My hands clench. "Um, yeah." I fumble for words. "A humpback was spotted."

Goddammit. I lost my sister and now I'm losing my dad.

"The tourists must've liked that."

I peer up at him, seeking eye contact, wishing he would stay the same person who'd raised me and loved me. My chin wobbles, so I bite my bottom lip to still it. "I love you, Dad."

"Goes without saying, sweetheart."

"Remember, stay away from the stove, okay? By the way, I brought you apple-cinnamon muffins."

His eyes light up. "Hand 'em over. Your muffins are snack crack."

"*Crack?*"

He smiles, showing his dentures. "Natalie taught me. Hey, gotta keep up with the kids."

"Okay, see you soon." With that, I step out the door.

CHAPTER TWENTY-THREE

Boston Public Market
4:15 p.m.
Rachael missing: 35 hours

Half an hour later, basket in hand, I move from stall to stall at the Boston Public Market, a year-round indoor sanctuary selling local produce, seafood, and gourmet food. I stop every so often and look around, as though coming out of a trance. The combination of lack of sleep and Valium gives everything a dreamy, movie-like quality, undercut by the hum of conversation as customers discuss their preferences with the vendors. Market shopping is the ultimate calming activity, an antidote to the stress of Rachael's disappearance and Natalie's emotional turmoil. There's nothing like this in the Cape.

On the way here, I called and checked in with Natalie. She sounded okay, said she and Kristen were fine, and I reminded her to let me know if she needed anything or wanted to talk later. Mom also called to say her plans had changed and she'll be home at eight or nine tonight.

So much for one-on-one time with Dad.

My mouth waters as I enter the deli section, breathing in the earthy aroma of freshly baked bread mingled with the scent of pungent blue cheeses and nutty, aged Gouda. I buy some parmesan and keep strolling. I'll make garlic bread tonight, thick slices with slabs of butter and crushed garlic. As I'm hunting for a baguette, something makes me look up. A head in the crowd. Dark hair, muscular arms, a crystal necklace.

Is that . . . ? No, impossible.

The man turns and spots me. "Em!"

What in the world is Guardie doing here? Legs a little rubbery, I walk toward him, unable to hide a grin.

"Hey," he says. He's dressed in camel-brown shorts and a sweater, while I'm sporting more of a beer commercial vibe — jeans, sneakers, one of Dad's Red Sox jackets, and a baseball cap.

"Are you stalking me?" I ask, straight-faced.

His eyebrows raise. "Maybe you're stalking me."

"Why are you here?"

He points to the deli window showcasing wheels of cheese neatly arranged on wooden boards, artisanal bread loaves, and cured meat. "I was hungry."

"I mean, *in Boston*."

"Excuse me" — the plump gray-haired woman behind the counter passes Guardie a brown paper bag — "here are your olives and cheeses. Can I get you anything else? Free samples?" The woman, who must be in her seventies, bats her eyes — Guardie apparently has the same effect on young and old.

"You're a star, Mary. These olives are going to make my day. Have a wonderful afternoon."

We step aside, and stand in a quiet enclave, away from the stream of shoppers.

"You're such a flirt," I tease.

"Friendly." He touches his heart. "Nothing wrong with making people feel good."

I glance at the old lady, who is now fixing her hair and bustling around her stall as though stung by a love bee.

He touches my arm. "How are you holding up?"

"I need more news about Rachael. I keep telling myself she could be fine. She could be anywhere. There's still a chance she's okay."

There is a long pause before he says, "I pray her family gets the answers they need."

He sounds like Li-Ping. Prayers, hope, lighting candles, going to church, and deals with imaginary gods — I know first-hand none of it makes an ounce of difference. "So, why are you really in Boston?"

"Getting spa supplies from my witch friend. Chai, massage oils. And I'm looking after her place while she's away." He repositions his leather satchel over his shoulder, which immediately makes me think of Rachael's bag at the beach and the missing notebook. "How about you?"

"I'm visiting my dad. Talk about a coincidence."

"Don't believe in those."

"Something more cosmic?"

He nods sagely. "By the way, I'm sorry you never got your chai."

"I'm sorry you got a full frontal." A blush eats me up as I recall flashing him my breasts.

He whistles. "Don't apologize. It was like witnessing one of the wonders of the world . . ."

"Oh, please!" I can't help taking the compliment to heart.

"I need peppers," he says. "Come with? There's a great stand around the corner."

We walk close together, weaving through the crowds, our strides matched, a bubble around us as though we're lovers. He goes to reach for my hand but then stops himself. As he should — you can't just go around holding a woman's hand before you've even kissed her.

A kiss does seem imminent. There's a spark, a buzzy kind of magic when you know a person likes you back. We're stealing glances, trying to play it cool while gauging each other's reactions.

At the end of the aisle, we approach a stall with baskets of peppers — green, yellow, purple-black, fire-engine red.

"Oooh," I murmur.

"You sound like a purring cat."

"Food shopping is my favorite pastime." There are so many peppers. Jalapenos, serranos, habaneros; they even have ghost peppers and Carolina Reapers.

"Favorite activity, eh? I can think of other things . . ."

I shove him. "Keep your mind on the task at hand, Oh Great Mindful One."

I'm drawn to the hot sauces on a table adjacent to the fresh peppers, the different shaped bottles, each with arty labels listing the heat level.

He selects a bag of fresh bird's eye chilis. After paying, he gives me a look.

"What?" I ask.

"I texted you about getting a bite . . ."

"I meant to reply." I couldn't tell him the truth — that I'd rather date a boring accountant than someone who could easily smash my heart into smithereens.

He gives me a disarming smile. "Maybe we should grab that bite tonight?"

There are a hundred reasons why this is a bad idea. One of which is he's a suspect in a missing woman investigation, but I guess I am too.

"I've got another date," I say, and his smile drops.

Miguel's orders come back to me: *I'll work Li-Ping. You work Guardie. Learn more about his secret.*

I suppose I could kill two birds with one stone.

"I have a dinner date with my dad," I say, adding quickly, "I could catch up, though, for dessert?" My mom will be home by eight.

"Hell, yeah. Your place or mine?"

We're in no way at the "bring a boy home" stage of our situationship, and besides, if I bring Guardie back to my parents' house, he'll be forced to watch — and I'll be forced to *re*-rewatch — Red Sox highlights.

"Yours, definitely. Give me your witch's address and I'll be there in a few hours."

"Can't wait."

We say goodbye and head in different directions.

"You won't regret it," he calls, and I spin around, watching as he walks down the aisle, pumps his fist into the air, and says loudly to himself, "She said yes!" as though we're in an eighties movie.

Laughter bursts out of my mouth. He's adorable. Which means I'm in trouble.

CHAPTER TWENTY-FOUR

Diamond Pond, Walpole
7:15 p.m.
Rachael missing: 38 hours

After feeding Dad "the best pasta he could remember having in years, *but don't tell Mom, her feelings will be hurt*," I wait until Mom gets home then drive to the witch's house in Dad's truck. By the time I arrive, it's nearing dusk.

Oddly, Mom kept inventing reasons I should stay in. She even tried to guilt me into extending my trip by a few days — no doubt so I could help manage Dad's care, though she didn't say it outright. When I told her I was needed back in the Cape to look after Natalie, Mom wasn't happy. She's not used to me refusing her requests.

Walpole is only twenty-seven miles from Boston, but couldn't be more different: it's hilly countryside, blue and yellow wildflowers dotting the grassy landscape. The town overlooks a huge pond, which to my eyes looks like a lake.

From outside, the witch's house is nothing out of the ordinary — except for a serpent-shaped door knocker — but once inside, I'm speechless.

"What a place," I breathe as I step through the doorway.

Guardie smiles, watching me gawk at the entry room.

It's like being in a pine forest: dark green walls, large fallen branches on the floor, an altar with wildflowers and candles, and no traditional furniture whatsoever.

"Kylie has her own style, for sure. She's an old friend. We met at a reiki workshop. She's away doing a walkabout."

"A what?"

"Inspired by the Indigenous people in Australia, a long walk or journey, spending time alone in nature."

In other words, more New Age appropriation.

"I'm here because she asked me to water her garden and check on her herbs. That's her main business." And probably accounts for the scent in the air.

"How long are you staying?"

"A night or two." He tilts his head. "You're so pretty."

"Thank you. That's kind." I did have an extra-long shower, and I'm wearing pants that hug my butt, and a cute, scoop-neck top. I even braided my hair and put on mascara.

He's still looking at me, and I could get a little swayed by the romantic moment, but I need to think critically.

Fact: Guardie had access to Rachael's bag and could've taken her notebook.

Fact: Guardie mysteriously bumped into me in Boston.

Fact: His eyes are the most chocolatey brown and his biceps are— *Stop already!*

"Do I get a house tour?" I ask.

The rest of the witch's place is equally enchanting: The adjoining bedroom with dark blood-red walls and a futon on the floor is attached to a sparse white bathroom, while at the other side of the house, a large window dominates the kitchen. Pots, ice cream tubs, and milk cartons cut in half are full of heady-scented herbs catching the last light of the day.

I sneak a peek in the fridge and spot jars of broth lining each shelf, alongside tinctures and ointments. I turn back and rest my hands on the counter beside Guardie's brown leather satchel, which has been left open, a charger cord snaking out of it.

How am I going to get my hands on that satchel? Is it possible Guardie has the notebook?

He closes his satchel and hooks it on the chair. "Let me show you outside."

It's as though I've stepped into a painting: The backyard is overrun with wildflowers and a small fire is blazing in a fire-pit. The pond isn't far away, and a fat moon is on the horizon.

"What's that?" I point to a large structure near the firepit — sticks arranged in a dome over a hole in the ground.

"Kylie's sweat lodge."

"I've always wanted to try one." As I say it, I realize I've invited myself into an enclosed space with him for hours. "Saunas are very important in Swedish culture." I try to sound expert-y and not at all horny. "We visited family in Gothenburg, and after our 'get to know you dinner,' everyone got naked in the same sauna. Seeing my long-lost relatives' junk? Not a highlight."

Guardie laughs. "Kylie runs sweats based on the lunar calendar. It's a special moon ceremony tonight, but she had to cancel it, so she's losing business."

Oh. The already-blazing fire suddenly makes sense. He'd planned this. I'm more concerned about finding out if Kylie is Guardie's lover. "Well, you're a good . . . friend."

"I try to be. But I can't get this runaway academic off my mind."

I grin, flattered and more than a little nervous about the inevitability of what comes next.

I play to the script. "Let's do a sweat lodge."

"Fair warning: it's intense. Some people hallucinate or find it suffocating. It brings out the demons."

"Dramatic. What kind?"

"Anything you've repressed, blockages in your heart. It's a powerful exorcism."

"I'm in." *Heal me.* I have more than a few ghosts to exorcise.

"The rocks are already hot but need another half an hour." Guardie crouches by the fire and uses a stick to stoke the logs. I sit quietly and watch him in nature, his perfect backdrop.

"Okay, let's cover this baby up." He lays numerous green army woolen blankets over the dome before adding two white artist canvasses.

"Ready for dessert?" he asks.

"I'm a sucker for anything sweet."

The combination of "suck," "sweet," and our sparky eye contact makes me look away.

In the kitchen, I sit across from him and we sip chai, which is as delicious as he promised — licorice, cloves, and star anise mixed with creamy, hot oat milk.

I lick my lips. "I'd drink this every day, if I could."

"In that case, I'll get you an order and deliver it to you personally. What's your address?"

I give it to him then ask, "What's yours? You've never mentioned where you live."

"Ah . . . the East End."

"Alone?"

"Yeah, right now. I had a roommate, and sometimes people crash at my pad, or I stay at theirs'." He sucks in his cheeks and holds his mug in front of him. "It's just, you know, four walls."

He seems defensive, as though I might judge him for not having a fancy place, but I wouldn't — at least, I hope I wouldn't. I'd respect that he's content with his own standards of success rather than following society's definition. But maybe I'll feel differently when I see it.

I take another sip of chai. "Better watch out, some guy warned me this has love in the ingredients." Since sex is possibly on the cards tonight — who am I kidding? We're out in the country, alone, on the eve of a special moon, about to enter a sweat lodge with sexual chemistry that's been brewing for months — I want to know his intentions. Is he only after a one-night stand?

139

"I haven't been looking for anything serious or committed for a while," he says.

Fuck boy. I keep my face impassive. Precisely what I
expected him to say.

"But with you" — he leans back on the chair, shoulders
relaxed — "it's different. I'm definitely open to seeing where
it goes, without forcing anything. No agenda."

I exhale. My sentiments exactly.

The question is: can I separate "suspect" from sex? Shouldn't
I check his satchel before I get swept away in the romance? It's
hard to tell which drive is stronger: wanting to screw him sense-
less or wanting to confirm he definitely didn't take the notebook.

Next, he serves chia pudding with a blend of vanilla and
maple syrup.

A man who feeds me. This is living. But suddenly, my
inner Miguel taps me on the shoulder and whispers, *Double-
check details, look for any inconsistencies or aberrations.*

I need some kind of opener. "So, does your family know
you house-sit for the witch?"

I barely listen to his response.

And now the real question: "Tell me more about your
family. You mentioned a disagreement about shares, how
money-focused they've become . . . ?"

Guardie recounts the same story as before. No inconsistencies. He adds, "The family dynamic was never right because
they favor my brother for his achievements. He's a genius,
takes bold moves with his stocks. They're all about the status
it brings *them*. Classic narcissists."

Fascinating. He was the odd one out in his family, the
tredje hjule, the third wheel. But don't all families have alliances,
members they connect with more naturally, based on tempera-
ments or mutual interests? There's nothing innately wrong with
that . . . *Mom at the front door, tightly holding Britta's hand, about to
go off on a day trip hiking.* Except it hurts when you're left out.

Guardie shrugs. "I'm okay with not talking to them for
now. No mud, no lotus."

"What do you mean?"

"Without suffering through the mud, you can't appreciate the beauty of the lotus."

Leaving me with that imagery, he goes outside and checks if the rocks are hot enough to begin the sweat.

My phone beeps from inside my purse. I fish it out — my darn battery is low, and I don't have a charger.

Miguel texted: *Having after-dinner drinks with Li-Ping. Three sherries & she's SPILLING. Kudos to Gentleman's Personal Trainer. He coached me how to get info. Mirroring techniques, open-ended questions & playing drinking games.*

I text back: *What's Li-Ping's secret?*

It's so major, it MUST be accompanied by alcohol. Debrief in person. But she's got one helluva motive. I think she's our man. [[emojis of three champagne glasses and an eggplant]]

As I slip my phone into my purse, Guardie walks back into the room and playfully tugs my braid. "It's time. Ready for a spiritual rollercoaster?"

CHAPTER TWENTY-FIVE

The sky is a deep pagan purple now, and the pregnant moon sends white maternal light over the little house in the woods, the wild garden, and domed sweat lodge.

I'm in a borrowed T-shirt and shorts as I enter the cave-like space. Guardie closes the flap. It's so dark, the sole source of light coming from the embers at the center of the circle.

"Temp okay?" he asks.

"Just like being in the sauna at the Y."

"It's going to get steamy."

I hide a smile. I certainly hope so. Not now, though, but after the sweat.

He ladles cold water onto the embers — a hiss of steam — foggy mist hovers over the red rocks. "It reminds me of this quote," he says, "by that woman who wrote *Out of Africa*. About salt water being a cure for everything."

"I love that." The quote wraps up my whole life these days.

The heat engulfs us, the burning sage thickening the air, my skin sticky. Time shifts over the next hour, until I can't make sense of it. All the while, Guardie beside me, checking in, "You're good? Not too hot?"

I close my eyes . . . everything in my body slows . . . drifting . . .

. . . I'm lying beside Rachael on the beach, trapped, my mouth stuffed with sand, hands bound . . .

. . . I'm a kid, watching TV on the couch with Dad and Mom. The host makes a joke and Dad throws back his head and laughs — but instead of turning to me, Dad pats Mom's knee. I laugh louder, a fake sound. Dad still doesn't hear me. "I'm here!" I yell into his ear. "Pay attention to me! Me!"

. . . I'm swimming with Britta in the sea, the Kraken behind us, its tentacles swiping, nearly catching us . . .

. . . I'm the Kraken, my arms long powerful tentacles — and I'm pulling William's ship from the sea, creating whirlpools.

Are these the demons Guardie warned me about?

Steam rises, fumes from the smoking sage, Guardie, at my left, repeating, "Feel it in your heart, feel the pain, then release it to the fire."

The heat is strong. My throat and nostrils burn. I grip my knees. It's like I'm being broken in half, one part of me grounded to the seat, the other part moving upward . . .

Am I awake? Asleep? Some half state? I shouldn't have had a Valium and put myself in such extreme temperature.

"Em? Do you need water?" Guardie places a hand on my arm. "We can get out. You're breathing really heavily."

"I'm okay," the "sitting me" answers while the "other me" floats to a different dimension. As scary as it is to be locked in my mind in a waking nightmare, I need to keep going. Other messages are waiting for me. Other truths.

. . . Now I'm in a black dress, high heels pinching my toes. Crying . . . someone nearby is crying.

Britta's memorial service, a small chapel in Boston, the only sensible spot to hold the event as she moved from state to state so often and didn't keep in touch with friends. An uninspired funeral director is leading proceedings. How Britta would have hated how uptight he was — all his words about her sound hollow, wrong.

If it was up to my sister, she'd have an outdoor funeral with Metallica playing, with fireworks and spicy food, not this bland, lack-luster middle finger to her passions.

Natalie, inconsolable, is sitting between me and Mom on the pew. The three of us are in tears, holding hands, a chain of sorrow.

There's no burial, or cremation, no post-funeral reception with tea and cake.

Then we're walking . . . Dad, steely-eyed, leaving the church and heading back to our cars. "This would have never happened to you," he said, not disguising his bitterness. "You would never have been so reckless to swim in the Outer Banks. Irresponsible. She's a mother, for god's sake."

I'd thought the same thing numerous times over the last few weeks. How dare Britta swim in waters known to be treacherous, with shifting sandbars and riptides. It felt like a suicidal act: die or not, a dare, let the waves decide her fate.

"She caused this." Dad frowned as Mom supported Natalie, who could barely walk. "All this suffering."

I nodded because Dad was right — but, no . . . not right. Siding with him, being the good daughter, separated me from being the bad one, separated me from being on Britta's side. His favoritism caused division. Mom versus "the girls," and "the girls" versus each other.

He favored me and Britta knew it. I played a part: nodding, agreeing, secretly liking how Dad chose me to spend time with if Mom wasn't home. Smug in his affections.

Maybe my whole career path, maybe my whole life path, was to differentiate myself from my sister.

Guardie is speaking but I can't hear him. Am I crying? I touch my face. No, just sweat. I focus hard, trying to return to the present moment, to hear what he's saying. But I can only hear my internal voice.

My life is not Britta's life.
Her pain is not my pain.
Our journeys are our own.
Her journey is over. I honor her by loving Natalie.
Love Natalie.

"Em! C'mon, let's get out," Guardie's voice finally breaks through.

No, I'm not ready. I'm still learning, a student of the fire, of the hot, trapped air, of my spirit.

He lifts the fabric of the hut, and we crouch low and crawl into the night.

It's a shock. The sweet, cool air. The smells of trees and sky. The feeling of a deep breath in my lungs, as though I'm filled with water. Steam rises off my body and the breeze makes my skin tingle.

As my eyes adjust to the dark, I have new super-vision. The backyard flowers, bushes, and grass aren't objects but living and breathing entities — I can *see* oxygen coming out of them.

What's happening to me?

The moon pulls me toward her. Losing my balance, I wobble and turn to Guardie. "I was awake and asleep at the same time — I was hallucinating. I still am!"

"It's natural for perceptions to change during and after the sweat." He hooks his arm through mine to offer support. "Some people go into trances or see visions. The insights are a gift."

"Did you hallucinate?"

"Not this time."

I rub my forehead, still lightheaded. "I thought maybe you put mushrooms in my chai."

"Never without your permission. Here, have some water." He passes me a bottle and I guzzle, water spilling down the sides of my mouth.

"Let me get that, sweetie," he says, wiping the droplets from my chin. His fingers brush my skin as he draws the sweaty locks of hair off my cheek and forehead.

"Look" — I point at the blue wildflowers at my feet — "the petals, they're moving, breathing. And your crystal — it's fucking amazing!" Aqua light shoots out of the pendant like something from Superman's crystal cave.

He stands close. "After the sweat, many people feel connection to Mother Earth. We're all one."

Not in my family, not in his. Our families are fractured. Why can't humans get along? Why, despite loving each other, do we eat our own?

"Time to go from fire to ice?" He gestures to the shimmering pond in the distance. It's probably only a few minutes' walk.

"Déjà vu." I laugh, deep from my belly. When we were at his spa, he gave me the fire and ice option — a sauna, followed by an ice plunge — and now he's offering a sweat lodge followed by a pond dip. "That's a vibe," I say, a goofy smile on my face.

He lifts his eyebrows and returns my smile. "I'll grab some towels."

By the time we arrive at the pond, I feel more myself, grounded, and the hallucinations have stopped.

He shifts on his feet. "Uh, Kylie offers people the option to swim naked if they want, to purify and wash away whatever they've exorcised."

That's a no brainer for me. "Sure." I'm ready to take this further, to go all the way with him. All the fear is gone. "I'm Swedish. We're not hung up about things like that."

"Me either," he says, whipping off his T-shirt and shorts. "Although most Canadians are hung up."

Hung . . . I'm very distracted. He's exquisite, and certainly has nothing to be shy about in that department.

I toss my clothes onto a nearby shrub and tiptoe after him.

146

CHAPTER TWENTY-SIX

Oooh! The icy water splashes my legs as I chase Guardie into the pond.

"Colder than a mixture of acetone and dry ice," I call out.

"Colder than a mother-in-law's kiss," he sings back.

He dives in first. I take a gulp of air and plunge, breaking the water's surface, the sudden drop in temperature electrifying.

When I come up for air, Guardie swims toward me. "How's that?"

"Invigorating."

We swim side by side, my senses alert to the scent of damp earth and foliage, the calls of distant night birds, water lapping against my skin.

I paddle my arms. "Thank god we're in a pond where no sharks are lurking."

Guardie's stroke falters for just a moment. "You got that right."

This could be so awkward — Guardie and I naked in the water, houses nearby with their windows glowing in the darkness — but the trees and shadows provide some privacy.

Once we get out, we wrap our bodies in towels. Guardie looks up at the sky. "This is the best sweat lodge and swim I can ever remember."

"It's going to get better," I say from behind him.

"Huh?" He turns.

Stepping forward, I lift my chin, lean close, and shut my eyes. *Contact.* He tastes like salt and syrup and fire.

"Em." He says my name with reverence.

Our arms find each other, bodies pressed close, lips only leaving each other's for air.

I stumble on a rock. "Ouch."

"Should we take this inside?" he asks.

We make our way to the witch's house, to her bedroom, to the blood-red walls, to the futon on the floor.

Lying side by side, he moves slower than any other man I've been with before. A hand trails down the small of my back. Minutes are spent kissing my collarbone before he makes his way to my breasts . . . stomach . . . thighs . . . and murmurs how soft my skin is. Excruciating. *Enough foreplay!*

Guardie says, "Much as I don't want to stop, I better get protection. Where'd I leave my satchel?"

"Kitchen," I reply. "Hurry!"

I simultaneously fix my hair and check my breath. Thank goodness I shaved.

When Guardie returns, he asks, "Everything alright?" and I say, "It'll be better when you're back in bed." He laughs, and I laugh too, and before long, we're both naked, and he's on top of me, inside of me, pumping me, pure ecstasy, a primal connection. Then I'm on top, showing him who's in charge. It's all very caveman, cavewoman, and I'm down for it.

When faced with life or death, there's no other way to feel so alive.

We have sex not once, but twice. These Canadians sure have stamina. All those long, cold winters. He is generous and attentive. Even though it is our first time together, it feels natural, and I can confidently report back to Miguel that Guardie truly lives up to his moniker: Magic Hands.

Afterward, he gets me a glass of water and we lie together, him on his back, me curled on my side, head resting on his

148

gorgeous chest. We talk for a while, but the words become less frequent, and it isn't long before he falls asleep.

I can't sleep. I'm still awake from the heat of the sweat, the power of the moon, the icy pond, and our sex magic. I sit up and study him. Silver light from the open window paints his body, and his crystal necklace.

How strange that tragedy led me to Guardie's arms . . . losing Britta, running to the Cape, Rachael's disappearance. Being with him is like a holiday from the rest of my life, an island of peace, and comfort, and crazy-good sex.

I need to let my parents know I'm not coming home tonight (which, yes, feels very high school). I grab my phone and start to text them, but halfway through, my phone dies.

I vaguely recall seeing a charger in Guardie's satchel.

Beside me, Guardie sleeps on, his chest rising and falling in the dim light.

Tiptoeing through the house, I reach the kitchen and feel for the charger in his satchel. My fingers land on something else. *No!* The corner of a thin, rectangular book. Shaking, I pull it out.

Miguel's voice, *Ask yourself . . . who was guarding Rachael's bags at the beach?*

My heart thuds in my ears. The yellow notebook stares back at me. I open it to see Rachael's words covering the pages. I want to drop it. Shove it back in the bag. Unsee it.

Guardie can't be — did he—?

My breath is too loud.

Shhh. Don't wake him. I look over my shoulder.

Can't hear anything.

Think! Should I grab the notebook, get dressed, and hurry back to my parents' house? But then Guardie will know I took it. And if he knows I'm onto him, I might be the next Tragic Wife to disappear. I could read the notebook before he wakes. See which of our swimming group's secrets — or his own — was worth killing Rachael over.

I flip open the notebook to a random page and crouch against the wall, its coolness steadying me.

Rachael's handwriting — big loopy, messy letters — is so *her*, always rushing, always late. My eyes fill with tears.

I scan a few paragraphs but find nothing of note.

Rachael writes about a guy who works on the Cape ferry. *He always watches me, and on the last trip, he approached and asked if I was a writer. Must have a crush on me. Wherever I go, men find me intriguing. It's the combo of red hair and curves . . .*

Could this be the same guy who Guardie and I photographed? Too bad she didn't describe what he looked like.

I flip to another page, searching for Serenity's name. Maybe Rachael dug up more dirt about the Iranian sculptor's supposed history in sex work.

There it is: *Serenity wasn't hard to crack. Everyone wants to confess to someone, and I've made myself the someone.*

My agent said he needed the first draft of my manuscript by the end of the month, which has forced me to become pushier, not such a bad thing. Women are taught to please, and wait their turn, so it has been liberating to be direct. To have balls.

Serenity caved and told me everything. All I had to do was reveal my secret first. A technique to foster intimacy. Share, share, share — even if what you tell them is bullshit. Serenity said she's been having the relationship for six months, although I suspect it could be longer. (Just like their number of sex partners, women always underestimate their wrongdoings.)

At first Serenity wouldn't name the person she was seeing, said only that it was someone connected to the Tragic Wives—

Guardie calls my name from the bedroom.

Fuck, fuck, fuck!

"Where are you?" His gravelly voice makes my skin prickle.

I keep reading.

Serenity told me their chemistry was undeniable, and even though Serenity knew it was wrong, because of—

Sounds coming from the bedroom.

. . . the significant age gap — her own words, a "robbing the cradle" situation — she started a sexual relationship with—

Footsteps creak nearby.

I shut the notebook, shove it back into Guardie's satchel.

"Em?" He appraises me in the darkness, no doubt wondering why I'm out here skulking around with the lights off. "What's up?"

"Um . . . just looking for a charger."

"C'mere."

Each step toward him, my hands shake more. I hide them behind my back.

"You okay, beautiful?"

As our eyes lock, danger signals filter through my mind.

Rachael — *gone.*

The witch — *gone.*

And I'm alone with him.

CHAPTER TWENTY-SEVEN

Tragic Wives (secret) WhatsApp chat
Two days later, 8 p.m.
Rachael missing: 4 days

Hannah: *With all due respect, I vote for morning swims to start back up tomorrow morning. Thoughts?*

Miguel: *I'm in. Any more news about Rachael??*

Hannah: *No. Anybody else?*

Li-Ping: *Her family are here from out of town. I saw them at the grocery store, but didn't talk to them. They looked miserable, of course. Rachael's brother is cute. (Don't tell my husband!)*

Serenity: *I'm preparing for an exhibition. I'll be at the swim in morn but probably unable to come to other swims in the week.*

Li-Ping: *See you tomorrow. May the God of hope fill you with all joy and peace as you trust in him, so that you may overflow with hope by the power of the Holy Spirit. Romans 15:13.*

CHAPTER TWENTY-EIGHT

P-town, Cape Cod
8.15 p.m.
Rachael missing: 4 days

"It's okay, Natalie, just get it out of your system."

Natalie huddles over the toilet, and I hold her hair back as she vomits. Remnants of the Thai green curry I made her earlier gush into the bowl.

It smells so awful I feel like retching too. The irony isn't lost on me: feeding people is my way to show love, and Natalie is physically rejecting my one go-to tactic.

My phone buzzes in my pocket — probably another reply to Hannah's text about resuming cold-water swims tomorrow morning. Since she sent the message ten minutes ago, everyone is texting back and forth, including Guardie, who said he won't be able to make it because he's still in Boston.

Well, thank god for that.

After discovering Rachael's notebook, I took off from the witch's house, hightailed it back to Mom and Dad's, and popped one of Natalie's Valiums because I knew I wouldn't be able to think straight in the morning without sleep.

Guardie was taken aback by my sudden departure, but I reassured him it had nothing to do with him, that I just needed to check on my dad.

Earlier today, when I caught the ferry back to P-town, Guardie texted — *You left in such a rush. Catch up soon?* — and I replied with a vague message which seemed to placate him.

"It's coming!" Natalie lunges toward the toilet, emptying her stomach again.

I kneel beside her. "Honey, we need to get you back to the doctor. You can't keep anything down, and you've lost so much weight."

"I'm okay." She wipes her mouth with the back of her hand and slumps against the wall.

"Here." I pass her a warm facecloth. I could bang my head against the wall. I'm no mother, no parent figure — I'm an idiot who chose to sleep with a guy who, possibly, is Rachael's killer.

Here I am jumping to conclusions. Why the hell did Guardie have Rachael's notebook? The morning Rachael went missing, Guardie arrived after me at the beach — but he could've been there earlier. And those scratches on his hand . . . I can't reconcile the Guardie I know with the idea of him being a violent psychopath. He reveres nature, the divine universe. But then I thought about the witch — was she really on a walkabout, or had something more sinister happened to her? And wasn't it just too neat that he had that sweat lodge all set up and ready to go when I arrived?

Natalie is cradling her stomach, but at least she's stopped retching. "Feeling any better?"

"Sicker by the second."

That makes two of us. "Let's just sit for a few minutes."

It's possible there was more than one yellow notebook — the one in Rachael's bag, which one of the other Tragic Wives took, and the one Guardie has. Still, I read it. I know it's got at least some of our secrets in it.

Now I'm sitting on this information and haven't told a soul, not even Miguel. I texted him that we needed to talk, to put our minds together, but his toddler is sick, and he freaks out if she even has a sniffle, so he insisted we wait until we can meet in person because he wants to tell me what "receipts" he has on Li-Ping; in his words, "Trust! It deserves serious airtime."

So, I'll tell Miguel about finding Rachael's notebook after our swim tomorrow — he said he'd be there come hell or high water. His fear of missing out on gossip may be greater than his hypochondria.

A good citizen would contact Officer Winn directly and inform her they'd discovered the missing yellow notebook. But maybe not a good citizen who recently did it (twice) with the prime suspect.

Another option is giving Guardie the benefit of the doubt and slipping Rachael's notebook into the conversation to see how he reacts. Or I could ask him straight out. There could be an innocent explanation. Rachael may have given it to him for some reason. Someone else took it and dropped it by accident and he found it? Maybe he did take it to protect his own secret, or his friends. I glance at Natalie, sitting like a marble statue by the toilet. If Guardie's involved in Rachael's disappearance, letting on that I'm suspicious will potentially put me in danger — and put my troubled charge in danger too.

My throat tightens. In the sweat lodge, I realized the best way to honor Britta and to make up for my mistakes was through loving Natalie. To base my future decisions on love.

I take the face cloth from her hands, rise, and walk to the sink. "How about a nice warm bath?"

The giant bathtub is in the center of the room — a free-standing masterpiece positioned underneath a giant chandelier. Natalie nods, then winces. She really isn't well; seemingly even moving her head is difficult.

I touch her forehead, but there's no fever.

Once I get the bathwater temperature right — not too hot, not too cold — I let the water run, adding bath salts and a few drops of rose aromatherapy oil.

I'll decide what to do about the notebook tomorrow after talking to Miguel. Thankfully, Guardie won't be at the morning swim. I have no loyalty to him; he's just a hot guy with magic hands who shared an intense, spiritual moment with me. For all I know, it could have been typical salesmanship — after all, self-proclaimed healers often have questionable motives. Shame on me for letting my guard down with another man so quickly. And here I thought William had set the bar for disappointment.

The notebook burns in my mind. Hideous crimes are committed by the holiest of people, the ones closest to us, or those we least suspect.

Where are you, Rachael? Please be okay.

Natalie sighs, eyes downcast.

"Your birthday's in less than a week," I say, choosing to focus on something positive. "What would you like to do?"

"Dunno."

"There must be something?" She's already turned down all my ideas.

"I guess we could go out for dinner in Boston with Grampa and Mormor."

"Perfect. I'll try to make reservations at Camelina's." The last few times I've suggested it, Natalie has refused, but I'll put us on the waiting list anyway — even if it's impossible to get a table this late. "The bath's nearly ready. Maybe let the water run and fill it right up." I head down the hall to start a load of laundry, then remember my jewelry sitting on the bathroom counter where I took it off before cleaning up the vomit, so I turn back.

In the bathroom, Natalie stands naked with her back to me.

I gasp. "Natalie! Your legs!" Bruises as dark as plums, ten or so, dot her calves.

She covers herself with a towel. "What? I bumped into a log when I was walking on the beach."

But there are other bruises — her inner elbow, her ankles.

Britta, for all her faults, noticed details. How could I live with a teenager covered in bruises and be so utterly clueless?

Natalie glares at me. "Waiting for something?"

I take a deep breath, terrified to voice the thought in my head. It's preposterous but I need to know. Stalling, I pick up my rings and bracelet from the counter and cup them in my left hand. "I wonder if you're maybe . . . giving yourself bruises?"

"Great! You think I'm a fucking psycho!"

"No, darling! I think you're sad and you miss your mom. I get it — I miss her too. Grief makes us do strange things . . ." *The Valiums. My reduced hours at Barnard. Running away to the Cape.*

"It's not grief." Natalie shakes her head. "You don't know everything. I talked to my friends and then Serenity . . ."

Serenity? As Natalie keeps speaking, questions fire off. I was aware Serenity had invited Natalie to her studio. Were they alone? Serenity had also said she'd introduce Natalie to some New York powerhouses. How much time had they spent together?

"Oh, shit!" I rush to the near-overflowing bath and twist the faucet with my free hand.

There were specific details in Rachael's notebook about Serenity's secret relationship. Six months. Someone connected with the Tragic Wives.

I assumed Serenity was having an affair with a man, but there's a chance . . .

What had Rachael written in her notebook about Serenity's relationship? Something like, *The chemistry was undeniable between them, and even though Serenity knew it was wrong, because there was a significant age gap, she started a sexual relationship.*

One of the rings I'm carrying drops from my hand and clatters onto the floor.

Could it be with my seventeen-year-old niece?

CHAPTER TWENTY-NINE

Natalie stands near the sink, facing away from me, the towel wrapped around her bony body. I've spent the last few minutes trying to get her to open up about the bruises, but she's sticking to her story.

I gather my ring from where I dropped it on the floor. This isn't the best time to interrogate my niece, not when she's naked and covered in possibly self-inflicted injuries. Serenity is the one who needs to be interrogated. Adrenaline with a strong serving of *How dare you?* surges within me. I'll call her as soon as I'm alone.

"How about you jump into your bath before the water gets cold?" I suggest, trying to disguise my nerves. "I'll make some soup for later, something your stomach might tolerate. Chicken noodle?"

"Why are you so nice to me?" Natalie snaps. "Just — stop."

I've overstepped again; sometimes it feels like I haven't done enough, other times too much. "Natalie, I know I can never replace Britta and I promise I'm not trying to. I just want to make things a little easier for you."

"Well, don't. You're not my mom! You'd be an awful mom! You'd make your child fat! Stuffing them with food.

Moping around. You're miserable. Mom said you were jealous of her."

"Hardly." I put a hand on my hip, bristling. The truth is, I was sick with jealousy when we were young about how Mom favored Britta. But then Britta made one screwup after another — and honestly, there was nothing to be jealous about.

Natalie's blue eyes glint. "Mom *lived* — when a song she liked came on the radio, she danced! She stayed up late having life-changing, profound conversations. She told the funniest stories. You . . . you're the boring, sad sister. I hate living with you."

My breath is shallow, and I have to dig deep not to yell back, *How do you think I like looking after you day in, day out when I want to grieve — alone! — and find out what to do next with my life! Why should I have to coddle someone who is legally an adult in a matter of days?*

I can't understand where Natalie's anger comes from, unless it's deflection because I questioned her about the bruises. Usually, when she's angry, she's sulky and passive-aggressive, never confrontational. Just because I made different choices than Britta is no reason to put me down.

The Valium in my purse calls, a siren song, promising numbness and alleviation from pain. One pill and I could climb into bed and wipe this conversation and the rest of the night away.

Instead, I say, "Let's talk in the morning, okay? Everything will be better after a good night's rest."

She offers a small, guilty nod.

In the kitchen, I make a cup of peppermint tea, replaying our conversation. I suppose she needs someone to lash out at. Isn't being an emotional punching bag the unglorified role of mothers?

Still, I need to establish boundaries. We're treated the way we allow people to treat us.

I grab my phone and text Serenity: *Up for a quick chat?* I need to know asap about her connection with Natalie. Maybe

Natalie's bruises, and her acting out of character, is directly related to whatever's going on with her and the sculptor.

Serenity's answer comes a minute later: *Sorry, trapped in a basement setting up an art installation. See you tomorrow for the swim.*

Dammit. What now? Call and question her? No, better to catch her off guard in person, read her body language. I could drive to her house right now, show up unannounced — but until I know what happened to Rachael, confronting any Tragic Wife alone at night isn't smart.

I carry my tea to the front office and sit at the maple desk, still reeling from Natalie's harsh words and all the unknowns surrounding so many people in my life. I try to focus on my breath, to center myself, but the built-in bookshelves feel like they're closing in. I open my laptop. Unread academic articles from last week stare back at me, along with a mountain of emails and abandoned to-do lists. I rifle through the emails on autopilot, barely registering what I'm reading.

Oh, great. An email from my boss. She's frustrated with my extended remote work, understands my ongoing mental health concerns, but wants to know when I'm returning to campus. If I'm not back in the office more consistently by next month, she'll need to reassign my current research projects.

The real estate agent also emailed with a potential offer on the house. Dammit. Once William's house sells, that's it — no more hiding here, pretending this is still home. I'm not going to freak out because I've been here before. These things often fall through.

I sip my tea.

The sad, boring sister, huh?

William had once said something similar in the heat of a fight: that every day with me was like the day before — my moods, my habits, the kind of books I read, the European films I streamed, the way I held him — and that the only novelty came from what dishes I prepared. I was about to tell him to go to hell when he kissed me and with unbridled sincerity said, "Thank you. You're my anchor, Em. Whatever else is going on, I can rely on your constant love. It's the best feeling I've ever had. You make everyone around you feel safe and nourished. It's like coming home."

Was this steadfast person the natural *me*? Or the "me" created at a young age within the dynamic of my family? Bad sister, good sister, exciting sister, boring sister. How can I be thirty-five years old and not know if I'm the true version of myself or the product of a difficult childhood? With Guardie, I felt like the real me was emerging. Someone without all the weight on her shoulders. Someone who could step off course and make surprising decisions.

A tension headache takes hold and I massage the back of my neck. Those bruises all over Natalie's body . . . She needs help, which I'm not qualified to give. What do I know about teenagers?

My thoughts jump again. Could Serenity and Natalie be in a relationship? I picture Serenity during our beach swims in her white one-piece, her long limbs, a dark swathe of hair. Not impossible.

I remember Natalie texting someone a few days ago and I teased her that it was a boyfriend, and she replied, "What makes you think I'm only into guys?"

Deal with facts is something Dad always used to say — meaning there's no point wasting precious time speculating without concrete details. With that in mind, I focus on the tasks in front of me and catch up on paperwork. One of the letters is from a lawyer, probably about Britta's life insurance. Natalie will be eighteen in — I check the calendar — six days, then she'll have access to all the funds, which seems premature. The girl leaves period stains on her sheets and forgets to floss her teeth. How is she expected to handle millions?

From what Miguel has told me, several of Serenity's previous relationships were patron-artist scenarios, her very survival resting on being a muse to the rich. By all accounts, in six days, Natalie will be very well off, but that money needs to go to her studies and setting up her future, not supporting the sculptor.

I open a new Word document and start a fresh "to do" list.

—*Reschedule an earlier psychiatrist appointment for Natalie*

—*Do social media deep dive into Serenity's past relationships*

—*Try to make reservations at Camelina's*

—*Buy dill, cucumbers, mustard seeds, whole allspice berries, prepare pickling jars*

When I was at my parents' house, I was inspired by all those jars of food Mom had prepared, and ever since, I keep thinking about how beautiful they looked. Maybe as well as pickles, I should make jam. I add cranberries to the grocery list.

I finish my tea, gazing at the weathered ship's wheel on the wall beside the framed wartime maps. Once Natalie receives her funds, she'll start her life in New York. And me? Who knows if I'll return there too, stay in the Cape, or try something altogether different. For some reason, I wonder what it would be like to live in the witch's house, to cycle to the local café and cook people's breakfasts. Not glamorous — scrambled eggs and hash browns ad infinitum. Maybe I could retrain, study baking at some fancy New York school.

A ping from my phone reveals a message from Guardie.

I'll be back in P-town tomorrow late afternoon. How about an ice bath followed by dinner? Or we can skip both and do dessert.

The innuendo is obvious. My headache kicks up a notch, the bands around my temples tightening. Usually, I'd be pleased by the request for a second date, but not in these circumstances. I imagine him luring me to his spa, to the ice bath barrels in the backyard, holding me down, suffocating me under the ice. Later, he would blame my death on an undiagnosed heart condition triggered by cold-water immersion therapy.

Get a grip, Em.

Rolling my shoulders, I head to the bathroom. As I pass Natalie's room, I catch muffled voices.

"I can't do this anymore," Natalie whispers.

I step closer to the wall.

"Sorry," Natalie says. "I had to call. I know I'm not allowed to talk to you on the phone unless it's an emergency."

There is crying and more muffled words. ". . . I miss you so much . . ." Natalie's voice breaks. "I wish you weren't trapped in the basement all night."

The basement!

What the hell? Natalie and Serenity obviously have a secret something going on. Christ. If only I could sit down with Britta and ask her how to parent a teenager who is exploring her sexuality with an older woman who happens to be a gold-digger and may swindle her out of the life insurance money.

"Isn't there some way we can be together?" Natalie says through the walls. "I wish I could go back in time and change everything." A pause . . . "Bye." Natalie's voice is full of longing. "I love you."

Oh my god. Now what am I supposed to do? Another problem, another puzzle. Aimlessly, I walk through the house, unable to think clearly, unable to settle my nerves. Only one thing can help.

In my bedroom, I grab the bottle of meds from my purse. It's all too much, the stressors interlapping like waves — Rachael's whereabouts still unknown; Guardie in possession of Rachael's notebook; Natalie embroiled in a secret relationship, yelling how much she hates living with me after all my sacrifices.

I dump the pills into my palm.

I'm sick of being the good sister. It's a two Valium night.

CHAPTER THIRTY

P-town, Cape Cod
5:10 a.m.
Rachael missing: 5 days

Today will be our first swim without Rachael. I wait in the car in the parking lot across from the beach. It's predawn; the moon is still in the sky overhead when she should probably be somewhere else. She and I both. No more early mornings alone by the Sandbar Café for me, staring at the inky water, digging my toes into the sand, reflecting on life until the rest of the Tragic Wives arrive — those days are over. When a tragedy occurs in a location, sometimes the area is cordoned off with police rope, buzzing with reporters and concerned citizens, then for months the spot is tainted, considered dangerous, exuding a dark yet alluring energy. If the tragedy is horrific enough, statues may be erected, or a carefully composed plaque, but after time, it's just another place, and no one remembers anything.

If only tragedy could talk. If only there was a world map that lit up in every site where a murder took place, a rape, or a school shooting. But tragedy does talk, I suppose, in women's bodies, in the illnesses I study, and all the inexplicable pains women endure, invisible to others, as if they have collectively swallowed the universe's tragedies, small and large alike.

I lean back against the headrest, the heater on full blast. The Valiums I took last night are making my tongue heavy, leaving an unpleasant, sour taste in my mouth. But I had knockout sleep, and even now, my pain is dulled; I am separate from my anxiety, my Siamese twin.

Miguel's late. I glance toward the part of the beach where he and I found Rachael's bags, then further out near the pier, where we discovered her iPhone in the seagrass. My heart hurts. Why haven't the police found Rachael? Each day that passes, it's less likely she's gone on a madcap soul-searching adventure and more likely her body's bludgeoned and dumped somewhere.

My phone beeps with a message from Miguel:

Sorry! Almost leaving. Dealing with double vomit/poo situation.

I toss my phone into the car's console. So much for our plan. We decided late last night that we'd meet this morning before everyone else showed up, to share our secrets — his about Li-Ping, mine about Serenity. I also need to tell him I found Rachael's notebook in Guardie's satchel.

It's a lot.

My gaze shifts back to the Sandbar Café, thoughts turning to my impending talk with Serenity. Will she admit that she's involved with my niece? In Massachusetts, the age of consent is sixteen years old. It's nearly illegal. Pressure builds in my head. I hinge my jaw open and shut.

There's Carol, near the café. I can tell it's her by her walk — she looks angry even from afar, as if she's approaching a boxer's ring, shoulders hunched, chin down.

I slide out of my car, grab my beach bag, and lock up. The cold envelops me. Brine scents the air, saltier than usual with a strong whiff of seaweed. Beyond me lies the ocean, flat and dark, with only tiny waves breaking on the shore, white ripples in an otherwise black expanse.

I can't see where I'm stepping, so I walk carefully along the uneven sand.

My phone buzzes again — now what, Miguel bailing? The message is from Guardie: *I'll take your silence as a no to dessert. Hope you're ok. Here to talk, always* x

How am I supposed to respond to that? I already had trust issues, and now that he has Rachael's notebook, I know I should steer clear of him.

"Carol!" I call as I approach, not wanting to spook her. I shove my phone into my pocket.

She turns, and I spot Hannah behind her.

"It's good to see you both." I give them each a hug. Their faces reflect my own worry, that "rug pulled from beneath you" terror when someone is taken from your life unexpectedly. That's another thing about tragedy — it binds you in a locked state, not before, not after the event, but midstream, where you're always left wondering, *What happened?*, connected by the painful unanswered question.

Carol looks more disheveled than normal, her brown curls resembling those toy trolls, her eyes red-rimmed, and Hannah, who usually exudes alpha Virgo "in charge" energy, seems smaller than her petite five-foot-three stature. The stress is getting to us all, and the realization Rachael might not come back.

The others arrive soon afterward. Li-Ping has fierce hugs for everyone, and Peggy, for once, isn't spouting off true crime facts. I'm grateful — the last thing I can take right now is gruesome details of female homicides.

The sky has morphed from a vast black dome to a dreamy half-awake blue. But it's freezing. I wrap my arms around myself, scanning for Miguel — if he doesn't show up soon, I'm going to lose it. We have to find time to talk this morning, not later.

"Are you okay?" Li-Ping asks, standing at my side. "You don't look well."

I could say the same about her. No protein smoothies or jumping jacks this morning — she's subdued, dark bags

166

under her eyes, making me wonder about the "massive" secret Miguel discovered about her.

"Five days, no sign of Rachael. It doesn't bode well."

"If this is all too triggering, you can always talk to me, okay? *The Lord our God is merciful and forgiving, even though we have rebelled against him.* Daniel 9:9."

"Ah, I'm good, thanks."

Li-Ping's a model Christian: always ready to lend a hand, offering to move boxes, donate time to community gardens, or any civic cause. True, she often uses these opportunities to collect images and reels for her social media, but no judgment. Essentially, her business is *her.* Being a former-Olympian-now-exercise-influencer requires a steady stream of content.

Her phone rings in her fanny pack. "Sorry, Em, give me a minute."

As I'm getting a towel out of my bag, Carol charges over. "Did you see? It's all over the media!"

"What?" I keep perfectly still, imagining the headline *Body found in search for missing woman — local masseuse arrested!* And all the while, I've kept silent. The police could blame me for being complicit, for not sharing vital information. They might think I'm involved.

"Rachael's family has put up a $10,000 reward for information. Do you know anything?" Carol asks me. "Or does your *friend* know something?"

"Why would I know anything? Which friend?"

"I'm freaking out." Carol pulls at the roots of her hair. "Rachael's MIA, the book of our secrets is missing and none of us knows what's in it, and no one wants to admit anything. Everyone's acting weird. And I . . . I . . ."

"What?"

"No, I shouldn't say anything."

"Look, none of us knows how to act. There's no manual on a missing friend. Hopefully with the reward, someone will come forward soon."

Peggy, eavesdropping nearby, says, "Her family is staying at the White Porch Inn. Personally, I never stay in hotels. People use hotel rooms for prostitution and taking drugs, but I listened to this podcast about how people have started to use them as temporary meth labs, which leave harmful, toxic chemicals. According to the DEA, over a thousand hotel rooms were used as meth labs in the US last year."

I release a heavy sigh, fighting the temptation to tell her to stick her podcast where the sun don't shine.

"That reminds me of something," Carol says to Peggy. "You and Rachael went away for a weekend trip last year."

"So?" Peggy says.

"Rachael said traveling with you was her worst nightmare. You never shut up," Carol says. "Talked late into the night. First thing in the morning. Blab, blab, blab."

Peggy's eyes goggle behind her cat-eyed glasses. "I don't like the way you're talking to me."

"Well, I'm just wondering" — Carol hitches up her pants and widens her stance — "what secret Rachael knew about you. We all know your friend was *poisoned* when you were in high school . . ." She stops.

Peggy glares at her. Hannah has appeared at Carol's side and is pulling at her elbow, as if trying to get her to move away.

Carol points at Peggy. "Your neighbor last year, Mrs. Woolenshire, died of *mushroom poisoning*, didn't she? Coincidence?"

Oh, man. Carol is coming unglued.

"Bet Rachael was writing about the freak 'coincidence,'" Carol says. "What happened, Peggy? Didn't like how your neighbor mowed her lawn, so you resorted to your old habits? Made her a *secret sauce* mushroom risotto or something?"

Hannah yanks Carol's arm harder. "Carol! Stop it."

For Christ's sake. This is ridiculous. Where is Miguel?

A dog walker with a large black Lab romping ahead of him on the beach passes us, and Carol calls, "The National Seashore requires dogs to be *leashed*."

The man flips her off without breaking stride.

"Dog walkers!" Carol snarls. "Most self-righteous people. Tourists let their mutts crap everywhere and act like they own the place."

Carol's obviously spiraling. Tragedy points fingers, creates mountains out of molehills, makes friends turn on each other.

Out of the corner of my eye, I spot Serenity nearing the café's bench. Despite the cold, my blood runs hot.

Time for a showdown.

CHAPTER THIRTY-ONE

I observe Serenity's every move: How she carefully sets her black-and-white Chanel beach bag on the bench, the way she floats around in her all-white outfit and tilts her head, greeting each of us with her eyes. Graceful, yes, but is it artifice, with the beach her stage? The nerve — she doesn't look one bit uncomfortable considering last night she was on the phone wooing my seventeen-year-old niece.

"Hi, Serenity," Carol says with a shy glance, her moods switching faster than I can keep up. "Sorry, I'm not going to be able to attend your opening show on Friday. I've managed to get a meeting with the mayor, and she's only available then. Couldn't turn it down — it's a great opportunity to talk about climate change."

"That's fine," Serenity says.

I approach Serenity from the other side, adrenaline firing up my nervous system. "Can I talk to you for a moment?"

"Oh. Okay."

We stand a little away from Li-Ping, Hannah, Peggy, and Carol, who have all struck up a conversation about something . . . hopefully not poisonous mushrooms.

"How's the preparation for your art installation going?"

Serenity nods, her dark topknot like a buoy in the sea. "Good."

"What's it about?" My throat is tight, strangling the words.

Earlier this morning before I left the house, I did some cyber stalking. Serenity's Instagram and TikTok accounts revealed she lives large — yacht trips in Miami, black-tie events in New York, luxury items and shopping trips, interspersed with quiet Cape Cod seascapes and her own harsh, abstract sculptures. It was difficult to tell if any of the people in the pictures were boyfriends or girlfriends, as most snaps were group shots, and Serenity seemed affectionate with everyone.

"The installation is called *Cross Wires*." Serenity's eyes dart around as she speaks. "It'll be on for the next month if you want to drop by."

"What themes are you exploring? And which materials best convey your message?" I've lived in New York long enough to talk art.

"Strings, all knotted and intersecting" — she lifts an elegant hand in the air — "how our digital and physical worlds are increasingly tangled. The juxtaposition of chaos and order. How we're all more involved with each other than we know."

"Ha! You don't say."

She looks at me like I've just made a loud noise in a crowded movie theater.

Enough fucking around. I think of Natalie huddled by the toilet, the bruises on her body — there's no way I'm going to let this parasite take advantage of my niece. As if she wouldn't be aware of the insurance money.

I step into her personal space. "I know about your secret relationship," I hiss.

Serenity blinks. "Ah . . . you do?"

In my periphery, Carol watching us.

"It wasn't meant to happen," Serenity says quietly.

I give her a sharp look. At least she's not denying it.

She shrugs, seemingly not ashamed, or embarrassed to be caught out, only defiant. "We didn't plan it. But the feelings came, no matter how unconventional the situation is."

Unconventional? Natalie's seventeen! My anger boils over, making me feel invincible, as if its force alone can alter her will. "You need to back off," I say, fixing a rigid smile on my face so no one can tell we're arguing. "Find someone your own age."

Her forehead creases momentarily but then she juts out her chest. "Whether you accept the situation or not, you can't stop love."

"Love? How dare you call it that? Money hungry, more like!" So, she and Natalie were in some twisted romance — and then what, Rachael discovered it? Rachael, like the rest of us, probably heard rumors about how Serenity bankrolled her lifestyle. Then Rachael could've dug more and threatened to write about Serenity and Natalie's relationship in her book and maybe . . .

Scenario one: Serenity made Rachael disappear. If it came out to New York society that Serenity was essentially a hustler, who stooped so low she seduced a seventeen-year-old orphan out of her dead mother's life insurance, she'd have little chance of future patrons. After all, the wealthy art collectors who fund her work probably expect discretion about their special "muse" arrangements.

Scenario two: Serenity roped Natalie in, and . . . it pains me to even think it . . . they were both involved in Rachael's disappearance.

Everyone needs to be treated like a suspect, even my own family.

Serenity towers over me. "Look, I can't say I understand your perspective on love, but to each their own. Besides, you shouldn't throw stones."

"What are you talking about?"

"What happened between you and Rachael the morning she disappeared?"

"Nothing!" My cheeks flame. "I found her bags on the beach. I never saw her."

"That's not what everyone else thinks."

"What?" Sweat breaks out on my forehead.

"Our whole group talks about it behind your back," Serenity says. "All the mystery surrounding you. Finding her bags, and the phone, your dead sister, your troubled niece."

I'm slammed by a wave of rage. "Don't talk about Natalie like you care about her!"

"Of course I care about her. She's a wonderful talent. Enchanting. Her costumes, extraordinary. I was quite taken by her. And now I'm committed to her."

Committed? I'm about to ask what that's supposed to mean when Hannah says, "All right, everyone."

I step away from Serenity, currents of disbelief rushing through me. This group — some of them my close friends — think *I* had something to do with Rachael's disappearance?

Hannah clasps her hands in front of her Star of David pendant necklace. "Well, ah, it's good to be together again. Uh" — she cringes and shakes her head — "that's not right . . ."

I've never seen Hannah anything but composed. If she's falling apart, the rest of us have no chance of keeping it together.

I glance at Serenity — then look around the group.

It strikes me that the blondes aren't here. Is a guilty conscience keeping them away? You'd think, given one of our own is missing, we'd all gather together and share information.

Hannah sniffs and looks up. "Rachael, I'm not sure where you are." She takes a deep breath and peers up at the sky then meets each of our eyes. "We hope with all our hearts that you're okay, and . . . we'll find you soon. Hang on and keep faith."

A sob among us. Across from me, Li-Ping makes a guttural sound which sets off a chain reaction of tears.

"Now we really are Tragic Wives," Carol says solemnly.

"Let's swim," Hannah says.

We trudge toward the beach, most of our heads bowed.

I sneak another peek at Serenity, perfect posture, staring straight ahead. Unresolved tension simmers inside me.

Li-Ping's crying is even louder now, crooning-at-a-funeral blubbering.

I link my arm with hers. "Everything's going to be okay."

"Yeah, right. Our friend's dead. And she wasn't even our friend, really, was she? I guess she only befriended us to get our secrets. I tried to reach out, to connect, but . . . none of us really knew her."

It's true that Rachael remained enigmatic. Throughout different stages of life, people have varying needs for connection: Forging new friendships obviously wasn't her priority, whereas writing, and making a name for herself, seemed to be what drove her. Plus mate hunting, hence her laser focus on Guardie, and all her activity on dating apps.

Once we all reach the shore, instead of going into the water, we pause, hugging ourselves for warmth, an unspoken moment of reverence for Rachael, in case this is where she last was. The waves crashing against the sand, Li-Ping's tears, and the cold blustering wind are the only sounds. Maybe it's too early for all of us to be back here, but I recall what my therapist said about Britta: a good way to process the tragedy is to return to the water, the scene of the crime.

Li-Ping whispers to me, "Are you worried about sharks after what happened to Rachael?"

"Sharktivity is on top of that." My eyes follow Serenity. What I am worried about is human sharks with model bone structure and magical vortex vaginas that seem to make people fall in love with them and give them all their cash.

Our group enters the murky blue water. No running, no playful splashing, no wide smiles, no "colder than" jokes — this is the quietest we've ever been. I barely feel the temperature of the water as it reaches my calves, or hear the birds, although part of me registers both.

"Hold up, hos!" comes an obnoxious scream.

We turn to see our favorite friend, the person who manages to put a silver lining on every last cloud, hurry over in his parrot Speedos, an unfastened Gucci robe flaring behind him like a bougie cape. "Don't think you're swimming without King Daddy!"

CHAPTER THIRTY-TWO

The Tragic Wives laugh at Miguel, a testament to his ability to lift the mood, even in the direst of circumstances. The water laps at my thighs, and I tense, shoulders scrunching as we wade deeper. I glare at him, silently communicating, *Where have you been? We need to talk. You screwed up the plan.*

Miguel bounds into the ocean, belly bouncing, then does a spectacular swan dive. Surfacing, he shakes his head like a wet puppy to more laughter. Everyone squeals and darts away, but his charm is lost on me.

The group forms a circle, our bodies bobbing in the water.

"Colder than the balls of a brass monkey," Carol says.

"Colder than a prissy Brit," Peggy follows.

"Colder than the soul of men," Hannah says.

"Colder than . . . than . . ." Miguel forces a smile. "Colder than a witch's tit." His eyes fill with tears as he looks far out at the distant boats. "Sorry, besties, this is hitting hard." His voice cracks. "I can't stay and have a coffee with y'all after because my bubby is sick, but I thought it was important to be here." He swipes the tears from his eyes.

"It doesn't feel okay doing this without Rachael," Peggy says, paddling to stay afloat.

Three seagulls swoop overhead, and Li-Ping raises her arms to the sky, "Jesus is watching over us. Psalm 147:3. *He heals the brokenhearted and binds up their wounds*."

Eye rolls pass between a few people.

After Miguel chat-swims with everyone, he front-crawls over to me. "Before you bite off my head about this morning, I did my best."

"It's okay. Do you really have to go soon?"

"Nursey duties. Ronald is in New York — what else is new — and the manny was up with my bubby all night. He needs to catch up on his sleep when I get home."

"When can we talk?"

"All we have is now."

"You sound like Guardie." My perfect-except-he-might-be-a-killer new flame.

I shoot a look at Serenity, who seems oblivious, maddeningly unperturbed while I'm still reeling with irritation.

Miguel and I paddle away from the rest of the group, our clumsy strokes making us look like out-of-shape synchronized swimmers.

"I've been dying to tell you Li-Ping's secret," Miguel says.

"Is it worth killing for?" In a sick way, I hope one of the Tragic Wives has a bigger motive for wanting Rachael to disappear than Guardie or Natalie, because then it's less likely they're involved. But nothing can change the fact her notebook was in Guardie's bag.

"Judge for yourself," Miguel says. "When Li-Ping was in the Olympics, she missed out on bronze by three points, right?"

"Yes." She's told us this. Many times.

"The person who won bronze — we'll call her Miss Bronze — was Li-Ping's main competition for years, lots of bad blood there. When I got Li-Ping drunk, she admitted what went down. Rachael knew about it too."

My gaze pivots to Li-Ping, who is doing water angels side by side with Hannah.

"Go on!" I'm kicking my legs underwater so hard — the proverbial duck — I'm starting to feel breathless.

176

"Li-Ping created an Instagram hate campaign on Miss Bronze, under a false name, obvs."

"That's bad!" Charity work and Christian values don't go well with hate bots. If this came out, it would be a massive fall from grace: Li-Ping's business, social media, and identity rests on her reputation, and she'd lose that big sponsorship she's about to get.

"Your turn," Miguel says. "What did you find out about Serenity?"

I paddle, accidentally smacking the water with my hand at such an angle that a spray of water hits my face.

"Well?" Miguel says.

My loyalties are divided, and I don't know who to protect: my troubled niece, the man I have feelings for, or Rachael, who needs dedicated sleuths — even the armchair variety — to get to the bottom of what happened to her. Above all, I have to make sure no one knows Natalie is connected to any of this.

Birds squawk overhead, and Miguel shudders. "Go away, assholes!"

I turn my head in Serenity's direction. She's beside Peggy, circling her arms in the water like she's dancing in Swan Lake. "Serenity is having a secret relationship with someone connected to the Tragic Wives."

"*Who?*" Miguel asks in the tone of someone jumping out of the darkness and saying, *Boo!*

"I can't say for sure."

He rubs his goatee. "I've always thought Compost Carol was hot on Serenity. Got anything else for Daddy?"

"Um . . ." Time suspends, my body weightless in the salty water, no longer requiring me to kick or paddle to stay afloat. I try to hear my inner voice, to receive guidance from my long-lost intuition, unsure whether I should keep the fact I found the notebook private or tell my best friend.

I can trust Miguel to help me see where I've been biased (or in his words, "dick-blind").

"It's Guardie," I say.

"What about him?"

Just as I open my mouth, Carol swims over. "What are you two conspiring about? You always seem like you're having the juiciest conversation. You never ask what I know."

Miguel and I exchange a look, and he says, "You're a little skewed to environmental issues, no offense. I like my free time to be more salacious."

"I can be salacious."

"Occasionally that's true," Miguel says. "Give me the sugar."

Carol is a self-righteous environmentalist with everyone, but Miguel brings out her gossipy side.

"I may have overheard a conversation about Rachael." The cold water has made the tip of Carol's nose red. "From someone who's officially connected to the case."

You'd have to be a dunce to not assume that means Officer Winn.

"The police have Rachael's manuscript." Carol's flabby upper arms slap the water like a kid doing the chicken dance. "They got it from her agent, so now they know all our secrets."

"That sucks," Miguel says, speaking for both of us. He sounds totally casual but I know it's his fake voice. Inside, he's freaking out.

The notebook — or notebooks — probably contain more damning information than the manuscript; considering factors like the writer's process and editorial suggestions, a lot could have been cut or exaggerated. Plus, of course, the manuscript was fictionalized, whereas the notebook is a record of all our actual conversations — and names.

"Also," Carol says, "they know what Rachael's last purchase from Toys of Eros was."

"What?" we ask in unison.

"A supersize vat of lube."

A beat of silence.

"Which would indicate lots of sex," I state.

"Not necessarily." Miguel sucks in his cheeks, which, from experience, means he can't wait to say something. "Lube has many uses — shining shoes, removing makeup, taking off a

178

ring, unsticking zippers, shaving, or taming frizzy hair." He gives a pointed look to Carol's damp curls plastered to her head.

"Enough, Miguel," I say. "We're talking about potential murder."

Carol looks over her shoulder before whispering, "Rachael's last phone call was to a Tragic Wives member who isn't here today, a guy the police are very interested to speak with . . ."

Guardie!

Hannah calls, "Time to head back in now."

"One thing I did catch" — Carol saves her juiciest morsel for last — "the last time Rachael was seen, two nights before we found her things on the beach, she went to someone's house."

My heart thuds. "The Tragic Wives guy you mentioned?" I already know what her answer is going to be.

Carol snickers. "And everyone thinks Canadians are so nice."

"Nice in a duct-tape-and-trunk-of-the-car kind of way," Miguel says as he treads water.

It's like I've forgotten how to swim, gravity sucking my limbs toward the sandy ocean floor. If Rachael bought lube and then went to Guardie's house . . . a lover's spat could've turned violent.

Carol grimaces. "Even though all the evidence points to the Canadian, and ninety-nine percent of serial killers are men, my bet's on Peggy."

"Why?" Miguel asks.

"Call it a hunch," Carol says.

"But we're not talking about a serial killer," I interject. "We don't even know if Rachael was murdered."

The list of suspects is growing though, and all too close to home. Serenity, Guardie, Li-Ping, and maybe — because of her connection to Serenity — Natalie.

"I agree with Em," Miguel says. "We don't know if Rachael is dead or off finding herself somewhere in British Columbia, mushroom foraging and vlogging under a pseudonym. Until then, *mis amores*, everyone is innocent until proven guilty."

CHAPTER THIRTY-THREE

P-town, Cape Cod
8:20 p.m.
Rachael missing: 5 days

The doorbell rings. It's about time. I walk to the door, my stomach growling in anticipation. The house feels empty with Natalie at Kristen's again — she won't be back for another hour or two. The quiet house and my boss's guilt-trip email pulled me into work until I had to order takeout clam chowder. Now I'm famished.

I flick on the porch light, and stop short. Guardie stands before me in shorts and Birkenstocks with socks, stubble darkening his cheeks. A bouquet of pink blossoms spills from one hand, a brown paper bag is clutched in the other, leather satchel slung over his shoulder.

"What are you doing here?" A gust of cold night air sweeps in.

"You asked for chai." Guardie gestures to the brown paper bag. "Hand delivered. And since I was stopping by, who doesn't like flowers, eh?"

As I stare at the generous bunch of dahlias and hydrangeas, the white wooden porch framing Guardie disappears, the walkway and trees recede into the distance. I'm back in time, seconds before my trust in William blew up, the bouquet in the entrance hall of his townhouse, my brief indulgence breathing in their floral magic, and how quickly that vanished when I walked into my bedroom.

Is my life to be a series of romantic episodes and shocking atrocities, flowers followed by . . . what?

"Can I come in?" Guardie asks, wind whipping his hair.

"I . . ." My mind fires off, reconstructing a possible sequence of events between Guardie and Rachael. Had he invited her to his house, suggested she pack her swimming stuff for the Tragic Wives meet-up in the morning? She brought lube from Toys of Eros, they had sex, and Guardie killed Rachael. He stole her notebook, and in the morning, planted her bags and phone at the beach. Guardie showed up minutes after I arrived at the Sandbar with those scratches on his hand.

It's only then I become aware Guardie is speaking, but I missed what he said.

"Pardon?"

"Sorry for dropping by unannounced." The iron porch light swings in the breeze, swaying shadows over us. "I understand if you want to catch up another time. I was trying to be, I dunno" — he shrugs self-deprecatingly — "romantic."

Obviously, after what Carol told Miguel and me at the beach, I won't let him in. But years of psychological female conditioning — be polite, never offend or act rude — make me hesitate. How do you turn away a man who's brought flowers to your door? I know I should make an excuse and plan to see him later in a public place, but maybe if we talk now, I can trick him into revealing information about Rachael . . .

"These days, who does unplanned visits, right?" He seems flustered, hurt that I'm not welcoming him with open arms. "I'll just leave you with this, and be on my way . . ."

As he takes an awkward step back, I realize I don't want him to go. Looking into his deep brown eyes and open face, feeling his energy, I tell myself this guy couldn't be a killer. He's my friend. He wears crystals, for goodness' sake.

He begins to turn away.

The normal me would tell him to keep walking, and I'd call the police the second I shut the door behind him. But the Britta inside of me — reckless, daring, not ruled by a "good-girl complex" — says, "Actually, come in," and steps aside.

Although I think he's safe, I'm no fool. "I have, um, friends stopping by in about twenty minutes, but I'm happy to chat until then. Excuse me, I have to text and remind them to bring . . . bread."

"No problem."

I accept the bouquet and lead Guardie to the living room, surreptitiously texting Miguel: *Magic Hands just showed up at my door. Call me in 20 mins. If I don't answer come to my house IMMEDIATELY. Confirm uv seen this!*

Guardie places the brown paper bag on the glass-covered map coffee table and stands self-consciously in front of the mantel. "Wouldn't mind a drink," he says with a cheeky grin.

"Wine or the hard stuff?"

"A beer, if you have it. Thanks."

Miguel texts: *Call you in 20. Btw the secret to a perfect BJ isn't deep-throating — it's EYE CONTACT.*

"Sorry, just need to reply to this," I say to Guardie as I tap Miguel back, *Stop! I'm trying to find out what Guardie knows about Rachael. He has her notebook.*

WTF?? Miguel texts, followed by a rapid-fire string of red alarm emojis. *How could you not tell me? Don't let him in the house. You might be in DANGER.*

Too late. He's inside already. Call me in 20.

My phone bleeps with messages from Miguel. *Abort! Abort!*

Guardie is looking around, his jacket laid out on the arm of the couch, his satchel on the ground by the blue-and-white-striped chair. He keeps moving, unable to stay still. Does he know people have discovered that Rachael was at his house before she disappeared? That it might be the last place she was seen alive?

"Nice pad," he says.

"It's my ex's." I lift my arm and nearly knock a seashell sculpture off the mantel.

How the heck do I slip the notebook into our conversation? *Quick question, babe. I happened to notice our missing friend's secret notebook hidden in your belongings. Did you brutally murder her or are you the good Canadian I think you are? And by the way, is the notebook still in your currently-on-the-floor satchel?*

"Going somewhere?" Guardie eyes my three-quarters-packed weekend bag on the coffee table.

"Boston, tomorrow." I zip the bag closed. "My dad called earlier sounding off. He said he needed to see me, that it was important."

"What about?"

"He wouldn't say exactly. Probably his health. He said he'll tell me when I see him. After everything that's happened lately, I'm trying to follow my intuition."

"And what's your intuition saying now?" His voice drops lower.

That you're genuine and gorgeous, and I'm in an old sweatsuit, hair still salty from the beach swim earlier, and even though everything is wrong about this situation, I want to be here with you, in bed with you, naked with you.

When I don't answer, he sits down. His tanned calves flex as he crosses his legs, and I have a sudden flashback to him kissing my thigh, murmuring how soft my skin was.

"So," he says. "It must have been hard being back in the water today."

"There was a lot of crying. Li-Ping's not handling it well." Of course, that could have been a deflection technique when really she was weeping over her guilt for offing Rachael before the world realized she was behind an Instagram hate campaign. "And Carol's freaking out. She even accused Peggy of poisoning Rachael *and* poisoning her old neighbor with mushroom risotto."

"*O-kay.* Sounds like I dodged a bullet."

Interesting phrasing.

"But I wish I could've been at the swim," he quickly corrects himself. "I would've liked to support everyone."

Is Mr. Nice just being Canadian or is he a conman?

"Yeah, you should've been there." *Carol is spreading rumors that the police are closing in on you.*

He squints at me as though he can tell something's not right.

I jump up from my seat. "Let me just put these flowers in a vase, and, um, get your beer." I hurry to the kitchen, fill a vase with water, and plunge the stems. I grab a beer from the fridge, and as I twist the cap off, it flicks to the ground. Clumsy.

"Can I get you a snack?" I call. Although my food delivery will arrive soon enough, my manners kick in; I can't resist offering a guest something to eat. Not even a murder suspect.

"Sure." He appears in the kitchen doorway, his shadow a menacing giant on the wall.

Is it weird that I feel both scared and a little turned on at the same time?

"Um, crackers and cheese? Leftover apple pie?" My voice breaks as I speak. Speaking of pie, I still have the pastry dough in the fridge for the pumpkin pie I was planning to make him before everything fell apart.

"I'll have some bread."

"Well, that's specific," I say in a half-jokey way, following it with a too-loud laugh.

The air feels charged and when he doesn't reply, I follow his gaze to the sourdough loaf on the cutting board. My stomach drops. Next to it lies the Chinese cleaver I'd left out for the parsley, its blade catching the overhead light.

Guardie steps toward me, an unusual look in his eyes — in fact, I've never seen him look so perturbed.

I cross my arms, paranoia washing over me when only minutes ago it felt right having him here. I was rash to let him in. What was I thinking?

"Em, are you okay?"

184

Yes. No. Do I have some kind of death wish? My hands clench and unclench at my sides as the thoughts rush in. Am I courting danger? Why? To fast-track reuniting with Britta in the afterlife? Who will look out for Natalie then? My parents probably don't have too long in this world, and Natalie's dad is a deadbeat. As Natalie's main carer, I don't have the luxury of letting bad men into her life.

I know what I have to do. "Listen, Guardie, I — um — it's better if we catch up another time. My friends are going to be here any minute, so . . ."

He goes still, his eyes narrowing as they search my face. But my resolve only strengthens. "You need to leave."

CHAPTER THIRTY-FOUR

Guardie backs me toward the counter. "What's going on?" His scent, earthy, with a hint of herbs, sends a jolt of heat between my legs.

Wrong! Bad reaction. I move away, bumping into the marble countertop. "What do you mean? Nothing's going on."

From nearby, there's the screech of the automatic garage doors opening — good, at least the neighbors are home and will be able to hear me scream if this goes south.

"I came to check on you," Guardie says. "To see how you were doing emotionally after we were intimate."

No East Coaster talks like this.

"You're jumpy." He touches my arm and I flinch. "You're dropping stuff all over the place. You're looking at me like I'm a stranger. And you lied about the bread."

Urgh, the sourdough. That's why he was staring at it.

"Um, as a matter of fact, I'm really confused." I check the wall clock above the stove — eight more minutes until Miguel calls, and if I don't answer he'll come racing over — and face Guardie. "You've left so much out. There's information from the police, unofficially, about Rachael. You were the last person she called."

He drops his head. "I thought that might be the case."

"Not only that," I press on, breath raspy. "They know Rachael went to your house. No one has seen her since." Stupidly, tears well in my eyes, raw emotions engulfing me. It's risky confronting him like this — I clock the potential weapons within reach: the cleaver, the knives in the block, the cast-iron skillet, even my rolling pin — but as much as all the arrows point at Guardie, as much as it's a gamble to give him forewarning, here I am, placing all bets on him.

He rocks slightly and says, "Fuck," in a quiet voice.

"You better have a good explanation." I hug my elbows to camouflage my heaving chest, my breath coming fast and furious. I peek at the wall clock — six more minutes before Miguel calls.

"Can we sit?" Guardie asks.

I nod and we return to the living room, my phone gripped in my hand.

He settles stiffly on the armchair, and I sit on the adjacent couch, the coffee table between us.

He wipes his hands on his thighs, nods silently as though summoning courage. "Rachael called me after hours. She had my number because she frequently canceled and rescheduled massages last minute."

The room seems smaller, the air heavy with what's coming. I don't know how he's going to talk himself out of this.

"She said her back was killing her. She'd been lugging around a bag of books and her laptop, all on her right side, and she was worried she'd popped a disc. I told her I could see her in the morning, although it would be better if she went directly to a back doctor, but she pleaded, started crying on the phone, said she'd give anything to stop the excruciating pain. So I agreed and gave her my address."

So far, his story seems believable, and I remember thinking once that Rachael shouldn't carry all those heavy books on one shoulder.

"She came to my house." Guardie rubs his mouth before continuing. "It's not recommended to have a client come to your home — and at night, alone, a woman to a man's house, it's rife with problems. My partner at the old spa in Vancouver got accused of sexual assault. He said he didn't do anything but because it was at his house, he didn't have a shot in the court of public opinion. Her word against his. Ended up ruining his business. Dude went bankrupt."

Really? He's opening with a story about sexual assault allegations?

"Anyway," Guardie says, "Rachael overreacted about my house."

"Why?" Was the shack a pigsty? A typical dirty bachelor's pad? Did she find his poverty too unpleasant?

He sighs. "It's a mansion."

"I heard you look after some rich family's house."

"Not quite. I don't live in the shack at the back. It's my house."

And . . . that makes no sense whatsoever.

"My family are a big deal in Vancouver," he continues. "That's my secret. I'm a trust fund baby."

Whaaat! I perch on the edge of the couch. All his comments about "manifesting" and "more to life than money," well, easy to say when you're cashed up. But had he actually ever lied to me and said he was broke? No. "So, does Rachael know something incriminating about your family?"

"I don't know how she found out about my situation. I guess, with her journalistic background, it wasn't hard." He slumps back in the chair. "My family are pissed off with me because I keep giving my money away anonymously. Charities, GoFundMe, whatever. We get biannual installments of our trust. My brother puts it into stocks, often triples the amount and reinvests it into our family trust. My parents wanted my brother to handle my funds. I said, 'No way,' because a lot of the stocks he buys aren't ethical."

"When did Rachael find out about your family?"

The wind whips against the windows, rattling the glass.

"Probably a few weeks after we first met. She was like, 'I know who you really are . . .' Later, she told me she was going to call me 'Secret Santa' in her book."

"I see. So the family fight at Christmas was about your brother investing unethically?" My skepticism is growing. This could all be a story to make Guardie seem even nicer than he already is.

He nods as the doorbell rings. "Your friends?"

"My food delivery," I answer sheepishly.

I rise, collect the clam chowder, its fishy aroma so strong it feels like I'm swimming in it. I bring it to the kitchen before returning to my place on the couch.

"Can I see a picture of your family?" Proof is what I'm after, and he knows it.

His lips form a straight line, but nonetheless he pulls out his phone, scrolls through it then passes it to me. An image of a newspaper article, titled, "Mitchell Family Celebrates Opening of Indigenous Art Gallery." The picture shows Guardie, his father, and brother in tuxedos, his mother in a sapphire gown. At least that part of the story checks out.

I cross my legs and place the phone on the coffee table. "What happened when Rachael got to your house?" *Did an argument escalate? Did you attack her, Guardie?*

"She was in a fragile state. I didn't work the area near her L5, just tried to relax the muscles around it. After the massage, I walked her to the door, said goodbye, and recommended a strong painkiller and rest."

"That's the last time you saw her?"

"Yeah." His neck is damp with sweat but it's impossible to determine whether it's because he's lying or because he knows the truth is damning. He didn't tell the police, he withheld important information. And he's a faker: this anti-materialistic hippie is actually a trust fund baby who lives in a mega mansion.

My phone rings in my clammy hand. Miguel, right on schedule. One ring, two, three . . . Any moment now, it will go to voicemail.

189

I look Guardie in the eyes, and ask, "Anything else?" because if he doesn't come clean about having Rachael's notebook, he's guilty of more than giving her a massage after hours.

"Yes."

I don't move a muscle.

"I should've told the police, but I knew how bad it'd look." A tendon in his neck pulses. "I have Rachael's notebook. I'll explain. But can you get me that beer first?"

CHAPTER THIRTY-FIVE

Hold off coming over, I text Miguel from the kitchen. *I'm talking to Guardie and getting the whole story. Call me again in 15.* Once I've armed myself with a whiskey on ice and grabbed Guardie his beer, I return to the couch, hyper-aware of his satchel near his right foot. Is Rachael's notebook in there? He must have read it. Will he let me?

"How did you end up with Rachael's notebook?" I ask, all my senses focused on his answer. If he stole it — unforgivable — there's no way he can sweet-talk himself out of that, but if he says he got his hands on it some other way, I'll try to be open-minded.

Guardie swigs his beer, and a few droplets miss his mouth. He wipes them off and sets the bottle on the coffee table. "People can get emotional when they're massaged. Happens all the time. Rachael cried. When I asked her what was wrong, she said her agent had rejected her manuscript."

I nearly spit out my whiskey. "*Secrets of the Tragic Wives and Guys?*"

He clasps his hands over his knees. "The agent approved her pitch, but when Rachael submitted the manuscript, her agent didn't think the material was 'loud enough.'"

"Meaning?"

"Not a big enough story, no X factor. Rachael talked about it nonstop during the massage, mumbling, furious. The agent thought she should change genres and turn it into a thriller, have some characters get killed off."

My mind is spinning like a boat's propeller. Rachael's agent's reaction left her a few options — scrap the manuscript and start from scratch, make it a gory mystery, or . . . hell, why hasn't it occurred to me before? Is this all an elaborate publicity stunt?

A missing author associated with the story certainly would give it an edge. I remember Rachael ranting once about the cut-throat publishing world — the tyranny of market trends, rising supply chain costs, sluggish print sales, the increasing cost of paper. Sick of rejections, maybe she became desperate and created the biggest buzz she could. Dying — or at least disappearing — for her art.

The euphoria of that idea fizzles as another replaces it. The failure could have stung so much that Rachael suicided, and the police are yet to find her body.

"Rachael said she was giving up being a writer," Guardie continues, "and she didn't want anything to do with the Tragic Wives book anymore. She gave me her notebook. Said it was full of toxic secrets, and she asked me to burn it. She couldn't trust herself to do it, but she knew I was a guy with integrity."

"That's crazy." He's lying. I should've asked Miguel to come straight over.

"There was a yellow notebook in her bag at the beach too," Guardie says. "My guess, she had lots of them. Maybe she started a new one."

"The notebook from the beach is missing. Only you, Li-Ping, and one of the blondes had access to it."

"It wasn't me. Hear me out." He raises his hands, palms outward. "Please. I know it sounds far-fetched, but it's the truth. I asked Rachael, 'How do you know I won't tell the group you've been collecting our secrets with plans to make them public?' I couldn't believe she'd exploit my privacy and our friends' pain like that. I wouldn't want things about any of us, about you, out there in the world."

"Did you read the notebook?" All this time, had he known whose secret was so bad they might have hurt Rachael? And who Serenity's lover was?

"For sure I thought about it," Guardie says. "But, no. Bad karma."

Yeah, right. "Do you have it with you now?" Reading it could exonerate him and suggest someone else is the culprit. And I could confirm Serenity is seeing Natalie.

"It's at home."

Convenient. "Why'd Rachael ask you to burn it?"

"Probably because I mentioned I was going to a sweat lodge run by a witch and Rachael had some poetic idea about turning the notebook into ashes, purification through fire."

I take a long swig of whiskey, processing everything. Rachael did lean toward the dramatic. Perhaps giving him her most private possession was a method to connect with Guardie, to lure him more into her life because she had feelings for him, although Guardie doesn't seem to have recognized that. Still, she could've burned the notebook herself and not risked people reading it.

"But you didn't burn it," I say matter-of-factly. He hid it in his satchel. Why refuse Rachael's wishes if not to protect his own secrets? And wouldn't it protect his secrets better if he did as she asked? Maybe he wanted leverage over someone else? Every word from Guardie's lips could be untrue, his charm lulling me into a false sense of security.

"I thought Rachael would cool down," he says. "I thought she'd, I don't know, revise the manuscript — isn't that what writers do? Work on the next draft. I was going to ask if she wanted the notebook back the next time I talked to her and try to convince her to make it a story about different swimmers, wipe everything out about us, but . . ." His words trail off into dead space. "Now I'm fucked. I'm probably the last guy who saw her. After my business partner in Vancouver got screwed over, I guess I wanted to protect myself. Selfish, I know." His shoulders curve over his chest, arms hanging at his sides.

"I didn't realize you and Rachael were so close. Ever want more than friendship? Did she?"

"Not my type. I'm into women from Boston who like to skinny dip."

I try not to smile.

"Anyway, like I said, people get emotional during massages. She confided in me. The last night I saw her, she told me she was about to shut down all her dating apps and had stocked up on supplies from Toys of Eros. I didn't ask what that meant."

But I knew — the vat of lube.

The pieces of new information float in my mind like flotsam in the sea, riding the waves to the shore.

Suicide. PR stunt. Foul play . . .

My phone buzzes. I expect it to be Miguel — although it hasn't quite been fifteen minutes yet — but it's a text from Natalie letting me know she's staying overnight at Kristen's. Not ideal. I'd rather have her safe and snug at home with me, and she knows that, but I need to balance my wishes with the benefits that come from her spending time with a friend. Natalie deserves a slice of happiness to counter everything else she's going through.

"If it's your guests," Guardie says, "I can leave whenever you want."

"Uh, actually, no friends are coming . . . that was my 'in case you were Rachael's killer' cover story."

He stares at me, stunned.

"Don't blame me for being careful." I refuse to feel bad. "Can you give me a minute, please? I need to reply to Natalie." I text her back reminding her I'll be in Boston tomorrow and let her know if she changes her mind about staying over at Kristen's (often she has last-minute anxiety and wants to sleep in her own bed), I can pick her up.

Something niggles in my mind . . . I lift my whisky glass to my mouth, and the sound of the tinkling ice amplifies. "What about the scratches on your hand?"

"Huh?"

"That morning on the beach, your hand had scratches."

He blinks. "Oh, right. I was gardening at the spa and brushed my hands against some plants with nasty thorns."

Were there any bushes like that in the courtyard? It's hard to remember.

Wordlessly we sip our drinks, and I mentally add up each thing he's told me, lining them up with the other facts we already know.

I rub my tired eyes. "The more I think about it, I'm leaning toward Rachael's vanishing act being a publicity stunt. Missing in Cape Cod — the area *Jaws* was filmed — writing a tell-all disguised as fiction about a swimming groups' secrets, it has PR all over it."

"You think?" He straightens up, then he sags back into the chair. "The thing is, ever since that morning on the beach, I've had this feeling she's not okay."

Miguel calls and I text him back: *It's okay, don't come over. I'll call you when Guardie's gone.*

Way to leave me in suspense, he replies.

I stare at Guardie across the coffee table. His story makes sense, but something still feels off. Dad would say trust the facts, not feelings. But right now, I don't know which facts to trust.

CHAPTER THIRTY-SIX

Guardie finishes his beer in one long swallow, his face pale.

"I'm glad you told me everything." His story is odd enough to be true — if he were lying, he'd have crafted something neater. "I believe you."

"What should I do?"

To me, there's only one option. "Go to the police station, hand in the notebook, and tell them what happened."

"I don't know . . ." He drums his fingers on the arm of his chair. "Rachael asked me to burn it."

"Honoring her wishes makes no sense now that she's missing. The notebook could point to the person who hurt her. If they did."

His gaze is fixed on the wall, shiny eyes showing tears aren't far off. "The police won't believe me."

"Well" — I lean forward on the couch, and try to pose my next sentence carefully — "it would make sense to read the notebook beforehand, so we know what we're dealing with. It's at your house?" The mansion I'm so curious to see.

"Nah, doesn't feel right. I don't want to find out all the devious, shameful things our friends have done."

I try again, "But we'd have a heads-up about who's behind everything." I need to get my hands on that notebook and find out what else was written about Serenity — and if Rachael knew Serenity was in a relationship with my niece.

In my mind's eye, I see the page of Rachael's notebook, the one I never got to turn: *Serenity was in a secret relationship with—*

Guardie clears his throat and reaches for his jacket. "I better get ready to go to the station."

"It's the right thing to do." I try to sound confident, like he isn't walking to the slaughterhouse

He meets my eye. "Guess this is it."

If the police don't believe him, this may be our last time together for a very long time. I kiss him, pouring all emotions into it, and he kisses me back, and after I pull away, his eyes darken, a look of lust I recognize from when we were at the witch's house.

He grabs my arm, spins me around, and pushes me against the back of the couch. The weight of his body presses against me as he leans over, and I'm jammed against the fabric. My skin prickles from his warm breath on the back of my neck. His hands circle my waist — oh! — and he slips off my sweatpants and undies in one swipe, yanking them down to my ankles.

I kick them off. Who needs clothes?

His hand roams in between my legs, probing, possessive. "You're so wet," he growls.

Still holding me against the couch with one hand, he reaches toward the satchel. What's he grabbing? A condom?

Then — what the hell? — there's something cold at the back of my neck. I jump, still pinned down, as goosebumps shoot down my arms.

He must have grabbed an ice cube from my whiskey glass. "Take off your top," he says.

I whip it off.

He moves the ice down my spine, from the base of my neck to my lower back. Droplets slide to my backside. My whole body clenches, bracing, as freezing droplets trail down my skin.

"Turn around," he says.

We face each other and he places the ice into his mouth and kisses me. Oh god. Our lips, hot; the ice knocking our teeth.

Holy hell.

I run my hands over his torso. Reach for the fly of his shorts.

He grabs another ice cube from my whiskey glass on the side table and draws it over my collarbone. As I arch my neck, he follows the ice cube with small, hot nips.

I groan, shutting my eyes. "Stop torturing me. I want you inside of me—" before I explode, the sensations too intense. Warm, cold, his hands and mouth, near then far. I'm desperate for more, for no distance between us.

"Not yet." His eyes burn into mine. "I want to give you something to remember me by." He places the ice on my belly button, then lower, slowly sliding it down, and I know exactly where this is heading.

Oooogh!

And . . . in it goes.

Yelping, I kick, fighting to get the ice cube out of me. "It's too cold!" But as much as I don't like it, I *do* like it. I swear I can't stand it another second when—

He smiles and scoops the ice cube out.

A rip of plastic. Standing behind me, there's a timeout as he puts on a condom. He positions me back against the couch before thrusting, filling me with life.

Afterward, we lean against the couch, his stomach warm on my back, both of us trying to catch our breath. He murmurs into my hair, "Thanks for the send-off." His arms tighten slightly around me. "From now on, let's hope it's not conjugal visits only."

"Not funny." I turn around so we're facing each other. "Are you scared to tell the police?"

"Scared shitless."

I cup his stubbled face and kiss him — because what else can I say or do? I know, I can feed the man. I slip my clothes

198

back on and after we've had clam chowder (reheated) and sourdough toast (multiple pieces slathered in butter), I ask if he's ready to go to the station.

"Ready as I'll ever be," he answers in a strained voice.

"I could go with you?" I offer, although I'd prefer to be here in case Natalie needs me.

"This is something I need to do alone."

"It'll be okay," I reassure him, hoping the police will believe his story. But as he walks out the door, giving me one last look, I get the feeling this just won't rock the boat. It's going to *Titanic* it.

CHAPTER THIRTY-SEVEN

Dorchester, Boston
12:20 p.m.
Rachael missing: 6 days

"I have to go," I tell Miguel on the phone. I'm in the back of a rideshare, my weekend bag on my lap, the streets of Dorchester passing by out the window. "I'm nearly at my parents' house."

"Okay, *mi amor*. I can't believe you slept with the prime suspect. It's so *Love Before Lockup*."

I roll my eyes. *Love After Lockup* is one of his favorite reality TV shows.

I've updated Miguel about Guardie's visit to the police station. Apparently, he handed in the notebook and Officer Winn was called in to take his statement. She asked him detailed questions about how and when Rachael gave the notebook to him. Guardie told her everything — how Rachael was frustrated about her book and how she wanted him to burn it. Following a three-hour interview, he was released but asked not to leave Provincetown. Guardie communicated all this by text late last night.

"Do you really think Rachael has it in her?" Miguel circles back to an earlier part of our conversation. "The grand vanishing act!"

"If it was all a PR stunt, she did a superb job. Hardly any breadcrumbs."

"Lots of artists pull off publicity stunts," Miguel says as my car screeches to a stop. The whole trip, it's been one red light after another. "Damien Hirst burned his own artworks. And Pussy Riot staged a guerrilla protest in Moscow's Cathedral of Christ the Savior to draw attention to the church's support for Putin's election campaign. By the way, just thinking aloud, what would be the male equivalent to Pussy Riot, I wonder . . . ? Penis Rampage . . . Dick Mosh Pit . . . Testicle Uprising . . . or how about Purple-Headed—"

"Stop! Speaking of publicity stunts, did you see that story in the news about the Indian influencer who faked her own death?"

"Poonam Pandey," Miguel says. "The model-slash-actress. There was a statement on her Instagram saying she'd passed due to cervical cancer. A day later, she fessed up her so-called death was only to raise awareness on cervical cancer."

"Good cause, bad method."

"Savage."

The driver slams on his brakes, shooting me forward in my seat. Thank goodness for seatbelts. The light turns green and the driver guns it, making me grateful we're only a block away from my destination.

"Well, I hope my Canadian crush doesn't get locked up."

"You're craving more ice sex, huh?" Miguel says.

"I mean, at first, I kind of hated the ice, but now I want it all over again." I know it's childish to share the details of my sex life, but Miguel peppered me with so many questions and it's not every day you're frozen from the inside out.

"Greedy bitch," Miguel says gleefully as the driver pulls up to my parents'. "I'm sure Magic Hands will clear his name."

"I wish I had your optimism." I thank the driver — for not *killing* me — and climb out of the car. "Talk later, Miguel."

As I look at the house in the bright sunlight, I do a double take. Details stand out that I haven't noticed before: chipped paint, a few missing shingles on the roof, overgrown plants, and weeds in the flowerbeds. My parents usually take great care in maintaining their property.

Mom's car is in the driveway, but that doesn't mean she's home. A lot of her social activities are local, and she prefers going by foot, visiting friends, undertaking charity work and all her art classes. I walk up the pathway to the house.

Even here in Boston, I can't escape thoughts of Provincetown. How is it even possible we still don't know what happened to Rachael?

During the ferry ride over, the same worker approached me again, rambling about *Game of Thrones*. This time, I was smart enough to get his name. A quick Google search revealed Angus Baker's Instagram — filled with disturbing cosplay photos and quotes like 'When you play the game of thrones, you win or you die.' His latest posts were vintage collectibles with googly eyes stuck on them.

I ring my parents' doorbell, knowing Dad will be home — Mom mentioned yesterday he'd be catching up on house projects. What was the important thing he had wanted to talk to me about? Had he gotten bad news from the doctor? I tap my foot as I wait. With the whole day ahead, after we had our talk, we could kick back on the couch and watch Red Sox highlights, and later I could whip up something delicious for dinner, perhaps Greek-style lemon-roasted potatoes, eggplant, hot pitta, and hummus.

I ring again. And again.

My heart speeds up. After what happened to Britta, I know how quickly ordinary moments can turn dark. "It's me!" I bang the door with my fist.

Dad might've fallen or had a heart attack. I don't carry a key to the house, but my parents have hidden one in the same spot since Britta and I were kids. I rush over to three garden gnomes under a mulberry tree: a mom, a dad, and a daughter. A few years ago, the "Britta" gnome, one in a red dress and orange hat, got smashed by the neighborhood kids when they were kicking around a football, and no one thought to replace it.

Kneeling, I lift the dad gnome and dig the Ziplock bag out of the soil. Once I have the key, and have dusted the dirt off my hands, I return to the front door and let myself in.

"Dad? Mom? Where are you?" I head down the hall, looking for any signs of trouble.

A fishy smell wafts from the kitchen . . . seafood? I walk through the living room to check.

The key slips from my fingers, clattering on the tile. There, sitting in Dad's seat, is Britta, my dead sister, EarPods in her ears, a tuna sandwich in her hands.

CHAPTER THIRTY-EIGHT

"Em," the ghost says, rising from the chair and walking toward me.

I touch my temple, dizzy, the floor moving under my feet. "Oh my god."

Britta stands before me, my mirror — same height, same hair color, same Dala bracelet, but her skin is so pale it's almost translucent, and there are sunken bags under her eyes.

"I don't understand."

"I'm so sorry, Em," she says, touching my arm. "Sit down." She leads me to a chair, pours me a glass of water, places it in front of me. "Take a sip. You're in shock."

Am I — am I hallucinating? I shake my head, uncomprehending, overwhelmed by the smell of tuna, the adrenaline coursing through me.

Maybe it's not really her. Some kind of trick. But then she sighs, like Britta does, wrinkling her nose before blowing air out of her cupid's-bow mouth. She brings a chair close to mine, sits across from me and says, "Drink."

I stare at her face — she looks ten years older than when I saw her last, with deepened crow's feet and marionette lines, her skin sagging like an ill-fitting suit. She's beautiful still, she's always been more beautiful than me — skinnier, elfin, like a magical creature. New tattoos mark her body, including a large one on her neck. Why is she wearing pink? Britta never wears pink. But, of course, the outfit, a pattern of crimson roses, is Mom's. So wrong on Britta . . . Mom. Dad. I flash back to earlier when I was worried he'd fallen or had a heart attack.

"Is Dad okay?" I try to still my whirling thoughts.

"He's fine. They're out for the afternoon with the Callaghans."

"Is it really you?" I stupidly ask.

She smiles, revealing her crooked left tooth, the result of the first of a string of abusive exes.

"I'm, um, glad you're here." She straightens her head and blinks, as though trying to remove a foreign object from her eyes. "I needed to talk to you."

"*Now?*" I blurt. A rush of anger rips through me, catching me unaware. "You needed to talk to me — after you've been 'dead'" — I make air quotes — "for what, almost a year?" I'm shouting but I don't care.

"Don't yell!" Her eyes swing toward the windows. "Don't draw attention to the house."

"Why? What is going on?"

Her eyebrows quiver, a tell-tale sign she's scared. "Listen. You need to understand why I had to pretend I was dead. It was the only way."

"*Fan,*" I curse, clenching my hands under the table, nerves crackling. "I'm all ears," I spit.

"Okay, so, um, where to start?" She fidgets in the kitchen chair, kicking her legs back and forth.

"Just start."

"My boyfriend, Mikey, back in Cleveland, was a pretty good guy, you know, but he ran with a dangerous crowd, including his brother, and dad. Drug dealers, it turned out, but I promise" — she looks at me beseechingly, lifting an arm to her chest — "I didn't know this when I fell for him. He was a bartender who used funny one-liners and played guitar in a band. You know I'm a sucker for musicians."

Drug dealers? What the hell did she get herself into? My body fills with dread, but another feeling surfaces too . . . relief. Whatever Britta is about to tell me doesn't matter. She's alive. A warm burst of emotion makes it hard to swallow. Within seconds, tears stream down my face, salty on my lips.

"Oh, Em," Britta says, and I can feel her fierce love.

I choke on my tears and start coughing. "Sorry — this is just . . ."

She rises and hugs me, and she's crying too, and I keep repeating, "Thank god, thank god."

My sister is back. It's the greatest gift I could have ever asked for. Whatever she's done, even if she's killed someone, I'll forgive it. Nothing matters but that she's with us again. Except . . .

"What about Natalie?" I wipe the snot and tears off my face with the back of my hand. "Does she know you're alive?"

"No." Backing away, Britta grabs the box of Kleenex from the counter and passes it over.

"But you need to tell her that because—"

"We'll talk about that later. Now, you need to listen. You gotta process a lot of information because we have huge decisions to make. Okay?"

I nod like a schoolgirl before an exam I haven't prepared for.

Britta pushes her hair out of her face. "Um, you know me and Nat moved in with Mikey. He kept weird hours, and sometimes his crew came over. I started to realize they weren't good people, and this one guy kept checking Nat out, asking her questions, giving her cash, so I knew I had to move right away. Somewhere better for Nat."

I purse my mouth. Anywhere would be better than a den of drug dealers. Classic Britta, making dumb decisions, putting other people in harm's way, and in this case, the most precious person.

"I just needed to save more cash first." Britta drops her gaze to the Formica floors. "I'd almost saved enough to pay for Nat's first year of school in New York. The tips were real good. But I should've left earlier."

"What happened?" I ask, foreboding tightening my vocal cords.

"One morning, I'd gone to work, and Mikey and the crew came over to the house. They thought everyone was out, but Nat had bad period cramps, and ditched school and came home. Then . . ."

A lawn mower starts up from somewhere outside.

"Then what, Britta?"

She twists her Dala bracelet, looking both nervous and masterful, a trickster, fooling me. How can this be real — I'm sitting with *Britta* at my parents' kitchen table?

She squeezes her eyes shut. "Then Nat went downstairs for a glass of water. She was at the kitchen sink about to call me, but changed her mind and put her phone on the side of the sink. We had those old-fashioned doily curtains, layers of lace that you can see out of, but people can't see in, so Nat saw the guys drive into the backyard. It's a huge backyard, real private, tall trees, a high fence, a garage, and . . ." Britta pulls her hair back again and exhales.

"Go on," I say.

"We had lots of fifty-five-gallon drums in the garage. Mikey told me they were for storing materials and waste disposal and stuff 'coz he worked in construction sometimes. I thought nothing of it. The men put on painter's suits and gloves and gumboots and dragged a bunch of garbage bags out of the trunk. One of the guys had an axe and they — they opened the garbage bags and took out b-body parts. They put the body parts into the barrels."

It takes me a few moments to process what she's told me. "Barrels of acid?"

"I think so."

Too sick, too hard to comprehend. "And Natalie saw this?"

207

"Yeah. Nat was so scared. She went to reach for her phone, but at the same time, the ringtone started blaring, and the guys turned to the window. Nat didn't know what to do. She ran through the house, out the front door, and hid behind the neighbor's tree. Their Doberman started barking like crazy. It always does when anyone walks by."

I swear under my breath.

"But I didn't know any of this," Britta says. "Mikey called me on the phone and said, 'I thought you were already at work.' He sounded freaked out and I knew something had happened. He said, 'I know what you saw. Trouble is, Dad and my bro know. You gotta get outta here. You seeing where they hid the body is gonna make them wanna hide you there too.'"

I lean closer to her, each word out of Britta's mouth more terrifying.

"I called Nat right away," Britta says, speaking faster now. "I asked her, 'Are you at the house? I know you've seen something. I told Mikey it was me who saw it. They don't know it was you.'"

My stomach roils. A dead body, limbs in barrels, Natalie witnessing all of it, now at our house in the Cape, unable to keep food down, her hair falling out.

Reckless, I hear Dad's voice in my head. *She's a mother, for god's sake. Sometimes I think you do a better job.*

Britta stands. "I have to go pee. Hold on a sec, okay?"

I nod, still piecing together everything's she's dumped on me. As horrifying as this all is, as damaging to Natalie's mental health, she'll be so happy to learn her mom is alive.

But why hasn't Britta contacted Natalie after all this time?

CHAPTER THIRTY-NINE

Steam rises from our mugs of chamomile tea as Britta sits beside me on the couch in the living room. An hour. That's all we have until our parents return, and Britta has just dropped another bombshell: Mom and Dad know she's been living in the basement. That's probably what Dad wanted to tell me, why he asked me to come here. She'll explain later, she promises. But I keep circling back to those men, those animals who dismembered a body. "Are you and Natalie safe now?"

"I think so." Britta blows the mug of hot tea to cool it down, readjusting her grip on the ceramic mug. "We're far away from Cleveland. No suspicious activity around the house, nothing in the news about Mikey's family or crew. Long as nobody figures out I'm here, I think we're all good."

All good, huh? A family severed, a daughter without a mother, not to mention the trauma of what Natalie witnessed. What a colossal fuck up.

I press my knees together, muscles tensing. "The whole Outer Banks trip, the drowning, you planned it?"

When she nods, I say, "How could you do that to Natalie?" *To me?* "Your daughter thinks it's her fault. One minute swimming with her mom, next minute you're gone."

"Look, once they got wind that I saw what I saw — or what they *think* I saw — I had to move fast," Britta says, a hardness in her voice I remember too well. "Take a vacation, stage an accident, vanish into thin air. Something that'd hit the papers and Mikey's crew could look up and see for themselves."

I take this information in, trying to put myself in her shoes, what I might've done. I drink my tea and burn my tongue.

"Dad got us both life insurance a few years ago, so I knew there would be a big payout if I died," Britta says. "Nat could have the money for fashion school in New York."

Each sentence from my sister's mouth swims over me, and I wish I hadn't taken so many Valiums over the last few days. My mind is like a fishing net with gaping holes.

Britta's eyes flash with intensity. "I'm not a dumbass, Em. I know I keep screwing things up for Nat. First her dad, then all these loser boyfriends, the dangerous situations. I couldn't make Nat's dreams happen without the insurance money. I only saved enough for her first year of school fees, not her rent, or living expenses." She stops talking for a moment, then mumbles something.

"Pardon?"

She lifts a hand and chews her finger. "I thought maybe it would be better for her if I was dead."

My temperature rises. "Save the self-sacrificing act." My sister is a lot of things, but altruistic is not one of them. "You don't think your boyfriend or his family will figure it out? What if they think you told Natalie?"

"Ex-boyfriend," Britta says sharply.

"Did he know about your life insurance?"

"Mmm, I guess."

"So, your criminal ex probably knows you're alive and your daughter is about to receive three million dollars in" — I glance at today's date on my phone — "five days. Clever, Britta."

"Fuck off."

No, you fuck off. I remain silent and compose myself because that's what I always do. Never fight back, never cross the line. One of us has to be an adult.

"Sorry," Britta says. "I didn't mean that. You gotta under-stand, Mikey isn't the smartest guy, and he loves me. If some-thing bad was going to happen to me it would've by now."

"No, it will happen *after* you get the money." She never thinks anything through! "Now what? You don't even want to see Natalie?"

Her eyebrows shoot up. "Course I do. But no way I'm risking it. She's too young — she'll slip up and say something to someone. It's safer for her to keep believing I'm gone and getting the insurance payout. Once she's set up in New York and has the money, I'm gone. Different country. Maybe in ten years, when everyone's forgotten about it, I'll find a way back into your lives."

"Wait . . ." I say as I consider my role in this fucking farce, the lawyers' letters on my desk, my signature. "I'm the executor for all the funds, which means, if I go along with it, I'm participating in fraud."

She keeps chewing her cuticle. "I know you like doing things by the book, but this sets Nat up for years. Keeps her *safe*. If it gets out I'm alive, Mikey's crew could come after me — could hurt Mom and Dad, you, Nat." She smacks her forehead. "I've brought so much trouble. I'm so sorry."

It's an old track. Cleaning up her messes, compensating, but this time she's put all of us in the firing line.

"What about the dead body? We should report it anonymously."

"Not now." Her cheeks darken a smidgen. "It'd bring too much heat."

"Who was it? Was there coverage about the person miss-ing in the media?"

She looks at me scornfully. "Some low-level dealer prob-ably. Not a major player, 'coz the people Mikey's family asso-ciated with aren't in big gangs or the mafia or anything." She shifts on the couch, tucking her feet under her body. "Will you help with the paperwork? You have to give me an answer."

I sip my tea. I won't be manipulated to respond on the spot. "I'll think about it. We can talk later."

"No, Em, this has to be our last communication."

As usual. Her mess, her rules, her timeline.

"Nat turns eighteen in a few days, and once the papers clear, I'm gone. But I'm not doing that until the money goes through."

"What difference does it make? What can you do if the money doesn't get transferred?"

She flips her hair, petulant. "I'm not leaving my daughter until she's got that cash in her hand."

We sit quietly as everything she told me slowly sinks in. Have we reached an impasse? If this is the last time I'm going to see her for years, each moment is precious. What does she need to know? "Natalie isn't well."

"I get updates from Mom. She's puking a lot?" Britta's skin bunches around her eyes and her forehead creases deepen. "Nat does that when she's anxious."

"She's only keeping down half of her meals. I've been taking her to a psychiatrist who has experience with stress-induced vomiting. She gives Natalie mindfulness meditations and progressive muscle relaxation, but it doesn't help." I consider telling Britta that Natalie's having a relationship with an older woman who may try to swindle her out of her money but I don't want to cause my sister more emotional distress.

Britta twists her small hands on her lap. "When Nat was sick, I'd make her artsoppa." The Swedish soup, yellow split peas and smoked ham, is a family favorite. "And she's big on old photos. Drags out the albums, wants to hear about every cousin and uncle, all their stories. Calms her right down."

"I'll try that."

My phone beeps and I check if it's Natalie.

A text from Miguel: *I lunched with Hannah and Carol and tried to get more leaked Rachael news. FAIL. Bitches be as tightlipped as nuns at a drag show.*

"What's that about?" Britta peers over my shoulder. "You look worried."

"A woman in our swimming group, Rachael Walker, has been missing for almost a week."

212

"What happened?"

"She left her bags and phone on the beach then disappeared."

Britta glances at the wall clock. "We can't keep talking. Mom and Dad will be home any minute."

"How much do they know?" My thoughts are scattered, in multiple places at once.

She toys with the edge of the quilt draped on the couch. "Yeah, well, I had to tell Mom everything."

My throat tightens. Mom's watched me grieve over Britta, struggle to parent Natalie, and yet she's said nothing. But I get it: her silence has guaranteed everyone's safety. Even so, it reminds me of when I was a girl — Mom and Britta going on their weekend adventures and not asking me to come along.

"What about Dad?" I ask.

"He doesn't go anywhere without Mom these days. With his brain scrambled like that, it doesn't matter what he says about me because people figure he's lost in his memories, right?"

"So, you spend all your time with him and Mom?" Jealousy edges into my heart.

"Yeah. But mostly I'm stuck in the basement bored out of my mind, watching crappy reality TV. Mom set up a kitchen down there."

The mini renovation now makes sense.

"I never get to go out in daylight." She pouts. "At night, sometimes, I walk the streets. That's why I look like a ghost."

"To be honest, you're kinda giving 'creepy Stephen King character.'"

"Ha!" She grins, crooked left tooth catching the light.

A car door slams outside. We both tense, but no footsteps follow.

My phone pings with a text from Natalie: Having really bad thoughts. Everything feels wrong. Can you come home?

What kind of bad thoughts? I text back, my stomach clenching. While waiting for a response, I add: I'll call you in five minutes, okay? Can you get Kirsten to come over?

"I should go." The trip back to the Cape is long, and Natalie needs me. I stand. "Dad did ask me to come all this way . . ."

"I'll explain to them that you know about me now," Britta says. "Let it happen naturally. Dad gets overwhelmed easily these days . . ." She's right about that.

"Okay. But you'll tell them soon?"

"Of course, yeah."

I carry our teacups to the kitchen sink. Her half-eaten tuna sandwich is still on the table. I grab it and swipe the crumbs away with a cloth.

We walk to the door, and she reaches for my hand, holding it in her own. "Thanks for taking care of Nat. I knew you would, just like you've always taken care of me."

Her words are kind, and I know she means them, but all the same, they feel flimsy, her eternal cop out.

"When Nat's in New York, take her out for real fancy birthday dinners, and toast me, okay? And I'll toast you both from wherever I am."

"I'll do that."

"And by the way, when I get this face redone, first thing going is this" — she jabs the bump on her nose. "Silver lining, right?"

She laughs, but all I can say is, "You're going to get plastic surgery? With what money?"

"The less you know the better."

The weight of what she's asking hits me. "At least going forward, I can talk to Mom about this." I'm stalling, not ready to walk through those doors and leave her.

"No." Britta's eyes narrow. "You can't. If you talk about it, someone's going to mess up, say something on the phone Nat might overhear. Please, don't say a word to anyone. Act normal, same routine."

"Where will you go?" I touch her white wrist near her butterfly tattoo. "Somewhere tropical?"

"All I can say is I'm leaving the States."

"But how? You need a valid passport."

"Some things were done before I disappeared. When you hang with the crew I did, these things are taken care of. Just in case."

"I don't want to say goodbye. This doesn't feel right. We might never see each other again."

"Hell yeah, you will." She juts out her chin — brazen Britta, cocky as ever. "Some time in the far future, I'll slide into the seat next to you at some dive bar or whatever, and tap your leg, and be like, 'Heeey, girl.'"

That's not enough, a promise of a meeting someday. I fight off tears.

"You need to go now," Britta says.

I give a single nod. What else can I do? I'm powerless, my brain fatigued, as though I've swum a hundred miles and got nowhere. But I can't accept this. There has to be another way, a solution. I need time to think.

"*Hej då*, Em."

"Goodbye, Britta," I echo.

She swipes the tears from my eyes and gives me a crushing hug before disappearing from my life. Again.

In the end, it turned out my sister didn't get swept out to sea and devoured by the Kraken, but if we're not going to see her until the far future — if *ever* — then she may as well have been.

CHAPTER FORTY

Tragic Wives (secret) WhatsApp chat
The next day, 3:55 p.m.

Hannah: *Have you heard? It's all over the news. I'm sorry if this is the first time you're hearing this, but they found Rachael's body washed up on Race Point Beach. The police report says the body was intact, no signs of shark attack.*

Em: *Heartbroken*

Li-Ping: *Pray for the soul of our dear friend. Psalm 34:18. The LORD is close to the brokenhearted and saves those who are crushed in spirit.*

Miguel: *NO! OUR DARLING FIESTY RACHAEL! RIP.*

Peggy: *Do they think she drowned? Any signs of foul play?*

Hannah: *No more details on the news. But there's lots of speculation. They even mentioned our swimming group.*

Miguel: *WTF!??*

Hannah: *The local news interviewed people on Commercial Street. Some old busybody told them Rachael was part of our morning swim group and claimed there were "whispers around town" that we might have wanted her dead because of some tell-all book she was writing. Can you believe this shit?*

Miguel: *Oh hell! Lock your doors, folks. Paparazzi gonna be on our ass. (Also time 4 Botox touchups. We'll probs be asked for interviews.)*

Hannah: *The only people we should talk to are the POLICE. Miguel, don't let 5 mins of fame go to your head.*

Miguel: *Insulting!*

Hannah: *The police are asking anyone who has info to step forward. The family has tripled the reward $.*

Em: *Lots of unhinged people will respond.*

Miguel: *Won't be surprised if someone claims they saw Rachael abducted by aliens. Imma head out, bitches. Emergency Botox appointment with dear Dr. Voldemort.*

CHAPTER FORTY-ONE

P-town, Cape Cod
4:00 p.m.

It's clear from Miguel's last message on our group chat that he's trying, in his own way, to lighten the mood, but cracking jokes while we're all in shock over Rachael only makes him look heartless.

I roll onto my side and toss my phone onto the bed, tears streaking down my cheeks. All this time, I've been praying Rachael's still alive — that her disappearance was a PR stunt, or she purposely got lost and reinvented herself in some fabulous place. Sniffling, I wipe my nose on a tissue, mind reeling. What happened that morning on the beach? She either went swimming and drowned, or something more sinister took place.

There won't be a funeral yet, not until the police do an autopsy. From the thrillers I watch, the autopsy will reveal its own story. I shudder, imagining strangers examining Rachael's body, cutting her open.

I curl into a fetal position on the bed, hit with the loss. My grief for Rachael merges with my confusion about Britta.

Fucking Britta. Hiding in plain sight. Both my parents kept it from me while I've been out of my mind with worry, obsessed with what happened to her, unable to move on with my life, busy taking care of other people's lives. When I got back from Boston yesterday, Natalie was fine — or said she was fine, claiming her dark thoughts were just body-image stuff she'd rather discuss with her psychologist. Just another thing I'm not allowed to help with.

I yawn and stretch my arms over my head. Last night, I didn't allow myself to take a Valium, so I only slept an hour or two at best. I dreamed about Britta's ex-boyfriend and a group of men in gloves and gumboots carrying axes, surrounding our house in the Cape, calling Natalie's name . . .

Christ! All Britta's other mistakes pale in comparison to getting involved with people who store bodies in barrels — and putting her daughter in such a sick environment.

My phone keeps pinging on my bed — all the Tragic Wives, no doubt, afraid their secrets will be outed, not just among us, but now nationally on the nightly news.

Miguel's secret. He has a better relationship with his AI than his husband. When he told me about his bot boyfriend, I laughed it off, but there's the car-keying incident too.

Li-Ping's secret. Mrs. Christianity is behind an Instagram hate campaign on her former Olympian rival. Her career rests on her "good-girl" brand, and she could lose the massive sportswear sponsorship, which is a big motive to stop Rachael's exposé from coming out.

Serenity's secret. She may have been a prostitute in the noughties and is having an age-gap affair with someone connected to our swimming group — possibly my seventeen-year-old niece, who is days away from inheriting three million dollars. Again, big motive.

Guardie's secret. Rachael's "Secret Santa," he's a trust fund baby preaching anticapitalism, at odds with his family about the most ethical way to spend their millions.

Carol's secret. Her hidden gun obsession, spending her weekends away fraternizing with gun folk when Hannah is a diehard anti-gun advocate.

None of those secrets are that awful, but it shows how for each of us, all starring in our own movie, we magnify our wrongdoings and catastrophize.

I still don't know Peggy's secret (and I certainly don't believe she killed her neighbor with mushroom risotto) or Hannah's, our undisputed Tragic Wives leader. The blondes may have skeletons in their closets. Any of our secrets could be connected to Rachael's death.

Then there's other potential suspects who aren't in our group — that creepy ferry worker, plus all the men Rachael dated and dumped in the last few months.

"Aunt Em?" A quiet knock on the door.

I dab my tears and sit up, pushing an avalanche of tissues off the bed onto the floor.

"Come in."

Natalie's skinny frame darkens the doorway. Her phone is clutched in her hand and she's wearing a maroon velvet robe, a wreath of crucifix necklaces, and thick, scrunched-up socks. Every time I see her, I want to grab her by the shoulders, and yell, "Don't feel so bad anymore! Your mom is alive! She just can't be with you for . . . a decade or so."

My eyes swing to the stack of letters from the lawyers on my side table. I reviewed them earlier, and after thinking about it nonstop, weighing up whether I could take part in something illegal, as there seemed to be no other option, I signed and posted them. Thank you, Britta, for forcing me into criminal activities. As for what happens if I get found out, I can't think about that now.

In three days, when Natalie turns eighteen, the money will be transferred into her account. Signing the papers ensures my sister's disappearance — once Britta knows Natalie is set up and ready to start her adult life in New York, Britta will leave the States, and we'll have no way to see her or contact her again.

"Did you hear?" Natalie asks.

"Hear what?" My mind leaps to Serenity — please tell me they've broken up.

"That woman, your friend from the swimming group . . . they found her body. It's all over my stream." Natalie raises her phone, her cheeks hollow, eyes wide and frightened. "I feel so bad for your friend." I know she's thinking about her mom, who she believes got swept away at sea, feeling guilty that she couldn't save her.

"At least they found Rachael's body," I say softly as my phone beeps with more messages. "It must be so hard for you not knowing what happened to your mom." *It wasn't your fault. She's eating tuna sandwiches at your fucking grandparents' house!*

Natalie's eyes well with tears.

This is too cruel. The truth hovers on my tongue — Britta is alive. I could tell Natalie. She deserves to know and be put out of her anguish. Why the hell should Britta dictate what's best when she's never had an ounce of smarts about Natalie's needs?

We haven't much time left until Britta disappears . . . maybe for good. But before Natalie's birthday, there's a window when Britta's whereabouts will still be known, a chance for Britta and me, at the very least, to have one more discussion about what's best for Natalie.

To keep the truth from spilling out, I focus on more immediate concerns. "Natalie, I need to know something."

Her body stiffens as though she can tell from my voice that I'm about to say something important.

"Can you come sit beside me?" When she perches on the edge of the bed, I say, "Do you have anything to tell me?"

"Um . . ." She shrinks into herself, swallowed by her velvet robe.

"You can trust me."

She drops her head into her hands.

"Natalie?"

"I–I didn't know that what I said would lead to anything like that," she mumbles. "To Rachael getting hurt."

Rachael? Goddammit, she's involved. I consciously force my face to relax. "It's okay." Foolish, farcical words that people say when it's anything but. "The important thing is you're telling me now." I pat her hand like a mother coaxing a child to reveal what awful thing happened at school. "What did you say that led to Rachael getting hurt?"

She parts her lips as if to speak, then clamps them shut.

"Please. I need to know."

She nods slowly. "Promise not to get mad?"

CHAPTER FORTY-TWO

Natalie isn't budging.

"Come on," I try again. "You'll feel better after you tell me. I won't judge you. I'll help you."

"It's bad," she whispers, chewing her cuticle the same way her mother does when she's nervous.

Nerves race through me, but I try to radiate strength. I can take on whatever problem she has. We're in this together.

"I shouldn't have told her anything," Natalie says, her finger still in her mouth like a binky.

"Told who?"

A tiny shake of her head. "Serenity." She refuses to meet my eyes.

How could she get herself in this mess? My heart palpitates as I scour my brain to figure out what Natalie could've said that would lead to — *fuck*. Are Serenity and Natalie responsible for Rachael's death? Did they kill her?

Beep! Beep! More messages land in my inbox.

"How long have you and Serenity been seeing each other?" I speak calmly, hoping Natalie doesn't get spooked and stop talking.

"How did you know?" Natalie's knees bounce, making the whole bed jiggle.

"I overheard you talking on the phone and put two and two together. Have you been dating for a while?"

"A few months."

I clench my teeth. "Serenity manipulated you. She's a manipulator. I found out she had lots of relationships in her past with wealthy people."

"It isn't like that for us! And I'm not wealthy."

You will be.

I cross my arms, holding back what I really think, but Natalie reads my body language.

"She *loves* me!" Natalie says hotly.

"Does she know you're about to receive Britta's life insurance?"

"Yeah, but that doesn't mean anything. You don't know how she feels about me!"

"You can't trust her."

"Shut up!"

"Natalie! Don't talk to me like that."

The fight drains from her face. She stares vacantly at the headboard, her lips trembling.

I lean closer and grip my niece's hand. "Listen. You need to tell the truth. Whatever you say, I'm going to protect you." I take a breath. "Did you have anything to do with Rachael's death?"

Her eyelids flutter, and she takes a few seconds before speaking. "No. I just told Serenity that . . . that . . ." She pauses. "Remember when Rachael came here for that dinner party, and afterward you walked Li-Ping home?"

I nod. About two weeks ago, the seafood feast.

"While you walked your friend home, I stayed talking with Rachael," Natalie says. "She poured me wine, a few glasses, and she asked me all these questions. I told her about my relationship with Serenity. I know I shouldn't have, but Rachael was such a good listener . . ."

I inhale through my nose, willing Natalie to keep talking.

"Then later, Serenity told me Rachael was writing a book about the swimmers' secrets," Natalie says. "Fiction, but based on all of your lives. Serenity said once the book was published, Rachael planned to leak that the secrets were real for publicity. So I admitted to Serenity that I told Rachael about our relationship."

"What happened next? What did Serenity say?"

"She went crazy. Said having a relationship with a seventeen-year-old girl would wreck her reputation." Natalie gulps, teary again.

My heart aches for her. No one deserves to be someone's dirty secret. "That must have hurt so much, honey. To have someone you love try to hide you away like that."

"Yeah, it was really hard."

I brush the tears from her eyes, remembering how many times I've done this since she was little. "Then what?"

"Serenity told me she'd get Rachael to not write about it. I asked, 'What if she doesn't listen to you?'" Natalie looks out the window and stops talking.

"And?" I keep my voice gentle. "What did Serenity say?"

"Serenity said, 'I'll make Rachael shut the fuck up.'"

"Oh . . . I . . . I see." The words sound normal coming out of my mouth, but inside, I'm shook: silent, sophisticated Serenity killed Rachael.

I place a hand on my stomach. What's to stop Serenity from hurting another person to keep her secrets? If Serenity killed Rachael to cover up her affair, might she also decide to harm Natalie? No, Natalie is a mark; the prize is her money. Serenity needs her alive to con her out of it. Still, I need to take every precaution and make sure Natalie is safe.

Serenity wouldn't want anyone around who could implicate her in murder.

"I don't want you seeing Serenity again. I need to protect you."

"*Protect* me? No. It's not like that. Serenity wouldn't ever do anything to me. I don't want you to worry. I'm fine. I — oh god, I'm going to—"

Natalie pushes a bed cushion away and falls onto her knees and pukes all over the Persian carpet.

On autopilot, I run down the hall and grab the vomit kit.

Back in the room, Natalie is huddled on the ground, rocking back and forth, crying, "I'm sorry, I'm sorry. I wish I hadn't told Serenity anything, then your friend would still be alive."

So underneath her defense of Serenity, she knows the truth, or at least suspects it.

"You're not to blame, sweetheart." I crouch and hug her tightly, trying to ignore the sour smell of vomit on her breath. "Serenity is a grown woman who makes her own decisions." I stroke her white-blonde hair — so like mine and Britta's — except for the thin patches.

My thoughts race. Could Rachael have somehow discovered Britta was alive? No. My mother and father are the only other people who know, and I only found out myself after Rachael disappeared.

In my arms, Natalie keeps rocking, hugging her chest as though it's the only thing keeping her intact.

"Everything's going to be all right. Soon, you're going to be with your grandpa and mormor, celebrating your birthday."

"I don't deserve a birthday. I hate myself."

"Don't say that. So many people love you."

"Whatever. Can I have a Valium?"

After I clean up the vomit, I get two glasses of water and the Valium and return to my room. Natalie is still sitting on the floor, resting against the bed. I pass her the glass and a pill, feeling awful plying a seventeen-year-old with drugs, but it's what the doctor advised.

I stare at the bottle. What did William say when he prescribed this? "Obviously, this girl is totally fucked up. I'll call and make sure she gets in with a psychiatrist and has supplies of Valium for at least a year." So easy. Too easy. Who else did he do that for? Just dishing out ADHD medication, Valium, Ketamine . . .

Turning away so she can't see what I'm doing, I down the pills — *one for her, two for me* — and slip the bottle into my pocket for safe keeping. "Come on, I'll take you to bed."

"No, I'm going to Cape Cinema in an hour with Kristen, remember? Can you drive us? It's a Marilyn Monroe double feature."

"It's probably best you rest." I can't trust what she's saying. She might be planning to meet Serenity.

She scowls. "So you'd rather have me trapped here, depressed, than out with my friend?"

The Valium makes her vulnerable. She could fall asleep, and I need to keep her where I can see her.

"It's just a movie. Drop us off and pick us up, okay?" She reaches for her phone. "I need to tell Kristen when you're coming."

"Why don't you watch a movie here, and I can make caramel popcorn?"

"Kristen already bought tickets. I'm not bailing on her."

Going out with a friend would be good for her mental health, but it's too dangerous right now. "Apologize to Kristen and tell her I'll pay her back for the tickets."

"I'm going!"

We face each other, a standoff.

"Why can't you understand? I don't want to be in this house. It's suffocating. I just wanna forget everything for a bit." She bats her baby blues and some part of me softens.

Oh, hell, what's a couple of hours? "I'll take you. But we need to share our locations on the family phone tracking app, okay?"

"Fine."

Driving after taking Valium is out, but we can rideshare. "If you're hungry, I made some artsoppa. It's on the stove."

"That's my favorite. How'd you know?" Her eyes light up, giving a flash of how she looked when she was a girl.

I'd also left out some photo albums on the coffee table, so over the next few days, we can sit together and look through them.

Once she's left the room, I pick up my phone. There are a few more messages in the Tragic Wives chat and a direct

227

message from Guardie: *I heard they found Rachael. Are you okay? I'm at the spa. Come over here after my shift finishes?*

It's all too much, I reply. *I wish we had more answers.*

His warmth, his touch. There's no one else I'd rather be with tonight. And since Natalie will be at the cinema . . .

Come, Guardie texts. *We can be sad together.*

I'll try, I reply, but there's something more urgent I have to deal with — I need to find out exactly what "make Rachael shut the fuck up" meant.

I text Serenity: *We need to talk.*

CHAPTER FORTY-THREE

P-town, Cape Cod
5:30 p.m.

Guardie wraps me in a bear hug.

"I can't believe they found Rachael's body," I say, my words muffled against his chest. The spa's sage and peppermint scents cling to him — woodsy and fresh.

"How are you coping?"

I draw away. "It's all so messed up." A killer's out there and just thinking about it makes me woozy — though that could be the Valium on an empty stomach. Rash, when I need to be thinking straight. Every day, I'm becoming more like Britta.

Serenity has texted back claiming a prior engagement tonight, so we've agreed to meet at the Sandbar Café tomorrow morning at eleven. My plan is to secretly record our conversation. If she's the intimacy expert people claim, skilled in seduction and artifice, she might try to pin Rachael's death on Natalie. I won't let that happen.

"Do you want some water?" Guardie asks.

I'm about to reply when it hits me. My body turns colder than any ice plunge. If Serenity thinks Natalie snitched to me, then the invite to talk tomorrow could make her suspicious. What's to stop her from hurting another person to keep her secrets? Like, say, a nosy aunt.

Just what I need, a homicidal sculptor after me.

Serenity wouldn't hurt Natalie — she needs her alive to get the money. But me? I'm just an obstacle.

"Is this — are we — okay?" Guardie asks, misreading my rigid body language. "Is something else wrong?"

I want to tell him everything. About Serenity, about Britta. The Valiums are dissolving my walls. And *him* — steadfast, kind, honest — he's dissolving them too. But my first priority has always been protecting my family. "There's a lot on my mind."

"You can trust me."

That's the problem. After Britta's resurrection, I don't trust anyone — not even my own parents.

"Hey, it's okay." His fingers graze my cheek.

I'm so mad at myself, for being tricked by my family, by Britta. For getting comforted when I should be with my niece, comforting her. After dropping her and Kristen at the cinema, I asked Natalie to text if she wants to get picked up early.

"I gotcha, Em." Guardie takes my hand and leads me to his treatment room, where we sink into the couch beside his massage bed. The lights are dimmed, shadows outline the plants on the walls, and relaxing music filters from the sound system.

He drapes his arm over my shoulder, and I cuddle up to him. My body starts to unwind, the awful fight-or-flight anxiety loosening its grip. His company is a salve.

We talk about Rachael, questioning what might happen next. I tell him Natalie is going through a hard time, and I won't be able to stay long.

Guardie studies me. "You don't look well, and you seem a little . . . spaced out."

"Can I give you a tip? If you want to get lucky again, stick with compliments." Makeup free, I'm in jeans, a tee, a gray mohair cardigan and sneakers, hair in a messy ponytail.

"I want to get lucky all right, and don't get me wrong, you're beautiful — stunning — but I get the feeling you could use a few more hours of rest." He cups my chin and peers into my eyes. "Hard time sleeping, huh?" I nod, and he says, "Sleep is the best healer."

"I've been taking Natalie's Valiums occasionally to help." From the expression on his face, I can tell he disapproves.

"They're a highly addictive benzodiazepine. Stick to natural remedies. Can I get you something now to help detox your system?"

"More grass-flavored stuff? No thanks." I scrunch up my brow. "All this talk is not what I had in mind when I came to visit."

"Ahhh," he says, holding my hand in his own. "You want to make love, to lie entangled in my arms, and not think about anything gruesome or worrying."

My mind flicks to tomorrow's meeting with Serenity. "Pretty much sums it up. But, FYI, I'm not a fan of the term 'making love.'"

"Noted. Is 'bang' better?"

"Shut up."

He gives me a sweet peck on the forehead. "You're the cutest."

"I was meaning to ask, has Officer Winn spoken to you again since you turned in Rachael's notebook?"

"No. But I guess now there's a body, they'll have more questions."

"Good thing you have nothing to hide." Unlike me.

My dead sister is alive. I committed fraud today. My niece may have something to do with Rachael's death. And here I am seconds away from getting it on (again!) with Guardie. He has that look about him, the darkening eyes, the meaningful touches, and I know he's seconds away from possessing me.

I smile; he smiles back. And like sexy Canadian clockwork, he leans over and kisses me on the mouth, long and slow.

"Can you give me a sec?" I check the tracker app on my phone — Natalie is still at the cinema.

You okay? I text.

I'm fine! Stop being a stalker.

I can pick you up now if you like?

Go away :) Do something nice for yourself for once.

At my side, Guardie says, "Babe, how about a hot stone massage? It'll help release your pent-up emotions."

"You don't have to ask twice."

He leaves the room, and I undress and position myself on the bed, lying face down. When Guardie comes back, his hands glide on either side of my neck. My skin tingles at his touch.

Then the thought slices through me: If he squeezed my neck right now, used all his strength . . . Stop it. But I can't. Because what if that's how Serenity did it — strangled Rachael with those artist's hands?

Guardie slips the elastic from my hair, letting it fall loose. "So soft," he says. "Like gold."

He works his magic, smoothing oil across my skin. Between strokes, he kisses my shoulder blade, my hip, the sensitive spot behind my ear.

"It feels wrong, getting pampered when I should be with my niece."

"I understand." He always understands, always does the right thing. Highly suspicious. No man — *even a Canadian* — is this considerate.

"Do you know Miguel and I have a name for you?"

"What's that?"

"Magic Hands."

He laughs. "Could be worse."

Then there's a *clack-clack-clack*, and he places stones along my spine.

"Ouch! They're too hot." My muscles seize.

"They should be fine. Try to relax and—"

"No, they're burning me." I sit up, disoriented, stones falling, some clattering on the ground. "I'm sorry." I wrap the blanket around me as Guardie collects the stones. Something's not right. If my sister could con everyone into believing she was dead, what other tricks are the rest of the people in my life pulling? Is Guardie who he says he is? Is he trustworthy?

"I'll go at your speed," Guardie says. "I just want to be with you."

"That's all I want too." The paranoia feels ridiculous now, faced with his certainty.

"Come here."

I scoot off the massage table. He kisses me and brings me to the couch, our lips not leaving each other's. He lays me down on a blanket and holds me.

I pull away. "I'm getting oil on you."

"Don't care."

Once he's whipped off his clothes, we move together slowly, no rush, no place to be, present for every swoon-worthy (slippery!) second. Our eyes stay connected, gentle and searching. I'm cocooned in safety — muted lights, candle wax, his sweet breath — and I don't know if it's the Valium, the massage, or the tender way he watches me as he moves deeper, but something shifts and I can't help wondering if we're falling.

We orgasm and collapse back onto the couch, his arm heavy across my shoulder, my head on his chest, rising with his deep breaths.

"I think about you all the time," he says.

"I do too. Like, in the morning, in the afternoon, before I go to bed — especially then." The Valiums make words come out before I've had a chance to veto them.

"How about that, eh?" He gives my arm a squeeze. "You wanna keep doing this?"

I fight back a grin. "What exactly?"

"Hanging out exclusively?"

"You want me as your g-i-r-l-f-r-i-e-n-d," I sing-song, and we both laugh, but the laughter dies on my mouth, because too many other worries crowd my mind — Rachael washed

233

up on the shore, my sister hiding in my parents' basement, Natalie tangled in Serenity's plotting. "It's bad timing."

"I just want you to know how much I care about you." He brushes the hair off my face.

"It'll definitely be nice having a boyfriend with perks. You can stone massage me any time. But make them less hot, okay?"

We kiss, sealing the deal.

I rub my arms. "I need to get this oil off."

"Want a shower under the stars? We have one in the courtyard."

"Sold. And speaking of, I wouldn't mind trying the shower at your fancy mansion soon."

"Sure," he says.

I want to know everything about him. Our growing connection fills me with hope. This could work out.

Together, we stand under the outdoor shower in our birthday suits, the greenery and trees offering privacy as the hot water pummels our shoulders.

"Water hog," he says. "Shove over and give me some."

I step to the left so the spray covers him. "See, I can share." Then I wrap my arms around his neck and wiggle my body against his. "But it's better when we're both under at the same time. You know what I can't wait to do?"

"Mmm. Tell me."

"Cook for you."

He grins. "My kinda dirty talk. Might be more empty promises. You talked a big game before about pumpkin pie . . ."

"Oh, you'll get your pie."

"I thought I just did."

Water drips down his glorious chest and we start making out again. Despite how good it feels, I can't stop worrying about Natalie.

"Woman!" Guardie groans, gesturing to his lower half. "Look what you're doing to me. Got one more round in you?"

"Uh-uh, I'm out of here." I don't need to be at the cinema yet, but my intuition is telling me to drive there and check on Natalie. She's probably fine, but I keep picturing the bruises on her body. She was so distraught earlier today. I should've forced her to stay home with me in case she tries to harm herself.

As Guardie and I get dressed in his rooms, my phone rings with an unknown number. *Please don't be about Natalie.* I click *accept.* "Hello?"

"Am I speaking to Emma Brennan?" the woman asks in an authoritative voice.

"Yes." Maybe it's a lawyer primed to cross-examine me about the fraudulent documents I signed.

"It's Officer Winn," the woman says. "We met before."

"*Officer Winn.*" I side-eye Guardie. "We were just talking about you earlier tonight." Urgh! Why would I say that? Dumb nerves.

Guardie frowns as the officer asks, "Who is 'we'?"

For some reason, I'm tempted to lie. When Guardie brought Rachael's notebook to the station, they must have considered him a suspect. I want to distance myself from that — but no, I need to be honest. "Guardie Mitchell."

A pause.

Guardie shakes his head and I mouth, "sorry." He steps closer, his warm hand on the small of my back. Though he's trying to comfort me, I can tell he's anxious the call might be about him — wait, maybe it *is* about him! After all, Officer Winn only interviewed him days ago. Maybe she found something linking him to Rachael's death. My head spins. How fickle am I, turning on Guardie right after we agreed to date? Serenity is behind this. Natalie practically spelled it out.

"We'd like you to come down to the station," Officer Winn says.

"*Me?*"

"Correct."

"Uh, I can come tomorrow morning after an appointment?" With Rachael's potential killer. "Say, noon?"

"We'd like you to come now."

"Now?" I glance at Guardie whose eyebrows furrow in concern. "I have to pick up my niece. Am I the only one who's been asked to come in? What is this about? Do you have more information about Rachael?"

"We'll talk when you get here." Officer Winn hangs up, and I'm left with the distinct impression everything is about to get worse.

CHAPTER FORTY-FOUR

P-town, Cape Cod
7:45 p.m.

"Evening shower, Ms. Brennan?" Officer Winn says when she enters the interview room at the police station where I've been waiting for the last ten minutes. She dominates the space, her frizzy brown hair as wide as her quarterback shoulders.

Another officer trails behind her, looking like an aging hound — hooded eyes, slumped shoulders, feet shuffling as though keeping up with his master is an effort. They take their seats across the table from me.

"Didn't your grandmother ever tell you, Ms. Brennan, going to bed with wet hair will give you a cold?"

Who goes to bed at seven forty-five?

Officer Winn sizes me up with a thin grin. She plops her phone on the table and spins it around. "I'll be taping this interview and taking notes. I'm sure you don't mind." A notepad and pen appear on the table.

I do mind, actually, given I have no idea why I'm here. It sounded urgent when she called and insisted I come to the station. I'd picked up Natalie with another rideshare and taken her and Kristen to Kristen's parents' house, where Natalie would stay overnight. I also googled a few lawyers and made some preliminary calls.

"This is my partner, Officer Jackson."

I cross my legs and place my hands on my lap, the tight confines of the room pressing in on me, the table, chairs, smudge-marked walls, lit by a double bar of florescent lights overhead. Not to mention the smells . . . stale coffee? Body odor? Disinfectant covering puke? Definitely puke, I'd recognize that smell anywhere.

"So, you're temporarily living here in the Cape. How long are you staying?"

"I'm not sure. I came here to reevaluate my career, but I'm afraid the insights haven't come yet." I wrap my mohair cardigan around me tightly.

"Lucky you." She smiles, showing her teeth. "Waiting for *insights* when most of us pound the pavement."

"I work at Barnard College," I say defensively. I bite my lip, annoyed I was provoked so easily.

"Good for you." Officer Winn adds under her breath to Officer Jackson, "Name dropper."

Far out. She's obviously playing bad cop. Is that her shtick?

"Have you immersed yourself in the local culture?" she asks in a pleasant tea-sipping voice.

Does she mean the art scene? "Yes. The Cape is a wonderful spot." Enough bullcrap. What does she want to talk to me about?

Tap. Tap. Tap.

The noise comes from somewhere nearby — but not the door. Neither of the officers pay it any attention.

Officer Winn says, "Word around town is you're in a *sexual* relationship with the Canadian masseuse."

I knot my hands. Innocent people get in trouble all the time. I don't want anything tied to me. I sigh. "I've been seeing Guardie Mitchell for a short time, although we've been friends for about four months. Why am I here?"

Officer Winn vigorously writes something on her pad, then she looks back up at me and says nothing. Her frightening dead eyes are awful.

Tap. Tap. Tap. That noise seems to be coming from the ground. I tilt my neck in time to spy Officer Jackson tapping the heel of his shoe on the floor.

"The Tragic Wives." Officer Winn turns to Officer Jackson. "I bet they wished they hadn't named their group that, huh? *Tragic* Wives . . ." Her manner of speaking irks me, her emphasis on certain words. "The press is eating this up."

On the drive over, the local radio stations reported that Rachael's story was being picked up in other states.

"What happened to your friend?" Officer Winn asks. "She *was* your friend, wasn't she? No bad blood?"

"We weren't super close, but we spent time together in our swimming group, coffee, having dinner."

"So? Swimming accident, a shark attack, murder?"

Why is she asking me? I cross my arms then quickly uncross them. Surely she knows more than she's letting on. The autopsy results could be back already. I try to keep my gaze level between the two officers. "No one in our group is capable of murder." In truth, I think there is a twenty-five percent chance Serenity hurt Rachael — with or without Natalie's help, but most likely without. "Rachael probably swam too deep and got caught in a riptide." After Britta disappeared, I did a PhD amount of research on ocean drownings. They happen a lot.

"You're either dumb or an optimist," Officer Winn says. "After you've been in our line of work, they're the same thing, hey, Jackson?"

Is this her interrogation technique? A mental game, ping-ponging from rude to friendly. Are all these questions to knock me off balance so she can start hammering in about — what? — Serenity and her relationship with Natalie? Whatever I do, I can't say anything damning about my niece or let on with my body language that I'm hiding something. It occurs to me that maybe this interview has nothing to do with Rachael or

Natalie and what we've talked about so far is to throw me off the scent — that Officer Winn has somehow found out about Britta.

"Let's play a guessing game. If one of your swimming group members wanted to get rid of Rachael, who would it be?"

I clear my throat. "None of us. But I've had a few run-ins with someone who seems suspicious."

"Oooh, another suspect," Officer Winn says eagerly. "More the merrier." I can't tell whether she's being facetious or not.

"Rachael . . . er, mentioned that a ferry worker talked to her a few times while she was onboard, traveling from the Cape to Martha's Vineyard." They would know this from Rachael's notebook, but there's no way in hell I'm owning up to reading that. "It could've been this guy who works on the ferry. Twice, I've caught him watching me and then he comes over and says odd things about *Game of Thrones*."

"Greatest show ever!" Officer Winn says. "The Red Wedding. Epic."

"Uh, anyway, Guardie and I saw the same guy the morning Rachael disappeared on Commercial Street. We took a picture of him because he was acting strange. Plus, he vapes, and there was a vape in the sand near Rachael's phone. Have you checked for fingerprints?" When neither answer, I say, "I did a little digging. His name is Angus Baker."

"Don't dig, darling." Officer Winn lifts her finger and scolds me. "Leave that to the *professionals*."

I clear my throat again.

"Nervous tic?" Officer Winn asks.

"Just thirsty."

"Jackson! H2O, pronto. We must make sure Ms. Brennan is comfortable. Don't want any more complaints. Ha!" She releases a throaty chuckle.

He rises and shuffles to the door.

"Quite a bit of tragedy in your life lately?"

I keep my mouth shut. So does Officer Winn — only speaking with her eyes — until Officer Jackson returns with a Styrofoam cup of water and takes a seat.

I knock it back too quickly, spilling a little on my skirt.

"First your sister vanished — swimming in the Outer Banks, of all places. Dangerous spot to body surf. Now you're taking care of your niece — the beneficiary of your sister's life insurance. Hefty sum." Her eyebrows wiggle.

Heat rises through my body, burning the tips of my ears.

"We looked into it, didn't we, Jackson?"

"Sure did." Jackson taps his shoes on the ground.

Oh, hell. I'm screwed. Fraud. Jail time. My breathing becomes too noisy as I picture Britta waving at me, dressed in Mom's clothes, feet up on the couch in the basement.

"My niece is still recovering from the loss of her mother." Saying it like that, I feel like a Bronte sister.

"The Cape isn't like New York, where people can go about their business and no one is any the wiser. Word around town is your niece is anorexic, bit of a head case."

Goddammit. What led her to think this? Compost Carol has a big mouth and could have jumped to conclusions about Natalie's panic-induced vomiting and told her sister.

"Mental health issues?" The police officer's face twists with mock concern. "All these girls thinking they're not pretty without filters. Or is your niece just clumsy?"

I'm about to defend Natalie when Officer Winn speaks over me, "Then your friend, Rachael — although none of you really seemed to be friends with her — ends up dead in the sea and you were there alone at the beach the morning she disappeared."

I say nothing. It was a mistake to come without a lawyer. *Tap. Tap. Tap.*

"Not so clever for an academic from *Barnard*."

"Do you really think I'd kill my friend then hang out at the scene of the crime?" I scoff, wondering how stupid she thinks I am. But I need to dial it back.

"No, *I* don't think that, necessarily," Officer Winn says. "The *witness* does."

241

CHAPTER FORTY-FIVE

Even though I know I'm not guilty, the way Officer Winn's eyes laser through me like a crème brulée torch causes my body to break out in a clammy sweat as if I held Rachael's head underwater myself.

"What witness?" I manage to say.

Officer Winn inspects her massive hands, checking her nails like a woman appraising her manicure before leaving a salon. "A witness placed you or someone matching your description at the scene of the crime."

"That can't be right."

"A fisherwoman came forward, who I, in fact, went to school with and trust very much."

The air leaves my chest as though I've been smacked by a boogie board.

"She said she saw two women arguing on MacMillian Pier the morning Rachael went missing. A tall redhead — Rachael — and a smaller woman in a black sweatsuit with blonde hair. She would've said something earlier, but she's been at sea. When she came back, she heard about it all over the media. Hope she gets a good reward for that info."

"That could be anyone . . . tourists or . . ." I struggle to make sense of this. A witness saw a short, blonde woman

arguing with Rachael on the pier the morning of her death. . .
Natalie? The noises of the room seem to magnify. My heartbeat, the buzz of the fluorescent lights, Officer Jackson's shoe
tapping on the floor, which is worse than any water torture.

"Do you have a black sweatsuit?"

"Who doesn't?" My fingers dig into my palms. Both
Natalie and I own black sweatsuits.

Officer Winn smiles and scribbles something on her pad.
"Officer Jackson and I will visit your house and pick that
up . . . You see, Ms. Brennan, Rachael Walker's phone records
corroborate the witness's account. Her last phone activity was
on MacMillian Pier, 5:14 a.m. The phone was turned off
there, but later found in the sand near the Sandbar Café where
you and your friend 'discovered' it."

This conversation isn't going well. *Turn it around!* I could
mention the other Tragic Wives' motives, but the police have
the notebook — they know more secrets than I do. I could
point them toward Serenity . . . no, that would lead them
straight to Natalie.

I need legal advice.

"Strike two, don't you think, Jackson?" He nods, and she
says, "The New Yorker is the first at the scene of the crime.
Then she finds the only other evidence."

"I wasn't there first — your sister was," I say breathlessly.
"And if I was guilty, I wouldn't want the phone found. Me
finding it doesn't make me suspicious!" Is this a game — say
preposterous things and see if I crack? "Were my fingerprints
all over the phone?" Because, of course, they wouldn't be, and
what can they pin on me without fingerprints or DNA?

"That would be too easy for us, wouldn't it, Jackson?
We like a good puzzle. Rachael's phone was doused in hand
sanitizer and wiped with black fabric before being dumped in
the sand. Who could've done that?"

"Well, not me!" I sit up in my seat. "The most violent
thing I've ever done is thrown a book across the room." My
vision sharpens, focusing only on their blank faces. "If you

were so sure it was me, you'd arrest me. What does the CCTV footage show? There must be cameras on the pier."

Which means it's only a matter of time before Natalie gets found out.

I look to Officer Jackson, who twiddles his thumbs.

When neither react, I keep going. "What did the cameras show?"

"The camera angles didn't work in our favor, unfortunately," Officer Winn says. "Most of the cameras pointed at doors of businesses not out into the 'wild.' We saw two different women at different times. A petite blonde first, then later Rachael. We know Rachael's height and were able to deduce the other woman was five foot six."

My height, Natalie's height.

"How tall are you?" she asks.

"Um, five foot six — but that doesn't mean anything."

Officer Winn snaps her head toward me. "First your boyfriend has the dead woman's notebook — then a witness saw you, or someone who is your height and with your hair color, arguing with the woman half an hour before she died. Is this a love triangle gone wrong?"

"No!" I shift to the edge of the metal chair, my knee knocking against the table. "Before continuing with this conversation, I need a lawyer."

A full smile appears on Officer Winn's face. "There always comes a point when the innocent 'I know nothing' person asks for a lawyer. It's when their story starts *crumbling*. Just one or two last questions. Tell me about your movements on the morning of Rachael's disappearance, before you got to the beach."

"I told you already."

"Jackson and I are like kids with a favorite bedtime story. We like hearing it again and again. Except our books don't usually have happy endings. Talk me through your morning."

"I woke up to my alarm, 4:55. Threw on some clothes. Had a glass of water. Drove to—"

"And your niece, Natalie Bianchi. I suppose you wouldn't have seen her at that time in the morning?"

Say yes — I give my niece an alibi.

Say no — Officer Winn might bring Natalie to the station and question her next.

The truth is, I think I forgot to check Natalie that morning, I really can't recall, but I nod, and say, "She leaves her bedroom door open and I check on her before I leave to make sure she's sleeping soundly because it's true, her mental health's been suffering since her mom passed."

Two lies to a police officer in one sentence. Fucking great. Add that to yesterday's fraud, and at this rate, I'll end up being a murderer by tomorrow.

After I finish recounting that morning, Officer Winn says to Officer Jackson, "This won't be too hard. We just need to figure out which five-foot-six blonde women were in Rachael's life, lived nearby, probably a Tragic Wives member or colleague. It shouldn't take us long to nail it down to one or two suspects, don't you think?"

How many days — or hours — do I have before the police hone in on Natalie? Thank goodness I'm meeting Serenity tomorrow morning. If I can get Serenity to confess to being the mastermind and record it, maybe I can minimize what happens to Natalie.

"Right as always," Officer Jackson says to his partner. "Like your last name, you always *win* the case."

"Thank you, hype man. That's why I keep you around." Officer Winn stands. "Ms. Brennan, if you were thinking of going overseas, I suggest you cancel your plans and stay in the state of Massachusetts." She slips me a card and says, "Call me any time."

CHAPTER FORTY-SIX

Tragic Wives (secret) WhatsApp chat
9:30 a.m.

> **Hannah:** *The police contacted me & asked for my alibi again. They said I might have to come into the station.*
>
> **Li-Ping:** *Same! Officer Winn showed up at my doorstep today and made me recount the morning Rachael went missing. (Btw I asked her to join my newsletter and she seemed offended.)*
>
> **Miguel:** *They haven't asked for my alibi yet. Obvs they think I'm less guilty. You two are in the hot seat.*
>
> **Li-Ping:** *Do you think someone in the group actually killed Rachael??*
>
> **Miguel:** *I guess we'll find out soon. BTW, if we figure out who killed Rachael before the police then the murderer might murder us! Knowledge is power and makes us ... murderable.*

CHAPTER FORTY-SEVEN

P-town, Cape Cod
The next day, 10:45 a.m.

"Explain what we're doing again?" Miguel asks.

I check my watch — fifteen minutes until Serenity's supposed to show at the Sandbar Café. "It's a fishing expedition. And you two are my hot decoys."

Guardie winks at me. "Compliments will get you everywhere."

"But to be clear," Miguel says, drumming his fingers on the table and shooting the evil eye to the waitress who hasn't yet delivered his caffeine fix, "you've asked us to be here but won't explain what happened at" — he drops his voice — "the police station last night?"

"I'm not trying to deprive you of drama, Miguel, but please shut your mouth and act normal when Serenity arrives. Besides, the police seem to be calling all the Tragic Wives into the station one by one."

Miguel mimes zipping his lips, practically vibrating with curiosity.

"Here you go." The waitress delivers our coffees, her eyes hanging on Guardie's tight T-shirt. Meanwhile, I seem to be the only one who's noticed Miguel's T-shirt, which reads, *Butt Slut*.

"Thank you. We don't need anything else." I hug the mug with both hands and take a gulp of the double-strength latte, suddenly aware I've shredded the napkin into confetti without realizing it. The less Miguel and Guardie know about Officer Winn considering me the prime suspect, the better. Any drama about me will end up bringing the spotlight to Natalie.

Innocent people are imprisoned all the time because of faulty or planted evidence. Given my "dead" sister is suddenly alive, I'm well aware things aren't always what they seem, and the police could easily think I'm guilty based on a few inconvenient details. I called some lawyers last night and set up two meetings for tomorrow. I need advice, stat, and until then I'm not sharing anything.

"You're sure you don't want something to eat?" Guardie asks me. "Keep your strength up?"

"I'm okay." I love how nurturing he always is.

"With so much on your plate, make sure you don't forget about your plate."

"Dad joke," I chide.

He smiles. "Sorry. I'll work on my material."

As the guys chat, I watch the door, searching for Serenity's regal frame.

I debated whether to keep my appointment with Serenity this morning after another virtually sleepless night.

Minuses. If the cops are following me, which I suspect they are, I'm leading them to Natalie's potential co-conspirator. Hence Miguel and Guardie — my decoys to throw off Officer Winn.

Pluses. The more I've mulled it over, Natalie is the only person who fits the witness description. Earlier this morning, I combed through our WhatsApp chat archive, analyzing every group photo — even those of members who only attended once or twice. No five-foot-six blonde women. I've already ruled out our two blonde members, who are both around five foot eight, and Serenity herself stands model-tall at five foot eleven. I also scoured Rachael's social media, hunting for anyone matching that description.

I know these attempts to prove my innocence are ridiculous, but I don't care.

If Natalie is responsible, I'll do everything in my power to protect her. She's still a minor — maybe she would be treated more leniently, especially if she was under an adult's influence.

When I picked up Natalie this morning, she bubbled with excitement about her birthday weekend in Boston — seeing my parents, her favorite Italian restaurant (we were lucky someone canceled at the last minute, allowing us to snag a table), our hotel stay (my parents' treat) — so I didn't see the point in bringing up her "confession" about Serenity, or any of the police's assumptions.

Serenity is smart, I doubt I'll be able to get much out of her, but I need to give it a shot because if Serenity does end up pointing to Natalie, my niece will flail in the interrogation room and Officer Winn will swallow her whole.

The squeak of the café doors makes me look over my shoulder. A family walks in, two moms, I assume, and a cute curly-haired toddler.

I take another sip of coffee. I have to find a way to talk to my sister during Natalie's birthday weekend to figure out a game plan, because one thing I know for sure is my skills as an aunt don't include criminal nous.

Guardie's hand finds my thigh under the table. I lock fingers with him, silently communicating my thanks that he's here. Even though he doesn't know all the details about my police visit last night — I gave him a vanilla version of events — his presence alone offers tangible support, and makes me a little less afraid.

"You look pretty," he says quietly in my ear, his warm breath dancing on my skin.

"Aren't you two hawt!" Miguel coos. "I can feel the sparks from here. Em, why didn't you tell me you guys are in lurve?"

"We're not," I mumble, probably turning as red as a lobster.

Guardie makes eye contact with me and shrugs, as in, *We might be . . .*

Miguel claps his hands. "*Felicitaciones*." He beams.

"Shhh!" I glower at Miguel. "You're acting too happy, given Rachael's body was only found yesterday. Eyes. Are. Everywhere."

Around us, vacationers gaze at the ocean view while small families linger over beautifully presented breakfasts, forks in hand.

I glance at the door again, then check my phone. "Maybe Serenity isn't coming. She should've been here five minutes ago." Regardless, I press *record* on my phone and hide it behind the saltshaker.

"She might not be, but they are." Miguel points to the window showcasing the street.

The doors swing open and in steps an older couple and two people in their twenties followed by a stampede of footsteps and flashing cameras.

"Enter Rachael's mom, dad, brother, and sister," Miguel narrates under his breath.

I study the Walker family, so familiar from their solemn news appearances requesting more information about Rachael, but it's different seeing them in person. They look terrible, a pale wash over them, as though they've applied the filter *Acute Emotional Pain But Keeping Stoic.*

My attention snaps to the brother. Skinny, blond ponytail, graphic T-shirt and baggy jeans, and — holy shit. How did I not see this before?

"How tall would you say Rachael's brother is?" I ask the guys.

"Five-seven?" Guardie guesses.

"He's closer to my height," Miguel says. "I'm five-six and a half."

"Do me a favor, Miguel? Could you go stand beside him?"

He gives me a heavy eye roll. "You owe me. I don't like being kept in the dark."

Miguel weaves through the café toward the Walkers, and I lean forward so far my coffee nearly spills. The brother shifts his weight, and even from here I can see it — the same height, almost exactly. My pulse quickens as another piece clicks into place.

Who's to say the five-foot-six blonde the witness saw arguing with Rachael on the pier wasn't actually her brother? Rachael had told Li-Ping about a recent fight with him, and Miguel found out he was an ex-addict. The real killer could have been right in front of us this whole time — and now he's twenty feet away, studying lychee cake like his sister hasn't just been found dead.

Looks like Natalie and I aren't the only suspects. And unlike us, this one has a history of violence.

CHAPTER FORTY-EIGHT

"Hi everyone," Serenity says in her clipped English accent. "Sorry to keep you waiting." All in white, her hair in a topknot as usual, she offers a small smile, and takes a seat to my right, hooking her Chanel bag over the chair arm. "Isn't it awful about Rachael?"

Also awful is you seemingly duping my niece into doing your dirty work for you.

I try to concentrate on Serenity, but my mind keeps drifting to Rachael's brother. As much as I want the killer to be him — someone with no connection to Natalie — my gut says it's Serenity.

If Serenity thinks it's strange I invited her here for "a private conversation," and yet have sprung two surprise guests on her, she doesn't let on.

"Are you holding up since the news?" she asks me, eyes soft with sympathy.

"More or less," I say.

"I haven't heard about any plans for Rachael's funeral. In Tehran, the family washes the dead and wraps them in a white cloth; then there's a procession to the cemetery — often in a silver Mercedes."

"Fascinating," I say. "The wakes on the Irish side of my family are a huge affair, with distant cousins coming from all over — storytelling, singing, and a free bar. So different from Sweden, where the dead are buried in pine caskets that loved ones write messages on."

I remember what I wrote for my mormor when we were in Gothenburg, just two years after we moved there, my fingers trembling as I held the marker: *Tack för att du lärde mig att baka alla smaskiga saker.* Thank you for teaching me to cook all the yummy things.

I let the funeral customs conversation fade, scrutinizing Serenity's face for any hint of discomfort.

The last time I saw her was before our Tragic Wives swim when I'd confronted her about her relationship with Natalie. What had she said . . . ? "We didn't plan it. But the feelings came, no matter how unconventional the situation." Then I warned her off, with something like, "Find someone your own age." But now she's acting like that never happened.

That's women for you — decades of people-pleasing means we can switch from bitch to bestie regardless of our true feelings. I wonder if that's what Serenity's doing now, masking whatever really happened between her and Natalie behind this polite facade. Sometimes I think that's what leads to women's invisible illnesses: all that repression of anger and other "ugly emotions" society still frowns upon as unladylike. Or maybe some people just hate conflict because it's uncomfortable, not because of how it appears.

After Serenity orders a green tea — claiming as she does that she can only stay for twenty minutes, conveniently — Miguel gives a few cute updates about his bubba, Serenity answers his questions about her recent art projects, Guardie adds an insightful comment here and there, and overall, it's like a normal conversation. Except every so often, one of us sneaks a peek at the Walker family, who sit a few tables to our left, chairs turned inward to form a protective circle.

Miguel strokes his goatee. "Any thoughts about what happened to Rachael?"

"An undiagnosed health issue?" Guardie says.

"Or she swam too far out and drowned." I keep changing my position, unable to sit still.

If Serenity's leaving soon, I don't have long to pry information from her that can implicate her as the mastermind behind Rachael's death — any slip of the tongue, contradiction, clue, or insight about what she may or may not have got Natalie to do to Rachael on that pier. My phone is still by the saltshaker recording absolute drivel.

Serenity traces the handle of her mug of green tea. "Everyone says it's murder."

"Is that what you think?" Miguel asks her.

"Most likely. Probably someone she knows." Seemingly aware of all our eyes on her, Serenity says, "Isn't it always? Some man whose feelings got hurt and he retaliated by bashing in her head?"

"Do you know if Rachael had any problems with anybody?" I ask her. *Did your feelings get hurt and you bashed in her head?* And why, precisely, are we talking about her head being bashed in? The news hadn't reported that.

"No one wants their secrets coming out," she says. "I'm sure we all feel the same."

"Guys" — I address the men — "do you mind talking among yourselves for a bit? Thanks." I lean toward Serenity, and say, *sotto voce*, "Were you worried about *your* secret?"

Serenity doesn't even flinch.

The café door opens. It's Officer Jackson, the hype man. I shrink in my seat. This is exactly why I didn't meet Serenity here on my own — all Officer Jackson can report back to his master is that I was having coffee with a few Tragic Wives. No big deal. Nonetheless, I ease away from Serenity and kick Miguel's foot under the table.

"What are everyone's plans for the weekend?" Miguel directs us to smoother sailing.

"Heading back to Boston," Guardie says. "Picking up some deliveries for our spa. I'll stay the weekend."

"Aren't you going to Boston too?" Miguel turns to me.

"Yeah." Dammit, Officer Jackson seems to be sizing me up. "It's my niece's eighteenth. She'll finally be an *adult*. When previously she was a *minor*." As I speak, I study Serenity for tells, darting of eyes, hands fidgeting, but she looks unperturbed. "I'll probably be busy with family the whole weekend, but" — I cast a shy glance at Guardie — "there's a chance we can catch up. If you're free."

"Are you two dating?" Serenity adjusts her topknot, an amused, slightly superior expression on her face.

"Is it that obvious?" I ask.

"I can read your body language."

"Well," I huff, careful to keep my voice low, "I'm not the one *hiding* my relationship."

Serenity purses her lips. "What are you doing, Em? Why did you ask me here with these guys?"

All three of them are watching me.

The fact that Serenity and I are not alone, and Officer Jackson has checked our table a few times, isn't ideal, but I have to grab the opportunity.

I move my chair closer to her. "Let's talk about your secret relationship," I say, lowering my voice. "How'd it start?"

She pulls a face, the V between her eyebrows deepening. "The usual way. There was an attraction. We have mutual interests, art and design, nature, and one thing led to another."

"Didn't her age put you off?"

She shrugs one shoulder. "Age is a state of mind." Says every sex offender everywhere.

Disgusting. "Are you still having the relationship?"

"Yes. But things have recently gotten more complicated and I'm starting to think maybe it's better we end things."

"Complicated how?"

Go on, say more. My phone's recording everything.

"Well," she says, looking at her hands, "they wanted to shout about our relationship. I wanted to keep things private, since there could be pushback because of its unorthodox nature."

What? The audacity.

I don't understand why she's so plainly discussing screwing my underage niece and expects me to sit here silently.

And why is she referring to Natalie as "they"? Did Natalie change her pronouns?

I unclench my jaw. "I just want to make sure you're not going to throw anyone under the bus. If shit goes down, you'll take responsibility, and not implicate a minor."

"I don't know what you're talking about."

"Bullshit," I say as Officer Jackson exits the café balancing coffees and muffins. It makes me sick, her manipulating Natalie, exploiting her age and vulnerability. Where did Serenity seduce her? At my house when I was out? In her studio-cum-love den?

Serenity's phone rings and a toddler at the nearby table starts crying just as I ask, "How many times did Natalie go to your studio?"

"Twice . . . I think," she answers absently, jabbing her phone. "Hello?"

At the same time I whisper, "*I don't want you seeing my niece again.*"

Serenity shakes her head and speaks into her phone, "Sorry, could you repeat that? There's too much noise. I can't hear anything."

The toddler's wails rise above the café chatter. I catch Guardie and Miguel exchanging concerned looks, clearly sensing something's wrong.

When Serenity finishes her call, she says to me, "You Americans are so uptight. I thought in Provincetown, of all places, there'd be less judgment. Love is love."

I fist my hands, anger pounding through me. "Love? That's rich." I'm about to lay into her when Miguel butts into the conversation. "Relationships take more work than humanly possible. Love! One day they say they love you, the next they leave you on 'read' . . ."

Is that a tear in his eye?

"What happened?" I reach for Miguel's forearm, guilty I didn't notice anything before.

"It's not a big deal . . . nothing compared to Rachael . . . that's why I haven't mentioned it." He lifts his head, trying to look unfazed, but the tremble on his lips gives him away. "I've asked Ronald not to bother coming out to the Cape anymore. If he can't find the time to visit his family, I'm done begging him to be with us."

"Oh, I'm so sorry, Miguel." I move closer and hold him as he cries quietly in my arms.

"That was the secret Rachael had on me," Miguel says. "Ronald is . . . is . . . in love with . . . if I tell you all, you can't say a word." We nod, and he mouths the name of a very famous, very heterosexual tennis player who's known for his thunderous grunts on the court. "They've been having an affair for nearly a year!"

"Wow," Guardie says, shaking his head. Even Serenity's perfect posture falters for a moment.

Well, Rachael sure got celebrity gossip for her book.

While I support my dear friend, who has now stopped crying, Guardie's hand lightly touches the small of my back, but more than that, his energy field envelops me like a warm towel after a winter swim. It brings me some comfort to know that whatever happens next, I'm not alone.

Serenity checks her phone, takes her Chanel bag and rises. "I need to go."

I rise too, stepping closer to her than I meant. "I've already given you a warning," I hiss into her ear. "Stay the fuck away from my family. You may call it love, but I call it depravity."

"What's wrong with you? You need help," she says before backing away.

The café door swings shut behind her with a decisive click, leaving me to wonder if I've just made things worse for Natalie.

CHAPTER FORTY-NINE

North End, Boston
6:40 p.m.

For tourists, Camelina's is an award-winning Italian restaurant in Boston's historic North End. For us, it's where life happens — birthdays, anniversaries, graduations, promotions. Our special place.

The last time I was here, I'd brought William to "meet the family." A lot has happened since then . . . and if my plan works, a lot more is going to happen tonight.

Mom, Dad, Natalie, and I are cozied up in a booth waiting for our main courses. Usually I love this place — Sicilian comfort food, family photos on the brick walls, chefs performing in the open kitchen — but nothing right now can take away my stress.

Mom takes off her spectacles and raises a near-empty glass of Prosecco. "Happy Birthday, Natalie."

We clink flutes. "To Natalie!"

We've been toasting all night, even with water, and it's a cute way to keep the mood up despite the elephant in the room: it's Natalie's first birthday without a mother. We're a party less its loudest member, less the one who used to lead the conversations, the one we often retaliated against. Our personal solar system is missing its errant sun.

But, of course, it's theater: Mom, Dad — who's been floating in and out of dementia tonight, talking about his childhood as though it's the here and now, then switching back to reality — and I know that Britta is only a ten-minute drive away. I haven't bothered asking Dad what he wanted to talk to me about during my last visit — his mind is too unstable right now. And I'm not even sure if Britta kept her word about telling my parents I know she's living in their basement.

On the surface, there's plenty to celebrate. Aside from Natalie crossing the threshold of adulthood, the insurance money cleared without a hitch, and during our appetizers — tuna arrabbiata and "exploding" Little Neck clams that lived up to their name — we chatted about what her life will be like in New York. If she makes it there. The thought of her being arrested for murder keeps me up at night.

I wimped out and postponed my meetings with the lawyers until next week. I'm not ready to own up to falsifying papers. I need more time to consider the smartest move.

"Prosecco?" the handsome Italian waiter asks.

Mom and I nod, and he says, "It's an honor to fill the glasses of three beautiful *sisters*, no?"

Mom smiles — we've received the "sister" comment before. She's still youthful, muscular from all her activities, with golden shoulder-length hair, and she dresses in a simple, Scandinavian style.

"Yes, please." Natalie holds her glass in the waiter's direction. "Fill it up."

He fills it with sparkling water instead, giving her an appreciative glance. What is with Natalie? She's flirtier than I've ever seen her, more carefree. My stomach twists — I wish she was still seventeen. If she's tried for what happened on that pier, she might be sentenced as an adult, even though the crime happened when she was a juvenile.

Natalie downs her water and fishes in her purse.

On the ferry ride over, I looked for that boy, Angus Baker, but I couldn't find him. Maybe when he heard the news that Rachael's body was found, he took off, or perhaps he's just working a different shift, and when Natalie and I travel back to the Cape on Sunday, we'll see him then.

I sip Prosecco, another headache brewing as I watch Natalie laughing. She looks lovely in a long-sleeved dress, chosen, no doubt, to hide her bruises. Foundation, bronzer, and highlighter mask her wan complexion, while fake lashes frame her eyes. She sure seems to find her way into trouble — the gangsters with the body parts in the backyard, her secret relationship with Serenity, and whatever happened with Rachael on the pier. Britta needs to handle this. As much as I love and care for my niece, it's beyond my pay grade.

My plan came to me during our walk from the hotel. Camelina's doesn't offer coffee or dessert — a great tragedy in my opinion — steering guests toward Little Italy's bakeries and gelaterias instead. While my parents and Natalie hunt for cannoli, I'll say I forgot Natalie's present at the hotel, and arrange to meet them in an hour and a half. Just enough time to catch a rideshare to my parents' home and talk to Britta about the situation before she goes underground.

"Nice dress, Em," my mom says.

"Thanks." A black velvet number with kitten heels.

"It'*sh* giving young Priscilla Presley," Natalie says.

Is she slurring? I check her glass — water.

My temples ache. I discreetly slip a Valium out of my purse and swallow it with Prosecco. Soon the jagged edges of my anxiety will soften.

My phone vibrates, and a quick read under the table reveals a text from my boyfriend. *Boyfriend.*

Missing you already. When can you come to witch's house?

I text back: *Hopefully tomorrow night.*

He's typing something. When I glance at the screen next, his message is in capital letters: *YOU ARE THE SEXIEST WOMAN ALIVE!*

A smile fills my face that not even extreme anxiety about being blamed for a murder I didn't commit or sneaking out to talk to Britta can erase.

Another text from Guardie: *If you change your mind, grab a rideshare and come visit me tonight. I've had a few or I'd pick you up.*

When our main courses arrive, Mom exclaims, "Look at that!" Her eyes are glued to her Tonno Siciliano — slices of sashimi, sautéed cherry tomatoes, and pistachio pesto with fusilli. My stomach growls as my dish is placed in front of me, Lobster Fra Diavolo — Maine lobster-filled ravioli, spicy tomato vodka sauce, and tiger shrimp. Natalie has ordered her usual, an Alfredo, but it's unlikely she'll have more than a few bites.

"You two should be more adventurous," Mom says as Dad is about to dig into his bolognese. "There's so many good things to try on the menu."

"I'm adventurou*sh*," Natalie replies with an obvious slur. "I'm about to move to the Big Apple!"

She's drunk! How is that possible? I take her glass and sip it. Vodka, straight.

"Where did you get that?" I whisper to her, glaring at the glass still in my hand.

"Hotel minibar."

"You shouldn't be drinking." As soon as you take on any sort of maternal role, you're essentially signing up for a lifetime of being the buzzkill.

"You're probably right." She smiles sweetly. "But I only turn eighteen once." She grabs the glass from me and gulps it.

"Not enough parmesan," Dad says gruffly beside me, oblivious to everything going on. "Britta, pass the cheese."

"It's Em," I correct him, handing him the bowl of grated parmesan.

Dad shakes his head at me. "Britta, I know it's you."

Mom, Natalie, and I all share a heartbroken look.

"You're such a trickster, Britta," Dad says. "When we were here last, you brought those novelty fortune cookies for dessert, with the funny sayings, like, 'I can't believe you're

261

going to eat my tiny home,' and 'Help! I'm being held pris-
oner in a Chinese bakery!'

"That was *sh*o funny," Natalie says.

"And the time before," Dad continues, "you pretended
you were Russian and wore that Cossack fur hat and acted like
you couldn't understand the waiter. And now you're pretending you're dead and living in our basement."

The fork slips from my hands. *Oh, shit.* My eyes swivel to
Natalie. Does she clock the truth or put it down to dementia?

Beside me, Natalie smothers another bread roll in a thick
slab of butter.

"Natalie," I say softly. "Dad just gets things mixed up
sometimes and—"

"It'*sh*, alright. I know my mom's living in their basement."

I stare at her unbelievingly. "But—" The muscles in my
body go weak.

"I've known since the beginning. Shh!" Natalie holds a
finger to her lips. "Guess the cat's out of the bag." Her eyes
sparkle, a flush on her décolletage. She's positively glowing.

I cup my hands over my mouth. This can't be real. So
much for my poor grieving niece!

"You all knew?" My voice comes out strangled.

Mom winces and Dad nods and says, "We did."

They all attempt to talk to me, stumbling over excuses
for their lies . . .

"Em!"

"Darling, listen to us . . ."

Everything tunnels, the noises of the restaurant disappearing, my vision blackening, only the three faces of my family in focus — all of them fucking liars. With each sentence
out of their dishonest mouths, I raise my hand, and say, "No,
not until we're with Britta. Get the check. Then we're driving
to your house."

And this time, everyone is going to tell the truth.

CHAPTER FIFTY

Dorchester, Boston
7:20 p.m.

We're mostly silent during the drive back to my parents' house. The sky's a dusky purple; there's a chill in the air despite the heater. Everyone is breathing more heavily, making the windows fog.

I try to keep my mind from spinning out of control. I need to think clearly, which isn't easy now with alcohol in my Valium-flooded system.

Why didn't Britta admit Natalie knows she's alive when I first saw her in my parents' house?

"Em, listen to me." Mom's driving; she peers at me in the backseat through the rear-view mirror. "We should have—"

"Save it. I'm not talking until we're all together."

"Tonight isn't the time for this conversation," she persists. "Let's have it tomorrow, when you've cooled down."

Always protecting Britta, her first priority.

To my right, Natalie's head rocks back and forth with each move of the car. She burps then giggles. "Ex*sh*use me. That was so gross."

The familiar brick buildings and corner stores of Dorchester appear foreign, as though I'm a stranger in someone else's life. I feel like the people in this car are not my family, not my loved ones. I've been used. Eleven months of caretaking — what a joke. Cooking meal after meal that Natalie puked up, worrying every day about her well-being because she was grieving over her mother, calling home and having heart-to-hearts with my mom about it, and the whole time—

How could I have been so stupid? Why did they lie to me?

Their house comes into view.

Mom pulls up to the curb and before she has a chance to turn off the engine, I undo my seatbelt and swing open the car door.

I stand at Mom's car window. "Give me the keys!"

"This isn't the proper time to do this," she says while Dad watches on nervously.

Just try to stop me.

I run through the garden, stomping on Mom's tulips underfoot, the lack of light making it hard to see. When I reach the three gnomes, I kick them with my kitten-heeled shoe, the dad first, the mom, then mine, and they shatter into pieces, ceramic cracking.

"Em!" my mother cries from behind me.

I dig in the dirt for the keys.

As I get up, Mom stands before me, her eyes white in the darkness, like an animal cowering.

"Em, you need to calm down. You need to—"

I run up the stairs to the front door. Stick in the key, twist.

Inside, I bolt down the hall, fly down the basement stairs, wishing I could move faster and wasn't wearing a constricting dress and heels.

Urgh, I nearly trip on a small plate left on one of the bottom stairs. Britta is such a slob.

Her bedroom is empty except for suitcases jammed full of unfolded clothes. Ready to leave our lives. To take the money and run.

Steam billows from the half-open bathroom door. I hurry toward it. At first, the bathroom seems empty too, but then I see the bathtub. I move closer.

Britta. I loom over her naked body, her head submerged underwater, eyes shut. So defenseless.

How dare she tell me Natalie didn't know she was alive! How dare she trick me!

Britta's eyes blink open and for a horrible second, I register her fear.

And I like it.

She sits up, water sloshing in the tub, spilling over onto the floor. "What the hell? Are you trying to scare me?" She stands unsteadily, face blotchy from the hot water, her thinness exposed, skin and bones. She wraps herself in a towel just as Mom bursts in.

"What's going on?" Britta asks Mom. "Where's . . ." She trails off.

I stand aggressively in front of Britta. "You wanna know where Natalie is? Because for almost a year, I've been looking after her, never feeling like I'm doing a good enough job, driving her to psychiatrist appointments about her dead fucking mother."

Britta and my mom exchange a panicked look. Conspirators, always, the two of them. Three bags of candies rather than one.

"Yes, Britta," I spit. "I *know*. Your daughter's here. Get dressed, then we're all talking." I turn on my heel and charge upstairs.

I spot Natalie near the liquor cabinet, opening a bottle of gin.

"Give that to me!" I wrestle it from her hands. "You've had enough. Get a glass of water and meet me in the living room."

Natalie nods, gaze lowered, having the good sense not to disagree. Clearly, I am not in the mood to be messed with.

I watch Natalie weave toward the kitchen, questions burning my lips. I don't understand. Why would Natalie be so upset about losing her mom all this time — unless she only just found out she was alive? At the restaurant she'd claimed she'd always known . . . Which version is the truth?

Now where's Dad? I search the house only to find him on the back porch, pacing, and mumbling to himself. Sometimes he does this when the dementia is bad, aggravated by stress. Another thing to thank Britta for. The shadows from the latticework cage his body in diamond patterns.

"Sweetheart," he says to me, his face lighting up. "It's so good to see you. Were you at church with your mother? Come, have some breakfast."

It's not morning! I want to shout. I need his help. I need him to correct whatever foul shit is happening here. Did Mom, Britta, and Natalie play me for money? Was this all about collecting life insurance? Am I the gullible one, who looked after my niece, and signed the papers, and is being blamed for Rachael's death?

I blink away my tears, not wanting him to see me cry. Besides, the neighbors often sit on their porch, and I'd hate to be overheard. They probably already have footage of me massacring my parents' garden gnomes.

"There, there." Dad walks over and holds me tight. "Did those sneaky girls take credit for one of your school projects again?"

I've lost him. I need him so much right now, I need his sharp, analytic mind, and he's talking like we're back in 1998. The tears fall harder.

"Don't cry now, darling," Dad says. "The rising tide lifts all boats."

"What does that even mean?" I pull away, unable to hide the frustration in my voice.

"In baseball, both the offense and defense need to step up." He leans his hand on the railing. "One person doesn't carry the entire team. The collective effort makes the difference. Everyone has their part to play. You, my kind, clever one, just always end up with the biggest role."

What if I don't want that part? What if I never did? Mature, sensible, the cleaner-upper — that's me all the time, except with Guardie. With him, I can be someone else. Someone who lives in the moment, who follows her whims.

"C'mon, Dad. Let's bring you to your room." I wish he could take part in the conversation we're all about to have, but it would only confuse him. "Why don't you lie down and watch a replay, okay?"

He reaches for my hand. "I want you to promise me something."

"Anything."

"When the time comes, remember about the rising tide. If I'm not with it" — he gestures to his head — "you steer the boat, okay, princess? Do what's best for the family."

I want to say, *Why can't Mom steer the boat? Or Britta? Why do you all keep expecting me to take on this role?* But looking into his eyes, I answer the way I always have: I nod, and say, "Okay."

"Is that what you wanted to tell me when you asked me to have a talk before?"

He nods.

Once I've put Dad to bed, I make my way to the living room, my jaw aching from grinding my teeth. Britta is on the couch, legs folded like a yogi, her wet hair in a bun on top of her head. Natalie lazes beside her, a drunken, dumb expression on her face. Mom, in her own chair, sits prim and proper, hands on her lap.

I have to stop myself from kicking something else. "It's time for a family meeting."

"Em, I'll tell you what happened," Britta says. "But you need to listen and ask questions later. If we're going to do this, we need to do it my way."

I make a scoffing sound. "When is it anything else?"

"Just sit down."

I take my place across from her.

"I guess I should just start with that night," Britta begins. "Ten days ago, I made a decision that changed everything. I snuck out of the house and took a ferry to Cape Cod . . ."

CHAPTER FIFTY-ONE

Britta

Harbor Beach, Cape Cod
5:02 a.m.
The morning of Rachael's disappearance

Man, I could use a shot of vodka right now. Courage for what I'm about to do. Here I am sneaking around in my black sweatsuit, like some junkie with this backpack on my shoulder. Standing at the edge of the ferry pier, looking at Provincetown all spread out. Weird to think my sister and Nat are so close, just sleeping in their beds.

Nobody else around. Just this big circle where cars turn around and those ferry ticket booths all locked up tight. Couple of trucks parked nearby, and the pier bending like a long fishhook. Behind me, the black ocean ripples, boats bobbing in the water.

On the beach, I spot someone beside the Sandbar Café. Rachael? That's where Nat said Em swims with her friends. Swimming in this cold-ass water? Like Dad always says, it's for the birds.

I shiver, and check every direction; nothing stands between me and the freezing Atlantic to the west other than an ankle-high cement curb and a few metal pillars. They should have some kind of divider to protect the tourists. I'd hate to be out here after a few margaritas.

I'd never normally come to a place like this alone in the dark. My habitat is the basement of my parents' house, stuck in the jail of my mind, rewinding the last ten years of my life, and replaying it so I can finally get it right. But I had to come. Protect Nat — protect all of us.

My daughter trusted the wrong person. A few days ago, Em had a dinner party and afterward walked her friend home, leaving Nat back at the house with Rachael. That snoopy bitch got Nat drunk and played therapist. Nat, easy prey, had a weak moment, spilled everything — the bodies in the back-yard, me faking my death. The guilt's been eating at her and the alcohol loosened her tongue. It could cost us everything — the money, our safety. If Mikey's family found out we did a runner, and we're cashed up . . .

I'll never forget one of the last things Mikey said to me about his family before I went on "holiday" to the Outer Banks. "They don't leave loose threads. You, baby, are the loosest thread around Cleveland. They all know you drink and talk. Your mouth is gonna get you and your girl hurt."

He was right about the drinking. It had snuck up on me — weekend drinking, to nightly drinking, to day drinking. My parents' basement has been my own personal rehab.

I stare out toward the Sandbar Café, where Rachael — if it's her — makes her way to the shore, carrying a big bag which looks heavy from the way her shoulder stoops.

I blow into my hands, steadying my nerves. I have to do what I have to do. No way around it.

It's just past five now — their swimming group doesn't meet for another twenty minutes. Cutting it close, but it had to be like this.

From here, I can see the backs of town buildings, the Pilgrim Monument tower rising above the town. A sliver moon hangs in the sky, providing some light. Darker would be better. Less chance of being seen. Google said there are CCTV cameras, but this area's got less of them. I'd have to be unlucky to be caught on tape.

But, fuck. Odds are I'll be unlucky. No four-leaf clover life. Every move I make backfires.

Rachael leaves her bag at the shore and takes forever to reach the pier. Hurry up. Let's get this over with. Sweat breaks out on my forehead and along my bra straps.

"I can do this," I whisper into the cold air. "Don't be chickenshit."

Rachael steps onto the pier. It's definitely her — I can tell now from the curvy body and red hair. Just like Nat described her. Jessica Rabbit in the flesh.

I took the last ferry out here last night and slept in the bushes north of the beach, my first adventure after nearly a year of being locked inside my parents' home. Felt human again with the ocean spray in my face on the ferry, then later, wrapped in a sleeping bag, staring up at those stars. Better than some fancy vay-cay to Boca, even if I was freezing my ass off.

Once I deal with the Rachael situation, and Nat gets the money, I'm starting over. Aguascalientes, in central Mexico, where a one-bedroom is only $169 per month. I'll be able to afford a great life there. Just gotta stay away from the tequila and the bad boys.

Rachael walks the pier, lined with US flags.

O say, does that star-spangled banner yet wave
O'er the land of the free and the home of the brave?

She nears the left side of the pier, which is flanked with shops full of local art. At this hour, everything is closed. Just lapping water and her footsteps break the silence.

She looks from left to right.

I draw back my hoodie and wave.

She waves back because, of course, she thinks I'm Em. From afar, it's hard to tell us apart. Nat "bumped into" Rachael yesterday, told her Em wanted to meet her this morning before their cold-water swim. Said Em had something so scandalous it would rock the Tragic Wives. Em was willing to share because she knew it would complete Rachael's book.

Cheese to a rat. Or, I guess, a seal to a hungry shark.

It was easy to come up with a reason to meet here alone, but it'll be tricky getting Rachael not to freak out when she realizes who I am. I have a plan. I'm not as dumb as my family thinks. Mikey said all the drinking had turned my brain to mush. Well, his brain's fucking mush, getting caught up in that dangerous Cleveland shit.

I roll my shoulders back and scan the beach, the long pier, the parked trucks. No one. If someone sees us, they might assume I'm Em, or maybe Nat, which sucks. I don't want to implicate them, but I'm doing this to keep our family safe, and right now they have legit alibis. As for me? Dead people don't need alibis.

Rachael passes the fishing charter kiosks, then the museum. She's only thirty feet away now. She walks under the Jaws head looming above the Shark Center entrance.

"Em?" Rachael calls out.

My face is in shadows and any second, she'll figure out I'm not her friend.

I take a deep breath and step into the moonlight.

"Oh — you're not . . ." Rachael looks behind her and frowns.

She's way bigger than I thought. Pink fluffy coat, sneakers. If we get into a fight, it would be hard to take her down. Not that I expect it to go that way, but Mikey taught me to always size people up, and know the nearest exit.

"Who are you?" Rachael asks. "You look like—"

"I'm related to your friend, Em."

As the moment of realization dawns, her forehead creases, hands clench.

That's right. I lock eyes with her. *I'm the mother who needs you to shut the fuck up.*

CHAPTER FIFTY-TWO

Adrenaline fuels me like a cage fighter, but I have to play nice. Make her see my side. "So," I say, real casual, "you're writing a book about the swimmers' secrets?"

"Yes — but I—" Rachael inches back. "I have to go. Something's come up. We can meet another time." Her hand sneaks into her pocket. Like I'm too stupid to see her going for her phone.

I stand in front of her. No phone calls, lady. "You got my daughter drunk — she's only seventeen — made her spill family secrets."

Too direct. Don't scare her.

"I have to go," Rachael repeats, seeming more pissed than frightened, the phone still in her hand.

"Just hear me out. The stuff my daughter told you is dangerous if it gets out. You can't put our secrets in your book."

"You can't tell me what the fuck to do." She whips her hair back, all high and mighty. She's a stubborn one. Reminds me of Mikey. Even when he should've known better, pride always got in the way.

"You don't understand."

"Yeah, I do," Rachael says. "You're the dead sister. Surprise. You're alive. Doing an insurance scam. Get out of my way. I'm going." She swivels on her heel and walks off.

I run ahead and block her. "Hear me out!"

"There's no point," she says in a shrill voice, waving her phone in the air like a weapon. "You can't stop me from publishing my book. My agent may have dumped me, but he's an idiot."

She's getting worked up, face almost as red as her hair.

"I rewrote the book opening and sent the manuscript straight to a publisher the next day. My contact there emailed me back in less than twelve hours. They already read the first few chapters and loved it! Do you know how hard it is to get a 'big five' editor to love your work? It's harder than winning a gold fucking medal at the Olympics."

She's too damn loud. Someone's gonna hear. I want to slap my hand over her mouth. Time to end this. I glance over my shoulder. Still nobody around. I turn back. "I'm not trying to stop you from publishing your book. Go ahead. I'm asking, real nice, take out my part. If this comes out, my daughter's life will be at risk. You want to be responsible for her death?"

"Look, I'm sympathetic. I'll think about your situation, but I'm not promising anything. It might be too late to make changes. Let me think about it."

Thinking about it isn't enough. Not by a long shot. Selfish bitch.

She heads off again.

"No, wait." I chase after her, our arms collide. "Don't go! Listen to me."

She fumbles with her phone. I grab her arm. She jerks free — the phone goes flying, clatters on the pier. I get in front of her, and she trips on my foot, her head smacking against the metal railing.

"God!" I say. "I'm so—"

Still on the ground, she blinks and rubs her head. "Oh . . . my . . ."

Think fast. No blood anywhere. Not on her hand. Not on her head.

As she crawls onto her hands and knees, I reach to help her up.

She jerks her hand away and stands close to the edge of the pier. "I don't want your — ahhh." She groans, staggers a little, touches her forehead. Then sways back and forth.

"Are you okay?" I ask.

"It really hurts."

When I step forward to help, she flinches. Her eyes flicker white, and she falls backward.

Everything goes slow-mo. She tips backward, arms wind-milling, then tumbles off the pier. A horrible crack echoes when her head hits the corner of the boat below.

No, no, no. I'm shaking, knees rubbery. I check behind me. Should I yell for help? Maybe someone is nearby.

I force myself to look back at the water.

Blood. Smeared on the boat. And . . . and she's floating. Face up. Her pink jacket spreads around her like some dead animal.

I gasp. Is she dead? My heart thrums in my chest. People can't die that fast. Can they?

I can't be here. Em's swimming group will be at the café soon.

I should jump in, pull her out, do CPR. Shit — I don't even know CPR.

Before I can decide, the current drags her further out.

I drop my backpack, my jacket, and jump into the water. Freezing! My clothes weigh me down. I swim to the boat and wipe away the blood with the cuff of my hoodie. Can't feel my body, teeth chattering like crazy. I freestyle hard to Rachael, fighting a current that's way stronger than it looks.

It doesn't take long to reach her.

But. Her face is underwater now, red hair twisted around her neck like seaweed. The bottom half of her body . . . sinking . . . disappearing into the black water.

My fingers are numb, losing feeling. I check her wrist, her chest — no pulse. Icy waves keep hitting me as I suck in salt water and spit it out. I check her pulse again.

Please be alive.

I gotta save her.

Another wave. I've swallowed too much water. Coughing.

Heaving her arm over my shoulder, still hacking up water, I pull her toward the pier. She's too heavy. And dead. I know she's dead. Crazy to even try.

But I keep swimming, keep hauling her.

Man, it's hard.

No! She slips out of my arms, starts sinking again . . .

I grab her, struggling with her weight, kicking my legs.

Another wave slaps my face.

People will think — they'll think I did this on purpose.

I need to get out of the water!

I look at her face, head lolling back.

I'm sorry. God, I'm so sorry, but I can't . . . I let her go and swim to a boat ramp. Drag myself up.

When I turn back, waves are already pulling her to deeper water. Christ. Can't move. But something deep inside, that survivor part that's kept me alive through everything else, screams at me to move.

I check my watch: 5:14 a.m. I can vanish. I've done it before.

I spot Rachael's phone where she dropped it on the planks.

Without thinking, I hit the power button — force of habit from all those times dodging Mikey's crew. Shit. That's stupid. If she went swimming, her phone would still be on in her bag. I'll put it back with her stuff.

Nat only talked to Rachael face to face about meeting, I made damn sure of that, so there's no messages between them on Rachael's phone. Now that I've turned it off, at least they won't be able to track where I take it.

As for the blood on the boat, people might think it's fish blood.

275

Backpack over my shoulders, and walk fast off the pier, head down, clothes dripping onto the wood planks.

When the cops check the CCTV footage, they might think it was my sister meeting Rachael. I have to believe they'll be able to tell it was an accident, and Em won't get in too much trouble. But shit, Rachael hit her head twice. Nobody would buy one fall did that. If they connect this to Nat, they might think Em did it on purpose. But Em's innocent. She'll have an alibi. It was an accident!

I reach the end of the pier, running down the stairs to the beach, unable to shake the image of Rachael's lifeless face staring up through the waves.

I'll put the phone in her bag, make it look like she went swimming. The cops will concentrate their search here. Everyone will believe she went for a swim and never came back. It worked for me once . . .

Hurrying along the sand dunes, I keep close to the shrubs, but once I near her bag, voices catch in the wind.

It sounds like . . . fuck, my sister. She's talking to a guy with a Canadian accent.

Now what? Can't put the phone in her bag anymore. I douse it in sanitizer, wipe it down with the edge of my hoodie, and chuck it into the bushes.

Then I run for it, disappearing into the shadows.

CHAPTER FIFTY-THREE

Em

Dorchester, Boston
7:45 p.m.

"It's a lot to digest." Mom rises, her voice wavering. "Let me bring everyone a drink. Akvavit or beer?"

A punch of nausea winds me. I lean over, desperate for my head to stop spinning.

"Em, would you like a drink? Britta?"

I take a few forceful breaths and look up at her. How can she act so normal? How can we lounge around in the living room — Mom, Natalie, Britta, and I — acting like we're not all complicit in . . . murder . . . involuntary manslaughter? I don't even know what to call what Britta has done.

"Akvavit," Natalie answers. A distilled Swedish spirit.

"No, water for you," I jump in, my protective instincts kicking in even though Britta should be parenting her. I'm on the edge of the armchair across from the couch, every part of me vibrating, my mind ringing, trying to process what happened to Rachael.

"Em?" my mom says again. "What would you like?"

"Beer."

"An akvavit for me," Britta says. "And some snacks would be nice."

I can't even look at my sister — pretending she was me, luring Rachael to the pier, leaving her floating in the water, hiding her phone. I know she was trying to protect herself, but she messed up beyond belief.

We are a tableaux of seething silence, until Mom returns to the room, drinks in hand.

"I'm *sh*-orry, Em," Natalie says, accepting the water. "For lying to y-you about everything . . ."

"I am too," Britta echoes.

I grip my cold beer bottle so hard I feel like I might crush the glass.

Mom fetches akvavit for Britta and a tea for herself, and once she sets the cup and saucer and a bowl of salted nuts on the coffee table, she sits in the armchair across from me. "Em, when Britta told me what happened to that writer, we didn't know what to do."

"So, you were in on this too?" The room tilts like a gut-curling amusement park ride. More secrets, more complicity. "You know where I was last night? The police station!" Each word comes out louder than the last. "They think *I'm* the blonde on the pier. They're probably going to arrest me!"

Not one of them looks surprised, their gazes on the rug.

When they still say nothing, I yell, "*Ursäkta mig?*" *Are you serious?*

Betraying me with their secrets, putting me in danger. I stare at our matching bracelets, the Dala horses that are supposed to mean faithfulness, wisdom, and dignity.

I want to upturn the table, break things, but I need to find out more. If Mom and Dad knew Britta was alive, why didn't they take guardianship of Natalie? If Natalie knew from the beginning, she would've insisted on living with her grandparents to be close to her mom.

278

"Why involve me in any of this — the faked death too? Natalie could've stayed here. You could've all been together, one big happy family."

Britta chugs her drink before answering. "It was safer having Nat away from me — you know, in case Mikey's family had eyes on the place."

Mom nods. "Cape Cod is much less accessible than Boston. They wouldn't think to follow you there."

"And Natalie? Why didn't she beg me to come to Boston all the time to have secret visits with you?"

Britta scoops up a handful of nuts. "She was under instructions."

"You" — I point at Britta — "should've told me."

"In a crime, you don't widen the circle. Each extra person you tell, the bigger the chance you'll end up in jail." She pops the nuts into her mouth and chews, her cheek bulging.

"Who even are you?" I don't recognize this person. I'm used to her causing ruin wherever she goes, but this — callousness — it's not her. "I asked whether Natalie knew you were alive and you lied."

"Like I said, don't widen the circle." Britta blinks. "Sorry. It's not personal."

"Of course it is! I could've cared for Natalie so much better if I had a full grasp of the situation. Did you think about that?" I take a long pull of beer, trying to drown my rage.

"I knew you'd do a good job," Britta says. "Maybe a better job than me. Even without knowing everything."

Classic Britta, complimenting and manipulating at the same time.

"The situation is hopeless. Unless . . ." my mother says.

I set the beer on the table with a sinking sense of inevitability and face her. "What is it you want me to do, Mom?"

"Oh, I'm not asking you to do anything. Just think through what will happen." Her hand shakes, rattling the tea cup. "If Britta comes out of hiding, it will be a sensationalized news story. Boston woman tricks system and pretends she's

279

dead so her daughter receives life insurance. Kills swimmer in Cape Cod to cover it up. Imagine the headlines, the frenzy."

I follow her line of logic. It would be a disaster.

"There will be no preventing Mikey's family from hearing about it," Mom continues. "Then what?" A red rash appears on her décolleté. "My daughter and granddaughter are at the mercy of these animals."

Mom's right, we can't draw attention from that family. Which means Britta's out: she can't turn herself in and take the blame for her own actions. Same old story.

Mom scratches her neck. "The government will take the life insurance money and prosecute Natalie and Britta — and maybe you. After all, you signed the papers, didn't you? The police could assume you're in on the scam. That we're all dividing the money."

Well, isn't that fucking great. How could they do this to me? I housed my lying niece before I knew about the scam. But I knew my sister's whereabouts when I signed the papers, committing fraud. I was set up.

Mom's speech sounds a little rehearsed. Did the three of them practice this?

"Natalie shouldn't get the life insurance money," I say. "She doesn't deserve it." It's a test, to see where their true intentions lie.

I'm met with silence. The three of them obviously think otherwise.

"It's illegal."

"I see what you mean, dear," Mom says. "But the money's already in Natalie's account. She'll need the down payment on her dorm in New York, the fees for her schooling, her whole life is about to begin."

This is what our family has all been working toward — securing our youngest member's path forward.

"The way I see it" — Mom stares straight ahead as though she's steeling herself — "we have three options."

"Go on." I don't break eye contact with her, despite my tsunami of emotions. "I'm all ears."

CHAPTER FIFTY-FOUR

After a break — Natalie to use the bathroom, Mom to refill drinks — we've returned to our seats.

Britta crosses her arms. "Court is now back in session."

Fucking hilarious. I glare at her, then turn to Mom. "What are the options?"

"Option one, Britta steps forward and tells the truth. Then Natalie will lose the money and Mikey's family may try to harm us. Britta will go to jail, not just for the unfortunate accident that occurred with the writer on the pier, but for faking her own death and life insurance fraud."

I roll my eyes. "Way to sell it to me, Mom."

"Two," Mom says, "and by no means am I recommending this, Natalie steps forward and says she met with Rachael on the pier. She takes the fall. This way, she keeps the life insurance money, but may get a small amount of" — Mom sniffs — "jail time."

Natalie waves an arm in the air. "I've seen *Orange Is the New Black*! I'm not having a cell mom or a cell wife." She dissolves into laughter, the alcohol, and probably fear, destabilizing her.

Britta readjusts herself on the couch and flicks her hair. "Natalie is not going to jail for what I did."

"So, what's your plan, Britta?" I snap as Natalie throws herself over the arm of the couch and laughs hysterically.

"I don't have a plan! I wish I could go back in time and—"

"Spare me." Her whole life is a series of retrospectives, of *if only I'd done this*. I eye my mother, who always coddled Britta, ensuring she never learned from her mistakes.

Mom peers back at me over her glasses. "None of us want the second option, of course. Natalie's just a child. She wouldn't know how to operate in those conditions!"

Natalie stops laughing as though the reality has hit her.

"They can't a hundred percent prove the blonde woman on the pier hurt Rachael," Mom says. "If Natalie comes forward and says she was talking to Rachael and left, there's no crime. Or she could say it was an accident, in which case she wouldn't do time, would she?"

I don't reply.

"Third option" — my mom's eyes dart between us — "I could say I did it."

Given the "three sisters" comments, the blonde hair, and the fact we're all the same height, she could get away with it.

"And I would, of course, girls, without question, but your father . . . right now, he needs me. He's not well, and we could take him to a care home, but how disruptive for him. It's best I look after him during his last years.

"Which leaves me," I say, slotting into my designated role. "That's what this is all leading to, right?" My chest is tight, the air trapped. "Option four, I tell the police I met with Rachael that morning because I didn't want her to write about something in her book, and then she accidentally hit her head — twice — and fell."

Mom gives a measured nod. "The autopsy will support your story, darling. This way, Britta and Natalie remain safe from that dangerous family. Natalie gets to keep the money to help her in New York. And you, always the responsible one, will carry this burden for our family, and we'll be forever grateful." Her eyes are glassy, the blue of a chlorine swimming pool: clean and pretty until you get close enough to see what the chemicals are hiding.

"You should do it," Britta says. "It'll help everyone."

Fuck you! I hold back the words. I want to bite off my sister's head. "Are you guys forgetting I was at the police station last night? I told them I wasn't on the pier. If I go in and say I lied and it was me on the CCTV, but it was an accident, there's no way they'll believe me."

Instead of offering another solution, they each look away.

Fury burns through me, shivery rage. They can't expect me to give up my life for them. It's always me making the sacrifice. How could they even ask me to do this? I grit my teeth and let the different scenarios play out in my mind, and try to match each option with each consequence, weighing the harm.

On the couch, Natalie is crying, her hands cupping her eyes, reminding me of those monkey figurines. *See no evil.*

The gesture might be genuine, but it's too late for innocence. "Natalie, I thought it was Serenity — that Serenity hurt Rachael," I say. "You led me to believe that."

She lowers her hands. "Yeah, I did the wrong thing there . . . among lots of wrong things. And after you've been so nice to me." She points to her sleeve, where the bruises hide. "That's why I'm like so mad at myself."

I won't be sucked into her sob story, her victimhood, in the same way I've spent my life being sucked into her mother's. I know Natalie's suffering is real, but I did everything I could to help her. Okay, she's young and impressionable, and Britta and my mom shouldn't have asked her to take part in any of this, but my niece betrayed me. All those walks on the beach, the meals we shared, our trips to New York . . . Lies. Tainted. Bullshit. "Were you even in a relationship with Serenity?"

Natalie speaks so quietly I can't hear her.

"Pardon?"

"I guess when you sorta put it out there, I thought if I went along with it, Mom wouldn't get in trouble. So, yeah, I lied."

I sit back, reeling. Details come back to me: Serenity saying she was in the basement doing an art installation, then overhearing Natalie crying on the phone saying, "I wish you weren't trapped in the basement," and, clumsily, I linked the two. Why did Serenity admit to being in a secret relationship? Presumably, she's seeing someone else, but who? It doesn't matter now.

"How well do you know Serenity?" I ask Natalie.

"I went to her studio, like, twice. And then talked to her at that dinner at our house."

I'm left with the stabbing truth. Natalie's looking out for Britta. My mom's looking out for Britta. Who's looking out for me?

My gaze returns to Natalie. Those weren't her only lies, were they? "What about when your mom got swept away in the sea? The search and rescue teams . . . You gave them false information?"

Natalie doesn't say anything.

"Answer me!" I shout.

"Fine! I told them Mom got taken in a rip in the opposite direction."

Rage tears through me. "How could you?"

"Don't yell at my daughter," Britta says. "I'm the one who told her what to say."

I shake my head, repulsed by their actions. "Think the teams of people searching, divers using expensive sonar . . ."

Natalie shrugs and starts chewing her cuticle.

Like mother, like daughter.

For the "smartest person in the family," it looks like I wasn't that hard to con. Sorrow washes over me. Why would they deceive me? They could've included me in the decision-making from the beginning.

Mom has been quietly watching all of this play out. "Em, we'd cover your legal costs. We could sell our house — it's worth a lot now, dear. We could downsize to an apartment. You could have the remainder of the money from the house sale."

It's too much — my synapses misfiring, head pounding. I can only catch fragments of what she's saying.

"Darling, there's not enough evidence for any deliberate harm . . . Can't be convicted without proof . . . I know it's a huge risk . . ."

My phone rings in my purse. I don't answer it. A moment later, it buzzes with a text. I check — Guardie. Sweet, wholesome Guardie.

I miss you. Sure you can't come to the witch's house?

At least that answer is easy. I text back, *Leaving right away.*

CHAPTER FIFTY-FIVE

Sad love songs play on the radio as I sit in the backseat of the rideshare, turning over Mom's "four options."

I don't have the energy to ask the driver to change the station, and besides, some masochistic part of me welcomes the maudlin mood the music creates. Except rather than just being on the verge of losing the love of my life like the singers on the radio, I may be losing the *life* I love too.

It's dark outside, clouds covering the moon, the town and country landscape lost by the freeway. Not much traffic tonight.

My phone rings — Mom. I ignore it. She'll only try to make me see her point of view, and right now I need a clear head.

The driver keeps a steady pace, a rhythmic rocking of the car, and as the singer croons, I replay the evening in a surreal loop. The birthday dinner . . . the waiter saying my mom, Britta, and I looked like sisters . . . my dad outing Natalie. Storming into Britta's quarters. Britta, naked, floating in the bathtub. Britta describing Rachael floating in the ocean . . .

While I was waiting for the rideshare to pick me up from my parents' house, I checked in on Dad. The game was still on, but he'd fallen asleep, so I turned off the TV and the lights and kissed him on the cheek before slipping away. I ached to ask for his guidance, wishing he could talk sense into my mother and sister, wishing he was lucid.

I sigh and look out the window, as if thinking harder about the four options may reveal a way out — a brilliant idea, a loophole — but by the time I'm ten minutes from the witch's house, only one answer remains.

Sick with nerves, I grab my purse and take Officer Winn's card out of my wallet. I touch the corners of the rectangular paper, digging the edges into the pad of my index finger.

The rising tide lifts all boats, Dad said. I have to make decisions based on what's best for the family.

The "responsible sister" may be the role I've tried to shake, but also, it could simply be me. As steady and reliable as the tide. My family needs me, and I can't turn my back on them. I wouldn't do this solely for Britta, I'm done going out on a limb for her, but I need to do the right thing by Natalie and Dad, especially since the last thing he needs is stress.

I punch Officer Winn's number into the blank message. My body fires with the rightness of what I'm doing, a familiar feeling I can't quite place, years of stepping in and taking the hits. I'll save my family one last time. Dad would be proud.

It's Em Brennan, I tap out. *I have information about the Rachael Walker case. I'd like to come into the station and speak with you.*

I reread the message. Send or delete?

Lights blur out the window and a truck zooms past so close that I instinctively lean in the other direction. The driver beeps his horn and swears.

A new sad song starts up, country twang. My velvet dress is too tight, making it hard to breathe.

"Do you mind if I open the window?" When the driver nods, I place my phone on my lap with the screen open, and use my other hand to lower the window a few inches, sucking in the cool, invigorating air.

If I send the message what will happen? Will they keep me at the station? Transfer me to jail? I don't know what to expect other than a loss of all the things I take for granted. If that's the case, I should enjoy some last splendors.

What do I want most?

Sex, first — Guardie's waiting at the end of this ride. Then food, real food, before it's all plastic trays and mystery meat. One last ocean swim? Another cocktail with Miguel, not admitting anything, just savoring his company. It's the small, precious things. Weirdly, I have thoughts about wanting to spend time with my family, yet they are the ones who got me into this mess.

As the moon breaks through the clouds, bathing the sky in a pale light, I rub my arms. This view is a luxury compared to being confined behind bars.

I look back at the open message on the screen on my lap.

It's nonsensical, everything I'm about to lose. *Worth it to save my family.*

Don't be such a *mes*, I think. Do it.

I press *send*.

Done. Set into motion.

I'm tempted to confess everything now, while I'm feeling strong. I type out, *It was me . . .* and stare at the words, my finger hovering over *send*.

"Miss? Miss?"

I look up at the driver.

"You're here." He gestures to the witch's house. "You've reached your destination."

Nestled among the trees, the cottage glows honey-yellow where Guardie, my lighthouse, waits.

I delete the unsent message, grab my purse, and climb out of the car.

If this is the last time with Guardie, I better make it count.

CHAPTER FIFTY-SIX

Diamond Pond, Walpole
8:00 p.m.

"Thanks for having me over," I say to Guardie. "And everything else . . ."

We're lying face to face on the futon in the witch's red bedroom, curtains drawn shut, clothes scattered like evidence around us, bare legs entwined, a condom wrapper discarded near the wall. Two white candles provide the only source of light. At least, before I go down for my sister's crimes, I had one last time with Guardie. I stroke his thigh and his cock stands at attention. Okay, maybe I'll make that two last times . . .

He traces my hairline with his thumb. "You're so quiet tonight."

"Mm-hm," I murmur, noncommittally.

He doesn't know this is our goodbye. Sometime soon — tomorrow, or the next day — I'll be at the police station, and who knows what will happen after that.

Guardie coughs into his hand. "I know it's early to say this, but, Em" — his eyes seem to shift color, a darker shade of brown — "I'm falling for you."

So quick, so reckless, something I never expected him to say.

He's studying me, gauging my reaction. In another world, where I'm not about to turn myself into the police, I would probably hold back to see how things play out. Screw it.

"I love you too." I tilt my head toward him for a kiss, just as reckless. It might be kinder not to say it. We're about to break up, but selfishly I want this moment for myself.

He holds me close, more soft kisses, our body heat enveloping us.

"I'm so happy," he says. "Being with you."

And I'm going to break your heart. We found love and lost it in the same night.

I don't want to imagine a life without him. A life locked up. My mom thinks I won't necessarily get jail time if I tell the police I met with Rachael on that pier, but she can't know what the police, courts, and press will think. There's no way Guardie and I will keep dating if I'm in jail. I know I need to reschedule a meeting with a lawyer, and I will, soon, but the lawyer will probably tell me to turn on my family. At this point, I refuse to do anything that can harm Natalie or Dad.

"Hey, you," Guardie says. "Are you crying?"

"Not crying." I wipe some sneaky tears off my cheeks.

The plan is not to tell Guardie anything — it would compromise my family's situation. But now, naked in his arms, after being so intimate, keeping this from him physically hurts — a sharp wedge in my chest.

"What is it, sweetheart?" The air has become cold on our bodies and he pulls the blanket over both of us.

He stares into my eyes, sadness shadowing his face as though he's absorbing my pain, then touches the scar on my cheek. "You can trust me with anything. I'd do anything for you."

I refuse to say a word, but more tears come like a riptide. I make a choking, sobby sound.

His pupils enlarge. He sits up and caresses my back while I remain lying down, tears still falling. "It's okay," he says. "Talk to me."

I grab one of his T-shirts from the floor and slip it over my head. It smells like his massage room — sage and lemongrass. I'll miss this smell so much.

"C'mon, Em. I know there's something you want to tell me. Something about your family."

My head snaps up. He must sense something's wrong.

His opinion could provide the insights I need. Pulling his T-shirt down over my thighs, I shift on the futon so we're facing each other. "If we break up, to your grave, you swear you'll never talk about this?" I stare at the floor, a traitor to my flesh and blood.

His fingers find mine in the candlelight. "I won't tell anyone."

CHAPTER FIFTY-SEVEN

"It's about Rachael, my sister, and my niece . . ." What's worse: telling Guardie now or letting him hear through the grapevine once I've confessed to Officer Winn that I'm responsible for Rachael's death?

"I'm listening."

His love surrounds me, radiating from his being, a conscientious, loyal man. My gut guides me to trust him.

The story pours out. He doesn't interrupt, just lets me talk, his forehead furrowing at parts, eyes widening at others — especially when I detail Mom's "four options." When I'm finished, he pulls me close.

"It's hard to believe," he says.

"Which part?"

"All of it. Your family keeping you in the dark." Anger fuels his voice. "Then expecting so much. Too much." I can see the wheels turning behind his eyes — processing, calculating.

Finally, having someone take my side, an achy, almost painful sensation fills me.

I breathe into his bare chest, and he embraces me tightly as if he can sense our coming separation.

"I feel so bad for Rachael," he says. "Can I get you anything? I need a beer."

"A 'get out of jail free' card?"

The same expression crosses his face as Natalie seconds before she's about to vomit. Picking up some sweatpants and a T-shirt, he leaves the room, and a tiny stab of doubt side-swipes me. An interesting time to sneak off to pee. See, this is what my family's done, made me suspicious of everyone.

Guardie returns, sitting beside me on the futon, our thighs touching. After guzzling half his beer, he runs his hand through his hair, pulling at the roots. "This is bad. But my family knows the best lawyers in North America. We need legal advice."

"You're probably right."

"Not probably, Em! Let me ask them about it."

"No, thanks." As much as I appreciate having him on "Team Em," the decision is made.

"Someone needs to look out for you." His cheeks are flushed. "I have to tell you something."

"I don't need more bad news."

"Before I went to the police station, I read the notebook," he says quietly. "I saw the part . . . about your family. What Natalie told Rachael, your sister faking her death. Here" — he gets up and pulls out of his satchel a few folded pages, holding them out to me — "I thought you should be the one to decide what happens with this."

The pages feel like they weigh a thousand pounds. "You read it? You knew this whole time?"

"No, only after we talked about it at your house, and they called me into the station. I couldn't turn these pages in. It would put your family at risk. But I also couldn't destroy them. They weren't my secrets."

"But why keep these?" I stare at the crumpled papers in my hand, Rachael's handwriting.

"Because I wanted you to have control over what happens next."

I get it now: this is why he's been so insistent about me not taking the blame — he's already been protecting my family, putting himself in jeopardy.

"Let's think," Guardie says. "Tell me again why Britta can't come back from the dead and own up to what she's done."

"She'll go to jail, potentially for what happened to Rachel, plus faking her death and committing insurance fraud, and Natalie will lose the money, but the main reason is because Mikey's family may try to harm us. It puts us all in serious danger."

"Can you talk me through your family's alibis?"

"Britta has the best alibi — she's dead. I already lied and told the police I saw Natalie sleeping that morning. I'm the only one without an alibi until you got to the beach." I pause, realizing the implications. "But the police won't believe you after I lied to them about not being there. And if they talk to you now, you'll be dragged in as an accessory, especially if they ever find out you took out pages of Natalie's notebook."

"Don't worry about me. What do you expect the autopsy will show?"

"I'm pretty sure autopsies can indicate if someone was dead before they hit the water. With a head injury like Rachael's, she was probably unconscious but still alive."

"So, the autopsy will reveal water in her lungs, proving she drowned."

"Exactly." The candles hiss, burning low in their holders. "That's why I'm going to cover for Britta and say it was me."

"What the hell? No." He jerks upright. "That's insanity."

CHAPTER FIFTY-EIGHT

"I'm afraid there aren't any other viable options." I shrug with false bravado. "I promised my dad that if anything happened, I'd step in and take care of the family."

"Do you hear yourself?" Guardie begins pacing, his shadow elongated to the ceiling.

He should support me, not ask rhetorical questions and make me feel worse.

"You told me your mom's 'four options,' but there's an option she missed."

"What?"

"She said she couldn't take the fall because she needed to look after your dad. But you could look after him. That's got to be a consideration."

"Good idea," I snap. "Would you let your mom go to jail for something she didn't do?"

"Think about it," Guardie says. "If you need to make the best decisions for your family, that means you too, the whole family, every member."

I look away, aggravated by his sharp voice, and his holier-than-thou attitude. "You don't understand. This is what I have to do."

"Why are you such a martyr? What's the payoff?"

How dare he take my selflessness and see it as something ugly when it only comes from love?

He takes a loud breath. "Your family putting you in this position — not okay. You accepting it — not okay. This could mean jail time. Obstruction, interfering with the investigation, and possibly involuntary manslaughter."

I jump up and grab his arm to stop him pacing. "It won't be that bad," I say, trying to reassure us both. "Britta didn't hurt Rachael. It was an accident. There's no proof of anything."

"Wake up! You have no idea what the police know. You're going to sacrifice this" — he swipes his hand between us — "your freedom, your life, and go like a lamb to the slaughter over your sister's so-called confession?"

My hackles rise. I've always cleaned up Britta's messes, defended her when people bad-mouthed her — kids at school, relatives, mutual friends. The protective feeling persists even now.

"Maybe nothing Britta told you is true," Guardie nearly shouts. "Have you thought about that?"

I don't answer, but it has crossed my mind. I have to believe that when it comes to something this important, my sister would be truthful.

An inner voice echoes back, *As if pretending Britta died wasn't important. As if telling me what Natalie witnessed in the backyard wasn't important.*

"Your niece could've done it," Guardie says. "She could've gone to the pier and hurt Rachael because of Serenity."

I keep my face neutral, refusing to share my thoughts, that there's a chance he's correct.

Guardie doesn't stop. "Your mom could have done it to protect Britta and Natalie. It's possible, right?"

"I can't answer that."

"Em!" He takes hold of my shoulders, staring down into my eyes, brow gleaming with sweat. "They've proved themselves to be unreliable. They're not looking out for you. This is wrong. You can't lie to the authorities."

"Don't tell me what to do!" I shout, all my anger about Britta aimed at him. "You're someone I met five minutes ago. They're my family."

"Yeah, some family — throwing you to the sharks."

"Screw you!" I yell back. It's one thing for me to think it, another thing entirely for someone outside the family unit to insult us. "They got caught in a series of compromising situations. And as for responsibility, well, you're not the poster boy for that."

Guardie's jaw hinges open, but I keep going.

"Being with different women each day of the week . . . wearing *crystals*, for god's sake! As if they do anything!"

"That all you got?" He crosses his arms, biceps bulging. He doesn't look wounded, he just stands there and takes it. He tucks in his chin and waits for more — my punching bag. "Em, stop deflecting, you know I'm madly in love with you . . . even if you bad talk my crystals." He touches his necklace and pulls a hurt expression, eyes huge like a puppy. The expression he used earlier when he begged me to get him a glass of water. "Listen, the crystal's crying." Without breaking eye contact or moving his mouth, he makes a weird little crying sound.

The corner of my lips twitch.

"But you can't do this," he says gently. "It's not the righteous path."

"Righteous?" I mock him, humor forgotten. "You're not a fucking preacher or some spiritual guru."

He squints. That one hurt, I can tell.

I twist the knife. "You're not speaking to your family because — what? — they're *too* generous. Talk about privileged. You've run away from your family — don't blame me for doing the opposite."

He closes his eyes briefly, taking it in. "I hear what you're saying, but no one in your family grows if you keep putting Band-Aids on everything and reenacting childhood scripts."

I back away from him. "I've already made up my mind. I've contacted Officer Winn. It's over. And maybe we are too."

"How can you say that?" His arms hang loose at his sides, his devastation obvious, but I don't let it soften me.

"After I talk to Officer Winn, I don't know what's going to happen. But I do know I don't want to hold you back. You're a free spirit. Go be free."

I won't drag him into all of Britta's drama. Shouldering the police's investigation alone might hurt less than getting closer and closer to Guardie, only for us to be torn apart. I grab my clothes from the floor, my shoes, my purse, my jacket, trying to hide my trembling hands.

"Let me help." He reaches to take the jacket from me.

"No, I'm fine." I avert my gaze. Although I'm grateful for his protectiveness, for his own good, I need to push him away, so I muster the nastiest voice I can, and say, "I'm calling a rideshare. I'd hate for you to waste your time with such a martyr."

"Don't do this," he pleads. "I don't want to lose you for someone else's mistake. I love you."

I touch him on the cheek. *I love you too. But it will be easier like this.* "I should go." I order the ride.

"Let me wait with you outside."

"I need to be alone."

I step into the night air, letting the door click shut behind me. The moon hangs bright overhead as I wait, praying Guardie doesn't follow to try changing my mind.

Dammit, the driver's canceled.

I'll walk, clear my head.

Without thinking, my feet carry me to the pond, Guardie's words ringing: *What's the payoff? Why are you such a martyr?*

Once I reach the water's edge, I request another ride, watching the moonlight shimmer across the surface.

My phone pings with an incoming text. Oh, crap. Officer Winn.

Even at this hour on a Saturday night, she's working the case. I guess in a small place like P-town, catching a killer would make her career.

Thanks for contacting me, she texts. *Can you come into the station on Monday? Noon.*

My nerves spike. I'm tempted to chuck the phone into the lake. Whatever move I make next, there's no going back.

My heart races. All the people I love, their opinions coiling around me. Mom's plea for me to step up and take the fall. Britta's assumption that I will, like I always have. Natalie, a witness. What kind of role model do I want to be? Guardie, begging me to fight for myself. And my promise to Dad that I'd do what's best for the family. But what's truly best?

I can come Monday, I type, but staring at the dark water . . . I can't cover for her. I won't.

I take short breaths, picturing Britta from her throne on our parents' couch. "You should do it," she said only hours ago. She never grew up, never took responsibility — my fault for always enabling her.

I twist my Dala horse bracelet. I'm not so different than Britta: When pushed, I did something illegal for Natalie — signed those papers. Both of us crossed lines for family. But it's up to each person to reap what they sow. Entwinement is a choice.

I unclasp the lock and chuck the bracelet into the pond, relishing the satisfying *plop*. No more shackles. Although what happened to Rachael was an accident, I cannot take responsibility — I didn't do it! Guardie is right. I won't give up my life because of their choices. Let Britta make the call and live with that. Dad told me to steer the boat, take care of the family. I always thought he meant them — Britta, Mom. But maybe he meant all of us. Including me.

My phone rings.

I jab the *answer* button.

"Em — Em?" my mom says. "Thank god you answered. It's your dad. He's had a fall, a bad fall — the ambulance is on the way. Meet me at Carney Hospital."

CHAPTER FIFTY-NINE

I see Natalie first.

Still in her party dress, she's slouching in a chair in the hospital lobby, nursing a Styrofoam cup, mascara smudged. She'll remember this birthday, her eighteenth, for the rest of her life.

"Where is she?" I ask her.

"Cafeteria." She listlessly lifts her arm and points to the left.

I round the corner, moving fast, searching for my mother. Why isn't she with Dad?

"Sorry!" I say, nearly walking into an elderly woman with a cane.

Slow down! I can't rush like this in a hospital. Forcing myself to take measured steps, I wait as an orderly passes, pushing a white-haired man in a hospital bed.

Down one hall, then another to the cafeteria.

I scan the food line — nurses laughing, a mother with a toddler on her hip, a man selecting Jell-O — then look toward a table full of doctors, and a couple by the window holding hands, heads bowed.

Where is she?

I spot my mother at the far side of the room, facing the gardens, her back to the entrance. I walk over. "Mom — where's Dad?"

Her chin trembles and she doesn't meet my gaze. "Sit down."

"I want to see Dad."

"It's too late." Her eyes shine with tears. "He — he didn't make it. Died as soon as we arrived. We were with him, Natalie and me."

No words form in my brain. I am perfectly still, not breathing, suspended . . .

"What happened?" I ask. Mom is crying openly now, dabbing a scrunched tissue under her eyes.

Somehow, I'm seated beside her, holding her hand, but I don't remember sitting. My purse is on the floor. Did I drop it?

"Mom, what happened? Did he slip in the bath?"

Her wrinkled hand lies limp in mine. "He fell on the basement stairs. Broken neck, head trauma, internal bleeding. In a lot of pain. I–I called the ambulance right away."

I grip the edge of the table, winded, body-slammed by a monstrous wave.

"Can I see him?"

She looks away, a tear splashing onto the hospital table. "Not a good idea."

"Why?"

"It's best to . . . what's the word? . . . preserve him in your mind as he was. He's in no state to be seen."

No. The wave sucks me down, deep and quick. I'm a rag doll, spinning underwater, held under by the terrific force, pain in my ears from the pressure, fighting for breath. "How did he fall?"

She shakes her head.

I speak louder. "How. Did. He. Fall?"

"Oh . . . ah . . . some dishes left on the stairs." Her nose twitches.

"*Whose* dishes?"

Mom jumps up from her chair, moving more quickly than I've seen in years. "You!" She jabs at my chest. "Stop blaming people."

Britta and her carelessness. Mom defending her. "I think it's time we *start* blaming people. Everyone in our family needs to take responsibility."

The doctors at the table nearby look over.

"Where was Britta when the accident happened?"

"Watching TV," Mom says.

"And when she found out, what'd she do?"

"She's — of course, devastated. She nearly passed out."

I stand and collect my purse, swinging it over my shoulder. Hot, nasty words shoot out of my mouth like harpoons. "She did nothing, you mean. As always. Dad would be alive if only Britta had put away her fucking tuna sandwich plates. Maybe now she'll learn that actions have consequences!"

CHAPTER SIXTY

I rush through the lobby to find his room. Fifth floor. 503 . . .
504 . . . There. 505.

A nurse with cornrows and wide hips stands at the
entrance watching me.

"It's okay. I'm his daughter. I know he's passed."

The nurse nods and steps aside and—

Fuck.

Daddy.

The waxy, unmoving man covered in bruises, neck
twisted the wrong way, is not my dad.

I make a crooning sound and hunch over in a half-crouch-
ing position.

Sit.

I make it to the chair beside his bed and hold his hand,
which is still slightly warm.

My breath is coming too fast. Hyperventilating.

I shut my eyes.

Turquoise and white tiles, the stench of chlorine.

Daddy? Daddy? Catch me!

When I was little I hated swimming classes, and Mom
got so fed up with me refusing to go into the water that she

changed the lessons from after kindergarten on Tuesdays to Saturday mornings, so Dad could take me.

"You're a fish, Em," Dad would say, water to his chest, holding his hands toward me.

Unsure, I'd hover at the edge of the pool, looking down at him. "Daddy, are you going to catch me?"

"Course. I'll catch you like a ball coming straight for Carlton Fisk. He never let the team down. My hands are like giant baseball mitts."

And then I'd jump.

The room is too cold. I tighten my sweater around me, but I can't stop shaking.

Sometime later, the nurse returns to the door. "You all right in there?"

I nod, and when I can't bear to stay any longer, I kiss Dad one last time.

I walk through the lobby — the chair where Natalie was sitting before is empty — and keep walking through the hospital doors, escaping outside into the night.

Fatherless. Sinking.

Wishing I could've been at the bottom of the stairs and caught Dad like he caught me in the swimming pool all those times.

I stand on the sidewalk as ambulance lights strobe red across the pavement.

Take out your phone, I tell myself. *Open the rideshare app.* Tears flood my eyes, making it hard to see my phone screen as I request a driver. I've just finished typing in my information when a body crashes into me from behind.

"Em!" Natalie hugs me tightly. She cries into my arms and I hold her. She's unsteady on her feet, no doubt from the shock of Dad passing, as well as from all the alcohol she consumed and the showdown with our family members back at the house.

A middle-aged couple walk past, averting their gaze at our display of emotion.

"I can't believe Grandpa's gone."

"I know." She's alone and fatherless too. I hold Natalie up as she quakes against my chest.

Natalie pulls back, her mascara even more smudged now, streaked down her cheeks. "You shouldn't take the blame for what happened to Rachael."

"Shh." I give her a look, imploring her not to be so loud with people in earshot.

"I just did everything Mom and Mormor told me to do. I'm sorry. I felt so bad not telling you everything. You've been a great second mom to me."

"Natalie, you don't need to say anything else. I forgive you." No matter how deep the betrayal cuts, I won't abandon her. That's how we teach unconditional love — it's on tap, no matter what. Besides, all we have now is each other. Dad's gone, Mom is emotionally unreliable, and Britta might as well be a ghost. I don't have to be Natalie's mother figure. I can be more like her big sister, her aunt.

The whites of her eyes shine in the darkness. "I was there, at home, when Grandpa fell . . . the noises he made . . ."

Bright lights stream over our bodies. The night is too quiet, I can't get away from her words. My ride's already here. I gesture to the car. "Are you coming or staying with Mormor?"

Mormor, singular — it hits hard.

She glances back toward the hospital entrance, wobbling on her high heels. "No offense, but I'm gonna stay."

"Wait. Let me fix your eyes. You look like Gene Simmons." I wipe her makeup away with a tissue and give her a hug. "Drink some more water when you get inside, all right? Water helps."

"Where are you going?" she asks.

"Back to the hotel tonight, then I'm catching a ferry to the Cape in the morning." I already sent the text to Officer Winn and I know what I have to do. "I've got an important meeting at noon on Monday."

It's time to steer the fucking boat.

CHAPTER SIXTY-ONE

Harbor Beach, Cape Cod
Monday morning, 11:15 a.m.
Plunge count: 82

Stepping over waves, I hurry out of the water to the shore and grab my towel from on top of my beach bag. I shrug the towel over my shoulders, moving from foot to foot to keep warm, sand caking my ankles.

The swim didn't help. There's only emptiness.

Even though it's mid-morning, the beach is almost empty, save a few lone walkers. Birds cluster near the water, leaving imprints in the wet sand, pecking at seagrass for hidden morsels.

I peer up at William's mansion, looming over this stretch of beach.

I pick up my beach bag, checking that the torn-out notebook pages are still tucked safely in the inner pocket. I make my way toward the dunes, where a little natural walkway will lead me home. Well, it's never actually been my home, and soon Natalie will be starting her life in New York. At least something good is happening.

Once inside, I check the time. Not long until I have to meet Officer Winn. Following a quick shower, I twist my hair into a bun, dress in black pants and a V-neck shirt — what is the ideal thing to wear to the police station? — and climb into my car and drive, only half aware of the cars on the road.

Yesterday I was talking with Dad, kissing his papery cheek, and today he isn't here anymore, and I'll never get another chance to cuddle with him on the couch and watch a game.

A horn beeps behind me. "Sorry," I mouth to the driver. I concentrate on the road and ten minutes later, arrive at the police station. A US flag snaps in the wind above the cedar-shingled station, its grounds dotted with seagrass and stone gardens.

I find a spot in the parking lot and rehearse what I'm going to say to Officer Winn.

At first, I thought I might tell Officer Winn to talk to my mom, that she "knows the answers." But I can't do that, nor can I sacrifice myself. Some random tidbits of information not related to my family will have to suffice. I'm buying time.

Crap, it's a few minutes to twelve.

I step out of the car, the breeze whipping loose strands of hair into my eyes.

As I start walking, someone calls my name.

I turn around. There, standing in front of Mom's Volvo, are Natalie and Mom. Like me, they're both dressed in black; Natalie in ripped jeans and an oversized graphic tee, Mom in a blouse and slacks.

"What are you guys doing here?" I glance at Natalie. "Natalie shouldn't be near this place."

But I know why they're here. They've come to make sure I actually go through with it and confess to Rachael's death and don't blame one of them.

"I'll handle this," I say quietly to my mom before checking over my shoulder. "How did you know I was going to be here?"

307

"Natalie told me you had an important appointment in Provincetown at noon," Mom says. "Knowing you, always putting others first, I figured out what it would be."

"I see."

"Britta and I had a long talk last night. She convinced me about the right next step to take." Mom nods and makes a little sniffing sound. "Britta said she can't live with it, her sister taking the blame for what she did. She wants me to do it."

Britta can't live with it so she tries to convince our mother, whose husband has just died.

Natalie stares ahead as though she's not listening to a word — though, of course, she is.

"And . . . ?" I ask, my voice shaking.

"Well," she sniffs again, looking indignant. "It seems the right thing to do."

"Wow! That's how much power Britta has over you? Snap her fingers, and you'll commit perjury? You were already okay letting me take the fall for her, but this takes favoritism to a whole new level."

"Favoritism?" Her brow furrows.

"That's the root of everything."

"Oh, dear." Mom dabs her eyes. "It's not that I favored Britta, necessarily. Dad favored *you*. It was always the two of you in those early years, so alike in personality. When Britta was born, she was such a fun baby and toddler, we just had a natural affinity. I thought it was okay. We always divided up in an organic way. You with Dad. Me with Britta . . ."

My face hardens at her revisionist history. "So, you're going to go in there" — I point to the station — "and say you're responsible for what happened to Rachael?"

"Yes. I'm going to say I heard about the book, and I wanted to stop Rachael from publishing anything about our family, about you."

"About me?" That has me stumped. "You'll need to make up a big, dark secret for me."

She winks at me. "I'm sure I can come up with something."

308

"Mom . . . I don't know . . ."

"Now, you take Natalie back to your house and help her start packing up her stuff. I'll call you when I'm finished here. I suspect it will take a few hours."

She turns to go but I reach for her hand. "Thank you. I know this must be really hard. I didn't expect this . . ."

"Well, it's about time, I suppose. I'm the mom."

As she walks away, I link my arm with Natalie's. Each step echoes against the pavement. Her figure grows smaller, more fragile, even as she walks with that familiar confidence. From behind it could be any of us: her, Britta, Natalie, or me. At the police entrance, she straightens up, pauses for a heartbeat, then steps through the doors.

"What happens next?" Natalie asks.

I watch those doors long after they've closed. Mom's in there alone, trying to protect us all.

"Em?"

"Right. Let's keep our minds off everything. Will you help me with something before we pack your stuff? I owe someone a pie."

"Sure," Natalie brightens. "My new closet is ant-size, so I'm going to rethink my wardrobe. Dark academia, for sure."

I press the button on the car key fob and force myself to turn away from the station. My stomach twists at how quickly life moves on, but isn't that what Mom's sacrifice is for? For us to keep living? "I'm thinking pumpkin pie. We could pile it high with meringue, give it a bruléed topping, drizzle it with warm caramel sauce, or add a chocolate magic shell."

"Mmm. They all sound good," Natalie says. "Which will you choose?"

"Whenever you cook, you need to keep in mind who you're cooking for. And this one's for someone who loves maple syrup. The Canadian kind, of course."

CHAPTER SIXTY-TWO

Tragic Wives WhatsApp chat
One year later

> **Hannah:** *Did you all see? Rachael's book is 13th on the New York Times bestseller list.*

> **Miguel:** *She's turned us into celebrities!*

> **Peggy:** *In case her book becomes a Netflix series . . . who do you think they'll get to play everyone?*

> **Miguel:** *Ooooh! I love dream casting! Em's easy, she'd be Queen Daenerys from GOT. How about me?*

> **Em:** *A wicked hot other kind of queen. RuPaul, but Latino.*

> **Carol:** *How about me?*

> **Peggy:** *Need skilled character actress. Jodie Foster?*

> **Li-Ping:** *Speaking of Rachael's writing . . . I need to confess something. Remember that yellow notebook that went missing from her bag? I took it. I was so scared it had our secrets. Inside was just notes about a new novel idea. I'm sorry.*

Miguel: *Girl! I lost sleep over that notebook!*

Em: *We all did. But I'm glad you told us.*

Miguel: *Hannah, who would play you?*

Hannah: *Lisa Kudrow if she dyed her hair brunette. A Middle Eastern model for Serenity, and someone with an awesome body for Li-Ping.*

Miguel: *Big Daddy, of course, can star as himself. [[shark emoji]]*

CHAPTER SIXTY-THREE

P-town, Cape Cod
Plunge count: 162

Miguel and I are lying on beach chairs that he set up just left of the Sandbar Café, discussing Rachael's posthumously published book. She'd be proud it became a *New York Times* bestseller, her artistic ambitions fulfilled. It gives me comfort to know she made such a big splash. The publisher she sent it to just before she died loved it.

"Can you please move the parasol over our legs?" I ask Miguel. "It's so hot."

"Thank you! I've been working out."

I roll my eyes.

Miguel is dressed in (his words) "French Riviera homo chic": red-and-white-striped Speedos and a navy sun hat. His whole look lately has veered into European holiday.

The beach is packed today with tourists and locals alike, families, and prowling sexy-suited singles, a big, colorful mix.

Clearing up my misconceptions with Serenity wasn't as hard as I'd thought it would be. It turns out Serenity was in a secret relationship, but I got the person — correction, person*s*

— wrong. Serenity, Compost Carol, and Hannah were in a throuple, which Serenity and Carol wanted to be open about, but Hannah insisted on keeping private — all this detailed in *Secrets of the Tragic Wives and Guys*, Chapter 6, entitled, "The More the Merrier." The throuple fell apart months ago, but Carol and Hannah are still going strong. Serenity's artwork has skyrocketed in value and Peggy now has her own podcast topping the charts.

"Pass me the baby oil, Mamacita," Miguel says.

"Baby oil? What, are we in the 1950s?" Reluctantly, I hand him his beach bag. "I'm surprised there's so many people swimming given the shark attacks." Two people were mauled last month, and unfortunately, one of them didn't make it.

"That's Cape Codders for you," Miguel says. "They love the beach so much, they're willing to die."

As Miguel coats himself in oil, I reflect on the Tragic Wives' secrets. It's a shame what happened to Li-Ping. Once it got out — and by out, I mean, went viral — that she was behind her former Olympian rival's Insta hate campaign, her Christian good-girl rep was tarnished, and people stopped wanting to be associated with her. Miguel thinks this isn't the worst thing in the world as she'll be able to reinvent herself free from the shackles of religious ideology — again, his words.

As for the rest of the secrets, Miguel is even more addicted to his phone. He cannot be saved. His SNAIL GIRL ERA business is thriving nonetheless as his brand celebrates "irony, parody, and pastiche."

My story about William's infidelity spawned all these "mouth pruning" memes on TikTok. His family is not happy, so William told me in a very terse phone call.

"Excuse me?"

I glance up, shading my eyes from the sun.

A young girl in a floppy red hat stands at the edge of our towel. "Um, is that sand dollar yours?" The hat slips over her eyes as she points.

Near the towel's edge, a sand dollar lies half-buried in the sand. "Nope. You can have it if you like?"

"Yes, please." She clutches some ladyslippers and periwinkles in her other hand. Scooping up the sand dollar, she scampers back to her mom, who stands weighted down with beach bags, wearing a long-suffering expression.

I lean back on the sunbed and sigh.

My mom ended up confessing to Officer Winn that she was the one who met Rachael on the pier. Mom served three months for obstruction of justice, and the whole thing was featured as the shocking epilogue of *Secrets of the Tragic Wives and Guys*. It has brought Mom quite a bit of notoriety among the pearl set, I hear. Apparently, she even gets fan mail from admirers. At this rate, she'll be "talent" on *Love After Lockup*, which would delight Miguel to no end.

Natalie is set up in New York, going to fashion school, and has a boyfriend who seems nice. She's still in therapy but off any medication. With her mom disappeared off the map, and her mormor letting fame go to her head, Natalie needs her aunt more than ever now.

As for Britta's ex, and what Natalie witnessed, I called and left an anonymous tip with police. Vague enough that it won't be traced back to me, but if they dig, they'll discover the rest.

When I'd originally moved to the Cape, I wanted to work through my grief about my sister's death and try to heal. Although Britta never died, she's now dead to me. I assume Britta has left the US and gone underground somewhere. I'm not close to my mom. The last time I saw her was at Dad's funeral. We shared a few words, but that's it.

But I don't grieve about that. My grief is now for Dad.

I stare out at the waves, mesmerized and a little motion sick as I watch them lap the shore. One grief gets replaced with another, until — if you're lucky — you get old, and look back at a life full of trauma and healing, collective pains, so many good moments, wins, and all the losses and betrayals.

Dizzy, I sit up on the beach chair and wipe my forehead.

314

"Em?" Guardie calls, walking in from the ocean, water glistening on his abs. "You want one of those Ginger Snaps?"

"Not one, like ten. Thanks."

Guardie squeezes his wet hair, which is longer now, past his shoulders, and drips water onto the sand. "Are you thirsty? Want a drink?"

"Sparkling water, please, babe."

Miguel coos, "Spicy margarita, please, babe. Thermoses are in the cooler."

Guardie brings me cookies and sparkling water and serves up margaritas for him and Miguel. Then he leans down to rub my stomach. "Don't make your mom nauseous, boy."

Yes, that's the other thing that happened. After our "pumpkin pie reunion" Guardie forgave me, and we got back together. Four months ago, a skinny dip at night led to passion getting the better of us, and no condom, so now we're expecting. Although I never wanted to be a mother, there was no question when the strong pink line showed up on the pregnancy test. Sometimes life decides for us. Miguel is the proud godfather-to-be. He's reunited with Ronald (who was dumped by the Grand Slam celebrity — a PR coup that significantly boosted Rachael's book sales), and their family has become our family now too, chosen families.

Guardie joins us, sitting beside me in the hazy sun. He's taken to wearing two crystal necklaces, Bloodstone, which is said to promote a healthy birth, and Malachite, the "midwife" stone. And although I don't wear the Moonstone necklace he gave me, I keep it safety tucked in my drawer that's now filled with baby clothes. (Who knew newborns need so many onesies?) Luckily, Guardie's mansion, where we've been living, has lots of closet space.

To offset the insurance money Natalie wrongfully received, Guardie has donated truckloads of funds into single-mom charities around New York.

As for what's next, while the baby is a baby, we're going to join the "van life." No vlogs allowed (that goes without saying — despite both of us being Millennials, we're not one bit follower-hungry). I left my university position to freelance, taking on research projects for various scholars. One day, I'll probably return to academia to work on my own area of interest. We also hope to drive to British Columbia and spend time with Guardie's family. After the book came out, they had a lot of open discussions, and being Canadians, of course, everyone made up and said sorry.

So, the plan is no plan. No worrying. No looking backward. Just living.

I yawn and stretch my arms. Ever since getting pregnant, I've started sleeping through the night. I'm going to enjoy every minute of it before the baby arrives.

Now, flanked by my favorite men, and the tiny avocado-sized one growing inside of me, I shut my eyes, basking in the warm sun.

The last year and a half hasn't been easy, but as Dad would say, "When life throws knee-buckler after knee-buckler at you, remember how much you love the game."

Guardie's fingers brush my knee. "Water's nice. You wanna go for a dip soon?"

"Mm-hmm. I do. What about you?"

"I do."

Miguel sits up straight, a hand on his cheek. "Did you two just exchange vows? Because one thing I'm good at is 'bitchy bridesmaid.'"

THE END

316

ACKNOWLEDGMENTS

Writing novels has been my dream since childhood, and I'm grateful to everyone who helped bring my second novel into being.

My steadfast and whip-smart agent, Jill Marsal of Marsal Lyon Literary Agency.

I'm deeply thankful to my writing friends and colleagues who provided invaluable feedback during the drafting and revision process: Andrea Barton, Kate Murdoch, and my fellow members of the Bayside Writing Group. Special thanks to Sophie Krich-Brinton, Lauren Griffin, Sharon Wishnow, Sarah Hawthorn, Stephanie Louise, Josh Moyes, Sunni Overend, and Anna George. I couldn't have done it without you. Additional shoutout to Peter Senftleben for his expert editorial guidance.

Narelle Warren, my academic island in the storm.

To the wonderful (and friendliest!) team at Joffe Books: Kate Lyall Grant, Kate Ballard, Sam Matthews, Matthew Grundy Haigh, and everyone in design and PR.

Finally, to my loving family: Stephen, Cohen, and Matisse — and our smallest, fluffiest member, Benson. Even on the hard days, writing with you at my feet makes everything better . . . and if I get stuck in a plot hole, you have your own brand of editorial advice: pleading eyes that say: *All plot problems can be solved with a walk.*

Follow Bella Ellwood-Clayton on TikTok and Instagram:
@bellaellwoodclayton

Visit Bella's website & sign up for her newsletter to receive free short stories and exclusive giveaways!

www.drbella.com.au

THE JOFFE BOOKS STORY

We began in 2014 when Jasper agreed to publish his mum's much-rejected romance novel and it became a bestseller.

Since then we've grown into the largest independent publisher in the UK. We're extremely proud to publish some of the very best writers in the world, including Joy Ellis, Faith Martin, Caro Ramsay, Helen Forrester, Simon Brett and Robert Goddard. Everyone at Joffe Books loves reading and we never forget that it all begins with the magic of an author telling a story.

We are proud to publish talented first-time authors, as well as established writers whose books we love introducing to a new generation of readers.

We won Trade Publisher of the Year at the Independent Publishing Awards in 2023 and Best Publisher Award in 2024 at the People's Book Prize. We have been shortlisted for Independent Publisher of the Year at the British Book Awards for the last five years, and were shortlisted for the Diversity and Inclusivity Award at the 2022 Independent Publishing Awards. In 2023 we were shortlisted for Publisher of the Year at the RNA Industry Awards, and in 2024 we were shortlisted at the CWA Daggers for the Best Crime and Mystery Publisher.

We built this company with your help, and we love to hear from you, so please email us about absolutely anything bookish at feedback@joffebooks.com.

If you want to receive free books every Friday and hear about all our new releases, join our mailing list here: www.joffebooks.com/freebooks.

And when you tell your friends about us, just remember: it's pronounced Joffe as in coffee or toffee!

www.ingramcontent.com/pod-product-compliance
Lightning Source LLC
La Vergne TN
LVHW032011160425
808835LV00029B/255